JAKE FOX

TIES THAT BLIND

MICHAEL STOCKHAM

Award-winning Author of *Confessions of an Accidental Lawyer*

JAKE FOX

TIES THAT BLIND

MICHAEL STOCKHAM

ISBN 978-1-7379584-4-4 paperback
ISBN 978-1-7379584-5-1 e-book
ISBN 978-1-7379584-6-8 audiobook
ISBN 978-1-7379584-7-5 hardback

Book shepherd: Aurora Winter, www.SamePagePublishing.com

Book cover designer: Richard Ljoenes

All cover photographs by Shutterstock: girl by Ievgeniia Dadabaieva; house by Milosz_G; Male, car and landscape by Raggedstone.

Author photographs by: Jamie House

www.MichaelStockham.com

BOOK REVIEWS

BOOK REVIEWS REQUESTED

Please leave an online book review! Your review will help other readers discover a new book by a new, award-winning author. You will also be encouraging Michael Stockham to write more novels for your reading enjoyment.

Rave reviews of Michael's novels:

★★★★★ *Jake Fox: Ties that Blind* is a fun mix of thriller, suspense, and personal redemption. Jake Fox is finding his footing in his life again after the death of his daughter, Lucy. It's through sheer chance that he gets involved in the drama that unfolds around Rose's father's death. He finds himself in charge of her defense and sees so much of his daughter in Rose, so it's more of a personal goal for him to not fail her like he failed his child. Rose, still reeling from finding her father dead, is sucked into the legal drama and doesn't know what to make of any of it. She's just a teenager, she wants her dad, and has herself yanked from one shock to the next—losing her dad to being the one blamed to her best friend, Beth, turning up missing. The more they try to save Rose from being tossed in prison, the more they uncover the truth of who really took Beth…and who was actually behind her father's murder. It turns out that a small town has plenty of places for snakes to hide. It's up to Jake and Hope, the sheriff, to flush them out. - Beta Reader [*Jake Fox*]

★★★★★ **I loved this book** [*Jake Fox*] from cover to cover. I reached the end of the book and couldn't believe it when I read 'Epilogue' as a chapter title. I couldn't believe it was over, I wanted more. Rose and Beth are the central characters, but you made Jake equally as compelling! A trial for a crime that wasn't committed, a lawyer who sees visions of his deceased daughter, and a young woman who is on the brink of being sold into slavery. Each one on their own could be a book in of itself, but together? They became **an utterly compelling masterpiece**. - Beta Reader [*Jake Fox*]

★★★★★ "**IT. BLEW. MY. MIND.** I want to read EVERYTHING from this author now. The book [*Confessions of an Accidental Lawyer*] is gripping to say the least. I cried, I laughed, I felt anger, I felt despair and I was on the edge of my seat…**I couldn't read this book fast enough!** If a book makes me FEEL emotions while reading, I'm hooked for life. It eloquently ties two worlds together through the eyes of a new lawyer and draws you in to each side of the story." – Goodreads 5-star review.

★★★★★ It's a strong story that offers mystery, suspense, corruption, and even court and police procedurals. As a beta reader, I found the novel engaging with strong elements of mystery, suspense, and character development, particularly in Jake and Rose, whose emotional struggles were empathetic. The plot provides plenty of tension. - Beta Reader [*Jake Fox*]

★★★★★ "The book is **exciting and intense**, with emotionally charged scenes and action that I didn't expect… *Confessions of an Accidental Lawyer* by Michael Stockham deserves **5 out of 5 stars for its exceptional writing** and delivery. It's a great story with **excellent characters** and an amazing story." - Amazon, 5-star review.

★★★★★ The murder of Marcus creates an immediate sense of danger and intrigue, especially with the sheriff's disbelief in the only witness. The kidnapping of Beth heightens the stakes, adding urgency and tension to the plot. Additionally, the unsettling stalker behavior exhibited by Zack adds an extra layer of creepiness and suspense, keeping readers on edge throughout the story. - Beta Reader [*Jake Fox*]

★★★★★ "*Confessions of an Accidental Lawyer* by Michael Stockham is an exciting novel that blends legal dynamics and personal turmoil with **thrilling** political drama into one **exceptional story**. I rate Confessions of an Accidental Lawyer by Michael Stockham a solid 5 out of 5 stars for it's **incredible writing quality and excellent**

narration, which makes for an exciting read!" - Amazon, 5-star review.

★★★★★ "**What is so huggable and lovable about this book is the depth of each character, warts and all**. You'll go quickly from reading to living the lives, feeling the desperation and complete fulfillment. The joyful highs and silent surrender in the same day. Even loathing at humanity's inability to treat each other with basic respect... I'm giving it a 5 out of 5 stars wishing I could give it more." - Amazon, 5-star review.

★★★★★ "**Couldn't put this book down**. I started it last night and finished this morning. The book pivots between the lawyer's work and his home life in a seamless way." - Amazon, 5-star review.

★★★★★ "*Confessions of an Accidental Lawyer* by Michael Stockham is **a fabulous thriller** that perfectly blends mystery, suspense, and drama. It is the ideal mix of situations that occur in most of our lives, which makes it highly relatable." – Bookbub 5-star review.

THANK YOU, KICKSTARTER BACKERS!

Thank you for much for supporting the launch of
Jake Fox: Ties That Blind.
It means the world to me!

Michael Stockham

DEDICATION

Significant credit for this book goes to my family for their infinite love and unwavering support.

Special thanks to Aurora Winter for her editorial wisdom and unlimited patience.

CHAPTER ONE

JAKE FOX STRUGGLED to escape the nightly vision ravaging his mind. His heart raced as he thrashed between consciousness and a delirious sleep, the sheets soaked with sweat. The dream always played in his head like a disjointed family movie reel. Night by night, he relived that fateful day and shuffled around his own frigid purgatory.

That morning, more than one year before, the stillness and silence from Lucy's room unnerved him. Cool air drifted through the house. The first birdsong leaked through the windows as dawn unfurled around him. He should have heard his daughter's music blaring and her hairdryer roaring. Lucy's voice should have spilled from the room as she sang along with her favorite tune for the day, like every other fifteen-year-old. But that day… silence. The hallway presented as a tunnel, growing as he walked it, one bare foot in front of the other on the carpet. The walls closed in as darkness enveloped him. Intuition and dread lurched forward with him. He padded down the hall, praying that Lucy had overslept. But no light peeked from under her door. Something was wrong. He swung open her door. Her bed lay empty, still perfectly made. The hair on the nape of his neck stood on end, and an eerie emptiness descended on him.

Behind him, his blue heeler, Ted, scratched wildly on something wooden. Jake chased the sound and found his dog pawing to get into the garage. As Jake opened the door, the pungent, acrid smell of death washed over him. Lucy's slender body dangled from a rafter, and a silver stepladder was knocked over on the concrete floor. Jake sprinted to her, a guttural howl in his throat. Lucy's deathly pale skin—almost translucent, with mottled purple veins now rising to the surface—forecast the ugly truth. Violet blood pooled in her dangling calves and feet. Jake righted the stepladder and climbed to help his daughter. Sweat blanketed his chest and sides. His fingers trembled as he tried to loosen the fierce grip of the brown leather belt looped around Lucy's fragile, innocent throat. The friction on the worn leather strap caused it to remain stuck. It refused to loosen from her windpipe. Jake's terrified pleas provided no help. Lucy, always so brilliant, had planned this out and executed it flawlessly. She would have made sure the belt would not give way—that there would be no way to reverse her decision. What a smart… tormented little girl. He held Lucy's swaying, vulnerable body. Jake's heart thundered in his chest. He pushed the savage, salty tears from his eyes, trying to focus on saving his daughter. A futile effort. Jake pleaded for it not to be true. He prayed to God. Demanded that He take it back.

Please, please, please.

Finally, he loosened the belt and lowered Lucy from the rafter into his lap on the floor, cradling her head. The cold concrete sucked the energy and warmth from his body. Jake smoothed her soft blonde hair. He traced his fingers over the porcelain skin of her face. The lack of oxygen had made blue-violet crescents under her eyes that amplified her penetrating stare. He passed his thumb over her cheek. His tears fell on her skin like raindrops. He knew he should call someone, but he could not let go. What was the point? Lucy was gone. He kissed her forehead. "I'm so sorry," he told her in a fervent whisper. "Daddy's so sorry."

His will to live drained away, and his body seemed to crumple into the floor.

Behind him, his wife's screams echoed off the garage walls. Her one and only child lay dead in Jake's arms. She clawed at him to release her. Momma wanted her baby. Shortly, she would blame him for not getting to Lucy in time, and that resentment would rot the roots of their marriage until it wilted into oblivion. Just another nightmare.

Jake screamed as he vaulted awake in bed, his shirt soaked, the acrid stink of perspiration all around. His breathing was tight and fast, and he took a moment to adjust to the present, to his room. The soft breeze from the ceiling fan froze him in place, his skin clammy, his pulse racing. Memories paralyzed him for a moment. In the cold, sparse room, regret seeped into him. Maybe he should have called an ambulance. But by the time Jake found her, she was beyond help. The pallor of Lucy's skin and the cloudy stillness of her green eyes had announced her demise. Jake could do nothing to help. Her fate remained irreversible.

Jake sat up in bed, placed his feet on the floor, and opened the drawer in his nightstand. There was Lucy's beautiful cursive script on the small ecru note he had found on her dresser.

I'm sorry, she had written.

He slid the drawer shut, unable to process the tiny message, unwilling to read it again.

Jake raked his palms down his face and tried to force away the nightmares and exhaustion. He stepped out of bed, clicking on the light in the bathroom. Jake drew a cool drink of water from the tap, the minerals from the well water giving off a slight metallic taste. The rumble of an approaching thunderstorm rolled across the lake outside his window. He lowered the glass to the counter and folded back the bath towel on the toilet tank, exposing the pistol. He picked it up, clicked off the safety, pulled the slide, and racked a bullet in the chamber. In the mirror, he noted the deep crags in his tanned skin. His shaking fingers traced the outline of his lips. The stress of losing Lucy had grayed large swaths of his stubble. These nights, he knew, would never, ever end. Slowly, he lifted the gun to his temple and held the cold metal there, trembling while he stared at his blue-eyed reflection.

One soft, slow pull with my finger, and it can all be over.

Jake closed his eyes for a moment. He let Lucy's short, brilliant life—and his own life—wash over him, while he dabbed away the moisture on his cheeks. As he steeled his resolve, tightening his tension on the trigger, the familiar perfume—sweet like spring flowers—surrounded him. He opened his eyes and let out a long, slow breath. Gazing in the mirror, he glimpsed her through the doorway, seated in a rocking chair, faint around the edges, mirage-like.

"Hey, Lu," he said, her name catching in his throat.

"Hey, Dad," she answered.

Jake lowered the pistol and set it on the bathroom counter.

"Taking some time off from being in Heaven?" Jake asked.

"I came to check on you. Someone told me you weren't doing so good."

Jake's jaw quaked as he struggled to regain his voice.

"It hurts, Lu… I can't make myself stop missing you. I want to be with you. Like old times."

"I miss you, too, Daddy. But you can't go. Not now. It's not your time."

"It wasn't yours, either."

"Someday you'll understand… Find the bright side."

"What's the bright side, Lu? It all seems so dark."

"They won't let me tell you. That, you'll have to figure out for yourself."

"What if… I don't want to?"

"You must. You're still needed here... You'll see."

"There's no one, Lu... No one."

Lucy stood and closed the distance between them. She took the gun, cleared the bullet from the chamber, and then tucked the weapon back into the towel. She stood on her tiptoes and kissed him on the cheek.

"There will be somebody," she said.

Lucy placed her palm across his eyes as if blindfolding him. Then Lucy and the scent of flowers disappeared. The room felt so empty. Jake glanced at the towel. After a moment, he picked it up and slid it into the drawer under the sink. He flipped off the bathroom light and crawled back into bed. Slowly, his breath stilled, and he slipped into a deep sleep. The sun would rise. Another day would be upon him.

CHAPTER TWO

MARCUS TUCKER GRABBED his daughter by the arm as if making sure he had her full attention. "Rose, I'm tellin' you to do this. I'm not askin' you. Go... sneak out the back door. Get to the well house. You know where to hide. Get in there and, regardless of what you hear or see, do not leave."

Her father's grip dug into Rosemary's elbow, his fingers strong from years of welding pipelines. It was a command and a warning all at once. Fear and caring illuminated his gaze, as did the shallow smile peeking out from his peppered mustache and beard. His pale-blue eyes brimmed with regret. Time, stress, and raising a daughter alone had aged him.

As she peered past the slit in the curtains, Rose's heartbeat thrummed in her ears. The headlights snaking up the access road meant trouble. She noticed the shotgun by the front door. Even at fifteen, Rose realized that evil was rolling up the drive.

"I promise: if I can, I'll come get you." Marcus lifted his necklace and slid it over Rose's head. He touched the medal that dangled from the chain. "Keep this safe. Don't let anyone take it. You will learn over time that Saint Michael will set you free. Trust me." Marcus rubbed a tear from Rosemary's cheek, and the scratch of his callused thumb was comforting. He was strong and always protecting her. "Right now," he whispered close to her ear, "you cannot be here. When this goes bad, I don't want you anywhere near it. You've gotta be somewhere safe."

"I'm staying with you. I can help." Rose's voice was a hoarse, hopeless plea.

"No! For now, you hide. When you can, run and find Margie Moore. She'll know what to do. She'll take care of you." His staunch expression pierced Rose.

In that moment, Rose regretted all the recent arguments she'd had with her father. Yelling, talking back… embarrassing him in front of others. Sorrow's apologies crushed her now.

A large black SUV pulled to a stop in the front of their house. Headlights fractured a cloud of dust. Bile rose in her throat, urging her to vomit in the face of it all. Rose placed a soft kiss on her father's cheek, squeezed his hands.

Peering through the curtains, she caught sight of a burly man sporting a jet-black ball cap and a belly-length beard woven in two braids. He banged on the front door and barked her father's name, his brilliant white teeth wolflike under his black mustache and fierce dark eyes.

"Marcus! Come out now. We can talk about this. Come out, and we'll have a seat. Get an understanding… You know, make a deal."

Marcus squared his shoulders as he turned to greet them. "Rose, leave!" His harsh whisper commanded her to run. Rose sprinted toward the back door. With a last look at her father, she grabbed her hoodie and exited.

The cool April air enveloped her as she crept along the back porch stairs. Rain threatened. The first tendrils of lightning webbed across the sky. She placed her feet near the edge of the planks so the warped boards wouldn't creak. She'd been using the trick to sneak out to see the boy she'd been dating, Tommy. Adrenaline fired through her, and her stomach roiled.

Thunder clapped. She struggled to calm her breathing, which came in a ragged pattern.

Rose spied the well house. It was a simple, forgettable concrete block hovel. Darkness covered the short distance to its door. Rose heard footsteps crushing rock on the driveway that circled the house. She couldn't stay put.

Is it too far away?

Rose scanned the tiny field between the house and the shed, looking for somewhere to hide. Panic blurred the edge of her vision. Beyond the field, Lake Haven extended into the horizon, a natural barrier to her escape. It emitted a sour stink as the oncoming storm began churning the moss. She could lie in the tall grass, or squat behind one of the large oaks, but they were both terrible hiding spots in a downpour. The man out front continued to yell for Marcus and bang on the front door. His booming, perfunctory tone caused the hair on the back of Rose's neck to stand.

A shadow appeared in front of her, stretching from the light around the corner. It stopped, as if the person was deciding whether to continue. Just then, Rose heard the front door open and her father's steel-toed boots clomp onto the wooden-planked porch. The shadow receded, as if drawn to the commotion. With everyone concentrating on Marcus, now was her chance. Crouching low, Rose hustled to the tiny shed. Her fluttering hands pulled the door open, working to keep the rusted iron hinges from screeching. Inside, she knelt against the wall and tried to calm herself. Tendrils of light seeped in through fissures in the walls. She reached for her phone in her back pocket.

I left it inside the house!

Worry coursed through her as she realized how disconnected she was from everyone. What had the school counselor taught her to halt her panic attacks?

Name five things I can see. Workbench, door, paint cans, a pipe wrench, pump. Four things I can touch. Denim of my jeans, dirt floor of the shed, a wisp of my hair in my fingers, the rough surface of the shed wall. Three things I can hear. My sneakers scuffing on the concrete floor, my breath, voices on the porch. Two things I can smell. Ozone from the storm, oil and gas in the shed. One thing I can taste. Bitterness in my throat as I listen to the voices outside.

A large crack in the mortar between blocks provided a perfect peephole. Her head pounded and her vision began to swirl as she scooted close to the wall and peered out at the scene.

Loud voices filled the air. She saw Marcus, rigid and strong, arguing with the tall man in the ball cap, but she couldn't decipher the words. The SUV's headlamps framed his silhouette. Their footsteps stirred up fine dust. The tall man's anger caused his braided beard to sway with the heated exchange.

Then the door of the SUV swung open, and a tall boot with a stiletto heel stepped out. A woman's curves followed. She was dressed in all black, and her long, straight hair fell well below her waist. The headlights behind her gave away its fire-red hue and her air of malice as she pulled on a pair of gloves. The distance garbled the woman's words, but her voice triggered memories for Rose. Marcus reacted to the redhead like he knew her.

I know her drawl. From where? Which town?

The redhead snapped her fingers. Without warning, two men grabbed Marcus by the arms and held him still. The man in the ball cap punched Marcus in the gut with a gloved hand. Rose winced. She wanted to cry out, to save Marcus, but fear robbed her of words. Marcus slumped forward to his hands and knees. One man kicked him in the ribs, and Marcus collapsed to the ground. The redhead laughed while Marcus lay heaving for breath in the middle of the driveway. Another man stepped up and yanked Marcus to his feet. Sweat poured down Rose's back in the cool night air. She sat helplessly in the well house as the men hoisted Marcus back to his feet, only to bend him again with another punch.

Rose clenched her fists and shifted, as if readying herself. A primal urge called her to charge from the shed and help her father, but she tripped over a tool bag Marcus had tucked in the shadows of the well house. Her thigh jammed against something sharp, and she bit her tongue to keep herself from yelping as something cut her. As she regained her balance, her elbow caught on empty paint cans, which crashed to the floor and banged against the wall. Fearful, Rose cowered as the clatter of the empty cans echoed through the night.

"Is someone here?" The redhead demanded to Marcus, who remained silent. She had grabbed his hair and twisted it in her fingers. "Go check it out," she commanded one of her men.

Through the crack, Rose saw the man in the ball cap turn and swing his flashlight beam over the field. He shined it at the side of the well house. The first drops of rain pierced the dangerous silo of light that threatened to expose her. The man stepped toward the shack, his leather boots crunching in the gravel. Shadows hid his face, but a cruel light smoldered in his eyes. Step by step, he approached, and Rose's heart pounded in her chest as a loud clap of thunder caused her to flinch.

The storm is here.

She grabbed the large pipe wrench she'd seen, hoping to God she wouldn't have to fight them off in the well house. The flashlight scanned the area between them. The man paused. The light beam pierced Rose's peephole, and she pulled away, setting her back against the wall, praying he hadn't seen her peering through the gap. The man outside took a few steps. The light vanished. With a breath, she glanced once more into the night. The man neared, his massive shape outlined by the headlights.

"Something's over here," he called out. He stepped

forward, as if surveying the grounds. Rose's ears rang as he approached the well house door. She massaged her temples.

Rose jumped up and felt along the firewood stacked against the opposite wall.

Come on… where are you?

A splinter gouged the end of her finger as she searched out a specific cylindrical log. Finally, she found it and pulled. A latch gave way, and a hidden door swung open, exposing a small landing and a staircase behind it.

Rose stepped through the doorway and closed the panel behind her. In the darkness, she faced the entryway, white-knuckling the pipe wrench, its metallic scent heady in her nose. She hoisted it to her shoulder, ready to swing if the bearded man breached her hideaway.

The hinges on the well house door creaked. Panic flushed through her as his boots crunched debris on the concrete floor. Rose held her breath, hoping he would go away. The light from the flashlight leaked under the panel door and painted the tips of her sneakers in a glow.

Please just go away.

Rose's lungs began to burn from holding her breath. She was certain the deep drum beat of her heart was loud enough for him to hear.

He's going to find me.

When she thought she couldn't hold her breath any longer, she heard his boots crunching on the gravel outside. The door to the well house creaked shut. She waited until the footsteps became distant and then gently opened the hidden door. She knelt against the wall and peeked out of the crack just as two furry flashes darted between the shadows, toppling boards and startling the man.

"Nothin' but racoons!"

The man paused again, sweeping the light from the field to the well house and finally to the lake's surface. He turned and walked back to the group. Warning drops of rain pelted the shed's tin roof.

"Let's get inside before we get soaked," the redhead said.

Rose watched as the group dragged Marcus into their home and slammed the door. Sobs of fear and helplessness overtook her in darkness.

Dad told me to run.

The skies ripped open, and fat raindrops pounded the well house. Sheets of water trapped her inside. The leading edge of the heavy storm blew in and dropped the temperature. She feared for Marcus, knowing she couldn't defeat the group that had him. The chill air drained her body heat. Rose shivered, her teeth chattering. Rain leaked in from a hole in the weathered roof and splattered onto her cheeks.

Rose opened the hidden panel again and stepped through, leaning the pipe wrench against the wall. Feeling for the shelf she knew was there, her fingers curled around a small packet. She tore it open and cracked and shook the plastic stick inside. An eerie, iridescent green glow lit up the landing at the top of a short staircase in their storm cellar. Her dad tended to prepare for the worst. Rose descended the stairs, observing all the supplies her father kept stocked. Food and water lined shelves on one wall, along with a small stove and several cylinders of propane. Rose pulled on a large hardback book of survival skills, and half of the bookcase popped forward. Marcus had installed a gun safe behind the false wall. It housed pistols, rifles, and ammunition. She could use a gun now. She could handle one. Marcus took her target shooting all the time. Just yesterday, they had been shooting targets with his pistol.

Always be prepared, Rose.

Rose pressed her palm flat against the safe as tears streamed down her face. Marcus had never told her the combination to this gun cabinet. She slapped the lock in frustration and pushed the bookcase back into place.

She could hear thunder through the ventilation shaft. Bunk beds ran the length of the other wall. Rose sat on the lower bunk, shaking out of control. An echo ricocheted in her head.

Get in there and, regardless of what you hear or see, do not leave.

Time passed. Adrenaline ebbed. Rose ran out of tears, and she fought to keep her eyes open. She lowered her head to a pillow.

Daddy, can I lie down for just a minute? I'm so tired.

Rose curled up with a blanket on the mattress. An image of the man beating her father swirled in her head. The faint edge of another panic attack threatened, but sounds from the storm outside drowned out her ragged breathing.

Name five things you can see…

Before she could respond, sleep dragged her into darkness.

CHAPTER THREE

ROSE TUCKER WOKE. An eerie stillness surrounded her. It took a moment for her to remember where she was. The glow stick's light ebbed on a stool beside her. She crawled out from under the scratchy woolen blanket. Her body ached from sleeping on the thin mattress. The cold from the rain and the adrenaline rush had sapped her. She stood and climbed the stairs, pausing at the top, holding on to the latch.

What if they're still here? What if they're waiting for me on the other side?

She reached for her phone in her back pocket. *Right.* It was still in the house.

Rose paced at the top of the stairs, worrying her fingers through her hair as she contemplated opening the door. She slipped a hair tie from her wrist and pulled the matted blonde mess into a ponytail.

Nothing ventured, nothing gained.

She picked up the pipe wrench and took a deep breath. Steeling herself, she assumed a fighter's stance, with the wrench resting on her shoulder like a baseball bat at the ready. She undid the latch, and the door swung open. She stepped through into the well house.

No one. Just Rose.

She turned and closed the door. Rose peeked through the crack in the concrete-block wall. The vehicles had left, though it was still dark.

Thank goodness… Daddy!

The hinges groaned as she pushed open the door and raced across the yard into the house. The wooden floors of their little clapboard home creaked when Rose walked in, as if giving up a secret.

"Daddy!" she called out.

Nothing. Panic coursed through her, and she turned to look for her phone, her lifeline to the outside world. She had left it charging, but the cord dangled from the wall plug and vanished into the gap between the cabinet and the refrigerator. Gingerly, she pulled the cord. She could see the glow of her phone hanging just a few inches below the countertop. Her heart rate ticked up.

Careful, Rose.

Two more inches. One more inch. Finally, it was free. Rose checked the battery. *100%*. She jammed the phone in the hip pocket of her jeans, then she tiptoed further into the heart of her home.

The acrid, sulfurous smell of gunpowder hit her senses, and a chill skipped across her spine. She slipped down the hallway. Through a partially opened door, she saw her father's booted feet on his bed. Rose pushed the door open and stepped into the room, the stillness unnerving.

She raised the back of her hand to her mouth and gagged. The pungent, metallic odor of death flooded her senses. Marcus's eyes stared back at her from his mattress—gray, clouded, and lifeless. Splotches and rivulets of blood and brain matter covered the headboard and walls around him. A gaping entry wound under his chin leaked crimson all over his pale bedding. The back of his skull had been obliterated by the bullet's exit. The pounding in Rose's chest became a gallop as adrenaline coursed through her veins. Ringing in her ears deafened her as the room swirled and tilted. Her hand quivered above her father's destroyed face, but she was too scared to touch him. Rose tried to scream from deep inside her lungs, but no sound came. The terror paralyzed her, and she collapsed to the floor, knocking over a bottle of bourbon on the nightstand. When she hit the ground, a sharp pain coursed through her right knee. Rose grabbed at what had bit her, and she stared in horror at the semiautomatic pistol that her father kept on his nightstand. She dropped the gun, and it skittered under the bed. Then she righted the bourbon bottle, which was dribbling the last of its contents onto the floor.

Dead. Her father was dead...

Get control of yourself, Rose. Get out. It's dangerous here. Run to Miss Margie's.

But she couldn't move. It was as if an invisible force tethered her to her father's almost accusatory glare, to the misery he must have suffered. She stroked Marcus's palm. The skin felt cold. Flecks of blood interlaced his fingers and stained hers. Her shock melted into tears, and she tried to push back the flood with the cuff of her camouflage hoodie.

Unable to control her insides, Rose vomited into the wastepaper bin next to Marcus's bed. As she pushed the bucket away, she saw the blood on her palms, from her father's fingers and from the gun. She rubbed her hands on the small rectangular rug, desperate to remove the sticky stain. Rose pulled her phone from her pocket and hung her head.

I should call the sheriff... But what can I tell them?

Rose pressed her phone back into her jeans pocket and stood up. She touched the tear in her pants where the sharp gun sight at the top of the barrel had sliced through the fabric when she collapsed. She rubbed her slick blood between her thumb and forefinger. She must have been cut, but she didn't feel it.

As she backed away from her father, she bumped into the

doorframe and stumbled down the hallway to their kitchen. The sun hid behind the clouds above the lake's surface; morning had arrived.

A truck's motor groaned as it sped down the road. She startled at the screen door clamoring in the breeze.

I've got to leave. What if they come back… come for me?

Rose filled a glass on the counter from the tap. She pressed it against her forehead, trying to steady her thoughts with the coolness. Drinking, she felt relief as the fresh liquid soothed her throat after puking. But her fingers, still numb from shock, lost their grip on the glass, and it smashed onto the tile floor, shards flying in all directions. She glanced around. Dizziness swirled over her. She thought about collapsing, and sleeping until someone found them.

That's crazy… Run, Rose, run. Go as far as possible from here. Now. They might be on their way back!

Rose sprinted down the hallway, slamming the screen door on her way out. She dashed toward the trails along the lake. She knew the back way to Margie's if she skirted along the shoreline. Twenty yards out into the lake, she spied a water moccasin gliding along with a baby ducking in its mouth. A pang of sorrow, and then empathy, washed through Rose. If she wasn't careful, she would be just as dead.

Rain had saturated the soil, and mud clung to the bottoms of her shoes, threatening to pull them off. The moisture on the long grasses soaked her jeans and hoodie, and the dampness robbed her body of warmth. Her teeth chattered. The rhythm of her heart pounded with the effort and stress. Panic threatened to swamp her. She couldn't quit.

Five things I can see. Loblolly pines, the water moccasin, the sun rising, a bass jumping from the lake, the smoke from someone's chimney the next cove over. Four things I can touch. The cool air on my face, the grasses in my hand, the hair against my face, and the breeze on my cheek. Three things I can hear. The wind in the trees, the quack of a mother duck distressed about her missing duckling, the sucking of my footsteps in the mud. Two things I can smell. The lake moss churned from the storm and the stench of some small animal long past dead in the scrub brush. One thing I can taste. The lingering sourness of vomit.

Fatigue plagued her as the roof of Margie's house came into sight. She slipped in the mud, collapsing on one knee, but pulled herself back up and soldiered forward to the edge of the forest, until the mown lawn was only a short distance away.

She couldn't just go waltzing in. She was a mess. *What am I going to tell Margie?* Rose hid behind a tree. Tears and snot ran down her cheeks and chin.

Daddy, what do I do? Please? Give me an answer.

As if on cue, she spied Margie's utility shed at the back of the lot, by the lake. Rose scanned the yard. The smell of cooking bacon wafted from the house, making her hungry.

I can hide in that shed for a minute. Just until I figure this out.

She took a deep breath to steel herself. After a beat, she crouched and made her way toward the small structure. Suddenly, she noticed Margie shuffling around the kitchen. Rose froze. When she noticed Margie was no longer in the window, she snuck to the shed and darted inside. Rose dropped to the ground and sat with her back to the wall, the shell of the building cool against her skin. The smell of oil and metal enveloped her. Rose released a long breath. She closed her eyes and focused on calming her heart and nerves. Outside, the rain drummed against the steel roof.

Daddy, who can I trust? Do I still go to Miss Margie? Tell me!

Rose rocked back and forth.

Margie will help, right? She has to help. Go knock on the door.

She wanted to go. Memories of Marcus swirled through her head.

I'm going. I promise.

CHAPTER FOUR

JAKE TURNED over in bed as the gray light leaked through the windows. Last night's storms had not fully dissipated. It had been a year since Lucy's suicide, but the horrors still chased him when he closed his eyes. He looked at the empty rocking chair in his bedroom.

Another day is upon us, Lu.

He groaned, not wanting to leave the warmth of his covers. The familiar chuffing of a pig greeted him as a round snout prodded at this elbow.

"Morning, Tiny," Jake whispered, rubbing the wiry fur on the potbelly's head. Snuffles, not to be ignored, propped his hooves on the mattress to root at Jake's legs, encouraging him to get up. Tiny and Snuffles were silly names for one-hundred-pound male potbelly pigs, but Lucy had named them when she was little.

"You boys hungry?"

The pigs grunted and squealed as they nodded their heads with excitement. Jake pulled himself up and dragged his palms down his face, the fatigue deep in his bones. His blue heeler, Ted, hopped up and wagged his bulbous docked tail to beg Jake for breakfast. Ted's sheer excitement shook the mattress, and he prodded Jake with his nose and a few wet licks of his tongue.

Knowing he would not receive any peace from the animals until they ate, Jake pulled on his sweatpants and T-shirt and shuffled down the hallway, trying to avoid being tripped by the critters circling his feet. On his way by, Jake pushed the button on the coffeemaker. Through his open window, the fresh April air flowed in with a hint of ozone. The thunderstorms had cleaned it. The briskness this close to dawn caused goosebumps that Jake worked to rub away. He heard the familiar clang of a cast-iron skillet on the gas range in Margie's kitchen next door. The familiar smell of bacon drifted from the main house to the guest house he was renting from her. Although Margie had been a librarian during her career, her parents had left her a large, estate-like parcel on the lake with the two homes, as well as a significant royalty stream from natural gas wells all over the county.

When he'd first returned to Haven, he'd eaten breakfast alone in the guest home. These days, he dropped in at Margie's for breakfast. She said that cooking for one was as troublesome as cooking for two, so he took her up on her offer. And he enjoyed having someone around to distract him from his thoughts.

Jake filled Ted's metal bowl with kibble, and the pigs' two rubber tubs with hay and feed. He tossed in a carrot, an orange, and grape tomatoes for the porkers: Lucy's precise recipe. She had instructed him in her final letter that Tiny and Snuffles needed fruits and vegetables, and that he must take good care of her pigs now that she could not.

The morning ritual, as usual, brought back the ache in his chest, a deep pain that stole his breath. Jake carried the two tubs onto the back porch. Tiny and Snuffles lost no time digging in, snorting as they devoured the fresh produce. Their thin, tufted tails joyfully swayed back and forth. Jake smiled. *Lucy would approve.*

With the pigs and Ted gobbling breakfast, Jake poured a cup of coffee and took in his surroundings. This morning a subtle fog—caused by the rains cooling the air—rose from Lake Haven. The sun peeked through a hole in the clouds. Its golden rays fanned out on the water's surface, punctuated along the shoreline by cattails. Haven resided north of Dallas, Texas. It was far from his previous world, where the other lawyers gossiped behind his back in the courthouse about his downfall. He had long given up trying to decipher the motive behind those whispers.

Thanks to a few favors from old friends, Haven—besides being where he'd grown up—had now become Jake's purgatory, a way station and a place to rebuild. A town of a few thousand, Haven was the government seat for Hawk County. A courthouse and cases awaited Jake to keep him occupied. But Haven was peaceful, a favorite spot for Dallas's wealthy to keep a lake house, hide away, and play on the water during an overcrowded Fourth of July. Indeed, from where he was standing, he could see his brother Britt's lake house, which was unused except for a caretaker. It was showy, as expected for someone who had discovered a fortune in a West Texas oil patch and wanted to flaunt it. But that was Britt. They had not spoken in recent years. When the brothers left Haven, they left each other, and focused on their own careers and families. Jake had called Britt a couple of times after Lucy's death, but the calls had gone to voicemail. Sometimes people just go their own way, and Jake was not sure he had the energy to piece their relationship back together.

These days, when Jake left the small law office he shared with another lawyer on the Haven town square, he could disappear on the lake or fish for bass and crappie from Margie's dock, lost in the silence and memories.

"It's ready, Jake," Margie called from the kitchen window.

"Be right there," Jake answered.

Jake slipped on his sneakers and crossed the yard with Ted,

Tiny, and Snuffles in tow. Ted curled up to nap on Margie's porch, and the pigs rooted for grubs in the wet grass, oblivious to the drizzle. Jake stepped through the screen door leading to the kitchen, his shoes squeaking on the tile floor. A perfect pair of eggs over easy and crispy bacon waited for him—his favorite.

"Morning, Margie."

"Mornin', Jake," she said, her silver hair in a tight, functional bun. A wild-patterned housedress flowed over her slight frame as she worked at her skillets. She pointed to his plate. "The toast is ready. Grab a piece or two and have a seat."

He glanced at his phone and noticed an email from Judge Maddix's clerk, Ginny, sent the evening before: *Jake, the judge wants to see you as soon as you get into town. Be sure you stop by.*

Jake emailed: *Just seeing this now. I'll be there.* He put down his phone and dug into his breakfast. Margie sat down at the table next to him.

"You've been too good to me, Margie," Jake said.

"Your mama would have wanted me to do it. She took my hand the night before she passed in the hospital and made me pinky promise—like we did when we were girls growin' up—that I'd watch over you boys. So I did it, and I'm still doin' it. I'm here, and I'm watchin' you and Britt… if he ever comes around." A wry smile punctuated her words.

"You sure you're not just gawking like a fan at a stock-car race, enjoying the wrecks?"

"You take that back, Jake Fox. Your mama's likely spinnin' in her grave at your horrible lack of manners."

"I'm just funning you, Margie. Mom knew a good joke." Jake mopped up his eggs with a corner of toast.

Margie smiled, trapped in memory, looking at Lake Haven through the window. "Claire had a great sense of humor." Closing her hand around Jake's, Margie glanced into his eyes. "You know she'd be proud of you, right? With all that's happened. That you didn't just give up. Nope, not you. You're gettin' back on your feet and movin' on. That's somethin' your mother would be proud of, yeah?" A beat passed as Margie's questions hit Jake in the gut. "She'd tell you to get back out there and start livin' again. Lucy would say it too. You deserve to be happy, maybe even find someone to move on with."

"Jury's still out on that, Margie, but I appreciate you saying it just the same."

"I'm serious, Jake. You must let it all go."

Silence fell between them, and it seemed that the world stilled for a heartbeat.

"I don't know how."

Margie patted his hand. "You'll learn. Give it time." Margie picked up Jake's plate and started washing up after breakfast. "What are your plans for today?"

"Judge Maddix emailed, said I need to come by the court." Jake rolled his eyes. "She's going to give me that ridiculous spiel about taking juvenile court appointments."

"You should help. I'm sure there're boys that could use your guidance and skills."

"Not sure I have the patience to deal with kids in trouble. I prefer it simple right now. No reason to search out trouble."

Margie glanced at her watch. "Well, trouble has a way of searchin' you out. Now, you'd better get ready for Judge Maddix. She's likely give you a tongue lashin' if you keep her waitin' until late in the day." She flicked the back of her hands at Jake to shoo him away. "Go on. Go back and get a shower and get dressed. I grabbed your shirts from the cleaners. They're on the far right of your closet. Also, pick a nice tie, will you? Something respectable."

"Margie."

"Okay, okay, I know you know how to dress yourself. But when you were little, you couldn't match an outfit to save your life. So try to find somethin' that goes together, will you? Now go... get." And with that, Margie hummed one of her gospel tunes and focused on rinsing dishes and cleaning pans.

A few minutes later, in the guest house, the shower's hot water spilled over his face. Jake wondered what crazy juvenile case Judge Maddix would try to foist off on him. He practiced saying no into the water spray. Tiny poked his snout around the edge of the shower curtain and snorted his appreciation for breakfast. Jake's thoughts turned to Lucy. The harrowing loneliness returned, threatening to cripple him.

No parent should ever bury a child, and no marriage could survive it.

CHAPTER FIVE

MARGIE WALKED toward the compost pile out back, her housedress flapping in the breeze from the lake. Ted wagged his docked tail and hind end while he and the pigs trotted ahead of her. Margie would have gone earlier, but the on again, off again rain had only now stopped briefly. Another band of moisture threatened from the other side of Lake Haven, and far-off thunder rumbled her way.

"Ted, don't you go swimmin' now. You've been trackin' in more mud than a pig because of the rain." Tiny grunted as if he knew she'd insulted him. "Sorry, Tiny. I understand you're a tidy pig. It's just an expression." Tiny wobbled forward, seemingly aloof and hurt. The long black mane on his withers shook in the wind, rocking with his gait. His potbelly swung from side to side, the bottom half darker from all the moisture in the grass.

Margie rounded the corner and dumped the peelings from tonight's dinner into the compost heap. She was making a pot roast with new potatoes and a nice peach cobbler, one of Jake's favorites. The rain amplified the smell of the fresh lawn clippings she had dropped on the pile yesterday. As she scooped the last of the peelings out of her bowl, she noticed that the door to the utility shed behind her home was swaying on its hinges.

"Now that's odd. I'm sure I shut that last night. The storm must have blown it open." Margie stepped toward the small building to shut the door. Ted scooted ahead, barking, planting his paws on the ground.

"Ted, what're you gettin' up to now? We can't have you gettin' sprayed by a skunk. You'll be sleepin' outside if that happens, no matter if it is rainin' and cold." Hackles up, Ted continued to bark and then emanated a low growl as he stared ahead, his body on point. Margie followed his line of sight straight to a pair of black high-top sneakers belonging to someone crouched behind the bulbous white propane tank next to the compact building. Margie's heart rate ticked up a notch. She looked around. She was alone except for whoever was behind the white cylinder. Jake had headed into town. Tiny and Snuffles grunted, as if sensing something had shifted in Margie's demeanor.

"Who's there?" Margie called, squaring herself for a fight and brandishing the ceramic mixing bowl in her hands like a weapon. "I can see your feet. I know you're back there. What are you doin' on my property?"

Slowly, a teenage girl stood up, looking exhausted and in shock. Her wet blonde hair clung to her face, and her dirty clothes suggested she'd trekked through the woods in the storm. The rain had soaked her, and her fingers quivered from either cold… or fear.

"Margie," Rose uttered, her voice barely audible.

"Rosemary, is that you, hon? What on earth are you doin', squattin' behind my propane tank?"

"Dad told me to find you. Told me you could help me." Rose's deep green eyes welled up with tears. They were red and puffy. Rose had been crying for a while.

"Why didn't you just come ring the bell?"

"Margie, he's dead." Rose's cadence sped up to a flutter. "They took him. I saw them beat on him, and now he's dead."

"Darlin', what are you talkin' about?" Margie slammed the shed closed. She walked over and reached out for Rose's hand. "Come on, come with me. We'll call the sheriff and get this wild story sorted out. Let's go into the house. Get you dry, and somethin' to eat. You look half-frozen." Margie took Rose's hand and half guided, half dragged her toward the house as she chattered away.

Inside, Margie sat Rose on a barstool at the kitchen counter. She grabbed a blanket from the couch, wrapped it around Rose's shoulders, and then turned with a flourish.

"Now, start from the beginnin'. Where is your daddy?"

"Last night, at the house. Men came to the house. Beat him. This morning I found him in his room… dead."

Margie drew in a deep breath. "Are you sure?" Margie already regretted her tone of disbelief.

Rose did not answer, the shock gobbling up her voice.

"Beat him, you say?" Margie continued. "Who was this? It just doesn't make sense. What could he have done that someone wanted to kill him? Rose, you must tell me what you know." Margie's question flowed out in a staccato rhythm.

"He wouldn't tell me. Just told me to run out back and hide in the well house. But he looked scared. Something was wrong. Those men were after something. I don't think they found it." Sobs wracked Rose. Margie scooted around the counter and rubbed the small of her back.

"Now don't you worry. We'll get it figured. I've got to call the sheriff, though, in case Marcus is still alive. Get him an ambulance."

"They shot him in the head," Rose croaked, horror haunting her eyes.

Margie embraced Rose and held her tightly, her own heart racing in her chest.

When Rose caught her breath, she said, "He was telling me

to hide. Then they showed up. I tell you, they are the ones that killed him…" Her eyes widened with fear.

Margie wiped a splash of mud from Rose's cheek. "Why didn't you call the police, Rose?"

"I almost did, but I couldn't. Dad didn't tell me to go to the law. He told me to come and find you. So I came. He said you'd know what to do."

"Well, we're callin' the sheriff, that is for sure. They need to get to your house now."

"I don't know who those people were. What do I tell them?" Rose asked.

Margie ignored the subject of Marcus's activities. She pulled her phone from her apron and dialed.

"Tina, it's Margie. I need Sheriff Stone or one of her deputies to come out here to the lake as soon as possible. No, no, everythin' is fine with me. I have Marcus Tucker's little girl out here, Rosemary… Yes, she has grown up. Tina, Rose is tellin' me some men killed Marcus last night. That's right. Dead. No, I don't know why… What do you expect? She's in shock. No, she's not goin' anywhere. She'll be here whenever someone gets here. Yes… yes, I'll keep her calm. She'll be here."

Margie hung up the phone and straightened her housedress. She pulled sandwich fixings from the refrigerator and a plate from the cupboard. Margie dropped the food on the counter and began to make Rose a sandwich. Across from her, Rose shivered under the blanket.

"Tina says they'll send someone out to your place right away. They'll call once the deputies have had a look around. She said it could be a while until they call back. In the meantime, they said for you to wait here with me. Let's get you a bath or a shower. You're chilled to the bone, and a few minutes' rest might do you a bit of good. I bet you didn't sleep a wink last night, did you? We have time 'til they call back.

Might as well use it." Margie winked at Rosemary, hoping a soft touch might calm the girl down. Once she finished making the sandwich, and without asking, she picked up the plate and headed down the hall, beckoning Rose to follow. "You can eat while you're washin' and gettin' warmed up." She led her into a guest room and placed the plate of food on the vanity.

"What if the sheriff thinks I did something wrong?" Rose asked.

"Sweetheart, you've been chased from your house, and you were out hidin' in the rain to reach me. How in the world could they think you did wrong?"

A pause floated between them as Rose looked out the window. "I should have helped him," Rose said, a small tear rolling off her cheek. "I just watched them take him and didn't help, and they killed him."

"Darlin', I'm sure Marcus didn't want you to get involved. He may have been mixed up with the wrong people, but he's not a fool. You said it was a group. How was little old you supposed to fight off a bunch of grown men? You'd have just got yourself swiped as well… or worse. Good Lord, you must be terrified. There are fresh towels by the shower. All the soaps you need. I keep a spare toothbrush in the drawers in there as well."

"Thank you," Rose said, still in a daze.

Margie sat on the end of the bed and took Rose's hands in hers. Margie could see the exhaustion enveloping her.

"The sheriff is going to figure this out, hon," Margie said. "You're safe with me. You try not to worry so much, yeah? They'll track them. For now, you try to relax and remember every detail you can for when the sheriff gets to talkin' to you. She's goin' to want to hear what you remember, down to the last detail. That's the best way to help Marcus now."

"I'll try," Rose said, her voice raspy, her stare blank.

"That's all we need, Rose. Just give them the best you have

got. I'm going to give you your privacy. I'll be out in the kitchen, waitin' for them to call. You holler if you need anything and come out when you're good and ready."

Margie closed the door and left Rose alone, with no actual answers and a lot of questions.

CHAPTER SIX

MARGIE HAD CLOSED the bedroom door behind her. Rose was alone. Anxiety scurried up her skin like a cluster of spiders. Sitting on the bed, she fought back tears with her hands. She was now a child thrust into adulthood. The grief promised to swamp her in unending waves. Silent sobs wracked her body until she became nauseated. The night before, there'd been no time to process what had occurred. She'd been scared and running for her life. Now, time had stopped, and emotions flooded her. Marcus was gone—truly gone. His lifeless stare haunted her. Rose's heart beat wildly, and her breath turned ragged with panic. She glanced at her hands as they shook. She interlaced her fingers and tried to start her grounding cadence. *Five things I can see.* But she failed to focus. Nothing would stop. Alone. She was alone.

Rose turned the images over in her head. The familiar laughter of that redheaded woman. A chill raced up her spine and niggled at her subconscious. The blood splattering the wall and soaking the mattress. Rose's heart sank. She wiped her nose with the heel of her palm and struggled to keep her sobs silent so Margie would not burst back through the door to comfort her. She wasn't sure she deserved any show of humanity, let alone love. Rose had left her father to his death. She had left his murdered body alone in their home.

Who does that? Who could forgive me?

Rose slipped to the floor and curled her arms around her legs. In her mind, she saw the silhouettes but not the faces of the redhead and the bearded man. They remained phantoms, their features faded into the darkness of her memory.

She shuddered at the thought of Marcus, injured from the beating. Then a flash of anger ripped through her as she realized that Marcus had known what was going to happen. He'd understood he was going to die. He'd saved Rose, sacrificed himself for her… given her time to run into a future. His gift overwhelmed her and made her angry at him too. She grabbed the medallion Marcus had hung around her neck and clenched it in her fist. She rubbed her fingers across the likeness of Saint Michael, trying to conjure up any sort of prayer. Her tears soaked the denim on her knees.

Rose stood and headed to the bathroom. She turned on the shower with quivering fingers and dragged herself out of her clothes, the chill making her shudder. She winced as she pulled off her jeans—the cuts on her thigh and knee were jagged, puffy, and angry. Rose would ask Margie later if she had something to clean them. Soap would work for now. Marcus had taught her how to mend her own scrapes years ago. He was always talking about being prepared, being self-sufficient. He was almost obsessed with it. Rose sighed and stepped into the shower. The steam fogged the glass until she could barely see the bathroom.

"I have to take care of myself," she whispered into the streaming water. "It's just me now."

The hot water enveloped her, and fatigue clawed at her. Absorbed in the warmth, her tears lost in the spray, she replayed the past few months with her dad, the stupid fights and ridiculous anger. Their recent battles seemed trivial now that he was gone. What she wouldn't give to hear his voice, feel his calloused hands wrap around hers.

She's been foolish. Just a dumb girl to cause so much trouble. He was only struggling to protect her. Her father hadn't much liked Tommy, the boy she was dating. He was suspicious of most of the boys she dated, like any father, but the moment he'd laid eyes on Tommy, he'd developed a violent dislike for him. He did not approve of Tommy's tattoos, or the fact that he'd dropped out of community college in the first year. He didn't figure Tommy was thinking about the future.

She'd argued that Tommy had a job. After all, he always had money. Her dad just didn't understand. Not everyone needed a formal education. Many roughnecks in the field did not.

Her father rode her for Tommy, telling her he was no good and that she deserved someone better. He had hoped she would head off to college and find someone there. He didn't want his little girl marrying a roughneck or a rail hand or some other blue-collar joe. Not to mention that Tommy was a few years older. Her dad said her boyfriend was only after one thing, and that comment had led to an awkward screaming match over the birds and the bees.

But none of it mattered now. She just wanted her father back. She wanted to curl up on the couch and watch television with his hands stroking her hair in the quiet of their little, broken family.

A knock came at the bathroom door.

"Rose, hon. You mind if I run your clothes through the laundry right quick?" Margie asked. "I don't want you being damp and cold."

The kindness in Margie's voice surprised her, and the hitch in Rose's throat interrupted her first effort to respond. Finally, she said, "No, ma'am. I'll be out in a while. Might catch some sleep if I can."

"You come out when you're ready, hon. I'll let you know when the sheriff calls back."

Margie fussed around the bathroom, then the door closed.

Rose's heart raced again as she remembered hiding in the storm shelter. Marcus had long been preparing for this possibility. That much she knew. But what had he been doing? And what did he intend for her to do? Rose mulled it over in her mind. No solution presented itself, at least not one she wanted to consider. However good his intentions, her father had brought trouble upon their home—and it had killed him.

Why did I dare to bring such danger into Margie's kind home? I should have kept running.

Rose remained paralyzed in the shower until the water grew tepid. Soon, it would turn cold. She didn't want to experience the morning's chill and become wet and frozen again. She shut off the water, toweled dry, wiped away the steam, and looked at herself in the mirror. Her pale white skin seemed to amplify her exhaustion. She'd always thought of herself as gangly unattractive. Tommy had changed that. He was the first boy to call her pretty. Rose twisted her damp hair into a long ponytail and twirled it behind her head, trying to pretend to be beautiful for Tommy. It wasn't working. She stepped into the bedroom and crawled under the welcoming, smooth linens on the bed. She only needed a few minutes to close her eyes, and her wet clothes would take some time to dry.

As she stared at the ceiling, fatigue pressed her into the mattress, and the annoying ringing in her ears returned as sleep started to consume her. The sheer weight of her situation numbed her in the calm of Margie's guest room. She worked to push all memories from her mind so she might rest, and she prayed she wouldn't bring trouble to Margie's door.

My father is dead. Where else can I possibly go?

CHAPTER SEVEN

JAKE WALKED into the law office he now shared with Hitch Mills. The bell on the front door clattered out its welcoming *ding-a-ling*. The familiar smells of strong coffee and cigars, already heady, anchored him in a bit of history.

"Jake, you're late," his secretary Darla said as she stood and grabbed a packet of unopened mail from the desk. She followed him down the hallway to his office. Her long brown hair flowed behind her, the gray at the temples giving away that she had worked for Hitch for a long time. Darla's perfume reminded Jake of the secretary at his former practice in Dallas. It smelled expensive—likely a Christmas gift from Hitch.

"Judge Maddix called this morning to remind you that you're due in her chambers today. She wants to talk to you," Darla said.

"I may or may not get there. There's still time for something to come up," Jake said with a playful smile.

Darla scoffed. "It ain't my place, but I'll tell you, Jake: don't hide from Maddix." A knowing glance passed between them. "We got that order back from Judge Thompson on the Estes will contest. And the clerk just sent through the deed on the house closing for Mr. and Mrs. Middleberry."

"Perfect, Darla." Jake stood at his desk and waited to see if she had any other messages or tidbits to provide.

After an awkward silence, Darla tapped her pencil on her steno pad. "Can I get you a cup of coffee? Black, no cream or sugar?"

"Darla, you don't have to get me coffee," Jake protested mildly. But he hoped she would persist. The errand would give him a moment to settle in before she returned.

"I insist. I've always brought Hitch his coffee. And he says I should treat you just like him—now that you're hanging out your shingle here and all."

Jake was now a small-town lawyer in Hawk County. It was a far cry from the skyscraper in downtown Dallas. He never thought he'd be back here, but some things, like Hitch's voice, made it seem like home.

"Speaking of Hitch, is he in?"

"Jake, you know he's always in. That boy, no matter what he drinks, always arrives at seven sharp. I assume he always will until the good Lord calls him home." Then Darla whispered over the back of her hand, as if shielding a deep secret, "He has amazing recuperative powers."

"Sounds like you might be a little sweet on him, Darla." Darla's cheeks flushed, and her hand rose to the diamond pendent on her necklace.

"You take that back."

Jake smiled, knowing he'd struck a nerve.

"I'll be right back with your coffee," she said, and shuffled out the door in a huff and a cloud of perfume, leaving Jake to his thoughts for a moment.

Jake spent time opening the stack of mail. A few minutes later, he picked up the coffee that arrived with a small flourish but no conversation. With the mail cleared, he ambled across the hallway to see Hitch, whose booming voice spilled out of the doorway. A melee was obviously underway.

"Harold, I don't care what you say. There's no way you can

get me dismissed at the outset of this case. You know good and well I'll be able to allege a claim sufficiently, and then we're off to the races. We're into discovery, and that'll just cost your client big dollars. Then you'll be lucky to get out on summary judgment on this one. Face it: you're going to trial whether you like it or not. And you shouldn't, because you got no facts and no witnesses on your side… You're gonna lose, Harold, so you might as well see if I can sell my clients on settling for close to your cost of defense… I don't give a rat if your clients say they did nothing wrong. You know, and I know, that the law is all about leverage. It's about what I can get the court to make your clients do. Right now, I think I can get them to pay me a pile of money… That's fine. You call my girl Darla when you got an answer. Dollar signs, Harold. You better be talking big dollar signs." Hitch slammed down the phone handset.

Jake knocked on the doorframe and walked into the large office. "Morning, Hitch."

Hitch was perched in his wide leather office chair. It was more of a throne than furniture. He took a deep puff of his cigar and raked his hands through the long gray hair he kept swept back with the comb in his shirt pocket. Except for a five-year stint working for a white-shoe law firm in a Houston high-rise, Hitch had been a fixture in Hawk County for his entire legal career. He'd made a small fortune suing trucking companies for eighteen-wheeler accidents that occurred on the highways that crisscrossed the county. For a time, he'd had a billboard out on I-35, but his reputation soon became sufficient advertising to keep his schedule busy and his wallet thick.

"Come on in, son. Take a seat." Hitch shot his cuffs, pulled at the cufflinks on his custom dress shirt, and flattened his bright-red silk tie against his chest. "Well, now, you look tired as a hooker at a truck stop on dollar night. You still not sleeping?"

"Working on it."

Hitch nodded, as if Jake's answer was satisfactory. "I had

insomnia once, way back. I'd just started out, had the first kid on the way with Wife Number One. Money was tight. I'd pace the floor all night and then drag myself through the next day."

"I'm not up pacing."

"Eighteen months."

"What?"

"Eighteen months was how long that spate of insomnia lasted. Toward the end, I was so exhausted I questioned whether it was better to just crawl out into the scrub brush and let the turkey buzzards get me." Hitch shook his head, as if to toss out a memory. "Ugly birds, turkey buzzard. Nasty beaks."

"My mind's not full of the best of dreams these days, Hitch."

Hitch's deep brown eyes took on a knowing, compassionate glint. "I assume not. I guess the only thing that takes nightmares like that away is time." Hitch leaned forward, resting his forearms on his desk, holding Jake's attention with a piercing stare. "You know, sooner or later, you're going to have to let all that hurtin' go."

Jake ignored the comment, cleared his throat, and pushed ahead. "Judge Maddix is hounding me to take juvenile appointments over at the courthouse. She told me last week at the diner that it would be good for me to help some kids around here."

Hitch leaned back in his chair and steepled his fingers just below his chin, as if taking Jake's measure. After a moment, he said, "I agree. Jake, you were one of the best. Still could be even greater. Some of those boys and girls could benefit from your talents."

"I've been avoiding her."

"Darla told me."

Jake thought, *Of course she did.*

"Thing is, I like it kind of simple," Jake said. "Estate planning, papering up a home sale, the occasional slip and fall, or a trucking accident. That's not a bad life, right?"

"Judge Maddix is gonna get you sooner or later, Jake. She vouched for you on your probation with the State Bar, and I expect she's calling to collect. Besides, what's the worst that happens? You end up defending a couple of dumb teenagers on a shoplifting bust. Easy peasy."

Jake paused for a moment, as if weighing something on his mind. "They won't all be shoplifting. Trust me, fate plays tricks."

"Can't hide forever, my friend."

Jake looked down and straightened the creases in his lap. "Well, telling a grown man he's headed to an eight-by-ten jail cell is one thing… I can't imagine doing it with a kid." Jake's voice dropped, and there was a slight catch in the back of his throat. "Failing a kid could wreck me. I'm not ready for that. I don't think I'll ever be ready for that." He looked back up at Hitch.

"Life takes it out of you, son. Nobody gets out alive, and most of us live tired. Might as well do something you're good at. Something that gets the juices flowing. Don't waste your talents."

For a moment, Jake remembered a familiar thrill. There is nothing in this world like the adrenaline rush that courses through the blood seconds before a jury foreman reads out the words *guilty* or *not guilty*.

Hitch took a long drag from his cigar and puffed out a smoke ring. They sat in silence for a moment, as if lost in memories of trials past.

"Jake." Darla's voice spilled through the doorway. "Margie's on line one, says she needs you up at the house right away. Says she has a problem, and it can't wait… She sounded flustered."

"You'd better git, then," Hitch said. "No one in this town leaves Margie hanging. She's been around too long, and she knows where all the bodies are buried."

"Darla, tell Margie I'll be right there. Call Judge Maddix

and tell her I had to run back home. Tell her Margie told me it was an emergency. That should get Maddix off my back."

"Will do," Darla called.

Jake stood up, but he turned back to Hitch, who was still sitting at this desk "Just a few shoplifting cases, huh?"

"Just a few," Hitch answered.

CHAPTER EIGHT

JAKE LOOKED down Margie's hallway as he finished his last bite of pie. Margie knocked on the bedroom door and called for Rose. Unease pulsed through Jake. *What on earth has Margie gotten into*?

"Thank you for the bite to eat, Margie," he said when she returned.

"You're welcome." Margie took his plate, rinsed it, and placed it in the dishwasher. "Thanks for comin' home."

"You called the sheriff like I said to?"

"I called when she first showed up and again after I got off the phone with you."

"What are we going to do with her?"

Margie ignored the skeptical tone in Jake's voice. "Do you think she'll be all right?"

"You said she's upset, so I imagine something happened. Once we hear from the sheriff, maybe Rose can fill in a few holes. But it would be a bit nuts if someone shot Marcus like she claims. I'm sure she's not the first teenager to spin a wild story when a parent wanders off on a bender and comes back stone drunk. For all we know, she's just a runaway seeking attention."

"You should've seen her when I first found her, Jake. This isn't a wild story. No, I know Rose, and this is real. I can feel it."

"We'll see." Jake hated being jaded, but everyone's story changes, eventually.

Margie's phone rang.

"Hello? Yes ma'am… No, she's still here, right here in my guest room. Poor thing was exhausted… She hasn't said much, other than what I told Tina on the phone… That's right, she said some men came after Marcus last night. Beat him, too, and she found him dead this mornin'. No, no, we don't mind. Yes, ma'am, we'll bring her right over." Margie hung up the phone and turned to Jake. "The sheriff wants us to bring Rose over to the Tucker place."

"Us?"

"Yes, you're goin' with *us*." Margie turned before Jake could protest. He shook his head and let out a long breath. Margie shuffled out of the kitchen to get Rose, knocking gently again on the guest room door. "Rose, hon, the sheriff wants us all to go to your house… ask you a few questions about what happened over there."

Slowly the door open and Rose appeared, her gaze distant. "The sheriff?"

"Yes. She has some questions, and she wants you to visit with her at your house."

"I don't…"

"Now, don't you worry, hon. I'm goin' with you, and we're takin' Jake."

As Rose walked through the door, Jake gulped, and his heart raced as he took in her long blonde hair and green eyes. It was as if Lucy had walked right back into this world. Same size, same build—a ghost. One by one, memories pummeled him: his little girl laughing on the swings, chasing ducks at the pond, singing in the school play.

Margie's voice pulled him from the painful reverie. "Jake, grab your keys."

Margie snatched a blanket to wrap around Rose's shoulders and shuffled her out the back door. Jake followed, trying to keep up.

The ride to the Tucker place was short. It was a mile or so up the road on this side of the lake. Margie sat in the backseat with Rose. A few times, Jake caught Rose looking at him in the mirror. She didn't respond to idle chitchat, but remained silent, as if girding herself against an awful truth.

What isn't she telling us?

Rose's home was set back from the road quite a way. As they rounded a stand of loblolly pines, a simple ranch house came into view. The house looked like it had a fresh coat of paint. Marcus Tucker had obviously taken care of the place before he disappeared. In the rearview mirror, Jake noticed a moment of fear in Rose's eyes.

The sheriff, who was talking to a deputy, saw them pull up and walked toward them. As she recognized Jake, she gave a soft smile, but in the next moment her expression turned grim again.

Hope Stone had recently won reelection as sheriff in a landslide. She was a natural politician, gregarious and at ease talking to strangers, someone you liked from the word *hello.* She always had been.

Jake and Hope had dated the summer after they graduated high school, and time had only enhanced her beauty. Her auburn hair. Those ice-blue eyes. A familiar heat stirred in Jake as he remembered their final night together, sitting by a bonfire on the lakeshore the summer before he headed to college. He hadn't run into her since returning to Haven. Now a flutter in his stomach told him he wished he had. He pushed the thoughts from his mind and rolled down his window.

This is serious business, Jake. You're at a murder scene.

"Margie. Jake," the sheriff said.

Rose shouted as she reached for the door handle. "Did you find the men who killed Marcus?"

"Rose, I need you to stay in the truck," the sheriff commanded. "Please describe the men you saw last night."

"What's going on?" Rose asked, panic lacing her voice.

"Rose, *tell me* about these men." The sheriff's tone remained calm but direct.

Rose's gaze implored Jake and Margie for help. Then she answered the sheriff. "They shot him," Rose yelled. "Shot him in the head." When the sheriff didn't respond, she relented. "There were four, total. Three men and a woman. But that redheaded woman was in charge."

The sheriff nodded as she took notes.

"A man came and shouted for Marcus to come out," Rose said. "They took him around front and started beating on him. Then they took him back into the house."

"Where were you?"

"Marcus told me to run and hide in the well house. I was watching through a crack in the wall."

"Did you see their faces? Did you recognize them?"

"It was nighttime. Their headlights were behind them. I couldn't see with the glare."

"Sheriff, tell us what's goin' on," Margie said.

"You were hiding in the well house, you say?" the sheriff continued, focused on Rose.

"Yes. In the storm cellar underneath it. Why are you asking me? Why can't I get out?" Her frustration was tinged with fear.

"Jake, Margie, can we visit for a second?" the sheriff asked.

"Rose," Margie said in a calming voice, "Jake and I are gonna to step out and visit with the sheriff. You stay here for a minute. I'll get this sorted."

They all stepped out of earshot. Jake could see a weight seemed to press on the sheriff.

"I haven't seen him for a while, but I still recognize him."

She nodded her head back toward the home. "He's in the bedroom, just as she said, and appears to have been dead for hours. He's been shot in the head."

Margie gasped and raised her hand to her mouth. "I knew she was tellin' the truth."

"To me," the sheriff continued, "it looks more like a self-inflicted gunshot wound. I'll have to wait to see what the medical examiner thinks." Sheriff Stone turned to Margie. "Rose didn't say anything about Marcus being depressed or upset, did she?"

"No, Sheriff. She was quite clear about what she saw. About someone killin' her father."

"Well, I'll keep it open as a crime scene, but as of right now, I've got no reason to suspect that anyone else was out here last night."

"Look, Hope," Jake said. "I mean Sheriff. I don't know this girl at all, but Margie says she was pretty shook up."

"I don't doubt she was upset," Hope said. "I'm just not sure it's a murder. Maybe she's making it up, so she doesn't have to think about her dad offing himself with a pistol."

Jake pushed aside thoughts of his almost-nightly ritual with his own handgun. "What do you want us to do?"

"I could ask Rose for a positive ID now, but I'd prefer to wait. The medical examiner needs to work the scene and must transport the body back to the morgue. And since we're going to treat it like a crime scene, Rose can't go back into that house. I need y'all to help me keep her from running up there. I need to keep her in the car. I can't have her touching the body or mussing up the scene any more than she might have already. The techs are still taking photos and processing evidence. But I would like her to know that we're worried it was a suicide. I'll need her help to figure out her dad's state of mind recently."

"I'll tell her," Margie insisted. "It'll be easier comin' from me. She's already scared half to death."

"I appreciate it."

Jake and Sheriff Stone watched as Margie walked back to the truck and climbed into the back seat with Rose. She took Rose's hands in her own and spoke softly enough that the sheriff and Jake couldn't hear her. Rose's expression crumpled, as if being told that Marcus shot himself finally drove the full terror of his death through Rose. She clawed for the door handle, and her feral scream punctuated the air. Margie grabbed Rose by the shoulders and pulled her back around, binding her in a hug. Slowly, Rose collapsed into Margie's embrace. The sound from the sobs wracking her body spilled out the window. Margie stroked the back of her long blonde hair, working to calm her as quickly as possible. Margie looked out the windshield at Jake and the sheriff and closed her eyes as she grasped Rose. Jake turned away, looking up at the house.

Life was about to get more complicated.

CHAPTER NINE

THE NEXT MORNING, the dread that had been turning Jake's gut threatened to wash over him as they headed to town. Sheriff Stone had asked Rose, the only known next of kin, to identify Marcus's body. Jake was thankful they would be identifying an adult, not a child. Perhaps he would handle an adult corpse better. As the mile markers raced by, a scant fog from the lake indicated that the growing spring humidity had yet to burn off. Silence filled the cab like a meditation all the way to town. Finally Jake, Margie, and Rose pulled into the hospital parking lot, and Jake shut off the engine.

Hawk County Medical Center, the main hospital, sat at the corner of Lead and Elm Street in the center of Haven. It contained the only trauma center in five counties. As such, it collected the aftermath of any violent activity in the area. Crumpled bodies wrenched from tractor-trailer accidents, any knife or gunshot wounds—and the dead—all made their way to HCMC. With the morning sun low in the sky, the large, red-brick monstrosity cast cold shadows over those who came and went.

Jake opened the back door and offered his hand to Rose. She had maintained an even, stoic demeanor. Rose was much too young to face the horror of identifying a parent's lifeless form. But she seemed to gain strength from the gravity of the task. It was simply what the law required. Even though she was just fifteen, the responsibility fell to her.

"You sure you're up to this?" Jake asked as he helped her out of the truck. The hoodie she wore swallowed her body, as if she'd shrunk overnight.

Rose drew in a deep breath. Her response came slowly, as if girding herself. "It has to be done." She wiped a single tear from her cheek with the cuff of her sweatshirt and flipped her ponytail to one side.

"Hon," Margie said, "if this gets to be too much, Jake and I'll just whisk you right out of there." She gave Jake a knowing glance that suggested if this became tough, he had to be ready to step up.

"It should be brief," Jake said.

"Can we just go inside and get this over with?" Rose asked.

Margie reached out and rubbed the small of Rose's back as if willing her forward. They remained silent as they walked up the front steps of the hospital.

The county morgue resided in the basement of HCMC, down a long, industrial-grade hallway and behind two hulking, white automatic doors. The germicidal odor of the mopped floor permeated the air. Up ahead, Jake saw Sheriff Stone sitting in a plastic chair, staring at a sign on the wall. Under different circumstances, he would have been excited to see her. But she was slumped, as if from an unseen weight. After a moment, she spotted the three of them walking down the hall. She conjured up a light but professional smile. Then she stood, cowboy hat in hand, meeting them a step or two from the doors to the morgue.

"Rose, I'm sorry you have to do this for me. Maybe there's someone else that could do the ID?"

"No," Rose said, standing straighter. "He's my father. I should do it. I need to do it. I still can't believe he's dead."

"Fair enough." Sheriff Stone reached down and pushed the red button on the wall, and the doors swung open on their hydraulic hinges. Jake had always hated the smell of hospitals —their antiseptic nature was foreign to other kinds of human existence. But morgues have a perfunctory ugly stench their own, driven by their purpose.

Inside the doors, Shonda Dunkin, the county coroner and medical examiner, waited for them in green scrubs and a pressed white jacket. Jake tried to push the images of what Dr. Dunkin had been doing the past few hours from his mind. Jake had seen plenty of autopsy photos while defending his clients in criminal courts. The autopsy procedure was a clinical inquisition as the examiner cut into the body and then explored, calculated, measured, weighed. It was an incredible invasion of a human body, especially one already victimized.

Dr. Dunkin kept her focus on Rose. Her expression remained calm and all business. "He's this way." She led them to a bank of square stainless-steel doors on a cabinet deep in the bowels of the morgue.

"You ready, Rose?" Dr. Dunkin asked.

"Yes ma'am," Rose answered. Jake saw Rose's fists clench, her knuckles turning white as she dug her black-painted fingernails into her palms. Dr. Dunkin opened the door and pulled out a tray with Marcus's body. Jake let out his breath.

No turning back now.

Jake was grateful that the good doctor had covered Marcus with a sheet. Prior experience told Jake that unwrapping the layers of tragedy a little at a time could forestall the crush of loss… somewhat.

They watched Rose take in the magnitude of her new reality as Dr. Dunkin lifted the sheet from Marcus's head. The medical examiner had made an extra effort to clean up the body after the autopsy. Marcus's expression was stoic. His waxen skin and pale blue lips had a peaceful expression, as if he'd done his duty. His body in this world rested still. It would never move again, regardless of where his soul might take him.

Rose let out a gasp and brought a quivering hand to her mouth. Soft sobs mixed with her voice, and her words at first were too soft to hear. Large tears rolled down her cheeks, and her breath came hard, almost like dry heaves. Jake wrapped his arm around Rose's waist, reached into his suit jacket for a handkerchief, and handed it to her. He was surprised when she leaned into him.

Rose's voice came thick with emotion. "That's him. That's Marcus… my father."

Dr. Dunkin nodded, showing that Rose had satisfied the law's identification requirement. She moved to push Marcus back into the darkness of the cooler drawer.

Rose held up a hand to stop her. She placed a kiss on Marcus's cheek and then spoke in broken gasps.

"I'm sorry. So sorry, Daddy. I love you. I'll do what you asked… I'm going to miss you, Dad… so much. It was supposed to be you and me. Now, it's just… me. I promise I'll be strong. I promise, Daddy, I'll be strong. You'll be proud of me. You'll see."

Rose's speech swamped the stunned silence of the sterile room.

"Rose, darlin' girl," Margie said in almost a whisper, "you're gonna be okay. I know you don't think that now, but somehow it will work out. We'll help you get on with it."

Jake felt a flash of anger at Margie's statement. How could it be okay? What in God's name was Rose going to do now that she was alone in the world at fifteen?

Once they had Rose somewhat stable and Marcus back in the drawer, Sheriff Stone cleared her throat.

"Rose," she said, "I know this has been difficult. I appreciate you coming down to do the formal identification." Jake noticed the tension had not left the sheriff. In fact, she looked even more conflicted and worried than before.

Margie piped in, "If that's all you need from us, Dr. Dunkin, I'd like to get Rose home. Let her have the time to sort this out."

"Of course," Dr. Dunkin said. "We're done here."

"If you don't mind," the sheriff chimed in again, "I have a few questions that Rose might help answer. It won't take long, then y'all can take her home."

Jake looked at Hope's face, seeking a clue. Her expression remained stoic. But something in her gaze set off alarm bells. Jake stepped between the sheriff and Rose.

"What if I bring her by in a couple of days?" Jake asked.

Sheriff Stone stood taller. "No… I prefer we do this now. It won't take long, and y'all are already in town."

"I don't mind," Rose interjected, her fingers now interlaced with Margie's. "I'll answer your questions, if it will help you find who killed him."

"We'll be right there with you," Margie said.

The sheriff turned on her heel and walked down the hallway to the elevators. They followed, with Margie fussing over Rose like a mother hen.

Jake couldn't pinpoint it, but his gut told him something had changed, and the sheriff wasn't telling him everything.

CHAPTER TEN

JAKE OPENED the door for Margie and Rose as they followed Hope to her office. The sheriff's department resided in the city-county building across the street from HCMC. It took up the entire first floor. Once through the doors, Sheriff Stone led them into the guts of the bustle.

"Hi, Penny. Is the conference room still open?" The sheriff asked.

"Yes, Sheriff. Bottled water is on the table, and there's a fresh pot of coffee in the break room."

Jake recognized Penny Lambert from his childhood. She had worked for Sheriff Hogue back when Jake was in high school. In fact, Penny had been very kind to Jake when he had to sit in the hallway, half-drunk and tired, waiting for Margie to come pick him up. Sheriff Hogue had busted a bunch of them drinking beers around a bonfire by the lake. Jake remembered Margie's expression as she came through the double doors that day: disappointed to be there, but forgiving, as if boys will be boys.

"Penny, how is Burton?" Margie asked. "He still doing everythin' the doctors tell him not to do?"

"I won't never get him to listen." Penny flashed a friendly

smile at Jake and Rose. "Margie, I left out fresh cream in case you're going to get yourself a cup of coffee."

Sheriff Stone thanked Penny and led them through the bullpen. Deputies, detectives, and others on her staff sat at their desks, pushing forward the police work in Hawk County. Jake, Margie, and Rose followed Hope down a short hall, and Sheriff Stone ushered them into the conference room.

Something niggled at Jake. Polly leaving cream out for Margie? This little question-and-answer session has been planned before the sheriff left to meet them at the morgue. It might have been planned for a while.

The sheriff directed Rose to a chair and sat next to her, their knees nearly touching. She passed a bottle of water, and Rose loosened the cap and took a long drink.

"Rose, I need to ask you additional questions about the night your father died, okay?" Sheriff Stone looked at Jake as if asking permission. She turned back to Rose. "This is an interview. A conversation, if you will. You're free to go any time you want, you simply say so."

"I'm happy to answer any questions you have," Rose said, her eyes still red and puffy from the morgue. "I don't know much more than I already told you at the house."

"Understood. We just need some details confirmed." The sheriff reached out, placing her hand palm down near Rose's arm. "Before we get started, though, I want to tell you how sorry I am about what happened to Marcus."

The emotion returned to Rose's eyes. Jake grabbed a tissue box from the corner and slid it across the table. He took a chair, but didn't relax into it.

"You're gonna find whoever did this, right?" Rose asked. "I don't know what I'm meant to do now. Where do I go?"

"I'm sure it's a shock," the sheriff said. "Something tells me you and Margie and Jake will sort it out." The sheriff kept her close, intimate proximity to Rose. Jake shifted in his seat, recognizing the positioning as a tactic to build rapport with the interviewee.

"Rose, can you run me back through what happened that night?"

"It's like I said. I was home with my father. Some men, and that redheaded woman, pulled up to the house in a black SUV. One guy stepped up on the porch. He banged on the door and yelled for my father to come outside. Dad told me to hide in the well house. I hid in there and watched them beat him and then drag him back into our home." Rose glanced at Jake as if seeking guidance before she looked back at the sheriff. "I got spooked and knocked something over in the shed. That's when the big bearded guy almost found me, but two raccoons stumbled out of the bush. I guess he figured that's what the ruckus was. The redheaded lady yelled at him. That's when they went in the house."

"Did you get a look at his face?"

"No, ma'am. I couldn't see much. It was dark. I remember that redhead's hair. That I can't forget. Fire red. Almost like it was glowing in the headlights."

"Anything else?"

Rose pulled on a cuticle. "That man's beard was long."

Hope nodded and wrote in her notebook.

"What about the trucks? Do you remember anything other than that the vehicles were dark? A license plate? Were the men wearing T-shirts, any logos?"

"No. It was night. Pitch black outside. Wasn't much of a moon. The headlights from the trucks were behind them. And the storm had rolled in. The rain was coming down."

"How long were you in there?"

"I don't know… I didn't want to run out in the rain. So I stayed in there until the downpour stopped. I fell asleep for a while on a bunk in the storm cellar. When I woke up, the sun was an hour or so from coming up. The sky was turning gray."

"What did you do?"

"I left the shed and went into the house. That's when I found my father dead in his room. I ran out and headed for Margie's, like my dad told me. He told me she'd figure out what to do. When I got there, she called you."

"How did you get into the well house?"

"My father saw the men coming up the drive. He told me to sneak out the back, like I said. You've been to my house. There's not much back there but the woods, grass, and the lake."

"With the men in these trucks out front in the driveway, nobody noticed you?"

"No, ma'am. I don't think so. They'd have grabbed me for sure if they found me. I didn't hear anybody say they saw me. No one came to the well house, but the one man with the flash-light that got close... The raccoons fussed about, and they left."

"What did you do while you were in the shed?"

"I watched through the crack and saw what they were doing to my dad. I wanted to say something... to yell. But I knew it wouldn't do any good. I lost my balance, knocked over a paint can. Like I told you. That's what got the bearded guy interested in my hiding spot."

"Anything besides the usual in the well house?"

Jake spied a twinge of hesitation cross Rose's face.

"No, ma'am. Nothing that comes to mind. There were normal tools and such."

"Did Marcus store other things in there? Like valuables or money?"

Rose paused. "I don't remember seeing my father put any money in the well house. The only time I saw him handling money was pulling it out of a lockbox he kept under a loose board beneath his bed. Said it was our emergency money."

"You didn't find any cash lying around?"

"No. I said that already. I couldn't see much in the dark. I was looking through that crack. Why are you asking me about this?"

Sheriff Stone paused, as if she might challenge that answer, but she moved on.

"Did you by chance hurt yourself while you were hiding?"

Rose rubbed one of the tears in the right leg of her jeans. Jake knew the sheriff might see the cuts through the holes.

"I bumped into something. Something sharp. A nail or a piece of scrap metal, and I cut myself, but nothing big. It doesn't need any stitches or nothing."

"That does look like it hurts."

"Margie cleaned it. Said she'd take me to get a new pair of jeans later today, maybe go by the house and pick up some of my other clothes."

"Well, we should be done with your place later today or tonight," Sheriff Stone said. "I can let y'all know when we're done. That way Rose can collect some of her possessions."

"We'd appreciate that," Jake said as he moved forward in his chair, eager to get Rose out of the room. "Are you all done with her, Sheriff?"

"Yes, I think we're good for now, Jake."

"Well, I'd like to get her back to Margie's. It's been a horrible morning."

Jake stood up and motioned for Rose to do the same. "You can find us if you need us."

"I'll ride out to Margie's if I have other questions."

As Jake and Rose were about to open the door to leave, the sheriff asked, "Rose, you don't know your blood type, do you?"

A twinge flashed through Jake's gut, his instincts suddenly on red alert.

"Not exactly, no. But my dad said it was something fairly common."

"Makes sense," the sheriff said. "Do you mind giving us

your fingerprints, maybe a DNA swab? We need a set to compare to what we found in the house."

"I don't suppose it could hurt," Rose said.

"One last question," the sheriff said. "How long did you stay in the room with Marcus's body?"

Rose pulled at the strings on her hoodie. "A minute or two. I found him and ran out the back door."

Sheriff Stone nodded. "I think Jake's right. It's a good time for you to get some rest. I imagine the days ahead are gonna be difficult. I'll show you to a deputy who can take your prints."

When they walked out of the front door of the sheriff's department, Jake couldn't help but feel that the interview had done more than confirm a few facts.

CHAPTER ELEVEN

THE WIND WHIPPED the hem of Rose's summer dress as she sat next to Beth on the tailgate of Jake's truck. Honestly, Rose could not remember life without Beth Dubose, though they had grown up on different sides of Haven. Rose was raised where the men wore jeans and had dirt under their nails. Beth lived where the men wore suits and ties and worked at desks. Her daddy was a bigwig judge in town. But no one got Rose like Beth.

Exhaustion seeped from Rose. Her world became a tempest the moment her father died. Her only normal activity was calling and texting with Beth, and those conversations moored her in the storm. Rose spied Margie and Jake finishing up with the pastor at Marcus's gravesite. The number of people who had come to the graveside service surprised Rose. When the pastor invited anyone to speak, a line formed, with people eager to share stories of Marcus's help and compassion. He'd changed tires for folks who'd broken down on the side of the highway. Carried groceries to the car for a mother with her hands full with kids. A rancher relayed a story about how Marcus volunteered one Saturday to weld and patch sucker rod barn stalls damaged by an F-1 tornado that had torn through the area the year before. During the speeches, Rose had stared at the casket with a single white rose on top. Pride swept over her as the community reminded her of her father's greatness. And, for a moment, the aching hole in her chest shrank.

I promise I'll make you proud, Daddy.

Now, Beth reached out and interlaced their fingers, rousing Rose from her reverie. They leaned against each other. Rose brushed away her own tears with her shawl. A soft breeze cut the heat as it swirled around them, cooling her moist cheeks and kicking up the sweet scent of mown grass. It blew Beth's towhead blonde hair across her milk-white skin. A few strands hid the freckles on her cheeks.

"The service was lovely," Beth said. "So many people said such nice things about Marcus."

"It was.... My dad would have grumbled about it. He didn't like people fussing over him."

Beth smiled. "He *could* be a bit of a grump." Above them, a migrating osprey circled over the lawn, stretching out all around them. That raptor's effortless soaring hid its true intention to find, kill, and eat a rabbit or other helpless critter. "What are you going to do now?" Beth asked.

"I haven't thought much about it... Margie says I should stay with her."

"How long is that?"

"No idea."

"Can't you move home?"

"I doubt Margie will let me go back right now. She keeps pointing out I'm only fifteen. Besides, I'm not sure I can go back into that house after seeing my dad dead in his own bed... When I close my eyes, I see blood everywhere." Rose took a moment to regain her voice. "The people who killed my dad are still out there. I have nightmares about them. What if they come back?"

"I *am* scared for you." Beth squeezed Rose's hand. "Best stay with Margie then… I hear she's an excellent cook."

Rose grinned. "Some of the best food I've ever eaten."

"You know, if you wanted to move home, you could get Tommy to move in with you? I bet he would do a few things to chase away the nightmares."

Rose bumped her body against Beth. "I can't believe you said that."

"What?"

"You know my dad would roll over in his grave. He and Tommy weren't buddies."

"So? No reason you shouldn't be happy someday… And Tommy could make you thrilled."

"You find that funny?" Rose chided, but only in jest. Tommy was handsome, and she liked the way he held her. He made her feel like the only person around.

"Has he been keeping you *company*?"

"Haven't seen him."

"He's ghosting you?"

"Not ghosting. He sent a few texts. Checking in to see how I am."

"He doesn't want to see you?"

"He hasn't asked."

"Did you ask him?"

"How am I supposed to see him? Margie's like a mother duck smothering ducklings."

"Did they see you?"

"Who?"

"The men who killed Marcus."

"They didn't know I was there."

"Are you sure?"

"They didn't see me."

"So they don't know who you are?"

"I don't think so."

"Sneak out."

Rose cocked her head. "Why would I do that?"

"To go jump Tommy."

"Stop."

"You're not a prisoner."

"Maybe Margie's right. Maybe they are out looking for me."

"Now you're being paranoid. Besides, their problem was with Marcus, not you. They're long gone. Not looking for you at Margie's. Besides... Tommy could protect you if they come around."

"Not sure I'm up to it today."

"Fair enough. But maybe soon."

Margie and Jake started walking toward the girls in the truck.

"If you're so keen on it, why don't you sneak out to find your new Internet boy, Charlie?" Rose asked.

"I am."

"Shut up! When?"

"Tonight. My dad doesn't know, and I'm not telling him or the step-monster."

"Are you sure it's safe?"

"Yes, and tonight's the night we get to spend the night together."

"Where?"

"He's going to meet me in the park in our neighborhood. And then I get him all to myself. He's bringing a sleeping bag. So romantic... under the stars."

Margie and Jake had closed the distance between the grave and Jake's truck.

Rose rubbed her shawl across her cheeks again. "This sucks. I'm all alone now."

"Not alone. You got me, and I'm not going anywhere."

"Pinky swear?"

"Pinky swear."

Rose and Beth hopped off the tailgate and closed it. Beth wrapped her arms around Rose, hugging her from behind.

"What are you girls doin' up here on the hill?" Margie asked.

"Hey, Miss Margie," Beth said.

"How's your father doin'?" Margie asked.

Beth crinkled her nose. "He's always down at the courthouse."

"He'll give himself a heart attack, workin' himself to death. He should mind after you."

"I get along just fine."

"I bet you do. I'm sure you do. Beth, do you want to come up to the house for some lunch? We'd be happy to have you."

"I'd love to, but my stepmom is waiting for me in the parking lot. We have to go shopping this afternoon."

"Well, darlin', you know you're always welcome to come by and see Rose. I'm sure she'd love to have you over."

"I'll do that, Margie," Beth said as the girls hugged.

"You running off now?" Rose asked.

"Yep."

"You'll call or text me later? Tell me how your night goes?"

"You better believe it. I'll text you the dresses I'm looking at. I'll give you all the details," Beth said with a wink, her ice-blue eyes shining.

"I'd like that."

"Bye, Margie. See you, Jake," Beth said as she scampered off to a black sedan. Beth's stepmother rolled down the window, honked, and waved as they drove away.

"She seems like a nice girl," Jake said.

"Bethie? She's been my best friend for as long as I can remember."

"You should ask her over to visit sometime."

"Maybe I could go out and hang with her for a day."

"I don't know that I'm okay with that," Margie said.

"Who knows? It might be good for Rose to get out with a friend," Jake responded.

"No. Not yet. I want the sheriff to find those men who killed Marcus. We don't know why they killed him. We don't know if it was a grudge. Until they find them, I'm not taking my eyes off you."

"Margie," Rose said

"I'm serious. Marcus sent you sent you my way for safe-keeping, and I intend to watch over you."

CHAPTER TWELVE

BETH SLID OPEN the window in her bedroom and slipped outside. The sliver of moonlight through the tree branches cast the yard in shifting shadows. She pulled up her phone and texted Charlie that she was on the way. Wrapping herself in a jacket against the cool spring air, she ran down the driveway toward the large brick mailbox on the main road. He'd texted that he would meet her at the picnic tables down by the tennis courts in her subdivision. A sly smile slid across Beth's face.

She looked over her shoulder to make sure the lights were still off in her house. Her father would kill her if he caught her sneaking out at all, let alone to meet a boy she'd met on the Internet. He'd lecture her for hours, and she was tired of his droning speeches. But the windows remained dark as she turned onto the main road and picked up the pace to put some distance between her and her house.

Electricity rocketed through her, and she put in her earbuds to listen to her favorite singer. She twirled as the romantic lyrics filled her head. Beth was going to meet Charlie. She had been hanging out with him online for weeks. They had so much in common: music, food, places they wanted to travel. He was perfect, maybe her soulmate. She could not believe that he lived nearby, and that tonight she was going to be with him.

Her father, Judge Dubose, would have hated him. He hated everything she did and every boy she dated. But he saved his ire mostly for her. The judge acted pleasantly while campaigning, but his criticisms slammed into her behind closed doors, long after election day. He hated the way she dressed. Hated how she acted. Hated the music she listened to. *Face it,* she thought. *He hates you and always has.*

He loved Natalie, that shrew of a stepmother, though. The judge spent any amount of time or money to make Nat and her boob job happy, or at least smiling and perky in public on his arm. She had no genuine interest in spending time with Beth unless they were running up the judge's credit card.

No matter what Beth did, she could not convince the judge to love her, and she knew why. Her biological mother, Eve, the judge's one and only true love, had died in childbirth of a catastrophic hemorrhage. The complications had left her unresponsive and brain-dead. The judge often reminded Beth of the painful ordeal of removing his wife from life support.

He always calls her his wife—never my mother.

Up ahead, a single streetlamp illuminated the tiny parking lot next to the playground and tennis courts. Shadows danced across the park. She picked up her pace, the excitement building—thrilled she would meet Charlie in person. He was so handsome in his pictures. Slightly older than her, but that was fine. She was tired of dating boys.

The park was just ahead. A silhouette shifted near a tree. A smile crossed Beth's lips. She turned up the music in her earbuds and shuffled down the street. The drumbeat from the song drowned out everything else.

Instantly, her neck hair stood on end as a van skidded to a stop behind her. It had come out of nowhere, and the headlights were dark. A canvas hood slammed over her head. Two sets of arms ensnared her. The heavy fabric from the hood pinned her earbuds in place. The music from her phone flooded her mind and drowned her senses.

Stupid girl!

Beth had seen nothing, and she had heard nothing but the singer crooning in her ears. The sensory deprivation amplified her terror. Her heart thundered. She bit her tongue and choked on the taste of blood. Beth struggled to breathe—she sucked the canvas bag partially into her mouth with each futile gulp. The hand across her mouth secured the hood and silenced her, amputating her screams in her throat. Her phone fell from her grip and skittered across the road.

In an instant, someone else grabbed her feet, picked her up, and she was bounced inside the van. She grimaced in agony as her hip collided with the ridged steel floor beneath her. The door slammed shut. The van sped away. Her lungs begged for air. Finally, the hood loosened—but her scream echoed around the empty van. Adrenaline pumped through her, and her pulse galloped. The acrid taste of fear crept up the back of her throat. Where was Charlie? Who had taken her? And why?

Are these the men who killed Marcus? Did they see me with Rose at the funeral? What have I done?

Beth kicked out, and her foot connected with a large, soft mass. A man drew in a heavy breath and gave her a backhand in return. Then the invisible attacker slipped zip ties on her wrists and ankles and pulled them until they bit into her flesh. Thoughts raced through her mind. Who would do this to her? One thought pulsed through her mind.

This is because of my father, the judge.

It had to be a criminal he'd put in jail—maybe one recently released from the prison. Or maybe a family member was taking revenge for someone her father had locked up years ago. Maybe they took her for ransom money.

How ironic, she thought. *Don't they know I'm his least favorite thing?*

The thought of her father saying no to their ransom

demands and leaving her to the whim of these kidnappers overwhelmed her. She hyperventilated again. The canvas bag caused her extra distress. Her lungs burned, and the taste of iron flooded her mouth.

After a few minutes, the van's heavy rumble gave way to a low, steady vibration underneath her. The staccato rhythm told her they had made it out of her subdivision and onto the state highway. Who knew how far away she would be by morning? She might not even be in the same state.

Beth concentrated her thoughts on believing she would be okay. *This too shall pass*, the pastor had said.

Screw that. She wanted to call out to someone for help.

Daddy!

Would he ever come to her rescue? Despite her efforts, terror consumed her, and Beth lashed out in every direction. Two sets of hands grabbed her and pinned her to the van floor. A moment later, she felt a sharp sting in her thigh. And even as her heart pumped wildly, she felt drowsy. Reality shrank until she descended into darkness.

CHAPTER THIRTEEN

JAKE WAS OPENING the screen door to pick up the bowls for Tiny and Snuffles when he noticed the sheriff's white-and-blue truck rambling its way up Margie's drive. Figuring the pigs could wait, Jake pulled on a shirt and hightailed it for the main house. Tiny and Snuffles protested in the background with loud grunts and squeals. Jake met Margie just as she appeared on the porch. Sheriff Stone stepped out of her truck, tipped her hat, and walked toward them. Taking the steps in a measured way, she gave them both a reserved smile. Jake realized he had come over in a T-shirt, pajama pants, and no shoes. He felt woefully underdressed.

"Margie... Jake."

"Sheriff," Jake said. The sheriff reached out and handed Jake some papers folded in a blue wrapper. Except for a short-lived grin presumably at Jake's motley state of dress, the sheriff's expression remained stoic. Jake unfolded the parcel and began reading. It was a petition, filed by the district attorney, commanding Rose to appear in juvenile court. Jake's jaw dropped. The petition alleged that she had murdered Marcus. It spelled out the details. Jake looked from the petition to Sheriff Stone and back again.

How on earth did they turn this into a murder charge with Rose allegedly killing Marcus?

Jake perused the paperwork. Blood. Fingerprints. Opportunity.

But no motive.

Jake looked at Hope, trying to gauge anything from her expression.

"You're here to arrest her?"

"Jake, you know how this works. She's a juvenile. Yes, I can detain her. But I don't want to do it that way. I came out here as a courtesy to serve the papers. Nothing good comes from having a fifteen-year-old girl in my jail if I don't have to have her there. I trust you and Margie will bring her into juvenile court. That way, I don't think we have much to worry about, and I don't need to take her. We can work out her surrender… right? You'll give me your word?"

Through Margie's screen door, Jake glimpsed Rose standing in the living room, running a towel over her freshly showered hair. He was unsure if she understood why the sheriff had arrived this morning. She seemed younger, more frail this morning. But her eyes widened, rimmed with fear. Clearing his throat, he turned back to the sheriff.

"When do we bring her to you?"

"It's all there in the petition. There's a notice at the back. The court set an initial hearing for tomorrow, Friday, at 9:00 a.m. It's in front of Judge Maddix, the designated juvenile judge."

Great.

Jake felt a flush creeping up his back and shoulders as the reality of the charges against Rose hit him.

"Tell me this: did you all even look for the men Rose told you did this?" He asked with more force than he intended.

Hope blanched. She fisted her hands on either side of her duty belt and stared back at him. "Jake, don't be like that. You know the detectives are doing their job. They worked the scene the same as they ever would. This is where it led them. Now *I'm* doing *my* job. We gather the facts. The charge? Now, that's up to the district attorney's office and the prosecutor on the case."

A slight breeze kicked up, rustling the leaves in the pecan trees that dominated Margie's property and taking some of the heat out of the situation. The sweet smell of grass swirled around them. Jake tucked the petition into the elastic band of his pants.

"Who has it?"

"Krista Robb."

The dumb luck of it all.

Krista Robb had been a force to be reckoned with since she dropped from her mother's womb. On the playground, she'd been the ringleader for all the popular kids. In high school, she excelled as head cheerleader, student body president, and the one voted most likely to conquer the world. The class had voted for Jake as the class clown. Hope had earned the title of class mom for her watchful care of everyone. But the worst of it was that Jake and Krista had gone to the same college. They dated and became serious. She wanted to get engaged and married between college and law school. Jake didn't. Krista had a timeline for all the important events in her life, and she marched around as if racing to check them off. Jake realized Krista was a crass political animal, which left a bad taste in his mouth. He told her he thought they should go their separate ways, and she spat in his face for being "a spineless nobody." Soon thereafter, she moved back to Haven, and he thought they would never see each other again.

I couldn't have been more wrong.

Krista was on a mission in everything she did. Now she was on a mission to cook Rose, and spice it up with petty revenge on Jake along the way.

Hope's voice coaxed Jake from his thoughts. "Jake, you bring Rose in tomorrow morning, show up at that hearing, and everything will go smoothly. I can trust you to do that, right? You will not go on the lam, will you? I don't think you're dressed to be a fugitive." Hope chuckled at her own joke.

"I'll make it happen," Jake said, catching a glint of electricity in Hope's eyes. The scent of her perfume filled his head. Clearing his throat to cover his thoughts, he said, "Nine o'clock? Judge Maddix?"

"Yes," Hope said, giving him a brief smile as if reading Jake's mind.

"Sheriff Stone? Dispatch, over."

Hope reached for her radio. "This is Stone. Go ahead dispatch."

"We have a call from Judge Dubose for you to come by his house… immediately."

"Roger, dispatch. On my way, over." Hope sighed and looked back at Jake. "Gotta go."

"Duty calls," Jake said.

The sheriff touched the brim of her hat, turned, and walked back to her truck.

Man, that uniform fits her.

As she opened the door, she called back to them. "See you in the morning, Jake, Margie."

Hope's truck tires spun in the drive and the car ambled back toward the highway.

Jake opened the screen door. An air of inevitability had settled across the house. Rose was curled into the couch, almost in a fetal position, soft sobs wetting her voice.

"They think I killed him?"

"That's what the petition says."

Rose began shaking, and Jake wanted to pick her up and hold her against his chest. Instead, he reached out and rested his palm on her shoulder to reassure her. She recoiled at his touch and threw the pillow she was holding across the room, knocking over a lamp. Then she jumped from the couch and stared at him.

"How can they think I killed my own father? I told them. I told them all about the men that took him. I found him, and he was already dead. Didn't they listen to me?" She pumped her fists.

"Rose, hon... We'll get it—"

Rose rounded on Margie. "They say I killed Marcus. How dare they!"

"Darlin', I'm sure it's just a mistake. Jake will get this figured out."

Jake looked up from reading the petition and gave Margie a sharp glance. "This is no mistake."

"You can fix it, though, right?" Margie asked, putting Jake on the spot.

Jake deflected. "These *are* just allegations. The prosecutor will still have to prove every element of her case beyond a reasonable doubt. Besides, you're only fifteen. You at least have that going for you."

Rose's breath caught as she drew it in and wiped a tear from her cheek with the towel. "They think I killed him," she repeated with a defeated air, and slumped back into the couch.

"I know that's hard to hear. But yes, that's their theory of the case, unless we can convince them otherwise."

"We?"

Jake paused for a moment, his heart racing in his chest, the slight damp of sweat on his neck cool under the ceiling fan. He didn't want to be here at all. His nerves screamed that he never again wanted the responsibility for a teenage girl. He looked past Rose to a simple mirage behind her.... Lucy, with a kind and empathetic expression on her face. Her green eyes implored him, told him what to do.

Rose's trembling lip silenced all but one voice in his head.

"Yes, Rose, *we*. I'll be with you every step of the way."

Rose backed away from him. "You don't know me from a hole in the ground. Why do you want to help me now? Maybe

I should just get one of those county attorneys they assign you."

"A court-appointed lawyer?"

"Yeah.... I'm sure they're good enough."

"I'm not letting some has-been who signs up for minimum wage so they can keep themselves in bourbon represent you. Margie believes in you. So I believe in you, too." Rose relaxed some. He leveled his gaze at her and could see her fear. "But if we do this," Jake said, "you must tell me everything. No lies... no secrets. I cannot defend against what I don't know. So I need to know everything. Deal?"

Rose looked Jake up and down as if taking his measure. Jake had signed a lot of engagement letters over a career, had all kinds of clients gauge whether to trust him and his skill. But Rose's gaze had a certainty to it. It pierced to his core.

"Deal," she said, and she stuck out her hand to shake on it.

"All right, we'll just have to see what happens tomorrow."

"Let's go see what we have for breakfast," Margie said.

Rose's lips hinted at a smile. "I think I can already smell biscuits in the oven."

"Yes, you can," Margie said as she and Rose headed toward the kitchen. "Maybe some sticky buns, too."

Jake stared down at the petition in his hand. This flew in the face of everything he had decided to do—and not do—when he moved back to Haven. Be he was committed now. He stood and followed his client through the doorway.

CHAPTER FOURTEEN

HOPE TURNED off the road and drove up a long, curving gravel driveway. She had been called to the home of Judge Harlan Dubose and his second wife, Natalie, before, but this time was different. Dispatch informed her on the way over that neither parent had seen their daughter, Beth, since retiring to bed the night before.

She stepped out of her cruiser and walked up the steps to the grand white brick home. She took a moment to appreciate the manicured lawn, topiary shrubs, and the tall Greek columns that framed the entrance. Oversized windows across the front of the home reflected the midmorning sun. Judge Dubose descended from one of the oldest and most storied families in the county, and the family's wealth was on obvious display.

Hope banged the brass knocker hanging from a lion's mouth on the red double doors and waited. After a moment, she heard footsteps echoing on the other side of the door, then it opened. Judge Dubose was a tall, imposing man with salt-and-pepper hair. His stern expression and rapacious nose gave him an air of antiquity, like a marble statue. Hope noted the bloodshot eyes behind the round bifocals perched precariously on his nose.

"Sheriff Stone," Judge Dubose said, his voice strained. "Please come in. My wife is in the living room. Come this way." The judge turned on his heel and strode down the hallway, leaving Hope no choice but to close the door and follow. He turned and stepped into a sunken room with a large, plush couch. Two partially filled highball glasses and a bottle of bourbon rested on the coffee table.

The petite and delicate Natalie Dubose sat hunched over with her head in her hands as her bleached-blonde hair fell in soft waves to cover her face. As they approached, Natalie raised her gaze to Hope, who detected desperation in her eyes. The German shepherd lying at her feet was keenly aware of Hope but didn't move away from the dog's master.

"Sheriff Stone," Ms. Dubose said, her voice strained. "Thank you for coming."

"Can you tell me what happened?"

"This morning, we woke early to get ready for church. Normally, Beth would have been up with us. She's always punctual, sometimes ready before Harlan or me. This morning, I didn't see her. I knocked on her door, thinking maybe she didn't feel well and was still asleep. When she didn't answer, I opened the door to check on her. She wasn't in her bed. I checked the bathroom and the rest of the house. She was nowhere to be found."

"We went around the house and outside, calling out for her, but she didn't answer," the judge said. "We came inside and checked our phones to see if the location apps revealed her whereabouts. I found her phone on the street. It's right there." There judge pointed to the coffee table. "You can see that the screen is cracked."

Hope looked at the roughed-up phone. "May I look around her room?"

"Of course," Judge Dubose said, waving her to follow him

as he hurried down a hallway. "Nat and I are on the upper floor, but Beth's room is here on the first floor."

Hope stepped through the doorway and looked around Beth's bedroom, which was decorated as she would have guessed. A large canopy bed set in the center of the room with elegant neutral bedding. None of the blankets had been turned down. Nobody had slept in that bed. She stepped by the desk, looking for a diary or any material that could give a clue to Beth's whereabouts. As she scanned the room, the curtains on the window moved. Hope stepped up. The window was open.

"Would Beth have left this window open when she slept?"

"Not always. Sometimes in the spring, when it's cool outside, she might sleep with it open. But in general, no."

"Is it possible she snuck out to meet someone?"

"Before today, I'd say she would do nothing of the sort, and we would not have approved of it. I think she knew she would be grounded. But now, I don't know what to think."

"Why would she go out the window? Since she's on the first floor, why wouldn't she go out the front door?"

"Fitz, probably," Judge Dubose responded. "He tends to bark at any movement in the hallway. Maybe she was trying to avoid him."

"I'd like to have crime scene techs come out and process the bedroom, windowsill, and grounds outside to see if we can find any clues."

"You think someone took her?" Natalie asked behind them. She had shuffled down the hallway without making a noise.

"It's a possibility."

"That's highly unlikely," Judge Dubose cut in. "Fitz would have allowed no one in the house."

"Is he a guard dog?"

"Yes. Being a judge, you can never be too careful."

"True. But right now, I'd rather be safe than sorry. We'll issue an amber alert. See if anyone has spotted her. Do you have a current picture of Beth?"

"I do on my phone," Natalie said. Hope noted Fitz standing beside Natalie, watching Hope's every movement. She pulled out a business card from her shirt pocket and handed it to Natalie.

"You can text it to me here. My phone number is on the bottom. Has Beth been under any distress? Any reason to believe she ran away?"

"Never," Natalie said. "Beth was happy here with us. We had just finished shopping for a dress, and she couldn't wait for the school dance." Mrs. Dubose wiped her tears and took a deep breath. "Sure, there have been growing pains, but nothing that would make her run away."

Hope wrote a few notes. Beth could have run away, but something felt off. There was more to this than just a rebellious teenager.

"Can you think of anyone who might seek to harm Beth?"

"No, of course not," the judge said. "Why would anyone want to harm our daughter?"

Hope had no answer for them. She requested technicians to work at the scene and then proceeded to question Judge and Mrs. Dubose, who had no additional information to provide. Each question only inflamed their desperation. After another half hour, her inquiry had exhausted Beth's parents. She reminded them of her business card and headed out the front door. She paused on the porch overlooking the oversized lot. As she left the Dubose house, the weight of the situation pressed on her. She had to find Beth, and she had to do it fast. The first seventy-two hours were critical. Abducted children were often murdered within hours of disappearing. Those that survived were in grave danger as they are held or transported. Each minute that ticked by was a minute Hope could never get back in her effort to save Beth.

A deep ache settled in Hope's chest. As a mother herself, she could not imagine the pain of having her daughter go missing. Her maternal instincts tethered her to this case. She also ached for the Duboses, because wagging tongues would compound the couple's anxiety and hurt. They were well-respected members of the community. Soon the cruel gossip mongers would spread the story throughout the small town, causing all kinds of trouble. And if anything happened to Beth, some would be in an uproar, blaming the sheriff. Others would gawk at the Duboses' tragedy. Taking a deep breath, she resolved to do everything in her power to bring Beth home.

Hope stepped into her cruiser and started the engine, her mind already working on leads and suspects. Surely someone in town had information about Beth's disappearance. Someone must have seen something. Hope resolved to uncover the truth.

CHAPTER FIFTEEN

JAKE SAW the deputy walk into the courtroom. "All rise. The 192nd District Court in Hawk County in the State of Texas is now in session, the Honorable Linda Maddix presiding. God save this honorable court."

Everyone in the courtroom stood as a black robe darted from the chamber's door and took the bench. Judge Maddix was a fixture in Hawk County. The voters had reelected her more times than anyone could remember. The daughter of a local rancher, she'd grown up with early mornings and long days. Those experiences translated to how she ran her courtroom. Her stout frame confessed a life of hard work as a lawyer and then a judge, and her short gray hair gave her a no-nonsense air.

Jake and Rose stood at the defense table. Wood panels with ornate carvings surrounded them. Floor-to-ceiling windows draped with velvet curtains lined one wall, and light flooded the room. All the hard surfaces made for good acoustics, and any unwanted sound echoed through the space. Above the judge's bench hung a mural of a cattle drive that dated from the turn of the last century. One of the enormous beasts stared down at Jake. He touched the medallion of Saint Thomas

More, patron saint to attorneys, that hung from a chain around his neck, under his shirt and tie.

Just like riding a bike.

"Be seated," Judge Maddix said. "We're here on case number JC-22-1448, State of Texas versus Rosemary Tucker. The State of Texas's Council of Juvenile Justice has designated me, the Honorable Linda Maddix, as the juvenile judge for this county for a term of three years. Therefore, this is a juvenile court proceeding today, and the deputy cleared the courtroom to protect the confidential nature of this hearing and the identity of the juvenile. We are here on the State's petition alleging a crime of violence by one Rosemary Tucker, age fifteen, against one Marcus Tucker, an adult, who is also the juvenile's father. Counsel, make your appearances for the record."

"Your Honor, yes. Krista Robb for the State of Texas."

Jake took a quick gander at Krista. She was still slender and athletic, dressed in a pinstriped blue blazer and a matching pencil skirt. Her stiletto heels and black stockings screamed power suit, and she had styled her professional shoulder-length brown hair. Her likeness belonged on a hard-charging, law-and-order campaign poster. She was all business. Jake felt the familiar spark that had attracted him to Krista in the first place. That flash gave way to a pang of guilt for their complicated history.

"Mr. Fox, you with us?"

"Yes … Your Honor, Jake Fox on behalf of the respondent, Rosemary Tucker."

"Very well. Ms. Robb, it is your petition. How would you like to proceed?"

"Your Honor, the State would like to alert the court to our motion filed just this morning, just a few minutes ago actually, with the clerk's office. I've brought copies for respondent's counsel."

Krista's paralegal handed a copy to Jake, and Krista continued.

"Your Honor, the State's motion asks this court to waive its juvenile jurisdiction and transfer Ms. Tucker's case to the district court for prosecution. The State of Texas seeks to try Ms. Tucker as an adult. The heinous and violent nature of this crime, and the fact that she is fifteen years old, argue in favor of such a waiver. We lay out the details of the offense in the motion, so I will not discuss them at length unless the court believes that will be necessary. But I want to emphasize that Ms. Tucker allegedly shot her father in the head while he was asleep on his bed. Because of the depravity and clear disregard for human life, we believe this case should proceed through the adult criminal justice system, not in juvenile court."

Jake thought he noticed a slight grin on Krista's face.

Who enjoys going after a child? Or… was part of this going after him?

"Mr. Fox, what say you?"

"Your Honor. As you know, this is the first we are hearing of the State's motion to waive jurisdiction. We've had the petition for less than a day, but yet this last-minute motion smacks of gamesmanship. It seems a little suspect to believe that the State first came to this decision in the middle of the night last night, and thus could file it this morning only moments before the hearing. We've had no time to read the motion, let alone prepare a response. Therefore, we request the court abate this hearing to allow us a reasonable amount of time to review the motion and prepare. Indeed, I can tell from leafing through the first pages that Ms. Robb's motion is a little light on facts."

"Your Honor," Krista butted in. "The State's investigation of the underlying facts is still ongoing. But we will be ready for a full presentation at any waiver hearing and are ready to proceed immediately. The State believes probable cause exists to charge Rosemary Tucker with at least the crime of manslaughter or second-degree murder. Either would be a violent felony under the criminal statutes of Texas. As such, it is within the State's right to try her as an adult and secure a conviction for this serious crime."

"Your Honor, I believe Ms. Robb is being dramatic, and she just admitted that she intends to lie behind a log and spring the facts on the defense at the last minute… maybe even at the hearing."

"Enough!" Judge Maddix's tone cleared the courtroom of sound. Rose jumped in her chair. Jake placed his hand on her shoulder to calm her. She had been a wreck ever since the amber alert had gone out for Beth the day before. "Ms. Robb," the judge continued, "I agree with Mr. Fox that the motion appears to be very last-minute." Judge Maddix lowered her iconic octagonal red-rimmed glasses to give Krista a glare. "Let's not make a habit of that in the future. A motion to waive jurisdiction is a serious matter, and the defendant has constitutional due process rights. No games in my courtroom. Understood?"

"Yes, Your Honor."

"Mr. Fox, I'll set the waiver hearing for next Friday. That gives you a week to prepare. That should cure any prejudice. I'll remind both of you that a waiver hearing is not an adjudication of the facts. The statute requires me to find probable cause. Mr. Fox, at the hearing, you will question any witnesses that you like. If I rule the State can try Ms. Tucker as an adult, I will transfer this to Judge Dubose in the 113th. He'll decide on a trial date. Do you understand?"

Jake answered in the affirmative.

Judge Maddix cleared her throat and turned to her clerk. "Betty, what do we have open on the motion docket next Friday?"

"You have your regular docket in the morning, but the afternoon is all clear."

"Okay, so here's what we will do. We will have the waiver hearing a week from Friday starting at 1:00 p.m. Anything further?"

"Nothing from the State, Your Honor."

"Nothing from respondent."

"Very well. That takes care of the petition and the motion for the waiver. But I don't know that we're done with all the business here as it relates to Ms. Tucker."

"Your Honor," Krista blurted, "the State is moving to detain Ms. Tucker. The gravity of these charges and the level of violence of the underlying crime show that she is a danger to the community. And, with no family in the area, she is a flight risk. We recommend holding her at the county jail until trial."

"Mr. Fox?"

"Judge, we couldn't disagree more. Ms. Robb is getting ahead of herself. She presented no evidence that Ms. Tucker is a flight risk. Ms. Tucker has been a member of the community for her entire life and has deep roots here. The State has a petition on file for a juvenile charge. No grand jury has indicted Ms. Tucker, and the State has shown no probable cause sufficient to detain her. So we request the court deny any motion to detain."

"Ms. Robb, I agree with Mr. Fox on this one. Provided we can find a place for Ms. Tucker to stay that is satisfactory to the State, I do not believe that housing her in the jail is necessary. Now, the father is deceased, and as I understand it, the mother has been absent from Ms. Tucker's life for over a decade. Is that correct?"

"Yes, Your Honor," Jake responded.

"That opens the question of who's going to be appointed the young lady's guardian, right? The juvenile court has an obligation to see to her welfare."

"That would be correct," Krista said.

"Ms. Robb, have you been in touch with Child Protective Services about a foster placement and a guardian being appointed, or were you counting on winning your motion to detain?"

Before he could stop her, Rose was on her feet.

"I'm fifteen and can look after myself."

"Ms. Tucker," Judge Maddix said, "I'm sure you can, but in the eyes of the law, you are a juvenile until your eighteenth birthday. So I'm obligated to ensure you have proper supervision."

"My office has been in touch," Krista piped in, "and I believe they're putting forth potential candidates now."

Margie jumped up from the pew behind Jake and tugged on his elbow, whispering in his ear.

The judge raised an eyebrow. "Mr. Fox, do you have anything to say?"

"If I may have a moment, Your Honor," Jake responded. Margie continued to whisper in his ear.

"Mr. Fox?" The judge's voice gave away her obvious irritation.

"Your Honor, Margie Moore, who's in the courtroom with me today, has indicated that she would be willing to step forward to foster Ms. Tucker and serve as a *guardian ad litem* for these proceedings."

"Margie, is that correct?"

"Yes it is, Linda … I mean Your Honor."

"Well, I must admit it's a little unusual—private citizens stepping up out of the blue to serve as a guardian. Ms. Robb, do you have any objection to Ms. Moore, provided CPS approves?"

Before Krista could answer, Jake interjected. "Your Honor, as you know, Ms. Moore has been a lifelong member of this community, and she served as a librarian at the local schools for over forty years. She was a surrogate mother to many in the community, including me. She has significant experience with children of Ms. Tucker's age. Indeed, she mentioned to me she used to look after Ms. Tucker when her father was out of town. Texas law does not require a guardian to be a lawyer or other professional. Indeed, it requires only relevant training, which Ms. Moore tells me she took as part of her work in the public schools. She has the requisite wisdom to serve as guardian ad litem and has a current relationship with the minor. She will be working with me and Hitch Mills to prepare a defense in this case. Thus, if the court sees fit, we support Ms. Tucker's request to serve."

"Hitch is on this with you?"

"Yes ma'am, he will be."

"Let me know how that goes, Mr. Fox. Nobody's been able to tell him what to do for years. Ms. Robb? Any objections to Ms. Moore?"

"Your Honor, if Ms. Moore wants to step forward and serve in that role, the State has no objection, provided Child Protective Services approves."

"Ms. Tucker, do you have any objection to Ms. Moore serving as your temporary foster caregiver and guardian?"

"Your Honor," said Rose, "Ms. Margie is like family to me. If she'll have me, I'd prefer to stay with her."

"Very well. I'll issue an order by the end of the day to appoint Margie—I mean Mrs. Moore—as temporary guardian ad litem, at least until CPS can finish its review. Margie?"

"Yes, Your Honor?"

"Over the next few days, the State will have to evaluate Ms. Tucker's situation. She needs to be interviewed. They need to look at her background. I trust the court can count on you to make sure she makes all the appointments?"

"Yes."

"Ms. Robb, anything further for the State?"

"Nothing."

"Mr. Fox?"

"Nothing, Your Honor."

"This court will stand in recess."

Jake looked back at Krista. The State had just thrown down the gauntlet, seeking to lock Rose away.

CHAPTER SIXTEEN

ZACH PARKED his black truck in the alley behind the hardware store. The slot gave him a clean line of sight to the courthouse. He left the engine off and reclined in his seat, not wanting to attract attention. Haven's streets remained quiet, except for a few locals dodging in and out of shops and eateries. Haven was an older, quieter town, slow to wake. The town's quaint façade helped hide Zach and Lilith's business activities.

April rains had faded to the first hot days of May. The Texas heat smoldered in the truck. His strong, black morning coffee turned tepid and bitter, and the sausage biscuit he'd scarfed down for breakfast was wreaking havoc on his stomach. Zach popped two antacid pills in his mouth and swallowed them dry. He leaned back to wait for the burning in his gut to subside and for his targets to exit the building.

The radio spewed out morning talk shows, punctuated at the half hour by agricultural reports. Pork bellies and cotton futures were rising. Coffee had fallen because of an overabundant crop from Brazil had hit the market. A half hour passed, and Zach lit another cigarette, the smoke billowing against the windshield and wafting across the crumpled cigarette packs and fast-food wrappers jammed along the dashboard. Zach's heartbeat ticked up from the strong smoke and nicotine. He tried in vain to will his stomach to stop gnawing at itself, and the frustration and languid pace caused a headache to bubble to the surface. He rhythmically blew smoke rings and stared at the courthouse door.

Another half hour passed. Zach cracked his knuckles and thumped his fingers on the gearshift. He craved painkillers for the migraine throbbing behind his eyes; he would have to hit Lilith up for a few. A hungry grin grew on his face as the radio called out an amber alert for Beth Dubose, the daughter of Judge Dubose, one of the judges in Hawk County. He ran his palm down the long beard that he'd washed and woven into the Devil's Vikings' signature double braid again this morning. He knew they would not find Beth.

The door to the courthouse opened. Zach spotted them and leaned his seat forward, wetting his lips with anticipation. Rosemary Tucker, Jake Fox, and Margie Moore stepped into the sunshine and descended the steps. Fox's glower belied a tough day. Perhaps the hearing had not gone well.

The court had sealed the juvenile proceeding from the public. Zach could have quietly entered and listened from the back row of the old courtroom balcony. He had access. But he chose not to risk being seen—better to hang in the shadows. As the trio moved down the sidewalk, Zach turned the key in the truck's ignition and the powerful engine rumbled alive. The air-conditioning belched a chill, welcome reprieve.

He focused in on the attorney's face. A snitch had recently told Zach that Jake would be representing Rose Tucker. Zach could not believe his dumb luck. It was a small world. Years ago, fresh out of law school, Jake Fox had been a green defense attorney, practicing on poor people and mucking up cases as he learned. Most of Fox's clients went to jail as he worked to perfect his craft of criminal defense. But what were the chances that the greenhorn who had screwed up Zach's drug case years ago was now walking down the street in front of him? Zach grinned. Sometimes fate did smile on you.

Welcome home, Jake. We have much to talk about—like the three years you cost me behind bars.

This was going to be fun, and Rose was now only half the equation.

The night before, Zach had scoured online articles on his phone, occasionally glancing through the windshield, keeping an eye on the courthouse door. Fox had turned himself into a hotshot criminal defense attorney in Dallas, making a big name for himself in the papers. He'd defended accused terrorists, several members from a motorcycle gang shootout in Waco, and one of the largest Ponzi schemers in history. Jake had a deep resumé, and the criminal defense ranks admired him as talented beyond his peers. Until they didn't. He'd run into trouble with the Texas State Bar, and the disciplinary committee had suspended his license for six months, with a year of probation.

Oh, how the mighty fall.

The State Bar's public announcement reported that Fox had failed to keep clients informed of their cases. He'd missed court dates and deadlines. Rumors filled the press that liquor ruined him. Still, they'd granted him a second chance based on extenuating circumstances, and placed him on probation. They reasoned he'd been under unimaginable stress because of a family tragedy.

Zach read the online obituary with morbid curiosity. Fox's kid had hung herself, and his law practice had suffered after that. Fox lost focus, despondent in the grief of burying a child. The online obituary mentioned a wife, but Zach had seen no sign of her in Haven. Zach had found the divorce decree filed in family court in Dallas. The daughter's suicide had gutted more than Fox's law practice. It had rocked Fox and his family to his core.

Zach grunted to himself in the truck's quiet. He had no

remaining family except for a kid brother in the Navy. And he could not imagine the pain of finding his brother hanging from the rafters. He shook his head to push any soft feelings aside. Fox was the enemy, and Zach needed to treat him as such. He refocused on his mission.

The group of three strode toward Fox's truck, Rose flanked by both adults. His higher-ups continued to debate whether to nab Rose now or to wait to move on her until after the murder trial, but Zach tuned out all the squabbling. This operation had a bonus, now that he knew it would be a reunion with his former attorney. Once they finished with Rose, Zach could pursue a personal vendetta against Fox.

Over the past few days, Zach had monitored Rose. He had followed her into town several times and watched from the bluffs above the lake house, trying to pick up a routine. There was no clear rhythm to her activities, and Rose was never alone. She always had company, whether in public or at the lake. Maybe he could trick her into coming out alone at night. Zach wanted to nab her when she was by herself. He wanted it clean, with no witnesses. It's possible that the cops would assume she'd skipped bail and fled. They would reclassify her from fugitive to runaway, and she would just fade away like all the other girls. If he had his way, she'd be long gone and turning tricks in Vegas or New Jersey before anyone noticed. But if he took her sooner, he could sample her for himself. See if he could put that sweetness she exuded to good use. Rose liked baggy jeans and a hoodie, but Zach could discern the shape of her lithe body. After undressing her curves, he could fill himself on her nectar. One week with him, and she would know every menu item, including the exotic requests.

He quieted his impulse to finish it right away. She was bound to make a foolish move, and he would be there to nab her. Then he could square up with Fox. He watched them cross the street.

Jake removed his suit jacket and tossed it in the back seat as

Rose got in on the opposite side. As Fox's truck pulled away from the curb, Zach lit another cigarette, dropped his truck into gear, and edged forward. Fox headed out of town to the state highway that ran along the lakeshore. Zach followed well behind them, always keeping a car or two between him and Fox. As the unsuspecting trio pulled into the driveway, Zach scooted along the blacktop behind them. Soon. He watched and waited for Rose.

Patience.

CHAPTER SEVENTEEN

JAKE'S EYES FLUTTERED OPEN, and it took him a moment to gain his bearings in the silence… the loneliness. No Ted, Tiny, or Snuffles. The light sifting through the blinds announced the sun was well above the horizon. He had slept later than normal. Where were all the animals poking him for breakfast? What the…?

Jake pulled himself from bed, rinsed off in the shower, and threw on sweatpants and a T-shirt. The familiar sound of Margie cooking breakfast spilled from her open window into the cool morning air. Jake crossed the lawn, beckoned by the heady scent of bacon and some sweet baked confection that he hoped was caramel and pecan sticky buns.

Margie was in her kitchen as usual, flitting here and there, her bright-red floral housedress billowing around her. She wore her long gray hair in a low bun. Jake noted three plates set on the table. Rose's image rushed back to Jake, and his heartbeat ticked up.

Jail will eat that little girl up.

The potential horrors of incarceration flooded his mind. Jake shook the images from his head and plodded toward the coffeepot. Margie's black java with a pinch of cinnamon would help clear the cobwebs and worry from his head.

"Morning, Margie," Jake said.

"Rough night?" Margie asked, glancing up while keeping one eye on the scrambled eggs in the pan.

"What gave it away?"

"You left your window open. I heard you shoutin' in your sleep." Margie turned off the gas burner beneath her cast-iron skillet and gave Jake's hand a knowing, soft squeeze. Her motherly warmth seeped into his cool skin. "It's a good thing you slept in some this mornin'."

"I didn't have animals prodding and snorting all over me. Where are they, by the way?"

Margie pursed her lips in the lake's direction.

Jake peered out the window. Rose sat on the slight slope of grass leading to the lakeshore. The sun lit her long blonde hair, caught in the breeze. Her likeness to Lucy was uncanny. Ted trundled toward Rose with a tennis ball in his mouth. Tiny and Snuffles lay on both sides of her, on their backs, enjoying the belly rubs. Everything seemed peaceful.

Jake took a big swig of coffee, burning the roof of his mouth. "How is she this morning?"

"Not sure she slept much last night, either."

"I guess that's understandable. Did she say anything more about the hearing… about Marcus?"

"She hasn't said much of anythin' this mornin'… not to me, anyway. I'm guessin' she's in shock. Krista Robb wants to try her as an adult, convict her of murder, and throw her in prison. I can't imagine what is goin' through little girl's mind."

"I can't say I'm surprised. Krista has always been aggressive."

"She can go chase real criminals. Why does she have to go after Rose? Marcus was all she knew. That girl's mother abandoned her when she was no more than a toddler."

"No one knows where she ran off to?"

"Occasionally, rumors surface here and there. About her runnin' with a rough crowd. But she never came back."

"I wouldn't put any stock in idle chatter."

"You know, one time while he was waitin' to pick Rose up from school, Marcus told me that for a whole year after that woman skedaddled, that little girl waited in front of those large windows out at their place for her momma to return. She'd sit there, play with her toys, and keep a watch on the drive—just hopin'."

Jake grunted at the anecdote, a pit forming in his stomach at the thought of a towheaded Rose plunked down on the floor, one eye on a doll, the other scouting for Mommy. Jake believed every word Margie uttered. She would know the family tree and their history. Before she retired, Margie worked her entire career at the library that the junior high and high school shared. She was also the archivist for all the town gossip. She no longer went to the library but somehow maintained her firm grasp on everything that happened around Haven.

"I've been meaning to ask you about all that you told me at the hearing yesterday. How well did you know Marcus?"

"Marcus did his best as a father," Margie said. "He welded pipelines for various outfits around here. Most times, he had a job. But he tried to make it to everythin' Rose had at the school too. Sometimes he'd ask me to watch her after school when he was goin' be late pickin' her up. She'd do homework in the library until he got her. I lost track of them a bit when I retired. I'd run into them in town, at the grocery and such. But I had no inklin' she or Marcus was in any danger."

From afar, Rose looked peaceful stroking Tiny's belly, and the pig looked downright blissful, his black skin soaking up the sun. Ted dropped the ball and circled her, begging her to throw it again, his docked tail frenetic.

"What do you think Krista is up to?" Margie asked.

"Let's wait and see what evidence they put on at the waiver hearing."

"No, I mean why is she goin' after Rose so hard?"

"Stepping stones. Rose is just another feather in Krista's cap, to mix my metaphors. She's a political animal."

"Since the day she was born," Margie spat.

Jake let the sour expression on Margie's face ease and then spoke up. "We still have the fact that somebody killed Marcus. They may also have been after Rose. She could still be in danger. Do you think it's wise to have her stay out here with you? She might only bring trouble… draw it like a moth to a flame."

"I can't believe you just said that, Jake Fox. If you think for a second that I'm gonna turn that little girl out of my house after yesterday, then you ain't got a lick o' sense. I told Linda—Judge Maddix—that I would take care of Rose, and I aim to do just that."

"I'm just saying."

"Well, don't say it again. I don't believe Rose murdered her father, and I am goin' to protect her from those who did. And you… you are goin' to get her off."

Margie's proclamation floated off into a silence between them. Jake stared into his near-empty coffee cup, then out at Rose, his expression distant.

Margie picked up the coffee carafe and poured Jake another cup. "She looks like Lucy, doesn't she?"

Jake winced. "I don't know what you're talking about, Margie."

"The heck you don't. The hair, the slight features. Those emerald eyes. Look, my heart aches every mornin' for what Lucy did. It breaks for you. But you can't live your life, can't judge everythin' you do, by that one awful choice Lucy made. That's what it was. An awful choice. And Lucy was the one responsible. Not you."

Jake's expression turned grim.

"That girl's gonna need us," Margie continued, pointing toward the lake. "She's gonna need *you,* Jake. *All of you.* With Marcus gone, she has no one. We're her people now. I haven't ever turned my back on a child." Margie squared her shoulders as if ready for a fight. "I rather die than do that now."

Rose stood, brushed a few grass clippings from her jeans, and walked back toward the porch. Jake could tell she had been crying. Who could blame her? She'd woken up this morning in a world that was trying to devour her. Tiny, Ted, and Snuffles followed Rose like a parade, begging for more attention. Something in Jake told him he should run away from this problem as fast as possible. Then Rose's gaze caught his through the window. Margie was right… Those eyes, just like Lucy's. Jake closed his eyes, fighting back emotion. Determined, he vowed to never let another little girl down, no matter what. Jake turned to Margie and gave her a small peck on the cheek. "You can climb down off your soapbox, you old coot. I hear you."

Margie patted him on his wrist and said, "It's about time. Now breakfast."

CHAPTER EIGHTEEN

JAKE DOODLED on a legal pad while he waited for the waiver hearing to resume. Judge Maddix had recessed for fifteen minutes, and court was due back in session any second. The courthouse's air-conditioning was already struggling with the May temperatures, and sweat ran down Jake's back. The tepid streams of air would be insufficient when the heat index hit one hundred and ten in the summer. Jake could only imagine how the stifling atmosphere would increase the frustration all around.

Great, just in time for trial.

The first hour of testimony had been perfunctory as the social worker from Child Protective Services testified about Rose's upbringing. Krista seemed to fight the empathetic and positive portrait the witness painted of Rose and Marcus. The mother had abandoned her at three years old, and Marcus raised Rose as a single father, doting on her until his death. Rose proved successful at school and dreamed of being a nurse. Teachers took a shine to her. One instructor emphasized how she succeeded in math and science, but she also excelled at art.

Jake agreed with the testimony. He had noticed Rose

sketching some around Margie's house. A drawing here or there on a slip of paper, and the beauty and care she put into them was obvious. Jake stored that nugget in his mind. He should buy Rose a sketchbook and pencils. Going to trial would be stressful, and a distraction could prove useful.

The recess over, the door to Judge Maddix's chambers swung open. Out walked the deputy, calling everyone to order. The judge followed—a black flash in her robe, white sneakers poking out from underneath. She scurried to the bench, and as always was all business. Jake noticed Rose stiffen as the judge began.

"Ms. Robb, I believe I have a full picture of Ms. Tucker's situation. And I've talked with the current guardian, Ms. Moore. Please make your record on probable cause."

"Thank you, Your Honor." Krista Robb stood up and straightened her pinstriped charcoal pencil skirt and sharp-angled blazer. Her perfume wafted over Jack as she grabbed a legal pad and folder and made ready at the lectern. "Your Honor, the State calls Detective Hendricks to the stand."

"Detective Hendricks, come forward and be sworn."

Jake knew Wes Hendricks from when they both went to Haven High School. Wes graduated from the local community college. He joined the sheriff's department and was promoted quickly to detective. He had worked in homicide for fifteen years. His once athletic build now carried the slight paunch of middle age. He was thorough, detail-oriented, and just jaded enough to view Rose as an adult.

"Detective Hendricks," Krista started, "I know you've testified many times before this court, but for the record, please remind us of your qualifications."

Wes laid out his distinguished career for the sheriff's department, peppered with the occasional special training he'd received from the Texas Rangers and the FBI. Jake scratched out a few meaningless scribbles on his legal pad. There was no impeaching Wes's credentials.

"Now," Krista continued, "In mid-April, did you investigate a homicide at the Tucker home?"

"Yes, ma'am. I'd just finished my morning paperwork when I received a call from the sheriff to head to the Tucker place. She said they'd discovered Marcus Tucker dead on the property. She informed me that Marcus had a lone gunshot wound to the head that appeared to be self-inflicted."

"Walk us through what you did after you arrived."

"I parked by the sheriff's truck and entered the Tuckers' home. I know Marcus and Rose from around town. Inside, I found Marcus's body in the master bedroom."

"What did you observe?"

"He lay in the middle of the mattress. His boots were still on. He appeared to have been dead for several hours." Wes looked apologetically at Rose.

"What conclusions did you draw from Mr. Tucker's injuries?"

"The blood-splatter pattern on the wall, headboard, and mattress revealed a single bullet wound inflicted under his chin while in bed. The medical examiner initially suggested that the death was a suicide."

"Did you agree with that assessment?"

"At first. There were no signs of forced entry found in the home. No defensive wounds, such as cuts or scrapes on his hands."

"Does that prove suicide?"

"No... Surprise could easily explain the lack of defensive injuries. Marcus could have known or trusted his killer, or he could have been asleep... or passed out."

"Did you draw any further conclusions from the blood pattern and volume?"

"I'm not the medical examiner, but from my experience, it told me the victim had died instantly."

"Was that important to your conclusion of homicide?"

"It was one factor. I've seen my share of suicides in this job. In a significant percentage, the person botches it. Their hand trembles with stress as they pull the trigger. Often what they hope will be an instant kill shot is not. The wound is severe and fatal, and the victim bleeds out over time. That leads to significant blood around the body. A gunshot wound causing immediate death results in less blood volume because the heart ceases to pump."

Jake reached across the table and covered Rose's trembling hand with his. He could feel her pulse racing. She stared at Wes, transfixed by this clinical description of what had happened to Marcus.

"Marcus was good with gun, correct? He was a hunter. He could have delivered a kill shot like you described."

"True, but further evidence suggested otherwise."

"Like what?"

"Marcus was right-handed."

"How did you come to that conclusion?"

"He had a computer on his desk. I spotted the mouse next to the keyboard. We had found the gun on the left side of the bed. Shooting himself with his left hand would be odd since he was right-handed."

"Detective Hendricks, what more can you tell us about the weapon that killed Marcus Tucker?"

"I identified a nine-millimeter pistol on the floor on the left side of the bed, two or three feet from the victim. Blood was visible on the grip, trigger guard, and trigger. The crime scene unit marked it as the potential weapon. I came to understand by reviewing the file that they confirmed this later through ballistics."

"What else did you see?"

"The bedroom and the rest of the house appeared undisturbed. No struggle was evident."

"Did you draw any conclusion from the lack of struggle?"

"Based on my experience, and the totality of the facts as we found them, it confirmed our reasonable inference that the victim knew the assailant."

"What else did you notice?"

"The team marked several drops of blood on the carpet, away from the body, near the bedframe. Blood smears on door and doorknob, also far from the body."

"Was the blood tested?"

"Yes. Techs collected blood samples from the carpet and door for lab analysis. The blood type returned as O-positive."

"Did the victim have type O positive blood?"

"No. The victim was A positive."

"Did you later come to learn that someone associated with the home had O positive blood?"

"Yes, ma'am. We later confirmed that Rose—Ms. Tucker—has that blood type."

"Was her blood next to the body and the door where you found the deceased?

"Yes."

"Detective, did you review any of the additional findings of the crime scene lab?"

"Yes. The team tested for fingerprints and found two distinct sets."

"To whom did those belong?"

"One set belonged to the victim, Marcus Tucker. The second set belonged to his daughter, Rosemary Tucker."

"Where were those located?"

"The weapon and the bedroom doorknob."

"Is Ms. Tucker in the courtroom today?"

Rose's nails bit into the flesh of Jake's palm.

Hendricks pointed at Rose. "She is. She's seated at respondent's table."

"Did you interview Ms. Tucker?"

"After she had made the physical identification for the Medical Examiner down at HCMC, Sheriff Stone interviewed her at the department."

"Had she spoken to law enforcement before?"

"After finding the victim, the sheriff had a brief conversation with her at the scene, followed by the formal interview."

"Was she able to explain her whereabouts on the day in question?"

"Ms. Tucker relayed a story about two men and one woman coming to the Tucker house and assaulting her father. On both occasions she was interviewed, she told us that men came to the house, searching for Mr. Tucker. Upon him exiting the house, they assaulted him and then they took him back into the house. According to Ms. Tucker, they left sometime later. She says she found her father dead after that."

"Where was Ms. Tucker at the time this alleged assault occurred?"

"She maintains she observed the events through a crack in the well house wall."

"Did you find any trace of the alleged assailants?"

"No. We found no observable tire tracks or indicia of a vehicle other than Mr. Tucker's truck, which was parked at the scene when responding units arrived. We saw no evidence of any sort of third-party involvement."

"Detective Hendricks, just to be clear: Ms. Tucker's fingerprints were found on the weapon that killed Marcus Tucker, correct?"

"Yes."

"Nothing further."

"Counsel," the judge said, looking at Jake, "questions for this witness?"

Several thoughts ran through Jake's mind about how to challenge Detective Hendricks. But he decided to wait. There was no need to alert Krista to any likely lines of cross-examination at trial. "None, Your Honor."

"Understood. Detective Hendricks, you may step down. Ms. Robb, call your next witness."

"The State has no further witnesses. The testimony from

Detective Hendricks concludes the State's evidentiary offer of proof."

"Anything from the respondent?"

"No, Your Honor. We believe the State has failed to meet its burden, and therefore we forego any evidentiary presentation."

Judge Maddix let out a heavy sigh. "Counsel, the court is happy to hear you both argue, if you wish to put it on the record. But I believe I have my ruling." Krista and Jake shrugged as the judge plowed ahead.

"In the case of the State of Texas versus Rosemary Tucker, upon a motion made by the State to try Ms. Tucker as an adult, after an evidentiary hearing, the court finds the following facts and makes the following rulings. The State has met its minimum burden to show probable cause that one Rosemary Tucker did, by violent means, take the life of another individual, Marcus Tucker, her father."

Rose slumped forward and laid her head gently on her forearms on the counsel table, silent sobs causing her chest to swell and contract.

The judge continued, "After reviewing the relevant statutes, case law, and the evidentiary record, and because Ms. Marcus is fifteen years of age and the alleged violent nature of the crime, the court holds that Ms. Tucker should be tried as an adult as requested by the State.

"Ms. Tucker, look at me."

Rose sat back up and smoothed the front of her dress, the skin on her neck bright red and mottled. She wiped the tears from her cheeks with her fingers. Jake handed her his hanky.

"Ms. Tucker, as your attorney will explain in more detail, Ms. Robb now has the responsibility to take the facts to a Texas grand jury to see if she can indict you as an adult for the alleged crime. If the grand jury agrees with her and issues a true bill, an indictment will issue followed by a warrant for your arrest. I will tell you, though, that if the grand jury indicts, it may be unlikely for you to be arrested. I would like to think that Mr. Fox and Ms. Robb will work together to arrange for your surrender rather than have you arrested by the sheriff's department. Because of the court's ruling, your case is transferred to the 113th District Court, the Honorable. Harlan Dubose presiding. Judge Dubose, if needed, will issue the normal orders in due course for a criminal trial, including arraignment, bail hearing, and trial, whenever it fits on Judge Dubose's criminal docket. Ms. Tucker, do you have questions?"

"No, ma'am."

"Counsel, anything further?"

"No, Your Honor." Jake and Krista answered in unison.

"This court stands in recess." And with that, Judge Maddix left the bench.

CHAPTER NINETEEN

JAKE PULLED into the wide gray gravel parking lot that serviced two local stalwart businesses. On one end sat Wigglers, which boasted the largest selection of fishing tackle this close to the Texas-Oklahoma border—most of it on one discount or another. Old Man Thompson and Wigglers raised the healthiest, fastest minnows and sported a worm farm out back in a compost field, producing plump, irresistible earthworms. This time of night, however, the bait shop was closed, and Old Man Thompson was sitting in a wooden chair on the porch, drinking his nightly six-pack of beer and smoking his filterless cigarettes.

Jake rolled his truck into a parking slot in front of the lot's other establishment: the Hog's Breath Saloon, the main watering hole for townies—not a tourist trap. It claimed the best burgers in town and was the best bet for trivia nights. Jake needed a few hours to decompress and clear his head after the waiver hearing that had led to Rose being tried as an adult.

Inside, the smell and muted light immediately transported Jake back to his final high school years. Back then, Red, the owner and main bartender, would wink and nod at the ridiculous fake IDs Jake and his friends had scored from a local forger who operated out of a rundown doublewide on Magpie Road and who may or may not have been Red's second cousin.

They would drink in the back room, because the side door allowed for an easy escape if Red signaled a deputy's entrance. Red was old-school, having grown up on horseback, tending cattle on a ranch. He figured that the closer boys came to registering for the draft, the better they deserved a beer and the less the law should be involved.

"Old enough to die for your country, old enough to knock back a cold one," Red would say. And, per the equality of the open range where only hard work matters, he'd serve all the girls too, because there's nothing more brave or beautiful than a barrel-racing queen strutting her stuff in tight jeans at the local rodeo.

Dollar bills signed by patrons covered the walls of the Hog's Breath. It was a collage of the history of Haven. Those bills spoke proclamations of love, brotherhood, and simple human connection through the decades. It was a blue-collar worker's bar that smelled of sweat, horses, and the slag that clung to the welders and pipe fitters who serviced the wellheads and pumpjacks that pockmarked the landscape around the county. It smelled of metal, strength, and the muscle that makes the middle of America work. In a lot of ways, the Hog's Breath Saloon was the heartbeat of Haven.

A pang of loneliness hit Jake as he looked around, realizing he would likely be sitting at the bar alone for dinner. Then he glimpsed Hope Stone sitting in a booth by herself, reading a book. After a moment, Hope looked up, a kind smile gracing her lips. She beckoned him over. That unexpected warmth started swirling again in Jake's gut.

"A night on the town, counselor?" Hope asked.

"It's been a rough few weeks. I thought a beer and burger might be in order."

"Well, you're welcome here if you'd like." Hope signaled to

the seat across from her. "I'm just catching up on my trash novels. I could use some company."

Jake tossed his jacket into the booth and scooted in across from Hope.

"I thought you'd be out looking for Beth Dubose."

"Tough situation, that one. I can't say a lot about an ongoing investigation, but even the sheriff takes days off sometimes. Wes Hendricks is working on that case as well. He's dogged. It's in excellent hands for a few hours."

Hope was out of uniform, in a sleeveless shirt with mud stains on the front, and her hair was braided in two long pigtails. Jake chuckled to himself.

"Nice getup," he said. "You been rolling in the mud?"

With an easy laugh, Hope examined the stains on her shirt and twirled her braids.

"Parent Olympics down at the college. My daughter signed us up to compete as a team. You know, egg toss, three-legged race, tug of war, that sort of thing. It was silly, but fun. Matching pigtails was her idea." Hope gave him a big smile. "Too much?"

Jake could feel a slight flush on his cheeks, not knowing if it was her smile or the surprise revelation that she had a daughter in college.

"Daughter?"

Hope's eyes gleamed with pride. "Yeah, I know, and all grown up. She graduates this year with a degree in nursing. She's super smart. Great kid."

Jake quickly did the math in his head. She must have gotten pregnant at a very young age. She seemed to recognize the calculus behind his eyes.

"Life happens, Jake. We just take it one day at a time… No regrets." She picked up a menu and handed it to him. "You look hungry. Better get to picking."

Welcoming the chance to retreat from his judgments, Jake

spoke. "I already know what I want. One Disaster Burger with tater tots and a draft beer."

"Good choice on tots." Hope signaled for the waitress, and Jake ordered.

"I'll have what he's having," Hope said, looking at Jake. "What? I'm starving. That three-legged race worked up a hunger."

"We'll get those right out, Sheriff," the waitress said.

"No rush, Holly. You get it out when it's ready. No special treatment needed for me," Hope answered, and the waitress skirted around the corner.

"You're a celebrity around here."

"I'm just the sheriff. But it comes with some perks." A moment of silence passed between them.

"What's her name… your daughter?"

"Grace."

"Beautiful name."

"Beautiful kid."

"How?" Jake said, embarrassed the moment the word left his lips.

"The usual way." Hope laughed. "As I remember it, you don't need a lesson on the birds and bees, do you, Jake?"

"That was stupid… that's not what I meant."

"I know, I know. I'm just jacking with you. You should have seen your face. Long story or short?"

"I'll take whichever you want to give."

"Well, I turned up a young, pregnant, single woman in the middle of the Bible Belt. And you know Bert and Connie—they're practical. So my parents sent me to my Aunt Idris and Uncle Russ, who have a cattle ranch out in West Texas. I hid out there until I had Grace and raised her on the ranch for a couple of years. Then I came back to Haven and started community college."

"The father?" Jake regretted being too presumptuous.

Hope paused and stared into his gaze. Then, as if unafraid of any truth, she said, "He doesn't know. No need to create a ruckus. Maybe someday he'll want to know. Grace asks occasionally, but she doesn't push it. Besides, by the time I got back, he'd moved on, and Bert had it all worked out. Simple story. Ranching can be dangerous. So my supposed fiancée had an accident with an unruly horse on the open range and didn't survive. Nobody asked me much after that. Nobody questions the dead."

Jake lowered his voice almost to a whisper. "You don't worry about everyone finding out?"

Hope leaned forward, almost as if teasing him. "Jake, it's Haven. Sure, there're some whispers, and everyone already knows it's a fiction. But they're happy playing along because it's a simple story. So nobody cares. Besides, Grace grew up here. Everyone adores her, so they're happy to live my lie for her sake. And life in Haven just marches forward."

The waitress brought their burgers, and the conversation turned toward easy topics, like catching up on old friends. Most of the stories ended with weddings and someone working as a roughneck in the oil fields. Hope reached across the table with a napkin, wiping some ketchup and mustard from the corner of Jake's mouth. She paused, rubbing her thumb across a birthmark on Jake's cheek.

"Never had that removed? I figured a celebrity lawyer like you would have plastic surgery."

"That mark. No. I thought about it, but my mom told me, long ago, that it was an angel's kiss. Every time I thought about getting it removed, her words seemed to be a warning. So, no, … no plastic surgery."

"It looks good on you. Your angel's kiss."

A soft, uncomfortable silence fell between them, then Hope reached across the table and folded her fingers across Jake's hand.

"I'm sorry about Lucy… Nobody should bury a child."

Jake's words caught in his throat. Lucy's suicide was the last subject he thought would come up tonight.

"Nothing in life can prepare you for closing the casket door over a child's face." A solo tear leaked down his cheek.

Hope reached over again, wiping it away. "I can't imagine."

"Try not to... But Grace sounds amazing." Jake paused, gathering Hope's gaze. "You know, life happens. We just take it one day at a time... A whole world of regrets."

She shook her head, as if retreating.

"Just know my heart breaks for you," she said.

"Thank you."

"What was she like? What do you miss most about her?"

The blunt, penetrating force of Hope's questions took Jake aback. Nobody had asked an honest question about Lucy for a long time. After a moment, he answered.

"Her laugh. She was so joyous." He shook his head as if trying to calm a tempest. "There was no warning... no storm clouds on the horizon."

"Don't."

"Don't what?"

"Blame yourself, Jake."

"I should have known. Maybe I could have stopped it. Maybe she'd be right here having a burger with you, me, and Grace."

"Life is beautiful and cruel at the same time. All we can do is nurse the bruises and know they will heal."

"I'm not so sure."

"Time, Jake. Give it some time. Besides..." Hope winked at him. "Who knows? Something beautiful might be on your horizon."

CHAPTER TWENTY

FRUSTRATION ATE AT JAKE. Within the week, Judge Dubose accepted the waiver of jurisdiction from Judge Maddix, commenting on the "heinous nature" of the crime as he looked down his hooked nose at Rose. Jake realized then that Rose's friendship with Beth would curry no favor with the judge. By now, everyone in town knew of his daughter's disappearance, and the stress weighed on the jurist's face. It looked like he hadn't slept in days. He arraigned Rose as an adult and set bail at $250,000, which required $25,000 cash paid to the bail bondsman to keep Rose out of jail. Margie had the bank issue a cashier's check from her savings, which raised some eyebrows in the courtroom. Over Jake's objections, Judge Dubose set Rose's trial on his criminal docket for Tuesday, August twelfth. He had less than four months to prepare a murder trial defense. Dubose also denied Jake's motion to close the proceedings to the public because of Rose's age. He seemed to smirk at the thought of her being tried in the public square, and the gaggle of reporters in the back murmured while he signed his ruling. Jake could understand that Dubose was under severe stress with his daughter missing, but he was worried the judge's temperament was fraying. He could file a motion for the judge to recuse himself from the case, but such motions were left to the complete discretion of that same judge. The chances of the judge recusing himself were nil.

A day later, as Jake sat at the diner, he finished his tuna salad sandwich and contemplated all that was to come… and Rose's fate.

"Why the long face?" Tizzie asked.

Jake looked up at the waitress, her ample bosom in a constant tug-of-war with the corn-yellow dress and apron she wore during her shift at the diner. He assumed Tizzie could have purchased a larger one, but he also assumed she might still be trolling for a husband among the roughnecks that rolled through town and out to the rig derricks. Tizzie and Jake had struck up a relationship made of friendly banter since he had come back. He often ate his weekday lunches at the café counter because he enjoyed her company.

"Just thinking about how fickle life is."

"Tell me about it… I find me a man. He gets in trouble. I kick him out. He apologizes. Then I take him back. Then he runs off, and I move on to the next piece of work. I'm guessing it won't change 'til I learn myself some sort of lesson. The good Lord teaches us the same thing over and over until we listen. I guess I just ain't hearing him yet."

"Maybe so."

Winking at Tizzie, Jake tossed a couple of bills on the counter and headed for the door.

"You the one defending the murderer who shot her father?" A voice spilled out into the diner. Jake turned. Blue-haired Gertrude Winnie, who spun bingo at the VFW, and her cadre of busybodies were perched in a booth. Jake flinched because the words painted such a discordant picture of Rose.

"What did you say?"

"You're that big-time lawyer defending that girl that shot Marcus in cold blood, aren't you?"

"And what business is it of yours?" Jake asked.

"Oh, everything around here is my business, mister. Mark my words."

"Ma'am, I think you ought to stick your nose somewhere else," Jake said, and pushed his way out the door. The early summer heat and humidity hit him as soon as he stepped on the sidewalk, and the sweat was already pooling on the small of his back. The fragrance of hyacinth swirled around him. He crossed the town square to his office.

The bells jangled as he opened the door. The acrid scent of cigar smoke spilled through. Penny called out as she moved from the copier to her desk. "Prosecutor sent over a box for you. It's on the conference room table. Hitch is already rummaging through it."

"Thanks, Penny."

Jake walked into the conference room. Hitch, cigar jammed in the side of his mouth, sat with his sleeves rolled up, thumbing through Rose's file. Jake had not yet asked him to help with Rose's case. *No time like the present.*

Jake took in the sight of file folders fanned out on the conference room table. Krista had responded to his discovery requests. She had refused to send him anything until he filed a motion with the court. She was going to make him work and never give him an inch. All the evidence the State had, including exculpatory evidence, was in the box. But who knew what Krista would hold back? Jake was pretty sure she would sandbag him somehow, closer to the trial.

Hitch's face was all focus, his readers perched on the end of his ruddy, bulbous nose.

"You think you can help me with this one?"

Hitch didn't look at Jake, and kept gazing over his glasses at the pages in front of him. After a moment, he pronounced in a deep voice, "You're up against it. Krista's working overtime to put that little girl behind bars."

"I don't think Krista sees much beyond notching another conviction on her way to bigger things."

"I get that, but it seems like she's making an extra effort here. I'm not sure why."

Because she's trying to pay me back for not going along with her planned life.

On second thought, Jake had not heard about any husband, so maybe her life was not going to plan, which might make her that much more vicious.

"I think you hit on it before. She's excited about the potential press coverage. She wants to grandstand and wants this case to be high-profile. Besides, no matter what she's up to, the only thing between a jail cell and Rose right now is me."

"Now, wait a second. I've been meaning to talk to you about that. Trial is just around the corner. I may just have some extra time I could lend… if you'd have me?"

Jake smiled at Hitch. He was an old man, true. Bags under his eyes. Heavy drinker. But, as Hitch had once told him, the only difference between an old lawyer and a young lawyer is the old lawyer has been kicked in the teeth enough to know when to duck. Jake could use Hitch's wisdom and, frankly, a friend in the courtroom.

"Funny you should say that. I sort of already hinted to Judge Maddix that you'd be in this with me."

"And she didn't curse you?"

"No. She did not."

"You know, she was a real looker back in her day. Sure, she grew up on that ranch, as solid a cowboy as anyone, but she cleaned up nice… real nice. Good kisser, too."

Jake pulled out a chair and sat down. "Put the memories away. We have work to do. What do we have?"

Hitch kicked forward in his chair and became all business.

"On first glance, they got your girl pretty good. Says here there was no evidence of any other person having stepped on the property. They note it had rained heavy the night before, so all that water flushed the crime scene."

"Maybe the rain washed away the footprints of the men Rose says took Marcus."

"Let's hope so. Let's hope those men exist."

"You doubt her?"

"Son, all we have is her story. And it could be just that… a story."

"I believe she's telling the truth."

"Does your belief explain Rose's fingerprints are all over the scene and on the murder weapon? Can it tell us why the blood on the gun and the doorknob matches Rose… O positive?"

"So? She lived in that house. Nothing odd about her fingerprints in her own home. Plus, she told us she cut herself when she found the body. I've seen the gash on her knee."

"I'm just saying…"

"What? That Rose is a liar?"

"No. Just taking a skeptical gander at what's before us. You know as well as anyone that a lawyer that starts digging his own chili too much is headed for a loss. You gotta ask the hard questions. Keep your eyes open to other possibilities. That's all." Hitch took a long draw on his cigar and puffed out the smoke in several rings. "I tell you one thing I know. I don't think the prosecution is telling us everything yet. Krista's gonna drip it out. Not so slow that the judge can bust her. But she won't do us any favors."

"Still," Jake said, "her entire case is circumstantial. Krista has no witnesses."

"You and I both know circumstantial is enough when that jury shuffles into the box."

"That's where you and I come in."

"Well, it gets even better. Says here during the months leading up to the murder, the neighbor heard Marcus and Rose arguing quite a bit. Raised voices and all, pretty regular-like."

"This witness say what they were yelling about?"

"Only that it was angry."

"That's thin. Not much of a motive. Lucy and I used to argue. Teenage girls can be unruly."

"Maybe their dads aren't much better."

Jake tried not to let that sting.

Hitch continued, "They're gonna put her in the house at the time of the murder with her blood at the scene, fingerprints on the murder weapon, fingerprints on the doorknob, and tell the jury that she and Marcus had a crappy relationship."

CHAPTER TWENTY-ONE

BETH WOKE in a dim isolation that blanketed her. The chilled damp air wreaked of iron and grease. She hated this cellar. Beth struggled to adjust her vision to the darkness, but she could see only the faint outline of a thin stained mattress tossed on the floor for her to sleep. Time held no significance in this pit. She thought a day or two had passed. But she didn't know. Obscure etchings in the brick served as cryptic testimonies to the girls who had been here before her. Name after name.

She stood, pacing in the tiny cell, working to relieve the soreness from her bruised body. Her efforts to resist when they took her led to beatings she struggled to forget. Her captors responded to any defiance by doling out significant pain. Beth focused on her breathing, trying to slow it to keep the panic at bay, rubbing her palms on her arms to remove the chill. The door had no knob, solely a deadbolt, with no way to open it from the inside.

Footsteps sounded on the stairs. It would likely be her keeper, a man with a long gray beard and crooked teeth who brought her food and water twice daily. He switched out the bucket they gave her to use as a toilet. Then he would disappear until next time. He'd said little to her so far, solely grunting short caustic commands. Beth backed up and crouched in the corner, waiting for him to open the door. The key turned in the lock, but an unfamiliar voice floated in the darkness as the door swung on its hinges.

"Put this on," he barked as he tossed a sundress at her. "We're leaving soon."

Beth tried not to gasp as he stepped inside the cell. His imposing size caused her to flinch. A long, black beard in two braids flowed to his navel and a set of near-black eyes held a menacing stare. They pierced her… pinned her in place. She summoned all her courage.

"I'm not going anywhere with you."

"You are in no position to refuse. And you *will* do what I say right now, or we'll remind you who is in charge." He raised the back of his hand to illustrate his point.

Beth recoiled. "My father is a judge. I'm certain they're looking for me. The sheriff is looking for me. You have no idea what he will do once he gets his hands on you."

"I know who your daddy is, honey, and he can't find you. Besides, the sheriff isn't looking for you. They think you ran away. Nobody really cares that you're gone. Now put that dress on."

Beth trembled against his words.

They are looking for me… right? Surely he is looking for me. Has the sheriff searching.

She stood up straight, trying to bluff. "Get out, and I'll put that dress on."

"I'm not going anywhere." He stepped forward, his arm snapping out like a snake. His hand clamped onto her jaw. Pain shot through her skin and joints as his strike jammed her teeth together. He held her head in place and bent his enormous frame down until they were nose to nose. His acrid breath rolled over her. "You'd better shed that shyness. The sooner you get used to showing off that sweet little body, the better it'll be for you." He pushed her backward by her chin as he let go of her, almost knocking her off-balance.

Beth struggled to force her words out.

"You can't make me do anything."

She winced, preparing for him to strike her again for her disobedience, like others had so many times before. Instead, he broke into a deep, mocking belly laugh.

"You'll do it. Trust me, you'll do it." He pulled what Beth thought was a short club from his back pocket. At first, she thought it was a baton the police might carry. Her pulse raced when he pushed a button and sparks jumped from one prong in a forked tip to the other. Their sinister nature was vibrant in the dim cellar. "We use these to prod all you little piggies along when you talk back." He reached out, grabbed the collar of her shirt and yanked, tearing the top buttons free. Beth jumped, covering herself. She tried to hide from his lecherous stare. He stepped back, leaning against the wall.

"Now strip and put that dress on." He sparked the cattle prod again to punctuate his point.

Beth placed the dress on the mattress and locked eyes with him, trying to conceal her panic. Her heart raced. The smell of sweat and fear encircled her. She stared at his gaze and then lowered her eyes as she raised her hands to the remains of her shirt. She finished undoing the buttons and slid it off her shoulders, dropping it to the ground.

"That's right. Keep going." Her captor licked his lips while he slid the cattle prod into his back pocket then rubbed his palms together. There was a laugh tied up in his smile. Beth slipped off her sneakers. She undid the zipper on her jeans and tugged them down until they puddled at her feet. She stepped out of them.

"Good girl, now you're getting it."

Beth knelt down and picked up the dress to slide it on.

"Not yet!"

Stepping away from the wall, he picked up a small bucket

from outside the door. Holding the bucket in one hand, he approached Beth. When he was close enough for her to feel his heat in the cold room, he reached down and pulled a long-bladed knife from the sheath on his hip. He raised it so she could see the glint on its matte black, razor-sharp edge.

"Don't move. This won't hurt."

Adrenaline coursed through her veins and caused her ears to ring. Terror pinned Beth in place. He traced her shoulder with the blade, hooking it under the bra strap on her left shoulder. The knife made quick work of the soft, intimate fabric. Beth's breath caught in her throat as he continued cutting her bra away from her body with deliberate strokes. She reached to cover herself.

"No!" he barked. "Put your arms down." Slowly, he traced the cruel point of the blade down her cleavage and navel until it hooked into the curve of her panties on her left hip. With a flick of his wrist, the knife slid through the cloth. He sliced away the right hip strap, and the violated fabric fell to the floor, leaving her completely naked except for her short socks.

The dank cold of the cell caused gooseflesh to raise all over her body as she shivered.

He placed the knife back on his hip and reached into the bucket. Beth heard the water sloshing. He picked up a sponge and rubbed it across her shoulders, washing away the grime. She hated that the warm water this animal was washing her with gave her some comfort against the cold and stiffness blanketing her. Beth pressed her eyes closed. Tears leaked from them as he rubbed the rag over her a little at a time. As he scooped her socks off and washed her feet, she opened her eyes. In the light spilling from the hallway, she noticed a piece of polished metal hanging on the wall of her cell, functioning as a mirror. She stared at herself, shivering in the cold, and hated herself for a moment.

How did this happen to me? You are so stupid. You did this to yourself.

He stood and wiped the tears from her cheeks.

"No need to cry. You have a big future with us." He cupped her cheek with an open palm. "You're going to make us a lot of money. Now… put that dress on."

Beth pulled the dress over her head and straightened it over her naked body.

A woman's voice pierced the blackness in the hallway. "Is she ready to go?"

He did not flinch. Instead, he kept his gaze trained on Beth, and then nodded toward the female voice. He lowered his lips to her ear and whispered, "She's getting angry, Beth. You don't want to make her mad." He paused and wrapped Beth in a final lecherous glare. "We're leaving in ten minutes." He pointed at the bucket. "If you need to use the bathroom, do it now. We ain't stopping on the road."

Beth continued to look at her reflection. Sadness stared back at her. The dress was pretty and fit her well, but the hollowness inside threatened to pull her into a new and scary bleakness. She had no watch to see the ten minutes leak out from under her. She only knew she would soon be on the move without knowing her destination, following in the steps of all the other girls who had passed through this cell and etched their names on the wall.

CHAPTER TWENTY-TWO

LATE FOR A STRATEGY meeting with Hitch, Jake stepped out of his truck. He hopped on the sidewalk and rounded the corner onto Main Street, right in front of their office. Distracted by the headlines about Rose's trial at the newsstand, he failed to see Krista, who was steaming toward him. He smacked into her, almost knocking her cup of coffee from her hands. Her cheeks flashed crimson.

"Whoa there, killer, tap the brakes," Krista said, a predatory electricity flashing through her glare.

Jake wiped several drops of coffee from his suit coat. "Krista… I didn't see you there. I was—"

"Not looking out for me again."

Jake ignored the dig. "I *am* sorry. I just wasn't paying enough attention to notice you."

"Nothing new there," Krista said.

"Don't be like that," Jake said, feeling the familiar pit in his stomach.

"Like what?"

"I haven't seen you since I came back to Haven, and the first thing you do is chew on me."

"That's not the first thing I did," Krista said. Her eyes widened with her smirk. "I beat you in court… like a drum."

Jake shook his head. It had been years, but she was picking up right where she left off. The familiar knots formed in muscles in his neck. Zero to sixty in mere moments. "One small motion is not a victory," Jake said. "Trial hasn't even started."

"It's started for me. And it's not a small motion. Your defendant is going to stand trial as an adult for the very *adult* crime she committed. No, Jake, you're behind. We've been prepping. By August, I'll be ready to bury your client."

"She's just a kid."

"She's a fifteen-year-old violent murderer."

"You believe *that,* don't you?"

"That's what the facts tell me."

"You're not interested in justice?"

"Around here, I am justice. Besides, the facts tell me she's guilty. You should learn about facts. They can be stubborn things."

"And the men who assaulted Marcus?"

"What men? They're ghosts, Jake. She made them up to get herself off for shooting her father in the head."

"What possible motive could she have? He was her only parent. He raised her. There's no sign of abuse or neglect. He wasn't a rich man who had threatened to leave her out of the will. You're smoking dope if you think there's a motive here. You have an enormous gap in your case, and you know it. All *this,*" Jake said as he waved his hand at Krista, "this bravado is nothing but bluster, because all I need is reasonable doubt. And I have much, much more than that. And you're missing a motive."

"We'll see…."

Jake didn't like the way Krista smiled as she threw out that comment. Nothing good ever followed her pregnant pauses.

"I have an amendment to the crime scene inventory," she said.

"What?"

"You'll get it in due course."

"I'm entitled to any evidence you have in your file."

"I'll give you a preview. We found your client's bra and panties."

"So? Rose lived in the home. What does her underwear being there prove?"

"We found them tangled up in the sheets of her daddy's bed."

"What?"

"Just what I said. Your client's dirty intimates were in the dead man's bedding."

"What do random panties have to do with Rose? Marcus could have had a girlfriend."

"That's where you're wrong, Jake. They matched the sets in the girl's drawers. They are hers."

"You're saying…?"

"Oh it gets better. The bourbon by the bed tested positive for Rohypnol."

"The date rape drug?"

"Exactly."

"That doesn't prove anything about Rose."

"It proves means and motive. Rose got tired of him forcing her into his bed. So she waited until she could, drugged his booze, and then … bam." Krista mimicked firing a gun.

"You're nuts, Krista."

"You know my story holds together. It's simple, and I'm going to hammer her with it in court. You won't be able to stop what's coming. You won't be able to save this little girl, either."

Heat pulled through Jake, and his fists and jaw clenched.

"Why are you going so hard after this girl? She's a child."

"You're still such a softy. An incompetent pushover."

"Krista, did you search for the men who assaulted Marcus?"

"I told you, they are a ruse. There is no evidence they exist."

"Man, you are stubborn as ever."

"Oh no, you don't... Don't put this on me. I didn't shoot her daddy in the head."

"You are maddening. She didn't shoot him."

"Prove it."

"I don't have to prove a thing to the jury, and especially not to you."

"There it is.... There. It. Is. Get it out, Jake."

"What are you talking about?"

"That seething anger. Lurking beneath the surface, ready to strike. I don't know what I saw in you."

"You wanted me to be a sap that you could cram into your vision of a trophy husband for your political career. I wanted no part. I wanted someone less fake."

"At least I have a career. How did everything turn out for you? I came back to Haven as my first step to the governor's mansion. You... you slunk back to Haven with your tail tucked between your legs after your wife threw you out."

"Just drop it," Jake said.

"Typical Jake, running away."

"Krista, I'm warning you. Drop it."

"Or what? You going to rough me up in the middle of the town square? Think about how that will go over with the press. Reporters will eat it up. I can see the headlines now: 'Enraged Defense Attorney with Anger Issues Viciously Attacks District Attorney Trying to Bring Justice to Murder Victim.'"

Jake threw his hands up. "You're impossible as ever."

"No Jake, I'm a winner. And you missed out on me, on all of it."

"The only things I missed out on were psychotic rages."

"Ha! You haven't seen me mad yet. But someday, I may let you see it. You'd deserve it. No. For now, I'm going to enjoy watching you go down in flames as I bury your guilty-as-sin client under the jail." Krista turned on her heel, flipped her hair over her shoulder, and said, "See you around, Jake."

Jake stood there, trying to quell the desire to toss something at her head.

"That went well," Hitch said from behind him. Jake turned to find the older man leaning against their office door reading the front-page article on Rose's trial. Hitch jammed his cigar in the crook of his jaw and raked his fingers through this gray hair.

"All I know about that woman is just when you think she can't get any worse, she does," Jake said.

"Same ol' Krista… She's gunning for Rose."

"That's so jacked up."

Hitch's gaze shifted, staring as something over Jake's shoulder.

"Gert, you and your posse get out of here. Nothing to see here, ladies, move on to hounding someone else."

"Hitch Miller, that girl is guilty as sin," Gert said, as if hurling an insult. "It's just an abomination, a child killing a parent. And you scum lawyers are going to help her walk free."

"As free as you, Gert. And when she is"—Hitch winked—"we might just send her up to shoot you. Now git."

"Well, I never…" Gert said and shuffled her and her three companions down the street. Hitch's eyes followed them until they turned left at the corner.

"I don't know what happened to her, you know. Gertie was a good kisser back in high school, but that fruit done spoiled somewhere along the way. She's about as pleasant as hemorrhoids." He shook his head and turned his attention back to Jake. "Now, where were we? Ah, yes. Are you sure you have all the facts here?"

"I'm telling you, that girl didn't kill her father."

"Remember the rules I taught you. Rule number one: clients don't know all the facts. Rule number two: clients lie about the facts they do know."

"She's not lying about this, Hitch. I can feel it in my bones."

"You sure that's not willful blindness or misplaced hope?"

"No. That's rule number three that you taught me: loyalty to others counts above all else. If you can't be loyal, then what else you got?"

"All I can say is that Krista is fixin' to fricassee you if you let her. And if she does, she's goin' to burn up Rose."

"How long were you eavesdropping?"

"You know me. I love a good fight. My pappy used to live by the saying, 'Is this a private fight, or can anyone join in?'"

"I noticed you didn't come to my rescue."

Hitch chuckled. "Come on now, *killer*, it looked like you had her right where you wanted her."

"You overheard the part about the bra and panties in Marcus's bed?"

"Yep… That's a bad fact."

"Sure would make it easy for the jury to believe Rose pulled the trigger."

"Like I said. Bad fact."

"At least we know Krista's intentions."

"Ya think?"

"Let's get to work and figure a way around this nightmare," Jake said.

Hitch waved his arm toward the door. "After you, chief."

Rose, what happened out at that house?

CHAPTER TWENTY-THREE

THE FAILING daylight over the lake took on the pink and orange hues of sunset. Soft clouds swept across the horizon like puffs of smoke from a giant machine chugging across the sky. Jake waved at Margie when she spotted him out her kitchen window. He crossed the lawn to her back door in long, crisp strides, and he started to speak before the screen door closed behind him.

"I swear," Jake said to no one in particular, "you'd think those pigs never eat. They seem starving every time I set the bowls down."

"They're pigs, hon. Not sure they know anythin' different. Can't change the nature of creatures."

"Good point," Jake said, rubbing Margie's shoulders and giving her a chaste kiss on the cheek. "It smells delicious in here. Is there something in the oven, by any chance?

"Pork tenderloin," Margie admitted. "I put it in before I went to bed last night. Low and slow is the best way to cook meat. It should be perfect just about now, if you're wantin' to eat with *us*." Jake noticed Margie had poured herself one bourbon for the night. Two fingers of the deep amber liquid in a highball glass with one cube of ice. Margie was no teetotaler. Indeed, before dinnertime she always had one snort—just one.

"How is she?" Jake asked.

"Rose?" Margie bristled. "Well. Someone murdered her father. The sheriff and county prosecutor want to put her in jail for a decade or more. Someone kidnapped her best friend. She's on the news every night. You know the school told her to stay home. 'Too much distraction for the other students,' they said. And, to top it off, she's havin' to learn to navigate life all on her own. Other than that, I'd say she's doin' just fine."

"You're here," Jake offered, then paused for a moment as if weighing his next words. "We're here."

Margie shook her head. "Sure, we're present. But can you imagine what's goin' through her mind? I can't. I'd wager neither of us knows what she's thinkin' when she's alone, and alone is somethin' she is quite a lot. I can't even imagine bein' adrift at that age." Margie stabbed a paring knife into an apple on the cutting board as if to punctuate her thought.

"We all understand loss, Margie."

"Well… of course we do, especially you. I'm not takin' away from that. Not a bit. But do you remember what it's like bein' a child with no adult? Are you sure you haven't forgotten some of that confusion and angst? She's rudderless, Jake. I'm just not sure an old lady is the best guide for her. She's goin' to need more… much more. She's goin' to need a parent, a family."

"I still remember what it was like to lose my parents as a kid. But Britt and I had you to help us. We leaned on you after Mom died. You were our family. And you're perfect for Rose. She seems to listen to you," Jake said.

"Jake, I will not be around forever. Raising teenagers is for the young at heart, anyway."

Jake felt the urge to say something, but held his tongue to avoid getting himself in any deeper.

Margie broke the silence. "Do you ever think of your father?"

A pregnant pause passed between them.

"I'm not sure my father deserves much thought," Jake said.

"He'll always be your father."

"No. He's gone. He took a coward's way out. Rather than stick around and do what a husband and father does, he took off. Why did you bring him up? My dad has nothing to do with Rose."

"Sure he does. Rose's mom abandoned her, and it looks like Marcus made bad choices that cost him his life. His poor choices led to Rose being alone. John's poor choices led to you bein' alone after your mother passed. You were younger than Rose when the cancer took your mother, but you may know more about what Rose needs than she does. And you know more than I do, too, because you lived it."

"Margie, I failed the last time I tried to help a struggling a teenage girl."

"I figured Lucy might be gettin' in the way."

"In the way?"

"Yeah, of you warmin' to Rose. Look, Jake, you're one of the most kind and helpful people I know, but with Rose, sometimes it's like you cannot wait to get her out of the house, get the problem off your plate."

"She's just a client. Besides, while I don't know what Marcus got himself into, I know it was trouble. If Rose is telling the truth, and that's a big if, then it sounds like some sort of gang hit on Marcus. Those killings tend to be over stealing money or stealing product, and we don't even know what shady business he was running. Trouble with a capital 'T' is something this house doesn't need. You're too old—heck, *I'm* too old—to be fussing around with whatever trouble she's visited upon this house."

"She didn't visit nothin' on this house. That little girl was in trouble, and Marcus sent her my way for help. I refuse to treat her like she's dangerous. And she's not just a client. She's family."

"You'd better think about getting in too deep with this kid, Margie. Who knows what is coming if she stays around here?" Jake said.

"She's stayin', so get yourself in order."

Margie paused the argument long enough to pull dinner from the oven and baste the meat in the Dutch oven.

Jake let out a sigh. "Who am I kidding? Rose isn't going anywhere... Judge Maddix boxed me in tight. I agreed to be Rose's lawyer. For me to get out, the judge would have to approve my withdrawal from representing her. Fat chance of that happening with Judge Dubose. He wants this case to move as fast as possible to keep his docket clean. He'd grill me about why I was ditching the case, and I certainly can't give him any reasons we've been talking about here today. With no good reason, he won't approve substituting counsel."

"But you're not goin' anywhere anyway, are you?"

Jake saw Rose on the lawn, throwing the ball for Ted. Lucy's profile briefly appeared, too, also to watch over Rose.

"No, Margie, I can't... I won't. Someone is after that little girl. So it's Rose and me until the end—and Hitch, of course."

"That old curmudgeon. You'd better keep him in line."

"You didn't seem that upset when he was here the other day, gobbling down your cobbler."

"I like it when folks enjoy my bakin', that's all."

"I'm just saying you seem to enjoy it more when it's Hitch. He brought you flowers and all."

"Don't you think for a moment I didn't notice that those flowers were out of my own garden... But I guess it's the thought that counts." Margie straightened out the wrinkles in her apron. "And before you go accusin' me of somethin', don't think I haven't noticed that little sparkle in your eye every time that sheriff comes around."

"Not true."

"True. She shows up her in her tight jeans with a gun on her hip, and you go trottin' out like Ted after a tennis ball to say hi."

"We went to high school together. I don't know many folks in town since moving back. Maybe I'm just catching up with her."

"Catchin' up," Margie said, using air quotes to punctuate her sarcasm.

"I'm not interested."

"Well, let me know what bein' interested looks like, then, because I'm confused."

"Nothing would ever happen there. Hope's got her life in order, and mine's a mess. She doesn't need me mucking up her good thing. Besides, she and her daughter seem to have it all figured out."

"Have you met her daughter yet?"

"No. She's down at the women's college, finishing up her nursing degree. I figure I'll meet her in time if Hope wants me to."

"You should meet Grace," Margie said with an impish smile. "Who knows, the three of you might hit it off."

CHAPTER TWENTY-FOUR

HOPE PULLED into the Quickie Mart out on Ring Road, right on the border of the county. The floodlights on the corners of the roof bathed the parking lot in harsh light, trying and failing to chase the shadows away. As beautiful as the lake and woods could be during the day, nighttime brought unease to all the dark crevices. Hope steadied herself.

The stifling June breeze whipped up as she stepped out of her cruiser and slid her baton into the ring on her duty belt. Hope pulled open the door and entered. The bell hanging above the frame jingled as she stepped inside. Smells of burnt coffee and boiled peanuts permeated the store. The air-conditioning squeaked out an effort to quell the heat. She scouted for the clerk, but no one was behind the counter.

"Hello. Anyone here? It's the sheriff. Someone called for me to come out?"

A gruff voice spilled out of the hallway to the back. "Don't get your knickers in a knot. I'm a comin'."

After a moment, a husky woman in a crop top walked out with a box of ramen to stock on the shelves. A filterless cigarette dangled from her mouth, wagging up and down as she talked.

"Hey, Sheriff." She set the box down, wiped her hands on the seat of her jeans, and then stuck one out to shake. "I'm the one that called."

"You're Frank?"

"Francine, actually, but most people call me Frank. It's me in the flesh. Although there's plenty more of me now than there used to be."

Hope appreciated the jest and shook Frank's hand. Several tattoos adorned the woman's arms and torso under the crop top. She looked as if she had been a practice canvas for the newbies at a parlor on the west side of Haven.

"I'm Sheriff Stone."

"I remember you, Hope Stone, from high school. You were a couple of years ahead of me, but we were in marchin' band together. You were a mean French horn, and I was a clarinet way down the wind instrument line."

Hope smiled, her eyes lighting up at the mention of the band.

"Now," Frank said, "you've gone and become famous and all. I mean, being elected sheriff is a big deal."

"I'm pretty sure it's not as much fun as marching during halftime with a French horn."

"Or foolin' around in the back of the bus on the way home from games," Frank said, and let out a chortle, lifting the cigarette from her lip so she could have a good laugh.

"True. There might have been some foolin' around... Did you call me out for a reason, Frank?"

"You betcha. It's about that girl that's missing."

"Beth Dubose?"

"Yes, that one."

"What about her?"

"I think I saw her."

"When?"

"Here... an hour or so ago."

Hope pulled a small notebook from the breast pocket of her uniform. "What makes you think it was her?"

"Well, at first I wasn't so sure. This guy comes in. I've seen him a couple times, maybe shootin' pool up at the Hog's Breath. Real ugly one. He has a long black beard, almost to his belt buckle. And somethin' odd about his eyes. They're black, almost as black as his beard. Not a real big talker either. He came in with her while he was filling his black truck."

"Here?" Hope asked, pointing at the pumps outside the windows.

"Right there on pump number one. When the gas was pumpin', they come inside. The girl asked to use the restroom, so I gave her the key. It's on that paddle hangin' behind the register. We have to lock it with all the tweakers around here doin' meth. Anyways, somethin' didn't sit right in my brain. You know, I'm always thinkin' too much. That girl, though, she looked familiar. I knew I'd seen her somewhere before, and not with him. But I couldn't quite place her."

"How long was she in the bathroom?"

"Not long. She came back out, always watching where that man was. And, come to think of it, he was keeping watch on the bathroom door while she was in there. She kept one eye on him, though, like she didn't want to upset him."

"Did she say anything else to you?"

"No, she didn't. She kept her mouth shut, and when she wasn't watchin' him, she was starin' at the ground. Like she was shy and all."

"She didn't make eye contact with you?"

"No, ma'am. She avoided it. I couldn't shake the feelin' that I'd seen her somewhere. That dude paid for his gas and a twelve-pack of beer. Then he barked at her to get back in the truck, and they left. About ten minutes after they left is when it hit me."

"I don't follow."

"Well, that girl in the store had shoulder-length black hair.

That hid her face some. I mean, the way she had it styled. So I didn't see the resemblance right away. Her picture in that flyer has long blonde hair, almost down to her waist."

"You think they altered her appearance?"

"Exactly. That's what I'm sayin' here. But there's no mistakin' that face… those blue eyes. The picture on the flyer was grainy, but I noticed the freckles on her cheeks."

"You're sure it was her."

"See for yourself."

"You have security footage?"

"It's not the greatest, but I have it."

Frank waved Hope behind the counter to a computer monitor. With a few clicks of the mouse, she called up the file. The picture was a rough, grainy black and white. She forwarded to the part she wanted to show Hope, and stopped when the footage showed a tall, burly man opening the door. He had woven his long black beard into two braids that extended to his belt. He was careful to keep the brim of his ball cap pulled low and to avoid any direct shots of his face in the camera. He knew what he was doing. He could not, however, hide the large Celtic crosses tattooed on his forearms. Hope's eyes quickly gravitated to the girl that stepped out of his shadow and asked for the restroom key.

"Pause it right there," Hope said.

Frank pulled the missing person flyer down from her wall and held it next to the monitor. "Well, as I live and breathe."

"That's her," Hope said. "Do you have cameras outside?"

"Nope, the owner's cheap. Just the one camera on the register area."

"Would you have time to come down to the station and work with our sketch artist? I'd like a better idea of what that man looks like."

"I'd be happy to help. I'll head over after my shift."

"Is that the key to the bathroom?"

"Yes, ma'am," Frank said, reaching for it.

"Wait!" Hope pulled a set of nitrile gloves from her back pocket and slipped her hands into them. "I'm going to want that dusted for prints."

"Right... lookin' for clues."

"Is the bathroom back here?" Hope asked, pointing toward the hallway.

"First door on the left."

Hope walked down the corridor with Frank at her hip. The door was ajar. She pushed it open with her flashlight. It looked, and smelled, like a typical one-hole gas station bathroom.

"I'll have the techs come out and work this area up. See if we can confirm it was her. If not, maybe it was some other girl in trouble."

"You just tell me what to do," Frank said.

Hope turned to leave when a small glint of light caught her eye. Someone had wedged something into the toilet paper dispenser. Hope looked more closely. It was a matchbook from the Silver Lake Casino, one of the large casinos on the reservation up the way. The metallic ink shone in the light. On a gut instinct, Hope picked it up and unfolded the cover. She drew in a deep breath when she saw the message inside.

PLEASE HELP ME!
– BETH DUBOSE

CHAPTER TWENTY-FIVE

LATE AFTERNOON in a Texas summer meant that the sun was still high and hot in the sky. Jake pulled his truck into the parking lot of the GasMart out near Rose's house. The asphalt had seen better days, evidenced by the large potholes. Krista Robb's file had notes of a potential witness who worked the register during the second shift—something about the witness having overheard Marcus and Rose arguing. As Jake and Hitch walked through the front door, an electric chime announced their arrival. The whir of a soda machine permeated the air. The store seemed deserted until a tall older man with a few days stubble and a few stains on his uniform shirt stumbled out of the back room behind the counter. Jake noted the television on mute behind him: a local reporter stood in front of the courthouse, reporting on Rose's case.

"You know where we can find Theo Hunter?" Jake asked.

"Who's asking?"

"I am. My name's Jake Fox, and this is Hitch..."

"Hitch Mills," the old man said. "I still remember you from your billboard out on I-35. You look older. I guess we're both getting longer in the tooth, you figure."

Jake flashed a curious glance at Hitch, whose expression confirmed he did not know who this guy behind the counter might be. But maybe they could use this perceived camaraderie to needle out information.

"Right. Yeah, I'm that Hitch Mills. We're hoping you might help us with some information about a police report you filled out." Hitch and Jake stuck their hands out, and Theo shook them, his skin dry and calloused from years of pushing a mop around this store.

"You'll have to be more specific than that. Unfortunately, I fill out a police report about once a week around here. You know... shoplifters, vagrants, you name it. We try to make a record the best we can just in case something happens. Insurance won't pay if we don't make a police report, so we report everything."

"Make perfect sense, Mr. Hunter."

"Call me Theo."

"Okay, Theo. This report would have been a few months back. You were reporting an argument between father and daughter," Jake said.

"Say, you're the one defending Marcus's little girl, aren't you?"

"Yes, I am. Can you tell me about the report?"

"It's pretty simple. I wasn't reporting them so much as I had called the deputy while they were here. I wanted to report some guy in a gray van come who'd come in, filled up, and driven off without paying for his gas. Before the deputy got here, Marcus and Rose were going at it, and got into it something fierce in the parking lot, yelling and all. They'd come to pick up a few things like bread, bologna, and such. Rose was yelling about some boy. She pitched a right round fit about it."

"Does the name Tommy ring a bell?"

"Yeah... Now that you mention it, Tommy could be the name of the kid they were going on about. Anyway, Marcus was telling Rose to get in his truck, that they were going home. That spun her up, and she was going on about how Marcus couldn't tell her what to do. She said she was an adult, and he couldn't boss her around no more. Reminded me of arguments I'd had with my daughters when they were that age. Well, Marcus must have had enough, 'cause he grabbed Rose by the arm and started walking her toward the truck. She bowed up, pulled away, and dropped all the groceries. About that time, the sheriff's deputy pulled into the lot, responding to my call on the gray van. But the deputy saw the dustup between Marcus and Rose. He jumped out of the car and went to work trying to defuse the situation. It took a while to calm them both down. Rose can get a bit riled up—reminds me of her mother that way. Anyway, the deputy must have noted something about Marcus and Rose after he took my statement on the pump jumper."

"Do you remember any specifics about what they were arguing over—what had Marcus in a lather about this Tommy kid?"

"Sounded to me like Marcus thought the boy was no good."

"Do you know Tommy?"

"Not really. He may have come in once or twice to get a soda or a pack of cigarettes. If I'm thinking about the right guy, he's got tattoos on both forearms. Mostly black lines designs. If that's him, he didn't say much and didn't stick around. I don't know much about him."

"Why would the deputy note a family tiff in a parking lot?"

"Well, when Marcus took Rose by the elbow, she took a swing at him, almost like it was a reflex… like she wasn't thinking. I think that's what got the deputy interested. Rose didn't connect very hard on Marcus, though. Best I remember, that swing landed somewhere on his chest, and it wasn't much of a hit. At least Marcus didn't seem to think so. I don't remember him getting mad about it. He kind of brushed it off... might have even chuckled."

"Did the deputy seem to take much interest in it?"

"Not really. He might have asked if everything was okay, and Marcus and Rose both said it was. Then it was nothing much to remember. Deputy turned to me and started asking about the gray van that skipped on paying for gasoline."

Jake took a card from his pocket and handed it to the clerk. "If anything else comes to mind, please call me." The clerk twirled the card in his hand and then read the name.

"Jake Fox. You wouldn't by chance be John Fox's boy, would you?"

Jake blanched. After a moment, all he could say was, "John was my father."

"I knew him from the VFW. He was always good at a joke. Shame, what happened to him. I'm sorry he up and did what he did, and the mess that must have made for you and your family. I guess it goes to prove that you just never know what's going on in a man's head, do you?"

Hitch stepped in as if to keep Jake from having to answer. "Well, Theo, you've been right helpful. Like we said, if you remember something else, please don't hesitate to give us a call."

"You can count on that. I'll ring straight away if something else comes to mind." As they turned to leave, Theo spoke up once again. "Mr. Hitch, I sure hope you'll be able to get Ms. Rose off of those charges. I can't figure she did anything to Marcus. Sure, she was fussing at him, but nothing worse than any other teenager in the history of teenagers. I don't think she did it, and I don't much think that the district attorney cares, if she gets a skin on the wall."

"Much obliged, Theo."

"One last thing. I hope they don't call me for trial. I didn't mention it to the deputy, but if they ask me from the stand after my hand's been on that Bible, I'll have to tell them."

"Tell them what?"

"Well, during that argument, like before the deputy showed up, Rose said that she couldn't wait to be rid of Marcus, and that she'd be better off without him."

CHAPTER TWENTY-SIX

STEPPING out of the blazing sunlight, Hope entered the sheriff's department and took a moment to adjust her eyes to the darker surroundings.

"Morning, Sheriff," Penny said from behind the front counter. She clicked a button to let Hope through the locked door into the bullpen behind.

"Good morning, Penny. Did you enjoy yourselves dancing last night?" As long as Hope had known them, Burton had taken his wife Penny to the Caravan to dance on Ladies' Night. They could scoot a mean swing waltz and two-step. Only severe illness or joint travel would break Burton and Penny's ritual.

How would it feel to have someone care for me as Burton does?

Hope shook her head at the twinge in her chest and the tendrils of loneliness nipping at her thoughts. A smile spread across her face, accompanied by a slight blush on her cheeks.

"You're thinking about him," Penny said, as if speaking to herself.

"What? Who?"

"Now, Sheriff," Penny said, cupping a flower on her desk from Burton. "I may be out of bounds, but I'm going to say it anyway 'cause you need to hear it. I see the way you look at that Jake boy… It's nice for you."

"Penny, he's a grown man."

"At my age, everyone's a kid. Besides, your answer isn't much of a no, is it?"

Penny had her there. Since the impromptu dinner at the Hog's Breath Saloon, Hope had been thinking about Jake quite a bit. She wondered if fate had brought him back to Haven. But as long as he represented Rose Tucker in her murder trial, she would have to maintain a professional distance. In the eyes of the law, they were adversaries. Admittedly, the idea of Jake brought a pleasant smile. It had been ages since a man, even in memory, made her flush.

Keenly aware of Penny's gaze, Hope said, "I don't know what you are talking about."

"Now I don't believe that for a minute." At that moment, the phone rang, and Penny answered it.

"Hawk County Sheriff's Department. How may I direct your call?… Yes, she's right here. I'll patch you through." Penny put the call on hold and turned to Hope. "It's the special agent from the Oklahoma State Bureau of Investigation that you called."

"I'll take it in my office." Hope headed to her office, picked up the receiver, and selected the blinking line.

"This is Sheriff Stone."

"Sheriff? Special Agent Strickland, returning your call. How can I be of service, ma'am?"

"I have a case that involves a kidnapping of a teenage girl down here in Hawk County."

"I saw it on the local news channels. It's a judge's daughter, yeah?"

"That's the one. Beth Dubose."

"You think she's in Oklahoma?"

"There's a good chance. Can I text you a photo?"

"Sure."

Strickland gave her his cell number. Hope sent him the photos she'd taken of both the matchbook and Beth's note inside.

"They're on the way."

"Just came through." Strickland let out a whistle on the other end of the line. "The Silver Lake, huh? Your hunch is she's somewhere up here in that casino?"

"Best lead I have so far. What can you tell me about the place?"

"If she's there, it might be tough to find her. It's a giant casino and resort up here by Lake Moore. On any weekend, gamblers from a four-state area cram the parking lots."

"It's a large facility?"

"Three thousand rooms in several buildings. The inside is a webwork of doors and hallways."

"Do you have any agents that work it?"

"Not regularly. That casino is on the reservation. Tribal police patrol it, and they don't like us, or anyone else, butting into their business. We have limited jurisdiction if we're pursuing a suspect. Otherwise it's by permission only. Unless..."

"Unless what?"

"You might get the FBI or Bureau of Indian Affairs involved if you think she's being trafficked. The Oklahoma State Bureau of Investigation may have an opportunity through a task force if there's organized crime involvement. Are you sure she didn't run away?"

"Positive. You see that matchbook?"

"Could be a hoax, somebody trying to mess with you, since the girl is still missing. Your amber alerts are over the area."

"Negative. I observed her on the surveillance footage from the gas station. It *was* her."

"Was she with anyone?"

"A man led her into the store. He let her run to the bathroom, but kept an eye out for her."

"What did he look like?"

"Tall. Muscled. Looked like he was no stranger to free weights. He'd yanked the brim down and avoided the cameras. He knew what he was doing. I didn't get a clear shot of his face. He had a long black beard woven into two braids."

"Devil's Vikings," Strickland said.

"The motorcycle club?"

"Chances are high."

"Aren't they more into drugs?"

"They are. They run drugs up from Mexico. Cartels bring product across the border near Laredo. The Vikings move it up Interstate 35. Distribute it in the Midwest. Mostly they run cocaine, fentanyl, and meth."

"And prostitution follows the drugs."

"Rumor has it they are big into trafficking girls out of South America. They smuggle them in and distribute them to clients who run escort services or massage parlors in Las Vegas or Atlantic City, and at all the casinos in between."

"Beth was from Hawk County, not South America."

"I know. If it's them, this would be unique. Risky. Especially so close to one of their main distribution areas. But, the double-braided beard is a classic marker for the Vikings. Any tattoos?"

"A Celtic cross on each forearm."

"That sounds like the Vikings."

"Why would they want Beth?"

"Crime of opportunity? Who knows? They might have a buyer seeking something particular. Someone young and American. Lucrative auctions exist on the dark web for virgins. Maybe the Vikings have expanded their business model."

"How do I check out that casino?"

"Good luck with the Tribal Police. They ignore anything that could be bad for business. And busting a sex trafficking ring in their casino would be a black eye."

"Perhaps I'll come and see for myself. I like to gamble."

"You can explore on your own, but if the Vikings catch wind of you snooping around, they'll move that girl. Or they'll send you a warning."

"I can handle myself."

"No doubt you can, Sheriff, but the feds suspect them of killing a US Marshal that was getting too close to a stash house down in Waco. The Vikings play by different rules. But it's a free country. I can't stop you from coming and gambling. If you come up, well, I might enjoy gambling, too. A date could be our undercover story."

Hope blanched at the statement. Had Strickland just asked her out, or was he teasing her during such a moment?

"Don't worry about getting involved because of me."

"Consider it payback. You pulled my younger brother out of his truck a few years back after a tractor trailer ran him off the road. His vehicle rolled several times in the center median, and you helped him out before the torn gas line sparked on the battery."

"I seem to remember some fresh-faced kid and a jacked-up red truck."

"That's my kid brother."

"It was my pleasure to help."

"Why don't we do this? I'm off tomorrow night. Send me photos of the girl, both old and new ones, from the surveillance tape. I'll do a drive-by, play a little blackjack, and see what I can find out. Check if any Vikings are present. How about we start there?"

"It's as good a place as any."

Hope thanked Strickland and hung up. She texted him all the photos she had of Beth. Strickland sent a thumbs-up in response.

Now we just wait. Beth, we're coming.

CHAPTER TWENTY-SEVEN

ROSE SLIPPED through the door behind Margie as Jake held it open. A woman with a placard on her desk that read *Judy* greeted them with a wide smile.

"We have an appointment with Rob Roberts at eleven o'clock," Jake said.

"Mr. Roberts is just now finishing up with his ten o'clock and will be right with you. Can I get you something to drink? Coffee? Water?"

Jake took her up on the offer of black coffee and then joined Margie and Rose on the couch in the reception area.

"Remind me why we have to be here?" Rose asked Jake.

"Marcus died without a will, so everything has to go through probate court before it can pass to you."

"I'm getting tired of lawyers and courts."

"Me too," Jake said. "It's only going to get worse before it gets better."

"Rose, we're going to help you through it. Every step of the way. Right, Jake?"

"Why can't you do this for me, Jake? Why do we need Mr. Roberts?"

"He's a friend of Hitch's and he offered to help. He was

also college roommates with the probate judge, and we need this to go as smoothly as possible," Jake said.

A door opened, and a spindly old lady labored out with a cane, followed by a gentleman in a dark pinstriped suit that made him look like a banker. Gray streaks punctuated the temples of his well-manicured brown hair. Judy stood up to help the ten o'clock out the door to her car.

"Jake, good to see you," the man said. "Margie, so good to see you, too. You're looking spry as can be. You can't be a day over twenty-five."

"I see you haven't changed a bit, Robert," Margie said.

"Just doing what I can to get by. You must be Rose. It's so nice to meet you," he said as he held out his hand.

Rose shook it, looking from one adult to another. The entire process—all the lawyers—left her breathless sometimes.

"Come on, let's sit down in my office," Rob said as he shuffled them to their next stop. They all took seats on the couch and chairs that surrounded a large wagon-wheel coffee table stacked with several manilla folders.

"Rose, I don't know how much Jake told you about my role, but why don't I give you a quick summary?"

"I think I'd like that. All I know is this is about my dad's house."

"True, true. It's about the house and more."

"I don't understand," Rose said.

"I'll start at the beginning. You stop me if you have questions. Deal?"

"Deal."

"First, Marcus, your father, died without a will, we believe. As of now, we cannot find one at the house, and we don't know of anything on file anywhere. I asked the other lawyers in town that do this type of work, and none of them had your dad as a client."

"My dad didn't much like lawyers."

"Fair enough. Most people don't. That leaves us, though,

with the presumption that he died 'intestate,' meaning without a will. I suppose he could have written one down somewhere himself, but since we couldn't find it, we'll go with the next logical deduction: no will."

"So I inherit nothing?"

"No, no. Quite to the contrary. You see, when someone dies without a will, the law tells us where to distribute all those assets. They would first go to a spouse, but there is no record of Marcus ever being married."

"That's right. My dad told me he and my mother were not married, which made it easy for her to abandon us."

"I'm sorry she did that, Rose. I did look for her."

At that statement, Rose's heart raced and her palms became clammy. *Has Robert Roberts found my mother?*

"Your birth certificate down at the Department of Vital Statistics gave us a clue. Your mother's name is—"

"Sally Jenkins."

"That's right, Sally L. Jenkins. She was born one county over and attended high school there. Her last known address is the one you shared with Marcus. But after she left there, she disappeared. We found no records of a Sally L. Jenkins in Texas, or anywhere else for that matter. Nothing that would fit with your mother's age and the identifying information we have. She appears to have become a ghost."

"So you're telling me my mom disappeared. I already know that."

"I'm telling you that to tell you this. With no spouse, Marcus's estate transfers to his descendants, of which you are the only one."

That statement flopped out into the middle of the room. Rose licked her lips. Her mouth was now dry. She tried to swallow, but coughed instead.

"Let me help," Rob said. He stood and retrieved a small bottle of water from a miniature fridge in the corner of his office.

"So what does that mean? I can't take care of a house. I don't have a job. What if something breaks? Who pays for electricity? Water?" Unease washed through Rose.

"Rose, hon. We can help," Marie said. "Jake will help," she continued, elbowing him in the ribs.

"We'll figure that out later," Jake said. "For now, you should listen to what Rob has to say."

"Yes, yes. I've worked with Jake and Hitch to figure out your future finances. There are, of course, the land and the house. The lake location gives both a nice fair-market value. Marcus also had life insurance through his work—one and a half times his last annualized salary. Welders make a pretty good living. The house and lot will be worth over one-half million, and the life insurance will pay a little over one hundred thousand in cash—tax free, mind you."

"She won't be able to live forever on that," Margie said. "With expenses and property taxes and what not."

"Well, it presumes that at some point Rose will graduate high school and either enter the workforce or go to college for some sort of career. But there's one more money item," Rob said, pausing for effect. "It seems Marcus had a keen head for business. The oil company he worked for allowed employees to invest a little of every paycheck in a profits-participation program."

"Tell her what all the jargon means, Rob," Jake pushed.

"I'm getting there right now. Rose, under the terms of the plan, you inherit that interest in the program. The program pays out a portion of the company's royalty interests in each drilled well. The share passing on to you pays over four thousand dollars a month at today's oil prices, and has been for a while. Marcus used that money to pay off the mortgage on the house, and he saved the rest. There is a savings account with about thirty-five thousand in it. That will go to you, too. In short, you should have sufficient funds to stay in that house and decide what to do next."

Rose's body relaxed at the same time butterflies filled her stomach. She would be fine in time. She could stay in her home, and this made it legit. No one be judging her, wondering where the money came from. No side glances from the gossip mill at the diner or grocery store.

"There is one final wrinkle, though," Rob said. "Jake and Hitch play a crucial role here. The law will not allow you to inherit if the district attorney convicts you of murdering Marcus. It is called the slayer rule, and it prohibits family members from profiting by killing others in their family."

"But I didn't kill him. You all know that."

"It will be the jury that decides that in the eyes of the law," Rob said. "It's all really in Jake's hands now."

CHAPTER TWENTY-EIGHT

HOPE MADE her way to the picnic table in the middle of Haven's town-square park. She waved at Shonda sitting on the wooden bench in her purple scrubs. Some might have considered it odd to look forward to hanging out with the county coroner, but even medical examiners need friends. Shonda gave Hope a quick, friendly smile and returned the wave. The soft morning breeze kept the July temperature bearable. The cool shade of a pecan tree was their usual meeting spot. It was the perfect location to drink a cup of coffee and engage in Haven's common pastime: gossip. Hope sat down, set her hat aside, and gently patted her friend's hand in greeting.

"Do you think God made perfect mornings like this just for us?" Shonda asked.

"I'd like to think He's pleased we became friends to enjoy each other's company. So... yes. I think He makes perfect mornings as a special gift just for us."

Shonda took a sip of coffee and then drummed her palm on the table. A moment of silence enveloped them, and Hope marveled at the ease of being with Shonda. Not once had Hope detected a whiff of judgment from her about Grace, or about Hope's decision to stay a single mother and raise her daughter on her own terms. Shonda never inquired about the father, because Hope guarded the secret. And Hope appreciated Shonda's quiet support.

After a beat, Shonda pointed over Hope's shoulder. "Don't look now, but we're going to have company."

"Who's coming?"

"Libbi Banderas."

Hope rolled her eyes. "It's too early in the morning for the press. Maybe she won't see me if I just stay still. She can't ask the sheriff questions if she can't find her."

"Pretty sure that ten-gallon cowboy hat and the large pistol on your hip are going to give you away," Shonda said. Hope smiled.

"Sheriff and Dr. Dunkin, do you have a minute?" Libbi asked.

"We were just headed to work," Shonda said.

"I won't keep you."

"Make it quick, Libbi," Hope said. Hope tended to shy away from talking with reporters.

"I want to ask you about Beth Dubose."

"Libbi, you know I can't comment on an ongoing investigation. Beyond the press conferences we've given and the updates, I don't have anything more to say."

"I'm just looking to keep the public informed."

"I bet." Hope shook her head at letting her irritation slip. "Sorry... but I cannot say anything beyond our prior statements."

"If you can't talk about Beth specifically, then I want to talk about her generally."

"What does that mean?" Shonda asked.

"I have a colleague just across the border in Oklahoma. She's doing an exposé on human trafficking. I've seen some of her drafts. She believes she has uncovered a syndicate involved in modern slavery, especially focused on the kidnapping and sex trafficking of girls in this area."

Hope thought back to her conversation with Special Agent Strickland and the Devil's Vikings. If Libbi had helpful information, she would listen. Occasionally, partnering with the press could be a help. Libbi had run with Beth's story and helped push it in the news, keeping it top of mind for the citizens of Hawk County and beyond.

"She thinks this group took Beth?"

"It's possible. I know most folks focus on sex trafficking at the Mexico–US border. The cartels can pick whatever foreign nationality of girls they want in Matamoros, Nogales, Tijuana, or other border towns. Czech, Columbian, Mexican, Russian, Vietnamese. They grab the girls and import them into the United States. They force them to work in massage parlors, brothels, and nail salons coast to coast. Tens of thousands a year. If it isn't sex work, it's indentured servitude. The girls work to earn money toward buying their freedom, but the gang's final price is always just out of reach."

"How does your friend's story connect with Beth? Does she—do you—think this syndicate took her?" The image of the Viking carting Beth through the convenience store flashed through Hope's mind.

"I was skeptical at first, too. Then I started reading her research on where the group operates. According to her research, this syndicate runs forced prostitution rings in casinos across the country, including right across the border on the tribal reservations in Oklahoma."

"I've read the bulletins on Native American girls being trafficked from the reservations."

"Highest rate of kidnappings of any demographic in America," Shonda chimed in.

"Does your friend think the syndicate is working in Hawk County?"

"My colleague believes they are picking up girls of all races around the country, including in counties in Texas and Oklahoma."

"But taking the daughter of a prominent local judge seems like a high-risk proposition. Why would they bother?"

"My friend stumbled across an online auction."

Hope turned and focused on Libbi's face. Her heart rate picked up, and she could feel the sweat on the small of her back. The thought of Beth suffering drew up a bitter taste in the back of her throat.

"Go on. You've piqued my curiosity," she said.

"From the online chatter, it appears some clients clamor for the all-American girl. They will pay top dollar for young and white. They are asking for virgins to deflower."

"I've given up being surprised by the depravity of humans," Shonda said.

"With an open market, the gangs have to buy their merchandise from somewhere. A rural county would fit the bill. In the dark web chat rooms, the public profile of the victim is part of the allure. The more prominent, the higher the risk of getting caught, which increases the fantasy."

"Has your friend gone to the police?"

"She is aware of a task force consisting of the Oklahoma Bureau of Investigation and the FBI, but obtaining information from them is impossible. Besides, the tribal police have jurisdiction over the casinos, and they shun the press."

"I bet they do," Hope said. "Unfounded allegations of sexual slavery would be bad for business."

"My source says it's not unfounded, and it's not just old-fashioned prostitution."

"What's worse than creepy men ordering up young virginal girls to deflower?"

"She stumbled across a chat thread last night that talked about buying a young white girl. The daughter of a prominent politician. The description fit Beth. I'm worried they're about to sell her to this group."

"Group?"

"Yes, she said it is more than one person interested in taking the girl."

Hope's insides roiled at the thought of sweet Beth being sold into a gang rape. "Any geographical markers or clues in the chat about location of the sale?"

"Nothing yet, but she's willing to come in and speak with you."

"Please have her do so right away. I'll clear my schedule."

Hope stood and placed her hat on her head. She looked around Haven's town square. Such a peaceful town. What on earth could have drawn such evil predators to Hawk County? She said her goodbyes to Libbi and promised to have lunch with Shonda later in the week. The morning sun had become harsh, as if the horror that awaited Beth was beating down on her skin. The faces of girls in Hawk county flashed through her mind. As she walked toward the door to her office, she pulled out her cell phone and dialed Strickland.

Please, God, do not let us be too late.

CHAPTER TWENTY-NINE

JAKE LEFT FOR THE OFFICE. Margie stepped out to run errands, including the grocery store. With the house to herself for a few hours, Rose jumped in the shower. Warm water and steam relieved her stress. She wrapped her long hair in a towel. Her phone vibrated on the dresser. It was a text from Tommy.

T: Can we meet up?

Tommy hadn't texted her for weeks. Not since Marcus was killed. She didn't blame him; she doubted he would want to get tangled in her screwed-up life. Now that she would be tried for murder, she didn't expect to hear anything from him. If their roles were reversed, she might not have stuck around either. But Tommy had ghosted her. Rose would have at least sent word about why she was lying low.

Briefly, Rose thought about being mad and telling him to go away. But right now, she was short of friends. If she wasn't having nightmares about going to jail, Rose lay awake at night fretting over Beth. Her imagination turned her stomach. The disrupted sleep made her exhausted and cranky, and she was alone in all this chaos. Her other friends' parents had told them to drop Rose from their contacts. They would not have their daughters hanging out with an accused murderer. So even though she was angry about Tommy abandoning her, it was nice to see a familiar name—especially one that could kiss like Tommy. A blush warmed Rose's cheeks, and eagerness flushed through her.

R: I can't leave.

T: Says who?

R: Jake and Margie. I'm staying with them.

T: C'mon. Just a few minutes? They won't know.

R: I can't.

T: Please. I'm dying to see you. I promise I'll make it worth your while.

Rose smiled at what Tommy might have in mind. A flutter passed through her belly.

R: How?

T: It's a surprise.

R: Where?

T: The boat launch out by Iron Gate Point.

Rose paused. Jake and Margie would be mad if they caught her.

Don't get caught, then.

R: I'll meet you there in 30 minutes.

T: Can't wait.

Rose pulled on her jeans and a T-shirt. She jammed her phone into her back pocket and walked into the kitchen. Margie's key rack hung by the back door. Rose flipped through the rings and chains until she found the keys for Marcus's truck—the first item of her soon-to-be inheritance. Jake had driven it to Margie's so nobody would vandalize it at Rose's unoccupied house.

She paused for a moment with the keys clutched in her palm. Technically, she had just a learner's permit. She was supposed to have an adult in the car with her when she was driving. Each passing day, though, moved her closer to her sixteenth birthday, when she could drive on her own.

I'm so close. It's like I'm licensed already. Besides, I've been driving with Marcus in the truck for years. I'll take the back roads, which should keep me away from prying eyes and the police.

Grabbing up a ball cap, Rose stepped outside and skipped to the red pickup. She could reach the boat launch and come back within an hour. Jake and Margie would never miss her.

Will they?

Even if she got caught, she could talk her way out of it with Margie. And Margie would help her wiggle out of any trouble with Jake.

She threaded her ponytail through the back of the cap and put on her sunglasses to look older and less noticeable. Out on the farm-to-market road along the lakeshore, Rose kept the truck under the speed limit to avoid unwanted attention. As each mile marker passed, she became more confident in her driving and more eager to see Tommy. Her mind drifted to the softness of his lips and the way he ran his fingers through her hair. Lost in thoughts about her rendezvous, she missed the black truck pulling onto the highway behind her.

Ever since Marcus had died, Margie and Jake had sheltered her. *A little freedom will do me some good—I'm not a child.*

As she closed the distance to the boat ramp, electricity welled up in her. She missed Tommy.

Rose spied the turnoff to Iron Gate point up ahead. She flicked on her blinker and slowed for the turn.

But her truck lunged forward. Something had slammed into her from behind. It was then she saw the truck in her rearview mirror. Its brush guard was almost touching her bumper. A man with a black ball cap, dark sunglasses, and a long beard in two braids stared at her through the windshield.

Adrenaline flooded her system. This was the man who'd stood on the porch the night Marcus died. It had been too dark, then, for Rose to see his face. But that beard was unmistakable. Next to him sat the woman with the fire-red hair.

They figured out I was in the well house.

Rose's heart galloped in her chest as she turned onto the circle road that made up the Iron Gate boat ramp. She scanned the area for Tommy's motorcycle, but didn't see it anywhere. He'd ghosted her. She was alone.

Rose slammed her foot on the accelerator and leaned into the turn as she whipped the truck around the circular dirt road and back onto the main drag, turning back toward the safety of Margie's home.

Shoot. No one is there.

Rose checked. The black truck had pulled back on the road behind her, and it was speeding up, closing the gap between them. Rose wiped her sweaty palms on her jeans. Her throat was now dry and scratchy.

Two hundred yards…. one hundred yards. Here he comes.

Fixated on the truck, Rose missed the flashing light up at the junction with another road. She blew through it, oblivious. A siren squawked, and blue and red flashing lights blew up behind her. A sheriff's cruiser darted out from behind a stand of scrub brush and pulled in behind her. Rose didn't want to stop—couldn't stop—until she made it back to Margie's. Only a mile away. Checking her review mirror, she saw Sheriff Stone behind the wheel, probably cursing at Rose for not pulling over. In the distance, behind the sheriff, the black truck was turning at the junction, hightailing it away from the cops.

Relief washed over Rose as her body tried to recover from the scare. Margie's property came into view. Rose turned up the drive faster than she should have, the tires skidding and kicking up dust when she finally stopped. She turned off the ignition and gripped the steering wheel, focusing on calming her breathing. Rose glanced in the mirrors. The sheriff's cruiser stopped behind her, and Sheriff Stone emerged from the truck, her face flushed. Rose bent forward and rested her forehead on the steering wheel, grateful the sheriff has scared off the man and redhead but dreading the knock on the window. She let out a deep sigh and ran through excuses in her head.

I have some explaining to do.

But her worry about getting in trouble with Sheriff Stone waned as a chill ran up her spine.

Whoever killed Marcus is looking for me now.

CHAPTER THIRTY

JAKE PULLED in into Margie's driveway. Hope and Rose were standing beside Marcus's red pickup truck. He coasted to a stop and stepped out.

"Rose. You're only fifteen! What were you thinking?"

"They've cooped me up inside here for weeks!"

"That's because you are on pretrial release," Hope said. "Margie is your guardian. She swore she'd make you come to court. She told the judge you weren't a flight risk. And here you are, zipping around the county without a license. Do you want me to take you in? Keep you in my jail? At least I can keep track of you there."

"No… I enjoy staying here. Jake, tell her!"

"Whoa, whoa, what's going on?" Jack said. He turned to Hope. "What're you doing, talking to my client without me?"

That comment caused Hope's eyes to flare with anger. "I'll tell you what's going on. I stopped on a service crossover to look at my notes, and little miss lead-foot here came blazing through the State Road 12 junction."

Jake looked at Rose. "You're driving?"

"Speeding," Hope said.

"It was just a quick trip." Rose said.

"I don't care if it was across the street," Jake said. "You don't have a license. You're only fifteen, and you're on trial for murder."

"You could've killed someone going that fast through the intersection without stopping."

"Hope," Jake said, more sternly than he wanted. "I've got this. Rose… inside, now. We'll talk about this in a minute."

"But I—"

"Inside," Jake said. Rose jammed her fists on her hips and stood her ground.

"This puts me in a terrible position," Hope said. "I cannot unsee what she did today. I must tell Krista."

"Wait a second. Why? Rose made a mistake. She won't do it again. Will you, Rose?"

"No."

"See. No harm," Jake said.

"She broke the terms of her release, Jake. If the judge finds out that happened—and that I let it slide without telling the district attorney—he'll hand me my head."

"It was one small mistake. Why does this need to become a big deal? You know Krista will try to revoke her release."

"She might. But that's on Rose. You'll just have to work your magic to keep her out."

"What were you doing out, anyway?" Jake asked Rose.

"I…"

"That's a good question. Have you been doing this all along?" Hope asked.

"Don't answer that," Jake said. "If you're taking this to Krista, then this interrogation is over. Rose, I mean it this time. Go inside."

Rose shuffled up the drive to the stairs. She turned back to Hope. "But you saw them, right?"

"Who?" Hope asked.

"That truck chasing me."

"Rose, you can't keep making up these ghosts every time you get in trouble," Hope said.

"I'm not making them up. They're real. The redhead and the man with the beard are both real. They followed me and chased me back here."

"Rose…"

"Believe me. They slammed into my truck, tried to run me off the road." Rose scampered down the drive and pointed at the dent and scuff marks on the heavy steel bumper Marcus had welded. "Right there. Tell her, Jake. Those marks weren't there before."

"I can't remember what marks were where," Jake said.

"You could've done that yourself by backing into something," Hope said. "You've been driving for what, a few days? Not the most experienced driver on the roads."

Rose puffed out her chest. "Marcus taught me. I've been driving with him on back roads since I was thirteen. I'm telling you, I didn't hit a thing. They hit me. The man that yelled at Marcus the night they killed him. I saw him in the rearview mirror. He was driving, and that redheaded hag was in the passenger seat."

"What did they look like, Rose?" Jake asked.

"Same as I told her before," Rose said, pointing at the sheriff.

"Tell her again," Jake said.

"The woman had on large sunglasses. But I won't forget that hair. It was fire red. Not dyed red, but natural. She was yelling at the driver and pointing at me."

"And the driver?" Hope asked.

"He had sunglasses and a ball cap. A long black beard. It was braided like the night he took Marcus."

"Braided?" Hope asked, turning quickly and focusing on Rose.

"I already told you at the station. He had a black beard he wore in double braids."

"You never mentioned braids," said Hope.

"I'm pretty sure I did."

"It would've been in my reports."

"What does it matter?" Jake asked. "The important point is the folks who killed Marcus tried to get Rose—maybe to shut her up about what she saw from the well house."

"Jake, how would they know?"

"She's on trial for murder as an adult," Jake said. "Everyone knows."

"Not about what she claims to have seen. Nothing in the public releases says anything about her being in the well house. Only you, my department, and the prosecutor's office know where Rose says she was that night." Hope stepped toward Rose, focused on her as if trying to read her truthfulness. "You're sure the beard had two braids?"

"Positive. A double braid, like in a Viking movie."

"Shoot."

"What is going on, Hope?" Jake asked.

"I can't tell you."

"Wait a second. These people are real. Something about that braided beard changed your mind about what Rose told you."

"I can't comment on an ongoing investigation."

"The investigation into Rose? Krista must turn over all her evidence. So spill it."

"Not that investigation," Hope said.

"Then what investigation? I need all the facts in order to defend my client."

"Rose, are you sure this was your first joyride?"

"Yes. I…"

"You what?"

"I got a text from a friend. He wanted to see me. I haven't heard from him in weeks. So when he texted, I decided I'd go hang with him."

"Just out of the blue?"

"It's not like any of my other friends are allowed to hang out with an accused murder. Beth was the only one, and she's still missing. You haven't found her." Rose's voice trembled at the mention of her best friend.

Hope seemed to ignore the jab. "Your friend texted you to meet him? Where?"

"At the Iron Gate boat ramp."

"Was he there?"

"I didn't get that far. Those two slammed into my truck before I could find him."

"Son of a..." Hope paced in front of them.

"What aren't you telling me?" Jake asked.

Hope let out a deep breath before answering. "I've got a lead on the man who took Beth."

"Where is she?" Rose asked, her voice trailing up with concern.

"I don't know yet. We're working hard on finding her," said Hope. "But the man that took her has a black beard he wears in a double braid?"

"Oh, man," Jake said.

"I don't know what's going on here," Hope said.

"Same guy?" Jake asked.

"What would they want with Beth and me?"

"That's what I'm trying to find out, Rose. But right now, all I care about is getting Beth back and keeping you safe."

CHAPTER THIRTY-ONE

THE CLAMOR of a motorcycle engine roused Beth from her sleep. Earlier, she had dozed off as the sun warmed the room. Upon waking, she was certain it was nighttime, but the dim bulb of the lamp in the corner provided sufficient light for her to gain her bearings as she wiped exhaustion from her eyes. The smell of cigarettes and stale beer wafted through the disheveled trailer. She tuned and sat on the edge of her bed, her legs leaden. She shifted, trying to ease the pain, and the chains clattered. Beth gazed at the empty water bottle on the nightstand, now certain they were drugged. She worked to rub the fog from her eyes, amazed at how she almost welcomed the haze and blackouts as long as she could ease her thirst. The drugged stupors made the time pass. A tear leaked down her cheek as she remembered that last night he had told her his name.

Zach.

She trembled, and her heart raced.

He's not afraid for me to know who he is. And he can't let me go now. I'm as good as dead.

The glare of headlights spilled through small gaps in the foil covering the windows.

He's coming.

Beth prepared herself for Zach's return. She hated to be alone with him. When displeased, he would strike her with a paddle in places she wouldn't bruise, often the soles of her feet. He spoke to her in brief grunts, always staring at her and licking the lips tucked under his long braided beard. But he had only touched her once, when he'd sponged her off in the cellar. In all those weeks, he hadn't raped her.

Why?

Something or someone was keeping him from assaulting her.

Thank God! But how? Who?

His leather boots thudded on the stairs as he climbed them, and the thin aluminum door creaked open.

Beth lay down on the mattress and pulled a sheet up over her—as if she could hide. The thin fabric caught on the manacles around her ankles. A chain extended to a floor-mounted U-bolt in the middle of the room. She felt like a caged dog pacing in circles for days on end. The sound of rattling glass bottles in the refrigerator leaked down the hallway. Then his footsteps. The doorknob turned. He pushed the door open and stepped inside, the pungent stink of sweat and fried food following him.

"Dinnertime," he said, and placed a Styrofoam box on the nightstand. Beside it, he placed a fresh bottle of water. He had already removed the cap. The liquid was already drugged. "Eat. We need you in prime condition." He lit a cigarette and stared at her with black, almost lifeless eyes. "Eat some of that salad."

"I'm not hungry," Beth said.

"You'll eat because I tell you," he said.

She said nothing in response.

"Now." He grabbed for the sheet as he towered over her.

Beth shrank into the crease where the mattress abutted the wall, her chains rattling. Cowering would offer no protection against him if he was mad. But she had learned about his moods. He wasn't mad enough to hit her… yet.

"Get up. I don't want to sit here and babysit you. We have things to get done."

"Like what?" Beth knew she was pushing her luck.

His eyes flashed wide, and he rolled his neck as if willing the anger to seep out of him. After a moment, he took a drag from his cigarette and exhaled a smoke ring in her direction. "You're trying to make me mad… You know what happens when you make me mad."

"Just let me go, please."

"It's just business, Viv."

Beth groaned at the name he'd chosen for her. *Viv.* He refused to call her Beth anymore. And amid the endless days, she felt Beth ebbing away.

"I have to go to the bathroom," she announced.

"You can use it after you eat."

"I have to pee now. I'll eat in a minute."

He grunted and removed a key ring from his belt. Reaching down, he undid the padlock, securing steel links to the bolt in the flooring. He grabbed the rest of the chain in his hand as if holding a dog leash.

"Go," he commanded. "Make it quick."

Beth moved to the edge of the mattress. She stood and wiggled her toes to drum the feeling back in them, staring down at the huge Celtic cross tattoos on his forearms.

"Why do you tighten them so much?" she scolded as she stared at the cuffs around her ankles. He smiled. Beth shuffled across the tiny hall to the toilet. Beer bottles and ashtrays littered the coffee table in the living room, if you could call it that. Nicotine stained the walls, and the smell permeated the trailer. She noted his rifle in a case on a chair.

"Why are you always shooting that gun out here?" she asked.

"I'm practicing for an old friend," Zach answered. "Now shut up and do your business."

Once she was inside the closet-like bathroom, Beth moved to shut the door.

"Leave it open," he growled. "You know the rules."

"I need privacy."

"No… Either the door stays open or I join you. Your choice."

"Fine," Beth said.

"I'm watching you."

Beth sat on the toilet, feeling the relief as her bladder emptied. She looked around the bathroom, the small space dank and hot. It would be her one change of scenery for the day. The shower dripped, leaving a ring of rust around the plastic pan and drain. She noted the box of tampons on the counter. At least he'd had the decency to buy those for her. She scoffed under her breath. Zach must have looked quite the sight at the store with his enormous frame, menacing beard, and a box of tampons under his arm. She looked at herself in the mirror. He had dyed her hair black. The dark color and the lack of sun gave her milk-white skin a pallid hue.

He yanked the chain, and the cuffs dug into her ankles.

"You're done," he said.

"I'm coming," Beth said. She wiped, flushed, and shuffled her way back across the hall. She grabbed the food box and perched on the bed. Supper was chicken tenders, mashed potatoes, and coleslaw—Zach's idea of salad. Her empty stomach grumbled at the smell of food. What she wouldn't give to eat at a restaurant salad bar with the judge and her stepmother Natalie. She opened the baggie with plastic silverware and a napkin. He would inventory these and the rest of her trash after he watched her eat her meal. He left nothing to chance. She took a bite.

"Don't watch me when I eat," she said. "It creeps me out."

A long silence fell over the room. The sounds of her chewing filled the void.

He broke the quiet first. "I was working on getting your playmate today."

Beth's appetite disappeared at the notion that some other girl might share her fate, chained in this dilapidated hellhole.

"I'm not enough, Zach?" Beth asked.

"No, Viv. My buyers wanted two."

Bile rose in the back of her throat at the mention of his "buyer." He taunted her often, but this was the first time he'd mentioned another girl. She hoped he was joking. He looked at her, as if enjoying her discomfort, but stayed quiet as she finished a few more bites of supper. She put it down and pushed it aside.

"Show me the knife and fork."

She held them up and then placed the box in the plastic bag from the corner Quickie Mart. He locked the chain in place, stood, and retrieved the trash.

"Now drink."

"I don't want to."

"Drink!"

Beth grabbed the water bottle and took a big swig. The distinct taste raised a panic in her.

I can't lose control when he's in here.

"Too bad I didn't get a friend for you. But time is running out. It's almost over."

Beth's heart lurched. "I don't need a companion."

"This one you would have liked," Zach said. "Trust me."

An engine's roar drowned out his last words. Another vehicle stopped outside the trailer. A wide smile washed over Zach's face. He flashed his bright white teeth behind his beard, like a wolf showing off its canines to its prey.

"Who's that?"

Zach's stare burned into her.

Waves of discombobulation from the drugs washed over Beth. He must have given her a higher dose.

"Who. Is. That. Zach?" she asked, as footsteps climbed the porch. Blackness crept along the edges of her vision.

"That. Is. Ted." Zach towered over her. "Showtime, Viv."

CHAPTER THIRTY-TWO

JAKE PUSHED AWAY his lunch plate and wiped the condensation from his iced tea off the table. The fans in the corners of the diner oscillated against the summer heat. Tizzie scooted by in her yellow dress, the fabric still wrestling with her bosom.

"You finished with that, Jake?" She asked.

"Yes, ma'am. It was delicious."

"Did you save some room for pie?"

"I did," Hitch said, as he passed his half-eaten sandwich toward Tizzie.

"You don't need another piece of pie, old man. You're getting a little porky."

"Say now. That's not very nice, Tiz." Hitch feigned hurt with his hand on his heart.

Jake had watched this little drama unfold again and again over the past few months. He was pretty sure Hitch had a bit of a crush on Tizzie and her girls. And Tizzie had a crush on Hitch's generous tips.

"I'll take a piece of the banana cream, please," Jake said.

"Same for me," Hitch said.

"Coffee?"

"Please," Jake and Hitch said in unison.

Tizzie whisked their plates off the table and disappeared into the back. Hitch pulled out his wallet and started fiddling with bills while Jake looked out the window at the folks walking around Haven's town square.

"Mr. Hitch," a voice said. Jake and Hitch looked up and saw an elderly black man standing in the aisle, a cowboy hat in his hands.

"Josiah," Hitch said, and he turned to Jake. "Jake, this is Josiah Reed." Hitch pointed to an open chair at their table. "Join us for some pie?"

"That would be nice," Josiah said, as he pulled out the chair and sat down, straightening the silverware in front of him.

Tizzie returned with Hitch and Jake's pie. "Josiah, you want a slice of the strawberry rhubarb?"

"Yes, ma'am. You know my favorite. Coffee, too, like the gentlemen here, if you still have some in the pot."

"Coming right up."

Hitch slapped Josiah on the shoulder. "It's been a spell. How have you been?"

"Real good. Business has been good. Cowboys still need horses, so I still have a job trailerin' them around."

"Good for you. You remember Josiah, Jake. Nobody could rodeo better."

"I remember. You could ride anything."

"That was years and a few broken bones ago."

Tizzie dropped off Josiah's pie. "I warmed it for you, hon, and put a scoop of vanilla ice cream, just the way you like it." She shuffled off again, clearing more dishes from the tables.

Hitch took a bite of pie and washed it down with a sip of coffee. "How can we be of service, Josiah?"

"You're defending Marcus Tucker's little girl."

"Yes, we're defending Rose."

"Well, I might have something you'll want to hear."

Jake and Hitch set down their forks and gave him their full attention.

"It was a while back. I was bringing a load of cutting horses up from near Houston. I'd run into a mess of traffic north of Dallas, so I was running mighty late when I got back to Haven." Josiah took a bite of pie and a swig of coffee. "It was well after dark before we started unloading. I was at the Applegate ranch there, across the road from the Tucker place. Some of the horses were skittish from being in the trailer all day, so it took a while to get them all put up in the barn. We fed 'em and then turned 'em loose in the paddock. Mr. Applegate paid me, thanked me, and then he and his hands turned in for the night. I was gathering up and storing my gear when I heard a commotion over at the Tucker place."

"What kind of commotion?"

"Yelling. Mind you, I was too far away to hear what anyone was saying. But the tone was angry. Someone was yelling."

"What time was this?"

"Close to midnight. And I was winding up my gear after that."

"Could you see what was going on?" Hitch asked.

"Nah. Marcus's home sits up in the trees there, back a ways from the road. So I saw nothing at first. I noticed there were lights on the property. But I couldn't much tell what they were coming from."

"And you didn't hear what the yelling was about?" Jake asked.

"No, sir. It was brief, you know. Then it stopped. I figured, whatever it was, it had blown over."

"What, if anything, happened next?" Hitch asked.

"Well, I went back to storing leads and ropes and such. I was done, and about to hop in my truck and haul myself home, when I saw several headlights working their way down the drive from the Tucker place."

"Go on," Hitch said.

"Well, something in my gut told me to stop and watch what was happening. So I did. The moon had come up by then, and I could see out on the road pretty well."

"What did you see?" Jake's anticipation made his words jump.

"After a bit, I saw a black SUV come out and turn on the state road there."

"Could you see who was driving?"

"I was too far away. I just remember thinking it was odd. It wasn't Marcus. He drives that old red pickup, you know. And it was an odd time of night for visitors, especially with the weather bearing down. But I didn't think of it as being wrapped up in Marcus getting killed that night."

"Have you told the sheriff?"

"Not yet. As soon as I figured out what I had seen, I wanted to come to you first. To see if you think it is what I think it is."

"You may have seen the folks who assaulted Marcus before he turned up dead." Hitch said.

"Why are you coming forward now, Josiah?" Jake asked. "Marcus died a few months ago."

"Been on the road, Hitch. Judge Maddix pays me to drive the hauler for the Arabians that she rides on the hunter jumper circuit out east. When she's not in court, she shows in New York, North Carolina, and Florida. After that I was hauling racehorses. I was on the road until a few days ago. When I come back to Haven, I heard about Marcus being dead and all. Then I heard about Miss Rose being indicted for killing him. That just didn't sit right with me. I've known her since she was knee high to a grasshopper, and she loved her daddy. There's no way she killed ol' Marcus. No way. Then I remembered what I saw that night. All those trucks and such leaving his place. The yelling. I thought you all would want to know."

A big grin grew on Hitch's face. "Josiah, you might have just become our star witness."

"I'll do whatever it takes to help Miss Rose, you know that. I'd love to help you too, Hitch. You have always been good people. I'd be happy to lend a hand."

"You'd be willing to testify?" Jake said.

"Place my hand on a whole stack of Bibles. I'm not afraid of telling the truth."

Josiah turned his attention to his strawberry-rhubarb pie, and all three men sat there, grinning at each other and enjoying dessert.

Jake looked outside at the clearing skies. A wave of relief flooded over him. They had their first big break for Rose.

Oh, Krista, wait until you hear what I found. Something tells me you're going to hate Josiah.

CHAPTER THIRTY-THREE

JAKE AND ROSE pushed their way through a gaggle of reporters on the courthouse steps. The intense press drumbeat was growing.

"Mr. Fox, are you going for an insanity defense?" one of them called out. "How do you feel defending someone who killed her own father in cold blood?" another asked.

Jake ignored them all, grabbing Rose by the wrist and leading her through the crush of bodies, cameras, and microphones jammed in their faces. Hitch and Margie followed in their slipstream. Hitch uncharacteristically refrained from popping off with some colorful statement. Suddenly the herd of journalists shifted as they saw Krista come into view, and they shuffled en masse toward her. She willingly obliged.

"Today the State of Texas will seek justice for Marcus Tucker. We are his voice, and the evidence will tell his tragic story. His daughter gunned him down at point-blank range, ending his life and ripping him from this community. The jury will bring him justice. We look forward to Rose Tucker's speedy conviction. I'll now take a few questions."

The courthouse doors finally closed behind Jake and company, cutting off the rest of Krista's impromptu press conference. "Ignore all that," Jake said to Rose. "Remember what we talked about. You must keep it together." Rose nodded, giving Jake a tight, brave smile.

A few minutes later, they sat in the courtroom as Judge Dubose banged his gavel. "The Court calls case number JC-22-1448, State of Texas versus Rosemary Tucker. Counsel, make your appearances for the record."

"Krista Robb for the prosecution."

"Jake Fox for the defendant, Your Honor."

The judge nodded kindly toward Gert Winnie, who was perched in the pews with the followers she had gained from badmouthing Rose in town. Then he glowered at Jake from the bench. His black robe made his imposing figure even more daunting. His round, tortoiseshell bifocals perched on his raptor-like nose, their gold temples disappearing into his salt-and-pepper hair that looked in need of a trim. Jake had not seen the judge since his daughter, Beth, had disappeared. Stress lines etched his face, and fatigue dripped from his every movement. Jake thought about Lucy and knew instinctively what the judge was going through: guilt and regret that he could not keep his little girl safe.

"I've set this case for trial next Tuesday," the judge said. "This pretrial hearing is for you to secure any needed rulings before a long weekend of preparations. Ms. Robb, what say you?"

"The prosecution is ready, Your Honor. We don't require any rulings today."

"Excellent news. It looks like you will be your usual efficient self, Ms. Robb. How about you, Mr. Fox? What do you have for the court? Are you as talented as Ms. Robb?"

Jake glanced at Hope, who sat in the gallery next to Detective Hendricks and looked upset. In the corner stood Libbi Banderas, the reporter from Channel 33. Everything he said today Libbi would blast across the airwaves. His next sentence would set off a powder keg. Despite his attempts, he couldn't see another option. His obligation was to Rose.

"Your Honor, the defense has one particular issue to raise, and you will see it has a significant impact on the strategy for defending Ms. Tucker."

"Don't be cryptic, Mr. Fox. Get to it. Tell me what this so-called important issue is."

"Your Honor, while investigating this matter, we learned that Sheriff Stone has critical information pertaining to the defense of my client."

"Call her at trial, Mr. Fox. Why does this concern the court?"

"I issued a trial subpoena for Sheriff Stone and served it this morning."

"I'm assuming you will go into her investigation of the crime and try to convince the jury that she failed to do her job. Again, I'm failing to see your point."

"Your Honor, we seek to compel the sheriff to divulge information from another matter that has a direct bearing on this case, and we need it before trial begins so we can prepare."

The judge shifted forward in his seat, tapping his pencil on the desk in front of him. "I'm listening."

"It relates to the sheriff's investigation into your daughter's abduction, sir."

The judge's eyes flashed wide, and a frown tugged at the edges of his mouth. "If you seek to absolve your client of murder by dragging my daughter's reputation through the mud, I would suggest you rethink your motion."

"Nothing like that, sir. We seek to ask Sheriff Stone about facts she learned in the investigation."

"Your Honor," Krista broke in. "Before Mr. Fox blurts out details that could harm the sheriff's efforts to locate your daughter, we would ask that you either clear the courtroom or that we take this up in chambers."

The judge surveyed the courtroom, briefly fixating on Libbi in the corner.

"Very well. We can take this up in chambers. Counsel, follow the bailiff."

Jake grabbed his yellow pad and pen. Rose grabbed his shirt cuff.

"Do I wait here?"

"Yes. For this, wait here."

"What if they are here… watching me?"

Jake scanned the courtroom. Nobody fit the descriptions Rose had given him of the man and woman from the night Marcus died.

"You'll be safe. Detective Hendricks is staying put."

Jake heard Rose whisper under her breath, "Five things I can see…" She tugged at her cuticles. Hope, Jake, and Krista followed the bailiff through a doorway. Judge Dubose had removed his robe and poured himself a cup of coffee into a dainty china cup, without offering it to anyone else. He sat back in his large chair and took a sip, observing the three standing in his office. A whiff of bourbon lingered in the air. Jake also noticed that someone was missing.

"Your Honor, should we have the court reporter here for this?"

"No, Mr. Fox, I don't think we need to fuss with a record on this just yet." He leaned back in his tall, leather executive chair. "Now, Mr. Fox, can you explain yourself?"

"Judge, Sheriff Stone has information related to the man they believe abducted your daughter."

"I know. I've seen the sketch they had from a witness."

"Well, that same individual tried to attack Ms. Tucker just a few days ago," Jake said.

The judge stood from his chair, fisting his hands on the leather blotter on his desk. "Why? How?"

Hope spoke up. "The details aren't important, judge.

Suffice it to say, Ms. Tucker described someone following her that is very similar to the man in the sketch I showed you."

"He attacked her?"

"Tried to abduct her, sir," Jake said.

The judge sat back down in his chair, took a sip of coffee, and tapped his index finger on his lip as he seemed to contemplate the issue. Then he shook his head.

"Even if that's true, this alleged attack or abduction doesn't seem connected to the case."

"It doesn't," Krista said. "It's a distraction, and it will confuse the jury. Ms. Tucker claims, with no evidence, that men attacked her father the night she murdered him," Krista said.

Jake stepped toward Krista, his voice teetering on a growl, "Rose didn't kill Marcus."

"I don't have the luxury of your false hopes and fairy-tale wishes, Jake. I have a murderer to put behind bars."

"I told—"

"Enough," the judge snapped. "I expect lawyers in my courtroom to acquit themselves with the proper decorum and not squabble like children. Do I make myself clear?"

Jake and Krista nodded.

"Now, Sheriff… am I to understand that Ms. Tucker is claiming that the man that you showed me in the artist's rendering tried to kidnap her—and is also somehow linked to her killing her father?" The judge asked.

"Your Honor," Jake implored, "at least pretend you don't want my client behind bars."

The judge flung the tiny china cup against the brick wall to his side. His neck flushed, a vein or two bulging.

"Evidently, I did not make myself clear, Mr. Fox! I'm not sure how the judges down in Dallas run their courtrooms, but you can be damn sure that here in Haven we will be running this court my way. Ms. Robb… I assume there is no evidence to corroborate the defendant's claim of near abduction?"

"Precisely," Krista said. "She has no proof of what she says. We believe it's all a fiction, and we think this latest boondoggle is also a fiction. She is trying to foist her guilt off onto ghosts."

"The description is too detailed," Jake said.

"How so?"

"Well, Judge, Ms. Tucker says that the man who confronted her father the night he died had a black beard he wore in two braids."

Realization dawned in the judge's eyes. He looked at Hope. "Is this true, Sheriff Stone?"

"It's true that she describes a man—"

"Almost identical to the man in the sketch," the judge said.

"Correct."

"But she only mentioned this 'beard' the other day," Krista blurted. "She conveniently omitted that until now."

"Are you saying she made it up?" Jake asked.

"I'm saying she could have heard about it somewhere and is now tossing it out as a smoke screen."

"How?"

"Gossip travels in this town, Jake. You should know that by now."

"No one in my office let this slip," Hope said.

"How do we know?" Krista said. "Mr. Fox plans to have the sheriff testify about the defendant's belief of a near abduction by a bearded individual. Even if you allow that testimony, which you shouldn't, it pertains to something recent. What Ms. Tucker did the night of the murder has no relevance to these recent events. The sheriff cannot testify about what happened the night Marcus Tucker died."

The judge paused, sighing. "That is true, Mr. Fox."

"Your Honor," Jake implored, "How many men wear their beard in a double braid?"

"It is hearsay and speculative as it pertains to the night of Mr. Tucker's death," Krista said.

"It backs up my client's story."

"Story is right," Krista said. "Judge, this tactic confuses the jury by involving the sheriff in both sides. It also relates to alleged events that occurred after Mr. Tucker's death."

"I agree, Mr. Fox."

"Plus, this could damage any chance of getting your daughter back," Krista said to the judge.

Krista's words seemed to knock the judge deeper into his chair. "How?"

Hope chimed in. "Judge, we have been careful not to let this detail of our investigation leak. If this reaches the press, the person holding your daughter may learn about our lead. That could cause them to run. They could disappear."

The judge looked at Jake. "Mr. Fox, the risk here is significant."

"Judge, you'll prejudice our defense if you don't compel this testimony."

"He can have Ms. Tucker testify," Krista challenged.

"The State can't force her to testify," Jake said. "It removes her right to refuse to testify under the Fifth Amendment."

"She doesn't have to take the stand, Mr. Fox," the judge said. "It's her choice. If she wants the jury to hear about the bearded man she claims was at her house, then she can tell them herself. If not, then I guess the evidence isn't crucial to her defense. I'm sure, as her wise counsel, you will guide her well about the pros and cons of taking the stand in her own defense."

"Judge…"

"That's my ruling, Mr. Fox. You will not jeopardize me getting my Beth back so you can create some circus with the sheriff on the stand. I won't allow it."

"Judge, I move that you recuse yourself from this case."

"Denied. This trial is going forward."

"Judge, you have no business—"

"You know recusal is within my sole discretion. I said, denied."

"I'll seek an immediate appeal."

"Go ahead. I'll be sure to let the appellate judges know about your complaint when I play golf with them later this week. And by the way," he continued, "let's discuss the duration of this sideshow."

"The trial?" Jake asked.

"Yes, the trial, Mr. Fox. Seems to me that, based on the record as I know it, the State should be able to put forward its case in an efficient and straightforward manner. Am I right, Ms. Robb?"

"The State will be ready to move efficiently."

"Good, good. So it seems to me that we could do this trial on a clock. I was thinking about twelve hours per side."

"A day and a half to defend a murder case?" Jake said.

"Twelve hours a side is fine." Krista smirked.

"Mr. Fox, the State does not object, and that should be more than enough time for you, by my estimate," the judge said. "If you need more time, and I doubt you will, I'd expect you to make your objections to preserve the issue for appeal."

"Your Honor—" Jake protested, but the judge held up his hand to quiet him.

"Twelve hours it is. Counselors, I believe we have finished here today. I must join my fellow judges for lunch. I bid you good day."

CHAPTER THIRTY-FOUR

THE AMBER SUN threatened to disappear behind the leafy live oaks framing the lakeshore. Tendrils of light stretched across the mirror-still water. Sunset. A simple wink to God's soul and intention that happened once a day.

But the nerves roiling Jake's gut forecast a sleepless night. In mere hours, Jake would pick a jury—twelve citizens who would hold Rose's future in their hands like a farmer holds a sparrow in a field, mending its wing. Then Jake would shoulder Rose's future and deliver an opening statement. Life would be beyond his control. Silently, Jake cursed the circumstances that had once again led him to this destination... someone's life in his hands. His ulcer seemed to flare. When the bailiff called for everyone to rise and the judge sat at the bench, planning and preparation alone wouldn't suffice. The situation would evolve. Jake would need a lot of luck. And a little magic. Hitch's words flooded back.

"In the moment... Stand in the moment."

Jake took a deep breath and leaned against a column on Margie's porch, trying to soak in the peace the lake brought. The wide, verdant lawn that led to the lakeshore splayed in front of him. His gaze trailed down the grass to the dock that stretched out into the water. Rose sat at the end of it, her legs dangling over the edge, hair in a high ponytail, presumably to keep the heat off her neck. The simplicity of it all suggested calm. Jake's heart jumped. From behind, in silhouette, Rose was the mirror image of Lucy. Long blonde hair, athletic build. Somehow, she seemed to keep the weight of the trial far from her in this moment. Rose could face years in prison if found guilty. Jake shook the image—of Rose sitting on a bunk behind bars, slumped in tan prison fatigues—from his mind. He noticed, about thirty feet in front of Rose, a large white-and-red bobber resting in the water… perfectly still.

Jake loosened his tie. Slowly, one foot in front of the other, Jake navigated the stairs and made his way to Rose. She didn't turn when his shoes clomped on the dock's planks.

"Good day to fish," Jake said, as if to no one in particular. Rose remained silent. "Hoppers or minnows?"

After a beat, Rose spoke as if talking over the lake's surface. "Minnows… Margie stopped by Wigglers on the way back from the grocery store."

"Good choice. Bass like them. They're too big for most crappie, so you can avoid catching all the dinks."

"Margie said the same thing."

"Well, she'd know. She's the one who taught me to fish."

Rose cocked her head as if just now catching sight of Jake over her shoulder and sizing him up beyond this moment. "Not sure I can picture her out here in a housedress, stringing up a mess of bass."

"Don't let that muumuu fool you. She's a fierce angler." Jake stepped up beside Rose, and then sat next to her, dangling his legs over the dock, his shiny black dress shoes a few inches above the water. "She can out-fish anyone on the lake."

"Well, will wonders never cease?"

Rose rested her hands, palms down, on her knees. She'd been biting her nails, nicking the bright-red polish. At least her choice of nail polish was hopeful. He resisted the urge to reach out and take her hand in his. Rose was still just a child. The law was prosecuting her as an adult, but the law did not consider all the things Rose had suffered and still had to learn… to experience. Heck, she wasn't even out of high school. If convicted, she'd leave prison as a hardened, cynical, middle-aged woman. A weight crushed down on Jake.

How on earth did I get back here?

"Have you seen the sheriff?" Rose asked.

"Not recently."

"So no word on Beth?"

"I'm sorry, Rose. No word yet."

Jake and Rose sat in silence for a minute or so, staring at the bobber for a short while.

"Nobody believes me, do they?" Rose asked.

"I'm not sure what anyone believes."

"The prosecutor thinks I'm guilty. She thinks I killed him. Thinks I killed my own father."

"She thinks you lost control and did something you'll aways regret."

"Well, I didn't. I never… Why won't anyone believe me?" Rose's expression tightened, and then her shoulders slumped. "The jury won't believe me."

"We don't need them to believe you. You don't have to say a thing. Krista must prove every element of the crime beyond a reasonable doubt. My job is to poke enough holes to let doubt seep in."

Rose turned to Jake, her gaze seeming to take his measure, and tears welled around her eyes. "Why won't 'I couldn't kill my father' be enough?" Her question fell silently on the water for a moment. "I want to tell them I didn't do this. Tell them about that night and all that happened. Who I saw. I didn't kill him."

"There's a risk, putting you on the stand. Krista will cross-examine you. Try to tie you up in knots. She'll be relentless, brutal. Make no mistake, she's in this to win it. Otherwise, she would not have sought an indictment. She'll try to make you mad and get you to show a temper, so the jury can see that you lose control. So they can picture you killing Marcus in a fit of rage."

"I can handle Krista," Rose said, pumping up as much bravado as she could muster and looking back out at her bobber.

"You shouldn't have to… I don't want to put you on the stand. I see no upside, and the downside is disastrous. If she gets to you, that could be it. Then what? You spend the next decade or so in prison."

"I'm not afraid of prison." The words fell from Rose in a halfhearted manner.

"You should be, Rose. Those women in there… Many have nothing to lose. They'll go after you as the new sweet little thing." Jake regretted saying it as soon as it came out of his mouth. He was supposed to be comforting Rose, building her up, not scaring her about spending her life with hungry convicted felons. Jake noticed a large bass swirling in the water clipped to a stringer through its silver gill plate. It was trapped, contemplating its fate.

Rose noticed his gaze. "You think jail will be like that? Me caught… always gulping for breath?"

"All I know is it will be rough."

"What if I take the plea deal?"

Jake felt his back bow up against his practical nature. "Why would you plead for something you didn't do?"

"We got nothing, Jake. Nobody's gonna come forward at trial and testify for me. They're going to lay out all that evidence they found in the house. You say I can't get on the stand… I got nothing that says I didn't do it. That's the truth." Rose paused and then let out a breath she seemed to be hanging on to. "Not sure the truth matters anymore."

"Rose… let's not be thinking that way. We still have time.

Things can happen." Guilt and regret sank into Jake as he wrote checks he possibly couldn't cash.

"You think any twelve people in this county is gonna give a rat about me? Some poor girl from out in the countryside? They're all going to believe I done it before they even sit in that jury box." Jake let her have her silence for a moment as she stared out at the sunset flooding the lake. After a few moments, she spoke again.

"Sunsets like this make me happy. I was raised outside, you know. Marcus loved to hunt and fish. Would take me with him. Pack me in with him whenever he could. I had to be in school as much as I could be. But… he'd find an excuse. Sometimes, if there was a special season—dove, quail, first part of deer season—he'd pull me out and write a note saying he needed me for some reason or another. Those are the times I felt the closest. With my mom gone and Marcus working as hard as he did, we didn't always have time. But those times in the middle of nowhere, doing nothing but waiting for an animal to come by, or fish to bite, it was just us. Just him and me, and we'd talk about stupid things."

"He taught you to fish?"

"You bet. Taught me to bait a hook and take my own fish off when I was younger than five. I could filet a bass and fry it up in a cast-iron pan by the time I hit middle school."

"Fresh bass is delicious."

Silence wrapped itself around both of them for a moment.

"I miss him," Rose said.

Jake let Rose's words float out into the calm and descend upon the lake. Rose was a scared little girl, same age as Lucy, facing an incredible ordeal. All at a time when she should have been hanging out with friends, going out to movies, giggling about which boy was cute in school. Instead, here she sat, on the end of a dock, watching a bobber with the weight of the whole adult world pressing down on her. The law would try to convict her. If it did, she would end up part of the prison system for years. With Marcus's death, her childhood was certainly over, but Jake was determined to make sure her adulthood wasn't a misery.

Just then, the bobber twitched and swirled... then it went full under. Rose set the hook. The rod bent, and Jake could tell a fish of some weight had taken the live minnow. He watched with a strange sense of pride as she worked the fish. It repeatedly leapt out of the water and splashed back down. Rose gave when needed to, took up slack when she could. She knew exactly what she was doing. After a few minutes, after the fight left the fish, she reached over the dock edge and pulled up a giant largemouth bass, holding it by the lower jaw, pinning it into submission. There, at the end of the dock, she stood with the sunset behind her, and a giant smile erupted on her face.

Behind her, Jake saw on the lake an apparition that looked just like Rose. Lucy smiled at him, too.

In the back of his mind, a steel door slammed shut. Krista would not take this little girl.

CHAPTER THIRTY-FIVE

AT MARGIE'S HOUSE, Hitch and Jake sat on the barstools at the kitchen island, reviewing their trial plan. In the living room, Margie worked to keep Rose calm. On the eve of court, as the sun set over the lake, reality overwhelmed Rose. She oscillated between fear, exhaustion, and grief—the graphic nature of the prep for the medical examiner's testimony about her father appeared to take her by surprise. Moisture welled up around her eyes. Jake prepped her to remain calm but not callous in front of the jury. But the sheer volume of grief spilled over into tears, inspired by the thought of Krista combing over the details of Marcus's demise in open court.

Jake leaked out his fatigue with a sigh. They had paused trial prep briefly to order deli sandwiches—the day's events had disrupted Margie's grocery shopping, and Hitch had grabbed the food on his way over—but by the sweet smells wafting from the kitchen, Jake was certain Margie had prepared some sort of baked desert. He pulled out a potato chip and tucked it in his mouth, the crunch distracting his thoughts. Strategy circled back to his mind like a mental boomerang.

"Who is Krista's first witness?" Hitch asked.

"She says she will confirm in the morning, but I imagine it will be the detective. Maybe the medical examiner. I don't know how much beyond that."

"The old man from the convenience store?"

"The one who overheard Rose yelling she'd be better off without Marcus? Perhaps."

"I'm not, you know." Rose's voice came as both a statement and a challenge.

Jake and Hitch turned toward Rose and caught her gaze from the doorway to the living room. "We know," Jake said.

"I hope so, Jake. I need the jury to know that."

"We'll get there."

"You know, he'd help with my homework when he was bone-tired after a full day on the job. He made sure I never missed an after-school activity that I needed, or wanted, to go to. He taught me to work hard at anything I did." Rose stood up taller as if remembering something that made her proud. "My Dad didn't know half measures. He insisted you do it right the first time or not do it at all. He'd say it takes more time to do it over."

"Those are good lessons," Hitch said.

"When I was sick, he would make sure I wasn't alone. He'd cook chicken soup. Reheat it, anyway. Watch me eat every bite. Now… he's gone." Her final words were almost a whisper.

"Sounds like an amazing father," Jake said, his voice low and measured.

"He was," confirmed. "Marcus was one of the good ones." She grabbed Rose around the shoulders and pulled her in tightly. "And he loved his Rose."

"I could never do what they accused me of, you know." Rose rubbed away a tear. "It's horrifying to think they'll try to convince people that I killed my own father." Her voice caught in her throat, thick with emotion. Her eyes pleaded with Jake and Hitch. "Why did those men do that to him? Why won't the police try to find them?"

Margie handed her a tissue and wrapped her in another soft hug. Rose tipped her head until Margie's arm cradled her cheek. Jake flattened his palms on the countertop, wrestling with a flash of frustration at Krista Robb.

"Rose," he said quietly. "I'm not sure why they stopped looking for other suspects. Hitch and I are trying to figure that out."

"I told them… That man chased me in my truck."

"But they're not listening," Hitch said, finishing Rose's thought for her.

"No… they're not listening," Rose said, the patina of defeat coating her words.

"Come on, Rose," Margie said. "Let's grab a couple slices of pie."

Rose nodded and followed Margie into the kitchen.

Hitch whispered to Jake, "You think that pie comes with ice cream?"

"Get to work, old man," Jake chided, pulling a folder of documents produced by Krista closer to him. He thumbed through it. "There's got to be something in here that we can use to make Hope rethink the investigation, or testify, or make Detective Hendrick restart his search for the man, or men, who killed Marcus."

"Give me some of that," Hitch said.

Hitch and Jake dug into the files. As the hours ticked by, they read back through the fine print that they'd digested seemingly hundreds of times before. As their energy ebbed, Margie scooted into the dining room and picked up the dessert plates, the forks clanging against the china.

"Margie, your pie is still the best," Hitch said, with a goofy grin.

"You'll be wantin' a pot of coffee, I imagine," she said. Jake noticed a slight blush on her cheeks.

"If it's not too much trouble, Margie. That would be most

welcome." Hitch worried his fingers through his gray locks to straighten them.

Margie hurried to the kitchen, pulled out her ancient percolator, and fixed up a pot. The grandfather clock in the hallway ticked away the time.

When it chimed midnight, Hitch raked his hands down his face. "I'm gonna have to call it quits soon. I'm not as young as I once was," he said.

Jake looked into the living room. Rose was fast asleep on the couch under a quilt, Margie watching over her and teasing her fingers through the young woman's hair.

Hitch leaned across the table and whispered, "Has she ever given you an explanation for why her undergarments were in Marcus's bed?"

"Not a good one. She changes the subject... denies anything was going on."

"It ain't gonna play well with the jury if we don't have an answer."

"Tell me about it." Jake turned and looked at Rose and Margie. "They both need to go to bed," Jake said.

"We could use some shut-eye, too." Hitch stood and gathered their coffee cups. "I'll make quick work of these before I head out." He washed them and placed them in the drying rack.

A moment later, Jake spied something on the floor. "What do we have here?" Jake asked. He stood and walked to the front door. Bending over, he picked up a thin envelope lying on the rug below the mail slot. Scrawled on the front in cursive were the words, "To Jake Fox."

Hitch peered over Jake's shoulder as he pulled out a sheet of paper. "What've you got there?"

"It was lying by the front door... Have we seen this report from the crime lab before?"

"What's it say?"

"It's results on some of the evidence gathered out at the Tucker place."

"We must have reviewed it. We've been through all these folders multiple times."

Hitch peered over Jake's shoulder, taking in the document. "Well, smack me blind," Hitch said.

A smile crept across Jake's face. "I don't know that we've seen this before."

Hitch looked through the glass pane in Margie's front door. "Well, someone wants us to see it now. You don't think Krista hid this from us, do you?" he asked.

"You told me she'd play sharp."

"But not producing test results… or, in this case, the lack thereof." Hitch shook his head. "How do we even know this is legit? It could be a plant. Without proof, it's a bomb searching for a place to explode."

"Yeah, maybe in our faces."

CHAPTER THIRTY-SIX

JAKE PULLED up in front of his office before sunrise, and his headlights illuminated Hope sitting on his stoop. The glint from the porch light shone off her long auburn hair. She stared back at him, spinning her cowboy hat in her hands. Her uniform cut sharp lines across her body, and Jake cleared his throat as he stepped from his truck. The sweet scent of lilacs mingled with the acrid smell of fresh mulch, and the humidity and heat caused him to sweat before he'd even shut the door to his truck.

"Still working or up early, Sheriff?"

"Couldn't sleep," Hope said, her voice distracted.

"Insomnia seems to be going around," Jake said. "I caught a fierce case last night myself. I got out of bed and started working until I felt like coming in to the office."

"You still get pre-trial jitters?"

"You bet. The day I'm not anxious about trial, I should quit. Don't you get pre-shoot-out jitters?"

"I try to avoid those… shoot-outs, I mean," Hope said with a slight smile, but something, maybe fear, seemed to lurk behind her gaze.

Jake unlocked the office, the familiar bells jingling as he opened the door. The smell of Hitch's cigars lingered.

"Can I get you a cup of coffee?" he asked.

"I'd love one," Hope answered. She stood, dusted off her jeans, and walked into the office as Jake turned on a few lights. The air conditioner whistled as he adjusted it to chase away the stale warmth of a closed building.

"Give it a few minutes. It'll cool off in here. Coffee's this way." Jake led Hope to the kitchen and turned on the coffeepot that Darla had prepared before she'd left the night before. The machine hissed and burbled, and the first pungent essence from the grounds scented the room. Pinned to the wall above the coffee maker, Jake noted a beautiful sketch Rose had drawn of the lake at sunrise.

"Is Rose going to take the stand?" Hope asked.

"You know I can't tell you that. You'd be duty bound to tell the prosecutor."

"I wouldn't," Hope said.

"I won't put you in that position."

"She could tell her story. Tell all that has happened to her."

"And Krista could cut her to ribbons on cross-examination."

Hope shuffled around the kitchen as if taking a quick inventory.

"You believe her?" Hope asked.

"That's she's not guilty?"

"About the bearded man and the redhead that came after Marcus."

"It makes more sense than her deciding to shoot Marcus in the middle of the night."

"Are you sure about that?"

"As sure as I can be. But it's not up to me. It's going to be up to twelve jurors soon. They get to decide whether that little girl spends a decade or more in a Texas state penitentiary. And without you testifying, they're likely going to send her there."

"The judge already ruled that you can't call me at trial."

"You're key, Hope."

"What would I testify to, Jake? That a man with a braided beard tried to chase Rose down in her truck the other day?

"That the man in her alibi exists," Jake replied. "The woman exists."

"If she's telling the truth."

"And you don't think she is."

"No... Maybe... I don't know." Hope sighed. "Her story is consistent. It fits..."

"Fits with what?" Jake paused and looked at the emotions washing over Hope's face. "Oh, I get it. You're worried that no one else has seen them. *You* don't believe they are real." The coffee pot beeped. Jake turned and yanked a cup from the cupboard. "Trust me, Krista's already clarified that you all believe they are ghosts."

"It's just—"

Jake rounded on her. "What, Hope? It's just what?"

"I have additional information on who took Beth Dubose."

"What? That's great. Do you know where she is?"

"Only who she was with."

"Now, what's that supposed to mean?"

Hope reached into her hip pocket and pulled out her smartphone. The screen lit up under her thumb and she scrolled through a few photographs. She stopped on one, paused for a moment, then handed it to Jake. He took the phone and zeroed in on the image. He gripped the device tightly as surprise ran through him.

"What is this photo? Who is this?" Jake's hands shook.

"I can only tell you I picked it up while interviewing a witness."

"Is this from a surveillance camera? Where?"

"At the Quickie Mart."

"Is this Beth?"

"Yes."

"That man in the photo… with Beth at the store. He has a beard in double braids. That proves Rose is not lying. Not about him chasing her in the truck, and not about the night Marcus was killed."

"All it proves is that Rose may have seen him around town once or twice. It doesn't prove a thing about what happened in that house that night."

"You can't be serious. It shows a kidnapper, a violent man, who fits the description Rose gave you. It's not a coincidence. Has Krista seen this?"

"Not yet. She'll say the same thing. It only shows what is happening to Beth. It does not show what happened at the Tucker house that night."

"Give this to her, Rose. That is exculpatory evidence. I'm entitled to that photograph under the law, and you know it. If I move to compel, the judge will have to give it to me, have to let it in. Then you *can* testify."

"I can't, Jake. If I do, and this leaks, then the likelihood of rescuing Beth drops to zero."

"So my client has to go to jail?"

"Should Beth disappear forever just so that you can set a murderer free?"

"Argh… We're never going to agree."

"Don't you worry about Beth?"

"Of course I do. I'm terrified for her. But I'm also terrified for Rose, and she's my client. I'm duty bound to defend her. To do what's in her best interest."

"Rose wouldn't want you to put her friend at risk."

"Of course she wouldn't. She's a wreck over Beth. Terrified of what's happening to her. The people who killed Marcus are serious, and time is running out for Beth. Unless you find her soon…"

"Don't say it."

"I must, Hope. I must push hard for my client, and we both know the chances of finding Beth diminish with each passing day. It's been weeks. But you can keep Rose out of jail today. Give her a future."

"I need to keep hope alive for Beth. I can't be sheriff without holding on to something."

Jake placed the smartphone on the counter. "You can't stop everything, Hope. You know that. It's the way it is." A silence fell between them. Jake poured her a cup of coffee. "Cream?"

"Please."

Jake pulled open the refrigerator and grabbed the carton. "Tell me this. Did you have this photo before the judge ruled you cannot testify?"

A tightness washed over his shoulders at Hope's silence.

"I can't believe it. I'm going to ask the judge to reconsider his ruling. Put you on that stand."

"He's going to deny it."

"I have to preserve it for appeal."

"Appeal? You already don't think you can get an acquittal, do you?"

"Hope, you've been doing this a long time. Before it even starts, any criminal trial can be lost. You know the government's win percentage. They have all the resources. The public wants to believe them, wants to see them as truth tellers."

"So, if it's such a lost cause, why put Beth at risk?"

"I've already answered that."

"Are you sure?"

"What's that supposed to mean?"

"Saving Rose will not bring Lucy back."

"Now you're talking crazy."

"Am I? Are you sure deep down you haven't made some promise to yourself that you wouldn't let her down this time?"

"Why would I—?"

"Because it's what I would do. You don't think that I'm scared, too? I have a daughter, Jake. I see her in Beth's story, and I see her in Lucy's story. It chills my blood to think of any of it happening to Grace."

"It should. Life can be ugly. And you're the sheriff. Every day, you see the worst of humanity."

"But not in my family!"

"What are you talking about? Hope, Grace is safe."

"Can you guarantee it? Whoever this man is, he took Beth. He came after Rose. What makes you think he wouldn't go after Grace?"

"I assure you, it's all in your head."

"I can't go to Krista!"

"You must."

Hope picked up her phone and called up another photo on her screen. She quickly zoomed in and rotated it with a shaky hand for Jake to see. She showed him a snapshot of a note inside a transparent evidence bag. The bag contained a photograph of a young woman with crosshairs drawn over her face —long blonde hair and green eyes, just like Lucy, just like Rose. Someone had included a note underneath: BACK OFF.

Anger flushed through Jake. "Is that Grace?"

"Yes. It's a picture of her outside the nursing college. Someone took it a few days ago… I don't know what it means."

"That you're too close to Beth?"

"Or maybe someone wants to keep me off the stand in Rose's trial."

"Nobody knows about you possibly testifying about her alibi except—"

"Except your office, my office, the prosecutor's office, and the courthouse. Jake, we cannot contain this information. If I give that photo to Krista, I lose control of it. I lose control of protecting Grace. I'm worried we have a mole. We have no way of knowing who it is. No way to defend against it. No one to trust." Hope pulled the phone back and jammed it back into her pocket.

"Where's Grace now?" Jake asked.

"I had my dad drive down and get her from the college.

She's out at their place with a deputy in the driveway and more guns than God. But she can't stay holed up there forever."

"What are you going to do?"

"I'm going to find Beth, Jake."

"And Rose?"

"She's going to have to count on you. If they are threatening to come after Grace, they could come for Rose… again."

"That thought had already crossed my mind."

"I just need time to figure out what to do next."

"Don't take too long."

Hope set her cup in the sink. "I should be going. Work to do, you know."

"I'll show you out." Jake already felt exhausted.

As he turned to lead her down the hallway, Hope grabbed his hand and pulled him toward her, placing a lingering kiss on his cheek. She flattened her hand on his chest, and the moment stood still. Her lips were warm, soft, and inviting. Jake listened to Hope's breathing and his own heart thundering in his chest. She paused for a moment, hovering near his cheek, and then pulled away, gazing into his eyes.

"What was that for?" Jake whispered.

"For luck at trial today," she said. She backed away and then walked down the hallway. Jake heard the bells on the front door jingle as she left. His eyes closed, and images of Beth, Grace, and Rose shuffled in his mind like a game of three-card monte.

CHAPTER THIRTY-SEVEN

MONDAY MORNING. "All rise. The 113th District Court in and for Hawk County is now in session, the Honorable Harlan Dubose presiding."

The judge appeared tired and pale, as if hungover. Jake remembered using bourbon to ease the pain after Lucy died. He could only imagine the fierceness of the anxiety if someone had abducted her. Judge Dubose buffed his round bifocals and looked down his hooked nose at the courtroom and wasted no time.

"We're here on JC-22-1448, the State of Texas versus Rosemary Tucker. Counsel, I've requested a panel of fifty prospective jurors, from which you will select your jury of twelve plus two alternates. I'll ask initial questions, then each side gets thirty minutes to question the panel. I intend to have the jury seated by noon and opening arguments after we come back from lunch. Is that clear?"

Jake and Krista nodded, neither speaking a word. Dubose was going to run a tight ship. There was no use in protesting.

"One more thing. This trial has brought about significant press coverage and interest from the community. Any outbursts, and I'll clear the courtroom."

Jake noticed the judge give a pointed stare Gert and her clucking hens ensconced in the first pew behind the prosecution. Behind them sat a gaggle of reporters, notepads at the ready.

The smell of ancient wood and furniture polish permeated the air. The judge spent the next hour grilling the panel about their general thoughts on crime and punishment, and ferreting out people who had legitimate conflicts with serving on the jury. One was the sole caretaker for her sick, bedbound mother. One had nonrefundable tickets for a cruise out of Galveston. And several convinced the judge that losing income for a week would see them tossed from their residences for failure to pay rent. The others waited for Jake and Krista, their faces sour.

After clearing away standard issues, the judge handed it over to Krista to examine the panel for the prosecution. She focused her questioning on whether any panel member objected to convicting the underage Rose as an adult. Krista never spoke about sending her to prison for years, but everyone in the courtroom knew that any verdict against Rose meant Texas would incarcerate her. The panel responded in typical law-and-order Texas fashion. Some women in the front row hesitated. But once Krista told them that Rose stood accused of murdering her father by shooting him in the head, they agreed they could convict... if that was where the evidence led. Several of the older prospects spoke of the moral decline in America and losing respect for one's elders. A few reaffirmed their fundamental belief in Old Testament justice and the Ten Commandments. Gert and her clan nodded in unison, as if sending out a hearty, "Amen."

To insulate the jurors she wanted from Jake's challenges of overt bias, Krista cajoled each of them into agreeing to follow the law as the judge explained, and to approach the trial with impartiality. Krista finished with a few questions to infuse the prospective members with a sense of duty. She explained they were the wall between chaos and civilization. The jury's verdict would send a loud message about what standards their community will set. Satisfied that she had salted the jury with sufficient platitudes about doing the right thing, Krista sat down, and Judge Dubose passed the questioning to Jake.

Jake used his thirty minutes to reaffirm the concept of reasonable doubt. He asked the jurors whether they could apply that standard and acquit if the government failed to provide sufficient evidence. He told him the decision required the level of certainty they would use in their most serious of personal affairs, like a decision to consent to a risky surgery on their own child. The prospective jurors all seemed to answer with sufficient ambiguity. No panel member confessed to an obvious bias against Rose or a desire to convict without evidence. In the end, Jake hoped they would end up with a fair jury. As he surveyed the panel, he noted an equal number of men and women and a mix of ethnicities. But the panel lacked jurors close to Rose's age. Indeed, the youngest prospect appeared to be in her mid-forties.

After Jake finished his questions, he and Krista submitted their strikes to the judge and selected twelve individuals and two alternates that would weigh Rose's future. Eight men and four women—half Hispanic with the rest a split between black and white—held Rose's future in their hands. As Jake sat down after the selection process, Rose gripped him by the wrist.

"That's a jury of my peers?" she whispered.

"It's the best we're gonna get with the panel we drew."

"The best we can do may very well get me convicted. How on earth are they going to believe me? All of them need a nursing home. They're going to think I'm just some nutty, lying teenager."

"They might surprise you, Rose," Jake said.

Judge Dubose called the jury members selected and instructed them to sit in the jury box. He issued the oath and excused everyone for lunch. Opening statements would occur as soon as they returned at 1:00 p.m.

Jake, Hitch, and Rose bumped into Margie in the hallway, then strolled toward a conference room nearby.

"You ready to go?" Hitch asked.

"I've lost my present desire to puke," Jake answered. "Give me a minute. I'm gonna scoot down the hallway to the restroom."

Jake sauntered to the restroom, hiding his trembling hands in the motion of washing them at the sink. Thoughts of Beth, Rose, and Grace swirled in his head. Alone, he stared at the mirror, at the age that seemed to creep further along his features every day.

The smell of sweet spring flowers washed through the open window on a breeze.

"You look scared." Lucy said from behind him.

A calm flushed through him. He noted her faint reflection over his shoulder. "There's a lot on the line, Lu."

"You know, you can't let that fear leak over into Rose," she said.

"I know. Cool and confident, right?"

"You're doing all you can do."

"Thanks for the vote of confidence."

"You have to believe in her now."

"I do, Lu."

"Are you sure?"

Jake nodded. "Yes. But I still wish I had some answers."

"You'll find them."

"How do I explain her underwear in his bed, Lu? She swears nothing happened. If something happened, maybe I could convince the jury that Marcus deserved to die, and Rose was the perfect person to do it. Go for jury nullification, you know. But a story we can't explain, it's…"

"What?"

"A motive with no answers from us. It's a fatal silence."

"You'll figure it out."

"How can you be certain?"

"Trust me. I have friends that whisper in my ear."

Jake turned around to face Lucy. Her kind emerald eyes gave him strength. "I want to believe Lu."

Lucy stepped forward, placing her index finger across his lips as if to silence him. "Then do," she said. He closed his eyes, and on the wings of another breeze, she was gone.

Splashing cool water on his face, Jake headed back towards the conference room. The door was open a crack, and he heard the voices spilling out.

"I hope he knows what he's doing," Rose mused.

"I'm sure you're worried to death as this all starts," Hitch said. "But there's nobody better than Jake. I've known him since he was a baby lawyer. If there's a way to get to reasonable doubt, Jake can do it."

"I didn't murder my father! I don't understand why no one will believe me. Those religious old farts on the jury won't believe me. We've lost before we've even started."

"I know you're scared. It feels like we're gambling with your life. But I've been doing this almost fifty years, and juries tend to get it right."

"Tend to? What happens when they don't?" Rose asked.

"Then we argue like heck on appeal."

"I don't want that. Wouldn't it be easier if I took off? Disappeared."

"Then what—live like a fugitive? You'd always be looking over your shoulder. What is your plan for money?"

"I have those oil royalties from Marcus."

"Darlin', they will freeze those accounts. You'll be as poor as the baby Jesus on the day he was born. Nope, you'll have no friends, no resources. And they won't give up looking for you. If you try to withdraw any of that money, they'll know right where you are. Running will only increase your guilt in the eyes of the law. To them you'll be a murderer on the lam. Who knows, they might shoot you on sight, thinking you're armed and dangerous. No, you make your stand here… now. Let Jake work his magic."

Prior to opening the door, Jake coughed.

"We talking about the weather in here?" he asked.

"Just talking about storms on the horizon," Hitch said as Jake entered.

"Well then, let's hope for clear skies ahead," Jake answered, and he shut the door behind him.

CHAPTER THIRTY-EIGHT

LILITH TUCKED her hair behind her ear as she looked down range through binoculars. A faint breeze tussled the tall grasses surrounding them, and the violent trill of cicadas pulsated through the foliage. Zach lay near her on a red blanket, peering through a scope. The red dot of a laser glowed inside the black outline of a man on a paper target down range. She heard him exhale. Then he steadied himself and squeezed the trigger. Lilith flinched at the crisp crack. The sound brought terrible memories of her family.

The bullet ripped through the target. Over the next few minutes, Zach fired five more rounds. All six shots formed a tight grouping in the target's head. He laid the rifle down on the blanket and stood.

"You've been practicing," Lilith said.

"Nothing to do at the trailer, since I can't take the merchandise for a ride."

"If you touch a hair on her…"

"Relax, Lilith. I know the rules. I know what buyers want. Virgins bring top dollar. I'm an entrepreneur, remember." He gathered up his casings, tucked them into his shirt pocket, and snapped the flap shut.

Zach field-dressed a cigarette, ripping off the filter and popping it into his pocket. He struck a match from the Silver Lake Casino and lit the tobacco. The bitter vapor overwhelmed the metallic smell of ozone swirling in the air. A thunderstorm threatened on the horizon. Unfortunately, the clouds were too far away to cut any heat from the fierce Texas afternoon, but the shade of several elm trees sheltered them.

Lilith stepped away from the acrid smoke. She hated the foul odor. It had wrapped her father in a blanket of bitter stench and marked his chronic foul moods and amorous advances. Zach took a long drag and blew out a series of white rings. A wide smile crept across his face.

"Those things will kill you," Lilith warned.

"If cigarettes put me in my grave, I'll have lived longer than expected."

Lilith pulled an elastic tie from her wrist, bundled her hair, and slid it on. Her long ponytail trailed the curve of her spine down to her waist.

"Two virgins would have brought more than double the price," Lilith said, a wisp of regret in her voice. "We were so close."

"Why don't we just take the Tucker girl tonight?" Zach asked. "I could sneak in, drug her, and be gone before anyone knows what's happening. We'd be doing the court a service. They'll think she just ran away." Zach twisted the braids in his beard. "I promise I'll be gentle with her." His toothy grin suggested otherwise.

"More money. But that girl helps us. They got their gal, so they aren't looking for who really shot Marcus. Keeps some heat off us."

"Then why'd we jump her the other day?"

"The higher-ups wanted her. So we took our shot. It was a good plan. Lure her out, take her. The sheriff finds an abandoned red pickup truck. Everyone assumes she ran off because of the pressure."

"It didn't go so well," Zach said.

"The sheriff mucked it up. Now they're watching her too closely. She's not going on any more joyrides. Besides, I may have another way to get her."

"We've got to unload the judge's daughter. You know we shouldn't hold on to girls this long."

"How is she? You haven't touched her, right?"

"No." Zach chuckled. "It takes willpower, though. She's mouthy. Someone's going to pay top dollar to teach her respect. Maybe I'll beat them to it."

"Don't. Bruises reduce her value."

"You could fix it with your makeup skills."

"Zach, I'm telling you!"

Zach lunged forward until he was in Lilith's face. "Telling me what, Lilith?"

"Back off," Lilith growled. Zach's stare bored into her. She did not look away. After a few seconds, Zach laughed as he held his hands up in surrender. "Relax. I'm just funning you." A moment passed. "Why don't we just sell her to our regular buyers? I like selling whores in casinos. It's a simple business. All cash. Slip some to the cops and they look the other way."

"No, leave all that to me. Just keep her a healthy, unblemished virgin."

"She doesn't have a mark on her, except from Ted."

"How's it look?"

"He's still the best tattoo man around."

Lilith let the silence sit between them for a moment.

"I don't like waiting," Zach said.

"Our orders are to keep her a couple more days. You'll need to move her from the trailer back to the safe house. Just don't be sloppy about it."

"I'm never sloppy." Zach licked his fingers and used them to crush out the ember on his cigarette.

A motorcycle rolled up behind his black truck. The rider cut the motor, removed his helmet, and shook out his mop of blond hair. Sleeves of jet-black Celtic knot work covered his arms.

"We're set for the day after tomorrow," the man said as he approached.

"You're sure?"

"Just spoke with them on the phone. They confirmed the timing should work."

"Good work, Junior," Lilith replied.

"You don't think they're on to you?" Zach asked him.

"No. There's no trail from me back to you two or the operation. They think I'm just a concerned citizen. They have no idea."

"I like that."

"How do we get Rose?" Junior asked.

"We let the trial play out. Our folks on the inside guarantee a conviction. We nab her once she disappears into the prison system."

"She's too young and pretty to be just a prison whore," Zach protested.

"We're not running her on the inside," Lilith told him. "She'll be another unfortunate statistic."

"They're going to shank her?" Junior said.

"They're going to fake it," Lilith said. "She goes down in staged a prison fight. They declare her dead, and her memory disappears in an unnamed cemetery plot, her death certificate forgotten in a filing cabinet. Then we sell her off under a new name."

"You think the sheriff got the message?" Junior asked.

"She better have," Lilith responded.

"We could sell *her* daughter for a decent amount," Zach remarked.

Lilith nodded. "All I want is for the sheriff to back off. Taking her daughter would create a real firestorm."

"Like taking the judge's daughter?" Zach quipped, and he and Junior laughed. Even Lilith cracked a smile.

"Worse," Lilith said. "We should leave before someone sees us." She turned to Junior. "Do your part well."

He flashed a sloppy salute. "Yes, ma'am." He stepped away, mounted his bike, and rolled it down the dirt road before starting it again.

Once Junior was out of sight, Lilith used the binoculars to inspect the target holes one last time.

"Why do you practice so much?" Lilith asked.

"I have an old friend to visit."

"Let's go, Zach. We have things to do."

CHAPTER THIRTY-NINE

"ALL RISE." The bailiff called the courtroom back to order. Nobody on Jake's side had eaten any lunch. Nerves had gotten the best of everybody. Jake, Rose, and Hitch stood at the defense table and watched as the jurors shuffled in. One by one, they stole a glance at Rose as they sat down in the box. Silence fell across the courtroom until Judge Dubose coughed to bring everybody back to attention. The air-conditioning leaked out a slow stream of almost-cool air. The humidity in the room had risen, and a heady smell drifted from the crowd. It was standing room only.

"Ms. Robb, is the State ready?"

"Yes, Your Honor."

"Then let's proceed with opening statements. The courtroom is yours."

Krista rose from her table and made her way to the court's lectern. She shuffled a few pages on her yellow pad, then faced the jury and plowed ahead with no notes.

"Ladies and gentlemen of the jury, we are here today because the defendant, Rosemary Tucker, murdered her father in cold blood one night here in Haven. It sounds unthinkable: a child taking the life of a parent—a parent who raised and nurtured that child. To the outside world, Marcus Tucker gave his daughter a good life. He was a hardworking single father. He wasn't rich, but Rosemary didn't want for essentials. It would seem to the outside world that, in a callous, ungrateful moment, she robbed Marcus Tucker of his life. But that home also kept a sinister secret. The evidence will show that her father was molesting Ms. Tucker."

A couple of members of the jury gasped. Rose dropped her head, and a single tear fell on her dress.

"To violate a child is shocking, repugnant… vile. But the law does not allow for vigilante justice or revenge. Ms. Tucker had the right to contact the sheriff, a school counselor, or Child Protective Services. She had multiple avenues to stop whatever unnatural acts Mr. Tucker did to her. However, she had no right to kill him for his sins.

"How did Ms. Tucker accomplish this murder? It's quite simple. As a storm bore down on Haven, Ms. Tucker ambushed her father in their home just up the way from the Iron Gate boat ramp. The evidence will show that Ms. Tucker waited until he was tired and getting ready for bed. With Marcus exhausted and distracted, and perhaps a nip or two into a bottle of bourbon, she entered his room and shot him at point blank range in the head.

"To cover her tracks, she concocted a wild story of a cadre of men assaulting Marcus at his home and then shooting. That is preposterous. No evidence exists to support that theory. No drag marks. No signs of a struggle. No defensive wounds. No evidence he tried to fight off an assault. No, ladies and gentlemen, Marcus knew his executioner very well. He loved her. And his fatal mistake was letting her get close enough to snuff out his life.

"The evidence will also show that Ms. Tucker has no alibi. The police found no unusual tire tracks at the home. The only footsteps came from Ms. Tucker's sneakers. At the time of the murder, she was in that house. They found her fingerprints all over the crime scene, including on the bourbon bottle next to the victim. They lifted samples of Ms. Tucker's blood from the carpet next to where the body lay in the bed. The wastepaper bin contained vomit from Ms. Tucker, who could not stomach the raw violence she had inflicted on her father. Her fingerprints are on the murder weapon, and her bloody fingerprints are on both the door and doorknob to the bedroom where the victim's body rested.

"The evidence leads to its logical end. In a premeditated and cruel fashion, Ms. Tucker murdered her father. The answer to what happened that night is simply that. And simple answers are correct.

"Ms. Tucker's age is fifteen. Let's deal with that right away. In Texas, the age of majority is eighteen. She is a juvenile being prosecuted as an adult. The defense will tell you she is a child. But the heinous nature of murder knows no age limit. Murder breaks the basic moral fiber of the community, especially the murder of a parent by a child. As such, the State can prosecute Ms. Tucker as an adult so the community can convict her for the very adult crimes she committed. The law in this case, as the judge will instruct you, requires that you treat her like everyone else. She is not to be given special treatment or sympathy because she's just fifteen. It is not her age on trial but her actions, and you must hold her accountable for the cold, premeditated slaughter of her dad.

"As the judge instructed you when you took your oath, we ask only that you weigh the evidence and then compare it to the elements of the crime. We ask that you do the job many other juries have done through history—find the truth. If you discharge that duty, we are confident you will return a verdict of guilty for Ms. Tucker."

Kristin nodded her head at the jury, turned, and marched back to the prosecutor's table with a bit of arrogance in her swagger.

"Mr. Fox," Judge Dubose said, "I'm assuming you have an

opening statement, or do you defer until after the prosecution's case?"

"Your Honor, I'll give my opening now."

"Very well."

Jake stood, straightened the lapels on his suit coat, and stepped past the lectern into the space in front of the jury. He let the silence continue for a few moments. He looked each juror in the eye before he began.

"The State cannot prove that Rose Tucker committed this crime because she did not do it. But let's also be very clear. In this courtroom, Rose has no obligation to prove her innocence, no obligation to take the stand. She has no duty to put on a defense. Indeed, the Constitution allows her to say silent and make the prosecution prove its case. You cannot hold that against her. Instead, the State must shoulder the heavy burden to prove, beyond a reasonable doubt, each element of the crime. And what they have produced is a rather lazy and fantastical story. They ask you to believe that a fifteen-year-old child plotted to murder her father for revenge. Without proof, they accuse Marcus Tucker of molesting his daughter, and then accuse her of killing him. I agree it can grab your attention, but it should not grab your verdict. Rather, when inspected, the State's case falls apart on the lack of evidence. No eyewitnesses exist. No confession exists. No cooperating informant that turned State's evidence exists. There is no evidence of improper contact by Mr. Tucker. Rather, the State's case rests on circumstantial evidence, innuendo, and supposition.

"Indeed, the prosecutor asks that you ignore the actual evidence of this case and guess what could have happened based only on their theory. They claim they have damning fingerprint evidence. But Rose lived in the home where Mr. Tucker died, so of course her fingerprints are on items inside. They say bloody prints show she was the culprit. But Rose found her father. In grief, she touched his lifeless body, a reaction any of us might have to such a loss. They say she vomited out guilt for slaying her father, but she vomited because the shock of losing her father in such a violent way rocked her to the core. Each piece of their case crumbles under simple scrutiny. You must analyze all evidence. You cannot engage in the blind faith the prosecution desires."

Jake moved behind Rose and rested his hands on her shoulders. "Rose suffered trauma in discovering her father shot, only to be victimized by her supposed protectors. Did the State try to help her? Console her? No. The State condemned her and rushed to judgment. Now they seek to convict her and prune her life before it grows. Based on their ill-informed guesses, the prosecution wants you to convict this child for the crime of murder on mere supposition. That cannot be the case. The law requires more in a criminal case. It requires proof beyond all reasonable doubt that each element of the alleged crime occurred. In this case, the prosecution cannot meet that burden."

Jake stepped back into the center of the courtroom.

"You will hear evidence in this case that the sheriff's department hurried the investigation. They failed to follow certain leads. Instead, the homicide detectives latched on to Rose as early as the night of the murder. They designated her as suspect number one. They never deviated from that preordained outcome. We will show through cross-examination that reasonable doubt exists in every turn in this case. When we come to you for a verdict at the end of trial, acquit Rose and allow her to grieve for her father, a process that has been interrupted by the State's rush to judgment and its desire to put her in jail."

Jake allowed his words to sink in as he looked across the jury, peering into their eyes and imploring them to hold faithful to their oath and to hold the prosecution to its burden. When he believed each juror understood the weight of the task in front of them, he gathered his papers from the lectern and headed back to the defense counsel table. He sat down and gathered a pen from his pocket to take notes of the testimony of Krista's first witness. Rose discreetly grabbed Jake's hand under the table and gave it a slight squeeze. Jake turned to her and gave her a faint smile. They were off and running now.

"Ms. Robb, call your first witness," Judge Dubose said.

Krista stood and said, "The State calls Wes Hendricks."

And so it begins.

CHAPTER FORTY

WES HENDRICKS DROPPED his hand from swearing his oath to tell the truth, the whole truth, and nothing but the truth. The detective straightened his plaid blazer and blue-and-red repp tie then sat in the oak chair. He pulled the microphone closer. Wes was no stranger to a courtroom, and he appeared comfortable, calm, and competent. He was the perfect witness for the prosecution.

Krista made quick work of his background, helping the jury learn to like Detective Hendricks. They could feel good that he was a person protecting their streets, especially against homicide. Jake looked at the jury's expressions, trying to read how much weight they might put on the detective's testimony. They seem enamored by the older police officer and all his exploits.

Krista ran through the same testimony as she did at the waiver hearing. Hendricks testified to finding Marcus in the house. He covered finding the murder weapon on the floor, and his opinion that Mr. Tucker likely knew his assailant. Hendricks testified that he'd found blood on the door and the doorknob, and that it matched Rose's blood type. He explained how the technicians had found fingerprints from both Marcus and Rose in the home at the murder scene, and that Rose's fingerprints were on the bourbon bottle next to the bed. Detective Hendricks framed the case against Rose the way Krista wanted it: short and simple. Hendricks made one point after another against Rose, but Jake took notes and had to believe in his strategy on cross-examination.

"Detective Hendricks, one last question," Krista said. "Were Ms. Tucker's fingerprints found on the murder weapon?"

"Yes, ma'am, they were."

"No further questions." Krista gathered her pad and pen from the lectern and strutted to her seat.

"Mr. Fox," Judge Dubose barked, "questions for this witness."

"Yes, Your Honor."

Before reaching the lectern, Jake asked his first question.

"Detective, did you see Rose shoot Marcus Tucker?"

"No, I did not."

"Did you come across any witness who claims to have seen Rose shoot Mr. Tucker?"

"We did not identify any such witness."

"So your theory that Rose killed her father is just that: a theory built on supposition."

"I'd like to believe it's a logical deduction of the facts at the scene and my twenty years of experience."

"That's right. You are piecing it together based on your history as a detective and what you believe your 'experience' has taught you."

"Correct."

"These experiences, they build up. Because you have seen more, you believe you can deduce what happened more quickly."

"My experiences inform my judgments. That is true."

"And your extensive experience makes you more efficient than a new officer. Is that correct?"

"I can analyze a homicide scene faster than a new officer."

"Experiences accumulate, don't they?"

"I don't understand your question."

"Let me ask it this way. Each new experience informs how you look at the next crime scene, correct?"

"Yes, I learn from each fresh crime scene."

"And from all this learning, certain patterns must emerge."

"That is correct."

"And those patterns are helpful."

"Yes, I've found criminal behavior rarely deviates from those patterns."

"You can decide which pattern fits which crime, as far as you're concerned."

"More or less."

"And you start with one of these patterns as your baseline?"

"Often, yes. Like I said, criminal behavior rarely deviates from the norm."

"And those patterns also inform how you investigate a crime, correct?"

"Not necessarily."

"You just testified that certain patterns have emerged to you over a career."

"That's right."

"And that makes you more efficient at your job?"

"Yes."

"But those patterns do not inform how you investigate a crime."

"I didn't say that…"

"That's right, because your experience, the patterns you see, they all inform how you investigate a case."

"They inform it, but that's not the only thing."

"So it's a baseline."

"You could say that."

"Could I say it's a bias?"

"I am not biased, Mr. Fox."

"How could you not be? You're only human. You look at a situation and slot it into one of your patterns. Even before all the facts have come in, right?"

"I wouldn't say that."

"In your experience, do you form an opinion when you arrive at a homicide scene? No hot takes on what you see?"

"We all form opinions all the time. We then use our investigative techniques to test those opinions to reach the truth of what happened."

"Those initial opinions shape the scope of an investigation… how you go about looking for additional facts."

"Yes, we build an investigative plan from the facts as we encounter them at the crime scene. We then adjust from there as additional facts come to light."

"So from the very first moment you arrive on the scene, you're already ruling in—or out—certain facts or leads to chase."

"Yes, we are sifting through the evidence."

"And your judgments can create biases that affect the scope of an investigation from the beginning."

"I told you, I am not biased against Ms. Tucker or any other suspect."

"How can you not be? We all set out to confirm what we believe had happened. We look for information to bolster our judgments and our patterns. And that is what you did here."

"No."

"Did you look for other potential suspects?"

"There were no other suspects."

"The morning after Marcus's death, Rose told the sheriff that several men and a woman assaulted Marcus the night before. Did you look for them?"

"There were no tire tracks, no footprints. Nothing at the

crime scene pointed to anyone else but Ms. Tucker being there that night."

"It had stormed, though, correct?"

"Correct. A big storm, as I recall."

"It's true that rain washes away tire tracks and footprints if they are in the dirt."

"It can."

"Detective Hendricks, is the driveway at the Tucker home paved or dirt?"

"It's a mix of gravel and earth."

"So it's dirt."

"Yes."

"And it was muddy when you arrived?"

"Yes."

"So the storm washed away any footprints."

"We did not observe any footprints in the drive area when we arrived."

"Since that evidence wasn't available to you, did you do anything else to find these people?"

"We did not believe they existed, so, no."

"Did you have Rose visit with a sketch artist?"

"No."

"Did you put out an APB on the descriptions of the vehicles she gave you?"

"No, I believed them to be too general to be of any help."

"So your experience, on first blush, told you not to bother."

"Objection," Krista said as she left from her chair. "Argumentative."

"I'll withdraw the question, Your Honor." Jake continued. "Detective Hendricks, did Rose live at the house where you found Marcus dead?"

"You know she did. She was Mr. Tucker's daughter."

"Is it unusual to find a person's fingerprints in a home in which they live?"

"No. It is not."

"Nothing further for Detective Hendricks, Your Honor."

"Ms. Robb, any redirect?"

"Just one question. Detective Hendricks, in your twenty years of policing and ten years of being a homicide detective, how often have you observed that it is a family member who kills the victim?"

"In my experience, most homicide victims knew their killer, who are often family members."

"Thank you. No further questions."

Detective Hendricks stepped down from the stand.

Dubose cleared his throat. "Ms. Robb, call your next witness."

"The State calls Dr. Shonda Dunkin, the Hawk County coroner and medical examiner."

"Dr. Dunkin, come forward so the clerk can swear you in."

Jake watched as the medical examiner positioned herself in the witness chair. She was dressed conservatively in an expensive navy business suit, and she exuded confidence and competence.

Krista took Dr. Dunkin through her credentials and expertise, and then through her experience both as a medical examiner and a testifier at trial. The jury hung on the doctor's every word, as if looking for someone to tell them what decision to reach. Dr. Dunkin could well be that guide.

With the preliminaries out of the way, Krista walked Dr. Dunkin through the core of her testimony.

"Dr. Dunkin, previously this year, did you have occasion to visit the Tucker property out at Iron Gate?"

"Yes, ma'am. I received a call at around nine o'clock in the morning from Sheriff Stone. She was on site at a homicide and needed me to assist."

"And you proceeded to the Tuckers' home?"

"Yes. When I arrived, the sheriff directed me inside the home to the master bedroom."

"And what did you observe?

"I observed a deceased male in his late thirties, early forties, supine on the bed. He appeared to have a gunshot wound to the head. I also noticed a semiautomatic pistol on the carpet, which I assumed to be the murder weapon."

"Could you tell the cause of death?"

"I waited until I concluded the autopsy to finalize the cause of death, but from my initial examination, the victim had sustained a fatal injury from a bullet fired in close proximity to his skull."

"What factors led to that conclusion?"

"I found the victim lying on his back in the center of the mattress. He appeared to have been dead for some time. The blood splatter and stains on the bed frame, mattress, and walls showed the injuries had occurred while the victim was possibly asleep. We noted an abrasion ring around the entrance wound on the underside of his chin, augmented by the inverted edges typical of a bullet entering the human body. The wound was circular in nature, suggesting the gun had been held perpendicular to the victim's head. The skin showed burns and gunpowder marks that indicated the gun was pressed below the jaw. The top of the head had a severe exit wound, showing major bone and tissue damage."

"This single gunshot proved fatal?"

"Yes. The bullet's path caused catastrophic damage to the brain tissue. Death was automatic and immediate."

"What else did you observe?"

"I noted the lack of defensive injuries on the victim's hands and forearms."

"Did your autopsy confirm the preliminary conclusions you made in the field?"

"It did."

"Did you perform any other procedures of note?"

"We processed the body as we normally would, including preserving any hairs or fibers. We scraped under the fingernails and sent clippings to the crime lab for processing."

"And the lab technician could explain those results to the jury?"

"Correct."

"Dr. Dunkin, in your expert medical opinion, was Mr. Tucker's death a homicide?"

"Yes, without a doubt."

"Your Honor, the State passes the witness."

Jake stood and walked to the lectern. He had watched the jury during Dr. Dunkin's testimony. They had warmed to her, many of them nodding along as she testified. He would score no points by trying to confront the doctor; indeed, it could backfire, and they could hold it against Rose. All he could do was pick around the edges.

"Dr. Dunkin, it's true that your examination explained how the victim may have died, correct?"

"That is correct. I would say my examination shows how the victim died, not how he *may* have died."

"Fair enough. And your examination concluded it was a homicide, right?"

"Yes."

"It's true, however, that your examination did not explain who may have committed that homicide."

"It is my understanding that the State has charged Ms. Tucker with the homicide of her father, Marcus Tucker."

"But your examination does not scientifically show that, does it?"

"No. I can say how he died, but I cannot testify as to who killed him. That is correct."

"You also testified that the gun was likely held below the jaw."

"That is correct. It was likely at a ninety-degree angle and held against or just adjacent to the skin."

Jake mimicked a pistol with his hand, holding his index finger to his chin. "In that position, would it be possible to commit suicide with a pistol?"

The doctor cleared her throat. "I testified about the firearm's whereabouts, not its holder."

"Nothing further, Your Honor."

As Dr. Dunkin stepped down from the witness stand and exited the courtroom, Jake continued to hope his strategy would be enough to raise reasonable doubt for Rose.

CHAPTER FORTY-ONE

JAKE GATHERED his things from the counsel table as he watched the jury disappear into their antechamber, the door slamming behind them.

"Counsel, do we have anything further to address before we go home for the day?"

Krista cleared her throat and held up a file folder in her hand. "Your Honor, may I approach?"

"Give whatever you have to the bailiff. He'll hand it up."

Krista gave the document to the deputy and turned back to deliver a copy to Jake. "We've become aware of a recent incident with the defendant that led us to file this motion to revoke bond and detain Ms. Tucker."

You've gotta be kidding me.

Jake glanced at Rose. A panicked curiosity flushed across her face.

"Judge, this is the first we are hearing—" Jake started.

The judge held up his hand. "Mr. Fox, when I'm ready to hear from you, I'll let you know. Ms. Robb, proceed."

"Yes, Your Honor. It appears a few days ago the sheriff intercepted the defendant traveling at a high rate of speed in her father's truck. She ignored the blinking red lights at a four-way junction and had to be pulled over by the sheriff to prevent further risks to other drivers."

What the…?

Jake scanned the courtroom for Hope. She stepped through the double doors and took a seat in the back of the courtroom.

"Judge, Ms. Robb wants to revoke bond and detain based on—"

"Mr. Fox, I will not warn you again. Let Ms. Robb finish. You'll have your turn. Now, Ms. Robb… what is your point?"

"Your Honor, it's twofold. The defendant must obey county and Texas laws as a condition for release. She has disregarded that condition. That alone is a reason to revoke her bond. She is not of legal driving age and she has no license. While driving, she showed no concern for the safety of fellow community members. Indeed, she could have killed someone else, adding vehicular manslaughter to her murder charge."

"So you're moving to detain her for a traffic ticket?"

"Mr. Fox!"

"No," Krista continued. "Ms. Tucker violated her conditions of release and has proven herself to be a danger to the community. Don't get me started on the lack of supervision. She has access to a vehicle and obviously feels comfortable driving off whenever she feels like it. That now makes her a flight risk. The guardianship didn't work."

The judge paused and tapped his chin with his glasses. "Mr. Fox, what say you?"

"Your Honor, this is preposterous. Ms. Tucker had a lapse of judgment—"

"That's what concerns me," the judge said. "It might not simply be a lapse of judgment. This sounds like more than a joyride." The judge nodded to the deputy, who slipped through the chamber's door and disappeared. "Does your client have a reason for driving like a maniac without a license in my county?"

"I think describing her as a maniac is dramatic."

"Are you sure, Mr. Fox? I see our good sheriff sitting in the back. Ms. Robb, do you intend to call her to the stand to make an evidentiary record?"

"Yes. If the court is ready, we'd call Sheriff Stone."

"Sheriff, approach and join our little shindig up here," the judge said.

Jake watched as Hope walked to the stand. She did not look at him. Rose grabbed Jake's hand and beckoned him to bend down so she could whisper in his ear.

"Jake, what is going on?"

"Krista wants to put you in the jail for the rest of the trial." Red splotches flushed across Rose's neck and face, and her hands trembled. Jake pulled a glass from the tray in front of them on the table and poured her a drink of cool water from the carafe. He listened to the court swear in Hope.

"Sheriff," Krista began, "please share with the court what happened between you and Ms. Tucker recently."

Hope stared at Krista with a slow burn in her eyes. Then she glanced from Rose to Jake, pausing as she looked at him as if imparting a silent message.

This has taken her by surprise, too.

"Sheriff," the judge prodded, "please answer the question."

"Several days ago, I was out on Lake Road near Klineman's junction. I'd stopped in the utility crossover to use the laptop in my cruiser."

"Did you observe Ms. Tucker in a red pickup truck?"

"Yes."

"And what did you see?"

"As I was looking up some information, I noticed a vehicle traveling at a high rate of speed."

"A dangerous rate of speed?"

"It was above the speed limit?"

"How fast? More than ten miles an hour over the limit?"

"Yes."

"Over twenty?"

"It's possible."

"Over twenty-five?"

"That is also possible."

"What did you do next?"

"I pursued the truck."

"Did it stop at any point?"

"I followed it for about a mile down the road. It pulled into the driveway at Margie Moore's place."

"The defendant's guardian?" Krista asked.

"That is correct."

"Was Ms. Moore home?"

"No."

"So the defendant was unattended, unsupervised... Did you confront Ms. Tucker about her driving at an excessive speed without a license?"

"I did."

"Did she explain her reckless behavior?"

"She told me the same men she witnessed assaulting her father the night he died were chasing her."

"Have you found these mystery men, these ghosts that she blames for all her criminal conduct?"

"Objection, Your Honor. Argumentative."

"Overruled. Sheriff, you may answer the question."

"We have not located them... yet."

Krista seemed to wave off Hope's caveat. "Ms. Moore, who's responsible for watching Ms. Tucker for the court? Who allowed her to disregard traffic laws and endanger the citizens of this county?"

"I don't know what Ms. Margie knew."

"Doesn't sound like much," Krista said.

"Objection."

"Sustained. Ms. Robb, is that all you have for the sheriff?"

"Yes, Judge."

"Mr. Fox, any questions?"

"Just a couple. Sheriff Stone, do you have any reason to

believe that Ms. Tucker is lying about the men she claims were chasing her?"

"I could not corroborate her story… but no. I have no reason to believe or disbelieve her. That is outside my personal knowledge."

"Any reason to believe Ms. Tucker is a flight risk or danger to the community based on your interactions and observations of the defendant?"

"Based on my personal observations, no. I have no reason to believe that."

"No more questions, Judge."

"Sheriff, stay there. We may need you some more. Ms. Robb, it's your motion. Do you have more to argue?"

"Judge, we'd ask that you revoke the defendant's bond and detain her for the duration of the trial. Not only have we demonstrated she is a potential danger to the community through her lawless behavior, but it is also apparent from the incident that the court-appointed guardian, Ms. Moore, cannot control Ms. Tucker's outbursts and propensity to break the law. Furthermore, Ms. Tucker's free access to the pickup and her willingness to drive without a license suggest that she can flee at any moment. She has the motive and the means. To ensure the State's interest in her trial, she must be detained in the county jail until the jury reaches a verdict. Thus, the court should grant our motion."

"Mr. Fox?"

"Your Honor, the State sprang this ridiculous motion on all of us. The court granted bail to Ms. Tucker and appointed Ms. Moore as the guardian ad litem. For months, Ms. Tucker has followed the court's conditions of release and has attended all hearings and this trial."

"So far," the judge interjected.

Jake saw a deputy enter the courtroom through the double doors. Behind the judge, another deputy entered the courtroom. Both slid their hands into nitrile gloves.

"I understand that the prior arrangement *had* been working," the judge continued. "But I'm concerned that Ms. Fox's erratic behavior will escalate the closer we get to an actual jury verdict. I'm not willing to take the chance that Ms. Moore's supervision fails and that Ms. Tucker absconds from the jurisdiction. Therefore, I'm granting the State's motion. The court revokes the defendant's bond and remands her to the custody of the county sheriff."

Rose grabbed onto Jake's hand. "What? Jake, what's happening?"

The deputies moved to either side of Rose, asking her to stand. She did, her body shaking as she looked at Jake.

"Why are they doing this to me? I was fine at Margie's. I... I take it back. Judge, I swear I won't touch that truck."

"Ms. Tucker, my ruling assures that you will not."

"Hope, tell them. Tell them about the men chasing me! Tell them about the man with the braided beard!"

One deputy grabbed Rose's wrist and tried to pull it behind her back. Rose punched him in the nose. Jake heard the cartilage crack.

Oh man, here we go.

The other deputy pounced on Rose, pinned her to the table, yanked one arm behind her, and snapped a cuff into place. The deputy with the broken nose wiped the blood away, grabbed Rose's free arm, and struggled with her second wrist as they finished cuffing her. Rose's face turned purple with effort as she screamed.

"I didn't kill my father! Those men! The redhead! Why aren't you looking for them?"

Jake grabbed Rose's jaw with his hand and held her gaze for a moment, willing her to calm down.

"Rose... we'll figure this out. You've got to stop fighting them. It's only going to make it worse."

"Let's go," one deputy said as he yanked her toward the

door that led to the holding cell. The other deputy was pinching his nose to stem the flow of blood.

"Jake!"

The deputies manhandled Rose through the doorway, and it closed behind her, muffling her struggles.

"Model citizen," Krista said.

The judge cleared his throat. "Looks like I made the right decision. Ms. Robb, anything else?"

"No, Judge."

"Then we stand in recess. Mr. Fox, I suggest you visit with your client and try to calm her down so that things go smoothly for her in the county jail. Trouble seems to have a way of finding her. I also suggest you try to convince Ms. Robb not to charge your client for assaulting a peace officer."

CHAPTER FORTY-TWO

THE STALE SMELLS of greasy institutional food and pungent disinfectant overwhelmed Rose when they thrust her in the county jail. A short, stout female correctional officer with a military haircut and the figure of a beer can took Rose's possessions, including her phone, while a tall blonde with her hair in a severe bun, who looked as if she lifted free weights, inventoried Rose's personal effects. They strip-searched her and smiled as they made her squat and cough to make sure she wasn't smuggling contraband in any body cavity. Both watched her scrub in a frigid shower. Then they shoved mud-brown prison fatigues and slip-on sneakers at her.

"Suicide watch," the more butch of the two said.

They marched her down the women's wing. A few catcalls and lewd remarks from the randier female detainees poured through the bars at Rose. The guards forced her into a cell and slammed the door shut. The clang of steel and the scrape of the lock echoed off the cinderblock walls.

Rose grabbed the bars as guards turned away. "I want my lawyer!"

"No visiting hours until the morning," they said in unison.

"I want to see my lawyer, now!"

The blonde banged a baton against the bars just above Rose's fingers, causing her to jump back. "If he wants to see you, attorney visiting hours start at seven in the morning. Until then, I suggest you get used to your new home. And don't make trouble." The guards turned on their heels and walked away.

Rose rested her head against the steel bars as the ultraviolet light outside the cell flickered, angering her migraine. She reached up and felt her hair still wet from the cold water, the chill not yet having left her. It had taken hours to process her. She'd spent most of her time in a small cell before the correctional officers arrived. She overheard one guard say they were letting Rose cool off after breaking the deputy's nose. When she closed her eyes, she could see his grimace as the blood leaked into his mustache. Exhaustion washed over her.

You've done it now, Rosemary Louise Tucker.

"It's best not to make them mad," a voice behind her said.

Rose turned and, for the first time, noticed another inmate in the cell, sitting on a bunk, tucked up against the wall. Her cellmate had white-blonde hair shaved short on one side, with long strands leaking down into her almond eyes. She did not seem much older than Rose.

"I think I'm a long way past upsetting them," Rose said.

"I heard." The girl smiled. "Nice job breakin' that deputy's nose."

"I'm not sure it's going to win me any friends."

"Not with the guards. But..."

Rose moved toward the empty bunk with a blanket and linens folded in the center. She sat down. The girl moved to the edge of her bunk and extended her hand.

"I'm Cassie Wolf," she said. There was a glint of mischief in her gaze.

"Rose Tucker." Rose shook Cassie's hand.

"You're the one on trial for killin' her father," Cassie said.

"I didn't—"

Cassie held up her hands. "I'm not sayin' you did. But you're a popular piece of gossip in here. A bit of a celebrity. Especially havin' been in the news."

"Because they say I killed my dad?"

"Yes, and no. It's more like a bettin' pool on whether the jury convicts you. You bein' a kid and all."

"Great."

"Each gal puts in one pack of cigarettes, and the winner takes all."

"I don't smoke."

"If they convict you, you'll learn. Nothin' better than a menthol cigarette in the yard."

Cassie stood and then sat next to Rose on the bunk, bumping their shoulders as if they were longtime buddies.

"Stick with me. I'll show you how it all works in here."

"I'm hoping not to be in here long," Rose said, noticing the two small holes in Cassie's nose. The guards must have confiscated her nose rings.

"Hope is good. But thinkin' about reality is good, too."

"Why are you in here?" Rose asked.

"My old man had me jacked for allegedly stealin' his truck."

"You stole his truck?"

"No, silly," Cassie said, slapping Rose on the leg. "*Allegedly* stealing. I drove to the GasMart for some cigarettes. I took his truck. We were fightin' something fierce, and he called the cops and got me pinched. I was out on parole for possession, see. So the deputies arrested me. Now I'm waitin' on a hearin' in front of Judge Dubose to see if they're gonna revoke my parole." Cassie's voice was high, almost like a bird's, and she talked fast but with a heavy southern drawl. Rose had to pay attention to understand her chatter once she got rolling.

"Good luck with that," Rose said. "Dubose just revoked my bond and put me in here with you. No offense meant."

"None taken. I've heard he's a real hard nose of a judge."

"And I'm pretty sure today I blew up any goodwill I had with him."

"The broken nose?"

"Yeah, the broken nose." Rose wiped a tear from her cheek. "I just… I panicked. I got so mad."

"Hey, now. No need to get all misty. He's a man. Tell him it was your period talkin'. Men run away from anything having to do with a women's period. Pansies. Who knows, maybe he'll write it off as you having a bad day."

Rose scoffed. "Bad day, bad week, bad life."

"Come on, you can't look at it like that."

"I'm going to look at it any way that I want," Rose said. "It's not like being shoved in here is making my life any easier."

"Did you hit him while the jury was in the courtroom?"

"The deputy? No, it was after they left. The prosecutor moved to detain me, and I punched the deputy when the judge ruled against me."

"See, that's somethin' good. You could have slugged him in front of the jury, so you're lucky."

"What are you, the eternal optimist?"

"In here, you have to be. Otherwise you'll go"—Cassie crossed her eyes and twirled her finger around her ear—"a little crazy."

Rose smiled. She had to admit that, even in her current funk, she liked Cassie. It had been months since someone had made her laugh. Months since she'd had a friend her age. Memories of Beth reignited her hurt and anger.

They keep coming after me. And who's looking for Beth? If I ever get out of here…

"What are you thinkin' about?" Cassie said.

"Huh?"

"You disappeared on me there for a bit. Where'd you go?"

"Thinking about friends."

"Friends on the outside?"

Rose nodded.

"I can tell you somethin' from experience. Even your best friends disappear fast once you're on the inside. They don't like comin' into the jail to say hello. I think it's a hassle they'd rather not deal with. It's good to start makin' friends in here. You can start with me."

Rose remained silent, recalling the last time she'd seen Beth's radiant smile—at her father's funeral.

"Hey, let's get you settled." Cassie stood and picked up the bundle of bedding in the middle of Rose's bunk. She dropped them on her bed, then shook loose a sheet and spread it on Rose's mattress.

Rose grabbed a corner of the sheet and tucked it in at the bed's base. As they spread the next sheet, Cassie cracked a few jokes, as if trying to get Rose to smile. She did in the end. Cassie flopped open the scratchy wool blanket. After tucking in the final flaps of fabric, they sat on the bunk. Cassie smoothed out a few last wrinkles.

"Nice tight job," Cassie said, admiring their handiwork.

Rose reached out and touched the tattoo on the inside of Cassie's wrist.

"I like that tattoo. It's a beautiful pattern."

Cassie turned her wrist up to show it off. "Thanks. I got it last year."

"How did you pick the design?"

"My old man liked it."

"The one who got you arrested for stealing his truck?"

"Allegedly."

"Right, allegedly. That old man?" Rose said.

"That's him." Cassie rubbed the intricate black design, and then her voice dropped. "He'll take me back when I get out," she said, but there was a twinge of sorrow on the edge of her voice.

"My boyfriend—maybe my ex now—has one on his chest like that," Rose said.

"They're popular these days. They call it a Celtic cross."

"Maybe I'll get one someday."

I could get one with Beth. We could be twins. Beth, where are you?

Cassie peered into Rose's eyes as if reading her soul. "I think we can arrange it. I know just the guy."

CHAPTER FORTY-THREE

JAKE GREETED the correctional officer at the jail's front desk. After signing in, he emptied his pockets into the gray plastic bin, placed it on the conveyor belt, and watched as it tracked its way into the black rubber flaps at the entry to the X-ray machine. He stepped through the metal detector and waited for officers to scan his personal effects. Once cleared, he reclaimed his belongings. Cameras loomed in each corner, their little green lights reminding him that the jailers watched his every move. A correctional officer escorted him into a large square room with benches and tables in a row.

"Wait here, Fox."

Jake nodded an answer and took in his surroundings. Vending machines lined one wall. He took out a dollar bill, fed it into a machine, and purchased a chocolate bar. He was the first visitor of the day. Attorney's hours started at seven that morning. Court began at nine. Jake had arrived at six-thirty and drunk a cup of coffee in his truck in the parking lot.

Sleep had eluded him the previous night as he wrestled with thoughts of Rose being torn away in the courtroom. The lock turned, and a door opened. Rose shuffled through with manacles on her wrists. The dark-brown jail fatigues hung on her like billowing clothes on a feeble scarecrow. Somehow, she looked older this morning—a mere twelve hours later. The officer led her to a room with a door and windows. He sat Rose down and locked her manacles to a ring on the table. Once she was secure, the jailer stepped out and looked at Jake.

"Fox, she's ready."

Jake stood and entered the closet of a room. He looked around. No cameras. This was a place safe from listening devices, safe for privileged attorney-client conversations. A fan churned in the ceiling, pushing around the hot air thick with germicide fumes.

"Twenty minutes," the officer said. He shut the door behind Jake.

Jake pulled out the chair across from Rose. He sat down, the silence between them now palpable. After a moment, Jake cleared his throat as he set the thin candy in front of Rose's hands. She hadn't yet glanced at him.

"How are you?" he asked.

"I'm in jail, Jake," Rose said.

"I'm aware."

"How's the guard?" Rose asked.

"Hope said he's going to live. Just a broken nose. It will heal… That was quite a swing."

Rose looked up. "I didn't mean to hurt him."

"I think he knows that. Hope talked to him. I doubt the incident will go further."

"Can you get me out, then?"

"I'm afraid not, kiddo."

"Hope won't tell them to let me go?"

"She can't. You punched a sheriff's deputy in the nose in the courtroom, and in front of the judge. The prosecuting attorney is an eyewitness. Hope may talk Krista out of pressing further charges, but she will not talk her out of reversing her motion to detain you here during the trial."

"I don't like it in here," Rose said.

"It's a jail. You're not supposed to like it."

"Did I upset you, Jake?"

"I wouldn't say upset, Rose. But you put us in a bit of a bind."

"You said they weren't pressing charges."

"For now. But it's a big part of our defense that you're not capable of violence, especially not rage-filled violence like shooting your father. And…"

"I gave them a show, didn't I?"

"Yep. You gave them a show."

"Cassie said it was a good thing that the jury was gone before I punched the deputy."

"Who's Cassie?"

"My cellmate."

"Great. Now we've got a jailhouse lawyer in the mix, too." Jake rubbed his palm across his face. "What did you tell her? They can use anything you say to her as testimony in the trial."

"I didn't tell her anything. She knew who I was, though."

"How did she know?"

"Saw me in the news. She said my case is all the gossip in the jail. Besides, the news that I broke a deputy's nose made the rounds."

"Jailhouse celebrity, huh?" Jake quipped.

"It's not funny."

"No, it's not. It's serious, Rose. If they convict you, then you won't be in this jail. They'll sentence you to ten years or more and ship you off to a Texas state prison in Iowa City or down in Huntsville. The inmates there will eat you alive."

"Why are you scaring me? You're supposed to be my lawyer. Supposed to be helping me."

"I *am* helping you. Now that you are in here until we get a verdict, follow the rules. You cannot step out of line one smidge. You can't strike a guard in there. If you do, they can try you for a different case, even if we get you off. Be very careful. No rash decisions."

"I don't—"

"What? Take joyrides? Punch deputies?"

"I'm just stressed, you know. I lost my temper."

"We're all stressed, Rose. I'm just telling you to mind your manners. That's all." Jake paused for a moment. Rose reached out and unwrapped the chocolate, nibbling at one end.

"How's Margie?"

"Blaming herself. She keeps thinking you punching that deputy is her fault."

Rose shifted in her seat. "It's not."

"She knows that, but she's Margie. She cares, so she frets. Margie will be better once she gets to hug you in court today."

"About that. How does it work? Do I get my clothes back from the jail?" Rose took another bite of the candy.

"They'll bring you to the court in your prison fatigues. You'll change into a dress in a holding cell. Margie has been picking out the perfect outfit for you."

"I didn't mean…"

"I know. Hopefully, this will be over in the next day or two. I think Krista will be done with her case today. Then we'll decide if we call any witnesses."

"Put me on the stand, Jake. I can tell them what happened."

"What if they don't believe you?"

Rose slammed her hands palms down on the table. "They have to believe me."

"Do they? What if you go up there, and Krista tears you to shreds on cross-examination, turns you into a sniveling shell on the stand? Or, worse, makes you look like a liar?"

"I'm not a liar," Rose said.

"What if she asks if you've ever struck a peace officer?"

"I didn't—"

"You did, though. I don't know that we can risk it, Rose.

Krista still must prove each element of the crime beyond a reasonable doubt. What if we think she failed? Do we want to give her a lifeline, put you on the stand, and offer her enough rope to hang you?"

"I can do it, Jake. Believe me. I can tell them. Tell them about the men that came for Marcus. *They* killed him, not me. I can make them understand."

"We have time to decide. For today, I need you to be calm." Jake took a piece of paper from his briefcase and set it in front of Rose. "You need to memorize that while you finish your candy bar."

"What is it?"

"The apology you are going to give to Judge Dubose and Krista for causing a scene yesterday."

"Do I have to?"

"Yes, and you're going to sell it. So practice while you're waiting to be transported. Krista can break any handshake deal with Hope, so put some feeling into it." Jake paused and gave his client a steady look. "I have to ask you one more question."

"Shoot."

"Are you sure Marcus never touched you in any inappropriate way?"

Anger flashed across Rose's face. "I can't believe you would—"

"Just answer me, Rose. I must know. Did he?"

Rose tightened her fists, her emerald eyes fierce. "Never."

CHAPTER FORTY-FOUR

TUESDAY MORNING, Judge Dubose banged his gavel, and the murmurs in the court died down.

"Counsel, I trust we can move this along. And you…" He turned his glare on Rose. "You, little lady, are going to act with decorum in my court. Do you understand?"

"Yes, Your Honor. I'd like to apologize—"

The judge pursed his lips. "I don't need your apology. You need you to behave. Pull another stunt like that, and I'll try you in absentia. I'll tell the jury why you're not in the courtroom, too. Do I make myself clear?"

"Yes, sir," Rose answered.

"Very well. Now, let's move this trial along. Counsel, control your witnesses and don't bore the jury with repetition. As best I can tell, we can finish this week. And I intend to see that happens. Ms. Robb, get your next witness ready. Bailiff, bring in the jury."

The jury shuffled in, keeping their gaze on the floor. Krista called Sam Timber, a technician from the Hawk County crime lab. Jake looked around for Hitch. He was nowhere to be found.

Come on, Hitch. I need to know if that note was correct.

To steady his mind, Jake took notes as Krista made quick work of Timber's credentials and sped to the meat of his testimony.

"Mr. Timber, were you the first crime-lab technician to arrive on the scene at the Tucker home?"

"That is correct. My colleague, Daniel Dietz, and I arrived after we had been called by the sheriff."

"You and Mr. Dietz gathered the evidence from the site?"

"Correct. We spent the better part of the afternoon photographing the crime scene and collecting potential evidence."

"And you later examined the evidence you collected?"

"Yes. We, and others, analyzed the items and reviewed the photographs. We isolated and identified fingerprints, fibers and hairs, and, where possible, we collected and typed human blood."

"You cataloged such items?"

"We did."

"Mr. Timber, please tell the jury what you found."

"Well, let's start with fingerprints. We lifted several prints from inside the home. We found some on the door handle and frame leading to the victim's bedroom."

"Did any prints match the deceased?"

"Yes, many matched Mr. Tucker."

"How about the defendant, Rose Tucker?"

"Yes, we found her fingerprints."

"Were there prints from someone else in the bedroom?"

"None that we found."

"Throughout the home?"

"Nothing. The universe of fingerprints we identified remained limited to the victim and the defendant."

"Were you able to discern anything based on where you found Ms. Tucker's fingerprints?"

"Most of the locations seemed innocuous. Since she lived at

the residence, we expected to see her prints in myriad locations. Some locations, however, were problematic."

"How so?"

"We identified the defendant's fingerprints at the murder scene in the bedroom. The doorknob and doorframe of the bedroom had Ms. Tucker's prints. Several of those prints were made with the victim's blood. We also found her prints on the bourbon bottle by the side of the bed."

The squeaking hinges on the courtroom door caught everyone's attention as Hitch slid through the opening.

"Mr. Miller, glad you could join us," the judge quipped. "By all means, have a seat at counsel table."

Hitch flushed, and he moved with purpose, taking a seat next to Jake.

"Did it check out?" Jake whispered.

"Yes," Hitch responded. "We are right."

Jake nodded.

"Mr. Timber," Krista continued, "before Mr. Miller interrupted us, you were describing the fingerprint evidence collected at the scene. Did you find other print evidence?"

"Apart from the prints on the bottle and in the room, we obtained fingerprints on a handgun found at the scene."

"The murder weapon?"

"Yes, we found Ms. Tucker's prints on the slide, trigger guard, and trigger of the subject weapon. We also identified a partial palm print from the grip."

"Had someone fired the gun?"

"Our examination confirmed that someone had recently discharged the weapon."

"At any point, did anyone test Ms. Tucker for gunpowder residue?"

"Yes. That sample proved positive."

"Did you identify other forensic evidence at the scene?"

"We did. We tested the liquor in the bottle. The sample of bourbon came back positive for Rohypnol."

"The date-rape drug?"

"Yes. The clinical name is flunitrazepam. Most people know it as 'roofies.' The FDA has not approved it for medical use in this country, and it is most commonly encountered in sexual assaults."

"What are the effects of *roofies*?"

"It's a powerful sedative, some seven to ten times stronger than valium. It soon disables any person who ingests it. Victims also report pronounced amnesia."

"Is it safe to conclude that this drug had incapacitated Mr. Tucker when the defendant killed him?"

"Yes."

"Mr. Timber, did you find any evidence near the body?"

"We inventoried the contents of the room. We discovered a pair of panties and a bra tucked into the bedsheets."

"Did you identify to whom the garments belonged?"

"We inventoried identical underwear in Ms. Tucker's dresser."

"Thank you, Mr. Timber. No further questions."

Judge Dubose turned to Jake. "Mr. Fox?"

Jake stood and approached the lectern.

"Mr. Timber, you were not present when Mr. Tucker died, correct?"

"Correct. The sheriff called us in after she found the body the next morning."

"You don't know who fired the gun?"

"That is true."

"During your efforts, did you find any footprints or tire tracks in the home's driveway?"

"No."

"Not a single print?"

"It rained the night before the sheriff found the body. As a result, any prints or tracks were likely washed away."

"Could others have been on the property, as Rose claimed?"

"The rain made it impossible to confirm or disprove Ms. Tucker's claim. No footprint or tire track evidence existed."

"In fact, Mr. Timber, you cannot rule out Rose's version of events."

"We found no evidence to support it."

"That wasn't the question, Mr. Timber. You cannot rule it out, correct?"

"Well… no."

Jake let the answer hang in the courtroom before grabbing a sheet of paper from the defense counsel's table.

"Your Honor, may I approach the witness?"

"You may."

"Mr. Timber, I'm showing you what I have marked for identification as exhibit thirty-three. Do you recognize that document?"

"Yes. The photograph I took is of hair strands found at the scene."

"And does that picture depict what you observed at the time?"

"It does."

"The defense moves to admit exhibit thirty-three into the record."

"Any objections, Ms. Robb?"

"No, Your Honor."

"Then it is admitted."

"Now, Mr. Timber, what color are the strands of hair in that photograph?"

"They appear to be a very light auburn or red."

"Did you run a DNA test on these hairs?"

"We did not."

"Why?"

"I believed it to be unnecessary."

"But you collected them."

"We collect all fiber and hair evidence. But, as anyone can see, Sheriff Stone has long red hair. It's rare, but not impossible, for a few strands of her hair to be found at a crime scene."

"Did you get a hair sample from Sheriff Stone to compare with the ones found at the scene?"

"No."

"This case didn't warrant one?"

"I know all the deputies and technicians who worked the scene. None of them have similar hair. Mr. Tucker and Ms. Tucker do not have red hair. In fact, no one involved in the case has red hair but the sheriff. We did not need to spend resources to exclude her when, based on what we knew about the scene and what occurred, a more likely answer presented itself."

"But you are aware, are you not, that in her statement to the sheriff, Rose described her father, Marcus Tucker, being assaulted by men led by *a woman with long red hair*."

"As I testified earlier, we could not corroborate Ms. Tucker's story of other assailants."

"You didn't compare these hairs to the sheriff?"

"We did not."

"You testified that Ms. Tucker tested positive for gunpowder residue, correct?"

"Yes."

"If Ms. Tucker had fired a gun the day before the murder, it's possible that could lead to a positive gunpowder result, right?"

"The connection would be weaker, but it's still possible she would return a positive test if she had fired a gun the day before."

"Your office identified Ms. Tucker's fingerprints on the handgun and in the room?"

"I testified we did."

"If Ms. Tucker handled the gun after discovering her father, that would explain her fingerprints."

"If that occurred, yes."

"If she touched her father in shock or grief, that could account for the blood and print evidence on the doorknob and door."

"It's possible. I believe it's unlikely, but it's possible."

Jake picked up a photo from the table and handed it to Mr. Timber.

"Do you recognize that exhibit?"

"It is a photograph from the scene of female underwear we found in the bedding of Mr. Tucker's room."

"And you said it matched a set in Ms. Tucker's dresser drawers."

"We found a few sets that are identical."

"Mr. Timber, did you perform any DNA analysis on these articles of clothing?"

"We tried, but couldn't."

"Why? Wouldn't DNA evidence further prove Ms. Robb's theory that Marcus was molesting Rose?"

"It would prove her DNA was on the fabric."

"Did you forget to do the test?"

"No. Our attempt to gather a sample failed."

"Can you tell the jury why?"

"I can render an opinion, but I cannot be certain within a reasonable degree of scientific certainty."

"What is that opinion?"

"Because someone had freshly laundered the garments."

"Does that mean it's possible that Ms. Tucker had not been wearing them before they ended up in that bed?"

"It's a strong possibility."

"No further questions."

CHAPTER FORTY-FIVE

JUDGE DUBOSE RECESSED thirty minutes for lunch but then sprinted back to the bench. "Ms. Robb, before we bring the jury back in, tell me how many more witnesses you have."

"Your Honor, the State will call Theodore Hunter as the last witness in our case in chief."

"And you, Mr. Fox? How many witnesses?"

"I want to reserve my right to call additional witnesses, Your Honor. I believe I'll be calling two."

"Ms. Robb?"

"Depending on that testimony, I may have only one rebuttal witness, if any."

"Very well, then. It looks like we should finish the evidence tomorrow morning. I expect we can close in the afternoon, and the jury will have the case before they go home tomorrow. With a little luck, we'll have a verdict before midday Friday."

Jake winced at the judge's eagerness for fast justice.

"Bailiff, bring in the jury, and let's get on with it."

The jury shuffled in and settled in their seats. Jake tried to discern any clues from their expressions. But they remained stoic. It appeared the judge's admonitions to remain neutral until he told them to deliberate had taken firm root. Jake hoped that meant they had no preconceived notions. Or perhaps they were good at hiding them. The judge exchanged pleasantries with the jury and informed them he hoped to have the case to them by the end of the next day, locking Jake into a short defense. He didn't want to provoke the jury's ire if a delay kept them from the freedom of their daily lives for longer than anticipated.

"Ms. Robb, with the jury now seated, call your next witness."

"The State calls Theodore Hunter."

"Come forward and be sworn."

Mr. Hunter walked to the front of the courtroom, took his oath, and mounted the witness stand. Krista covered Mr. Hunter's name and background and then jumped into the core of his testimony.

"Mr. Hunter, where do you work? "

"I own the GasMart over on Sullivan Drive, near where it passes by the dam on the western tip of the lake."

"As the owner, are you on the premises often?"

"It's a small business, and I'm the small business owner. So I'm there every day. I have a couple of employees who work occasionally, but you'll always find me behind the register."

"I'd like to take you back to this past spring. Did you have occasion to observe the decedent, Marcus Tucker, and his daughter, Rose Tucker, the defendant in this case?"

"The Tucker place is near my store. They would come in now and again. Mostly to grab a soda or a loaf of bread. Marcus filled up his truck at my place pretty regular."

"So you could identify them."

"I knew who they were, and we were all friendly."

"I want to focus on one evening in particular. At some point, did you overhear Marcus arguing with Ms. Tucker?"

"I did."

"Describe that argument for the jury."

"Marcus had parked at the pumps to fill up his truck. Rose came into the store. I could tell something was amiss."

"What do you mean?"

"Well, when Miss Rose came into the store, she didn't say her normal 'hello' or other chitchat. She walked straight back. She yanked a few items off the shelves. The whole time, she mumbled to herself as if she was keeping on with a conversation. You know, like when you're arguing with someone and you just keep on a fighting with them when they ain't there. It's like they get in and rattle around your head."

The jury smiled.

"Did you hear what she said?"

"Not the words. But the tone. She was angry, or at the least upset."

"Did you figure out what had Ms. Tucker agitated?"

"Not right away."

"But later?"

"When Marcus finished filling up, he came inside. He stepped up to the register, and at that same time, Ms. Rose joined him. She was buying sandwich makings. You know, bread, mayonnaise, some sliced deli meat. Maybe she had a jar of pickled jalapeños. They joined up there at the register so Marcus could pay. It was like I wasn't even there. They started bickering again."

"Did you hear what the argument was about?"

"It took little effort. Marcus was none too pleased about a young man named Tommy that Rose was seeing."

"Rose wanted to see the boy, but Marcus disapproved?"

"More or less. But Marcus seemed agitated up about it, as if he was worried about Rose. I mean, I have daughters. I had to wait up late at night as they started dating. It's rough on a father, not being right there to protect his babies."

"So he was angry?"

"I wouldn't say angry. More frustrated. I gathered he wanted Rose to stay away from this Tommy. She said she was an adult and would do what she wanted. Or something to that effect."

"Was the argument over before they left your store?"

"No… it spilled out into the parking lot once they'd paid and moved on. Once they were outside, Miss Rose raised her voice. I could tell she was getting more and more upset with Marcus. But he wasn't budging."

"Did something happen after that?"

"Outside the door, Miss Rose tried to walk away from Marcus as he talked to her. He didn't take too kindly to that."

"How so?"

"When she turned away from him, he grabbed her by the elbow to turn her back around."

"How did the defendant react?"

"She was angry and took a swing at him."

"She attacked Mr. Tucker."

"Well, it wasn't much of an attack. Marcus was solid muscle from working his whole life, welding pipe and such. He outweighed her by quite a bit. Plus, Miss Rose is a bit scrawny." Theo turned and looked at Rose at the defense table. "Sorry, Miss Rose, you just ain't that big." A couple of jurors chuckled.

"Mr. Hunter, did Ms. Tucker's punch connect with the deceased?"

"Yeah, she nicked him, but it wasn't much of a bother to Marcus. He didn't respond. I could tell it didn't sting him. He shrugged it off."

"How did Ms. Tucker respond to her father shrugging off her attack?"

"It made her mad. Under the canopy lights, I could see her face turn deep red."

"Did she say anything?"

"She did. She yelled it out."

"And what words did she say?"

"She told Marcus she'd be better off without him."

Krista let that statement hang in the air and shuffled through her legal pad as if checking her notes. After sufficient time, she said, "No further questions."

"Mr. Fox, do you have questions for Mr. Hunter?"

"Only a few," Jake said, moving to the lectern. "Mr. Hunter, were you at the Tucker place the night that Marcus was killed?"

"No, sir. I was not."

"So you cannot say whether Rose did anything to harm Marcus?"

"I wasn't there when Marcus died."

"At the time you overheard this statement by Rose in your parking lot, did you fear for Marcus's safety?"

"I did not. I chalked it up to a teenager blowing off steam. That's what it seemed like to me."

"Thank you, Mr. Hunter," Jake said.

"Ms. Robb?"

"Nothing further."

"Mr. Hunter, you are excused."

Theo stood and left the room.

"Ms. Robb, call your next witness."

"Your Honor, the prosecution has no additional witnesses at this time. We rest our case, reserving the right to rebuttal."

"Very well. Mr. Fox, I assume you have some motions you would like to make."

"I do, Your Honor."

Judge Dubose turned to the jury. "Ladies and gentlemen, we are going to need a bit of time to take care of some lawyer things. But please return first thing in the morning. Remember: do not talk to anyone about the case, and do not read any news or observe any media related to the case, including on the Internet and social media. We'll see you back at nine tomorrow morning."

CHAPTER FORTY-SIX

HOPE'S HEAD hurt with the constant noise and flashing lights from the slot machines. The Silver Lake Casino was a monstrosity set on the shores of Lake Moore in Oklahoma, just across the Texas state line. The cocktail waitress delivered a soda water with lime, and Hope placed a few bills on her tray as a tip. All around, patrons either stared glassy-eyed into their machines or paced the aisles, as if trying to divine which game was due for a payout. The buzzers and bells added to the frenetic atmosphere. A more than slightly drunk young woman next to her slapped the buttons in a frenzy, as if she could not lose her money fast enough. Hope played at a leisurely pace, more interested in scouting the crowd than spinning the digital wheels on the screen in front of her. This was not Hope's kind of place. She preferred a cup of herbal tea and a good book in her chair at home.

Beth hasn't been in a comfortable place for a while… What are you doing here, Hope?

Trying to push away her concern for Grace, Hope let out a sigh. Despite all her efforts, she had turned up no further leads into Beth's disappearance. The last true clue had been the matchbook note from the restroom at the Quickie Mart. Everything after that had led to a dead end. She'd heard nothing back from the tribal police, and no information had come from the Oklahoma State Bureau of Investigation.

Come on, baby girl, don't disappear. I'm coming for you.

Even with crowds all around her, Hope felt exposed. Nobody knew she was here. It was just a hunch, after all. Would Beth's abductors bring her back here?

She needed more information before she could justify devoting significant department resources to hunting down this lead. But she couldn't shake Beth from her thoughts, no matter how uneasy she felt. The laughing smile in a photo the judge had given to Hope had etched itself into her memory. It seemed to mock her inability to find Beth. Sleep now often eluded her, and the girl's face was an unrelenting shadow in her mind.

Hope had picked a location near the entrance to the casino, where all the gamblers funneled past security. In between lazy looks at her slot machine to ensure she hit the correct buttons, she kept an eye on who was coming and going, hoping to see any man with a braided beard. An hour passed. The waitress refilled her drink. Masses of people entered and exited through the main doors. Nothing.

"To what do we owe the pleasure?" A voice behind her asked.

Hope turned to see a man slightly older than her. His gray goatee accentuated a chiseled jaw, and his physique and posture gave him away as either ex-military or a cop.

"Excuse me?" Hope asked, a pulse of vulnerability flashing through her. Her heartbeat quickened, and sweat formed on her chest.

Nobody knows I'm here.

"The sheriff of Hawk County, up here gambling away her paycheck."

"And you are?"

"Sorry, sheriff," the man said. "I'm Special Agent Todd

Strickland. You and I spoke on the phone about your missing girl." He stuck out a hand.

Hope gave it a shake as a wave of relief washed through her.

"Agent Strickland. Good to meet you in person."

"Most folks call me Todd."

"Thanks, Agent Strickland."

"You couldn't stay away, huh?" he asked.

"I thought I would come up and check it out for myself. But I have to tell you, I'm not much of the casino type."

"Yeah? What type are you?" Strickland asked.

"I tend to be a bit of a homebody." Hope looked past him at the casino patrons still shuffling in and out of the building.

"Well then, there must be some irresistible pull to southern Oklahoma to get you out and into a casino. Maybe you just couldn't stay away." Strickland finished with a smile as he fiddled with the toothpick in the corner of his mouth.

Hope pushed a little further back in her chair. "You'd be surprised at my ability to resist."

Strickland pointed at the empty chair next to Hope. "Mind if I sit?"

"Go ahead."

He plopped down in the chair, his hands on his knees. He felt too close for comfort to Hope. "You have any further leads on your girl?"

"Nothing. The investigation has hit a dead end. Did you ever come out and look around this place?"

"I've been out here a few times. I have yet to see any of the Vikings out here. It's almost like they've disappeared, which is unusual. They're brazen. Don't much care about law enforcement. Maybe they've moved on."

"I doubt it," Hope said. "Something tells me that if they've been making money trafficking girls through the Silver Lake, they are going to keep at it."

"I agree, I just haven't seen any activity from them as of

late. Doesn't mean they aren't here. Maybe they're running the girls by proxy."

"How so?"

"The Vikings membership includes dozens of old ladies—club wives and girlfriends. Best as I can figure out, they're part of the operation. It's easier to get girls in and out of situations if they're being led around by women rather than men."

"That makes sense. It also makes it near impossible to spot them."

"They're good, I'll give them that." Strickland rubbed his palm across his bald head and stood again, blocking Hope's view of the doors. His cheesy smile was back on. "Let me show you the best steakhouse in town. What do you say?"

"Don't take this the wrong way, but I think I'll stay here and watch for a while longer." Hope picked up her glass. "I have several more club sodas to drink."

"You sure? It's just down the street."

"I'm—" Hope swallowed her voice as she spotted a man over Strickland's shoulder. Adrenaline coursed through her veins. "Strickland, behind you… headed for the door."

Strickland looked straight ahead as if waiting for Hope to describe the scene.

"Black beard. Double braids."

"Anyone with him?"

"A girl with shoulder-length black hair. Her back is to me. They're making their way to the parking lot."

Strickland turned, and Hope stood from her chair. The man in her sights was tall and muscular. He wore his ball cap low, but the double braids in his beard were unmistakable. From here, she could see the large black Celtic crosses on his forearms.

A Viking.

The thug yanked along a petite girl with milk-white skin in a little black dress and stiletto heels, her black hair jostling.

Beth.

Hope moved toward them, Strickland on her hip. As they stepped forward, the man looked at Hope, and recognition flooded through his expression. He said something to the woman and began pulling her toward the exit.

They're on the run.

Hope pushed past Strickland and ran after the Viking and the girl. She busted through the front door, searching for them in the parking lot. The mass of people coming and going created the perfect cover. They were like raindrops falling into a river. She heard footsteps behind her. Hope looked over her shoulder to see Strickland coming to a stop behind her.

"Which way did they go?"

Hope surveyed the area, looking for anybody moving faster than the surrounding patrons.

"There!" Hope said, pointing at a man navigating the maze of parked cars at a run, tugging the girl behind him. Hope and Strickland took off at a sprint. The flood of adrenaline and stress stirred up a metallic taste in her mouth.

I'm coming, Beth.

Hope dug in and increased her speed, sucking in exhaust from all the cars shuffling around the parking lot. The Viking continued in a straight line ahead of her, running toward the shadows. But Hope began to close the distance. The girl lost her shoes as her captor yanked her along behind him.

Forty yards.

Strickland followed along a parallel path, as if seeking to cut off their ability to escape to the right. The Viking tugged at the girl, who struggled to run in bare feet.

Thirty yards.

A rearview mirror on a parked car caught in the girl's dress, causing her to pitch forward and crash to the asphalt. The Viking cursed and stopped, trying to untangle the girl and her tattered dress as Hope and Strickland bore down on him. As they closed the gap, Hope recognized a mix of fear and anger on his face. In a split second, he must have decided to save his own skin. The Viking pushed off of the car and sprinted away. Unencumbered by the girl, he sped into the darkness.

"Take care of the her!" Strickland said. "I'll go after him."

Hope slammed to a stop, almost tripping over the girl lying face down on her stomach on the asphalt. The girl sobbed as she tried to scramble away from Hope.

"Get away from me! They'll beat me. Stay away!"

Hope held up her hands. "It's okay, you're okay. I'm not going to hurt you. I've been looking for you."

"No one is looking for me!" The victim buried her face in her hands and sobbed.

"I am. I'm a sheriff. I'm looking for you, baby girl. It's over."

Beth, it's okay. You can go home now.

Anguish flooded Hope at the animalistic wails coming from the victim. Hope took off her leather jacket, knelt, and gingerly draped it across the victim's nearly naked body. "It's okay, Beth, I'm here. We found you."

The girl sobbed. "Who… who is Beth?"

Hope pushed the hair away from the victim's face.

Oh, man….

Hope wrapped the unknown girl in her embrace and let her sob.

Beth… Where are you?

CHAPTER FORTY-SEVEN

THE LOCK to her basement cell turned, rousing Beth from a shallow sleep. Since they had taken her, true rest had eluded Beth, and each day left her more exhausted. The door swung open. Zach stood in the doorway, and the soft light of a single bulb hanging behind him spilled into the room. He had transported her back from the trailer to the cellar in this home. The musty room was chilly and damp.

"Get up. It's time," Zach said, his smirk showing off his eyeteeth.

Beth's heart pounded, and she scrambled backward on the mattress on the floor until her head slammed against the cellar wall.

"Where are you trying to go now?" Zach moved toward her and reached out. "Don't make me come get you. That would be bad. I might have to teach you another lesson."

Bile rose in the back of Beth's throat. Any lesson from Zach meant a beating. His favorite was a strip of garden hose used on the bottoms of her bare feet. With each stroke, the sting rocketed up Beth's legs and slammed into her hips. He left red marks that faded where no one would look.

His boss said not to bruise me. At least he hasn't raped me… Why?

"Come!" He thrust his hand toward her. Beth scooted toward him. "Good girl. Come."

Beth grabbed his large, callused hands and stood. Even though she was wearing sweatpants and a hoodie, the chill in the room made her teeth chatter. Zach led her from the underground cell to the bottom of a flight of stairs. She glanced down a long hallway with several doors on either side.

How many of us are there?

Zach pulled her by the wrist.

"Go," he said, pushing her up the stairs ahead of him.

"You're pushing me," she said as she stumbled.

"I'll push you even harder."

Rose struggled to get her legs under her and keep her balance while ascending the stairs. As she climbed, warm air cascaded across her face. Sunlight danced beyond the cellar door. Rose blinked against the bright light, struggling to adjust. Through the door, she recognized the kitchen from her prior move.

"You're looking good," a voice said.

Beth turned to the dining room table she knew was to her right. The redhead sat in a chair, her elbows resting on her knees. Assessing Beth's appearance, she closed the gap between them swiftly.

"You want me to get her ready, Lilith?" Zach asked.

They don't care that I know their names!

"No. I'll take it from here."

The redhead reached and held Beth's hand.

"No need to fight me, kitten. I'm here to help."

She knew it was a lie, but the fatigue of captivity distorted Beth's senses, making her receptive to the idea of help and hope. Beth followed Lilith to a bedroom down the hall. Bright lights flooded the space from a large vanity. A table was filled with cosmetics and hair styling equipment. Lilith pulled her inside and pointed to the ensuite bathroom.

"Come on, I already drew a bath for you." Lilith pulled Beth through the door, had her step on a scale, and then stood next to the tub. While looking Beth in the eyes, Lilith pulled the hoodie over Beth's head and removed her bottoms. "Hop in," she said as she pointed toward the water.

Beth stepped into the bath, sucking in a breath at the initial sting of the hot water.

This is all my fault. Maybe I deserve it.

After a moment, her skin acclimated, and she lowered herself into the water. The Celtic cross that Ted had tattooed on her hip still ached. She rubbed her thumb over the dark ink knitted into her pale skin. It *was* beautiful, maybe something she would have picked herself under different circumstances. Now? Nausea washed over her, and hope faded like the last dancing flames of a fire before they disappeared.

Lilith knelt next to the tub and grabbed a sponge. With slow, gentle circles, she cleaned Beth as if polishing a statue for display. The heady scent of lavender filled the room. Once she finished with Beth's body, Lilith picked up a red plastic cup and poured water over her head, careful to keep it from running into Beth's eyes. Over the next few minutes, Lilith massaged shampoo and then conditioner into Beth's hair, rinsing in between. With each gentle cupful of warm water cascading over her scalp, Beth allowed a small dribble of hope into her heart.

She said she was here to help me.

"Stand up," Lilith said with a soft command. "Let's get you toweled off."

Beth stood, and Lilith dried Beth's tired body before wrapping it in a robe. Then she held out her hand and presented Beth with a small white pill.

"Take this."

"What is it? I don't wany more drugs."

"It'll take the edge off." Lilith pushed the pill between Beth's lips and gave her a swig of water to chase it down. Beth closed her eyes and swallowed. She hoped the drugs would take her far away from here. She had spent days in that strung-out calm and had come to welcome the release.

Please… I need it.

"There we go." Lilith broke Beth's reverie and set the cup down. "This way."

Lilith led Beth to the chair in front of the mirror and gestured for her to sit. Beth noticed fatigue lines on the face in her reflection. Lilith blew Beth's black hair dry and then straightened it with an iron. She then picked up a small bottle of moisturizer and rubbed a dollop or two onto Beth's cheeks… then foundation, concealer, powder. Layer after layer, Lilith painted Beth's face like a canvas, until the woman sitting in the mirror looked nothing like the girl Beth remembered. Harsh shadows on her cheeks, dark eyeliner, and thick black eyelashes. Bright-red, glossy lips.

I look like a stripper.

A tear leaked from the corner of Beth's eye. Lilith caught it with a tissue.

"Now, now, kitten. Don't cry. You'll muss up my handiwork. We all have a role to play."

Once Lilith finished painting Beth's face, she had Beth stand up and remove the robe. From the closet Lilith pulled an outfit. If you could call it that. It featured no substantial piece of fabric other than a few leather straps and metal rings to accentuate parts of Beth's body. Lilith strapped it on Beth as if she were haltering a prize cow for the state fair. After that, Lilith slipped a pair of black stiletto heels onto Beth's feet.

How can I walk in these?

Lilith stepped back, admiring her work.

"You look stunning, kitten. You're going to do very well for us."

Lilith grabbed her by the wrist and elbow, helping her find her footing in the heels.

"This way."

Lilith led her down the hallway. Beth's heartbeat thrummed in her ears, washing out all the surrounding sounds with its vicious ringing. The drugs coursed through her body, giving her an edge of euphoric numbness. They stepped into the new room, and Beth's eyes widened.

No bed. What is going on? Aren't they going to rape me?

Adrenaline flushed through Beth. Her body trembled as Lilith walked her to a chair and pointed for her to sit. She wanted to run, but she could see Zach's silhouette blocking the door, so she complied. Glaring lights on one side hid half the room, but she could see the outline of computer monitors and hear the hum of the machines. Quick breaths overwhelmed her.

"Relax," Lilith said as she knelt. She buckled leather straps to each of Beth's ankles, securing them to the chair legs, then strapped her wrists to the wooden arms. Lilith raised a hand that held a gag in front of Beth.

"Open up, kitten."

Beth opened her mouth, and Lilith slipped the bitter red rubber ball between her lips and buckled the leather strap behind her head, careful not to muss her hair. Lilith stood, as if admiring a painting. Stepping back, she checked her watch, picked up a microphone, and nodded at the figure behind the glare. A small green light turned on.

A camera!

"Ladies and gentlemen," Lilith said, "lot number 00376. One hundred and seven pounds. White with creamy pale skin. Texas born and bred. Not yet sixteen. Beautiful smile and curves you will all want to caress. She'll make a perfect white slave—a nice, ripe virgin… Vivian. The bidding starts at fifty thousand dollars, plus shipping."

CHAPTER FORTY-EIGHT

AFTER THEO HUNTER'S testimony the day before, Jake had moved for a directed verdict, arguing that Krista had failed to present sufficient evidence for the case to go to the jury. As expected, Judge Dubose denied it.

Wednesday morning, after the jury took their seats, the judge cleared his throat. "Mr. Fox, call your first witness."

"Yes, Your Honor. The defense calls Josiah Reed."

The deputy at the back opened the doors, and Josiah entered.

"Mr. Reed? Join me up here so I can swear you in for testimony."

Josiah walked with a deliberate pace through the hushed courtroom, the only sound the clopping from the heels on his boots. He twirled his cowboy hat in his hands. Western stitching adorned his black suit. He was every bit a ranch hand. Josiah took the oath and settled behind the microphone at the witness stand. Jake stepped forward to the lectern.

"Your Honor," Krista started. "We object to this witness. Mr. Fox disclosed him on the eve of trial, and the prosecution has had limited access to him to prepare."

"Mr. Fox?"

"Judge, Mr. Reed was working out of town and only recently came forward when he returned. I disclosed him as soon as I learned of his testimony. Ms. Robb will have her chance to cross-examine him, and what he has to say is critical to Ms. Tucker's defense."

"Mr. Reed, is it true you were out of town?"

"Yes, sir. I just returned a few days ago."

"I'll allow the testimony, Ms. Robb. But, Mr. Fox, lay a foundation for why you designated Mr. Reed late. If you don't, I'll strike this witness from the record."

"Yes, Your Honor. Josiah, introduce yourself to the jury, please."

"My name is Josiah Reed. I've lived in Haven my entire life."

"How are you employed?"

"I run my own business. Mostly, I work for the ranchers in the more rural parts of the county. I haul horses or livestock for a living. Past couple of years, I've been on the road a lot, sometimes helping Judge Maddix take her Arabians to horse shows or hauling horses to and from their winter pastures. She can really ride."

Two of the female jurors smiled.

"Do you know why you're here?"

"It relates to the night someone killed Marcus Tucker."

"Tell the jury what you observed that night as you broke down your tack."

"I was out at the Applegate place."

"Is that across the road from the Tuckers' home?"

"Yes, sir."

"Mr. Applegate hired me to fetch a load of cutting horses from outside Houston. Once I had them settled, I was tending to my gear when I heard yelling over at the Tucker place."

"What kind of yelling?"

"Mind you, I was a fair distance away, so I couldn't make out any words. But the tone was angry."

"What time was this?"

"Late. A wreck north of Houston caused a traffic jam that strung on for miles. So I didn't get to the Applegate ranch until after ten. I'd say it was around midnight."

"Could you see who was yelling?"

"Marcus's home is away from the road behind some trees. I couldn't see who was making a fuss."

"What did you see, if anything?"

"Something was lighting up the place. More than just the normal house lights. Could have been headlights."

"Objection. The witness cannot testify by guessing at what occurred."

"Sustained. Please do not speculate on the stand, Mr. Reed."

"What happened next?" Jake asked.

"Well, I got back to work. I was tired and hungry. I wanted to get home. When I finished, I hopped in my truck. Just as I turned the key in the ignition, several headlights worked their way down Marcus's driveway."

"Was it Marcus?"

"Nah, he drives that red pickup he's had for years. I got a weird feeling. Something just wasn't right, you know."

"Objection. Feelings aren't facts."

"Overruled."

Jake continued. "What did you see?"

"A black SUV arrived at the drive's end. Then it turned onto the state road. It took off real fast. I remember because the tires squealed as the truck sped up."

"Could you see who was driving?"

"I was too far away. Plus, the windows were tinted dark. I just remember thinking it was odd. It wasn't Marcus. And was an odd time of night for visitors. Men like Marcus tend to get up before sunrise. So I don't imagine they have much use for staying up late."

"Objection!" Krista rose from her seat. "Strike that last

statement from the record. Again, Mr. Reed should not be testifying to his guess about Mr. Tucker's bedtime habits."

"Sustained. The jury will disregard. Mr. Reed, if you could confine your comments to what you observed."

"Yes, Judge."

"Did you go to the sheriff?" Jake asked.

"I wasn't aware of any need to contact the sheriff. I took off for work on the east coast early the next morning. Had to deliver Arabians to Virginia for Judge Maddix, and then I helped with racehorse transport between Florida and New York. That job kept me out of Haven for a few months. I just got home. When I did, I saw news about Marcus and his trial."

"Thank you, Mr. Reed. I pass the witness."

Krista almost jumped at the lectern.

"Mr. Reed. You did not observe what happened inside the Tucker house that night, did you?"

"I did not. I was across the road, like I said."

"You do not know who killed Mr. Tucker, do you?"

"I know it wasn't Miss Rose."

"But you didn't see anyone or anything inside that home."

"That's correct. I just feel it in my bones. That little girl wouldn't kill her daddy."

"So this is another one of your famous guesses."

"It's my opinion."

"You have a lot of guesses. You guess about the headlights? Guess about Mr. Tucker's sleeping habits? Guess about whether Rose could be a killer?"

"I tell you what I know."

"You tell us only what you think you know. You don't have any facts."

"Objection. Argumentative."

"Withdrawn," said Krista curtly. "No further questions."

"Mr. Fox, I suggest you move on to your next witness."

"Redirect, Your Honor?"

"I said you were on shaky ground by designating this

witness late. Most of his testimony has been mere supposition. I shouldn't have allowed it. I suggest you quit while you're ahead before I strike everything Mr. Reed said on the stand. Call your next witness. Mr. Reed, you may step down."

As Josiah passed him on the way out of the courtroom, Jake stood and buttoned his suit coat. He noticed Krista scribble a note and pass it to her paralegal, who exited the court.

Jake said, "We call Margie Moore."

Margie stood from the bench behind Jake and Rose. She passed through flapping doors in the pony wall that separated the court from the pews. The bailiff issued the oath, and Margie took her seat. Jake began.

"Ms. Moore, please give the jury a brief summary of your background."

"Jake, how far back do you want to go?" I'm gettin' older by the day." Several of the older women on the jury nodded at Margie's quip.

"How about we do the short version?"

"I'll try. I was born right here in Haven. My father was the janitor, and my mother was a secretary. Except for the few years I spent at the Texas Woman's College pursuin' a degree in library sciences, I've lived here my whole life. After college, I returned to town and got a job at the school library."

"Family?"

"Father and mother passed many years back. They were my immediate family. I have no siblings. I never married, so I had no family of my own. The kids and the parents at the schools became my family."

"How long was your career?"

"I worked until last summer. I still help when they call. But I spend most of my time up at my house, enjoyin' my golden years, as they say."

"As librarian, did you know Rose?"

"I knew Marcus and Rose. I watched them both go through school and grow up."

"Did you observe the relationship between Rose and her father?"

"I did. Marcus adored Rose. The mother abandoned them when Rose was just a toddler. The wife came from somewhere down south in Texas. I knew little about her. In my mind, Marcus raised Rose."

"Do you have an example?"

"Not one simple story. I know how he was with Rose. Marcus worked hard welding pipelines in the area. That's early to rise. He knew I arrived to the school early for work, so he'd drop Rose off at the library so she could do homework. Typically, he finished work and came to pick her up. If he ran late, she'd come see me. I spent many hours with Rose, sometimes tutoring her on one subject or another if I could."

"Were they close?"

"Marcus doted on Rose. He tried as best he could to be at all of Rose's activities. She enjoyed having her father around. Some teenagers don't appreciate their parents taking an interest in them. Rose took pride in their small family, just the two of them."

"You are her guardian during these proceedings."

"That is correct. She is still a child…"

"Objection," Krista snapped. "Your Honor, the court has already ruled that Ms. Tucker is an adult for this proceeding. You should strike any reference to her being a child."

"She is a child," Margie snapped.

"Judge!"

The judge banged his gavel. "Quiet! Ms. Moore, that will be enough. Ms. Robb is right. Rose Tucker is being tried as an adult."

"But Judge Maddix appointed me her guardian because she's a child."

The judge threw up his hands. "Mr. Fox, control your witness, and I suggest you move along. Ms. Robb, if you have a problem with the prior testimony, take it up on cross-examination."

"Would you call Rose and Marcus's relationship close or contentious?"

"Very close."

"Did you ever see them fight?"

"To the contrary. They seemed to get along famously."

"Let's move forward to the morning after Marcus died. Did you encounter Rose that morning?"

"I did."

"Describe that for the jury."

"Well, that mornin' I was taking scraps to my compost pile when I noticed a pair of sneakers—those high-tops that the teenagers wear—poking out from behind my propane tank. I called out, and Rose appeared."

"How did she explain her presence behind the tank?"

"Objection. Hearsay."

"Mr. Fox."

"Your Honor, the State has already introduced several of Rose's statements she made to the sheriff. The statements Rose made closer to the incident support what she told the sheriff. Her demeanor, as observed by Ms. Moore, would help the jury understand Ms. Tucker's state of mind in the relevant time frame."

"Overruled."

"Margie, did Rose explain how she came to be at your home?"

"She was all a-titter when I first found her. She was shiverin' from being cold and soaked. The night before, a terrible storm blew through. She was crying. It took her a moment to calm down and share with me the details of the incident."

"What did Rose tell you had happened?"

"She explained several people had showed up at her house and had beaten up Marcus."

"Did she say if she recognized them?"

"She did not know who they were. But she said it was several men and one woman."

"What about the woman? Did Rose relay anything specific about her?"

"She was certain that the woman in charge had long red hair."

"Did she tell you what happened next?"

"She said that after those men beat Marcus, they grabbed him and took him inside the house.

"What did she do?"

"By then, the rain had become strong. She hid in their well house. Rose found Marcus the next mornin' and then lit out for my place. Marcus had told her to find me."

"Objection, Your Honor. Now she's testifying for a dead man."

"Dying declaration, Judge."

"Overruled."

"Margie, on the morning Rose showed up at your house, did anything in her behavior suggest that she was making up a story?"

"No, sir. She seemed terrified about what happened to Marcus. She was confused, exhausted, and upset."

"Thank you, Margie. No further questions."

"Ms. Robb," Judge Dubose started, "you may start your cross-examination of Ms. Moore."

"I have no questions, Your Honor."

Both Judge Dubose and Jake did a double take. With her objections, Jake expected Krista to grill Margie. But she was just walking away. He didn't like it at all. She had something up her sleeve.

"Mr. Fox, do you have another witness?"

"No, Your Honor, the defense rests with Ms. Moore's testimony."

CHAPTER FORTY-NINE

JUDGE DUBOSE INQUIRED if the jury wanted a break, but they requested to move along. Jake could tell they were getting antsy.

"Very well. Ms. Robb, have you decided on whether you're calling a rebuttal witness?"

"Your Honor, I will call one. The testimony will be short."

"Let's get on with it."

"The State calls Tommy Dickerson."

Jake felt Rose tense beside him. She grabbed his hand on the table, her nails digging into his palm. He leaned close to her ear and whispered, "Keep it together.... Do you know what he will say?"

"No idea," Rose whispered back.

Jake stood. "Your Honor, may we have a sidebar, please?

Judge Dubose called Jake and Krista to the bench outside the hearing of the jury.

"We object to this witness, Judge," Jake said. "The prosecution did not disclose him."

"Ms. Robb, any response?"

"Well, Your Honor, Mr. Dickerson is a rebuttal witness, and since the prosecution did not know whether his testimony would be relevant until the defense presented its case in chief, the rules do not require the prior disclosure of this witness."

Jake countered, "Your Honor, the rules require Ms. Robb to disclose rebuttal witnesses, even if they are unlikely to testify. This is trial by ambush."

"Ms. Robb, he has a point. Why wasn't Mr. Dickerson disclosed?"

"I apologize for the delayed notice, but he just came forward, after trial started. I'm asking for some leeway here. His testimony is also impeachment evidence, which does not have to be disclosed."

"Impeachment as to what?" the judge asked.

"For one, the testimony from Ms. Moore. She tried to tell the jury that Ms. Tucker is a 'child' to garner sympathy. Mr. Dickerson's testimony goes to the issue that Ms. Tucker is not a child but a calculating killer. You should allow me to counter Ms. Moore's outbursts."

"Your Honor," Jake said, "that is rebutting her testimony. It does not impeach her for bias or truth telling. You should keep him from the witness stand."

"It goes to several relevant points," Krista countered. "Ms. Moore is either blind to Ms. Tucker's true character, or a dupe."

The judge worried his palms across his face. "Ms. Robb, you are putting me in a tough spot. But I'm going to allow his testimony for now. Provided it's narrow. Mr. Fox, you'll cross as you see fit."

"We renew our objection."

"Fine… Protect your record however you wish. What evidence to admit is within my discretion, and I'm going to let him testify. Be careful, Ms. Robb. I expect you not to waste the jury's time."

"Yes, Judge, I understand," Krista answered.

Jake watched intently as Tommy took the oath and sat down.

"Sir, please introduce yourself to the jury."

"Tommy Dickerson. I'm named after my father, so my friends call me Junior."

"Very well, Junior. How do you know the defendant?"

"We dated."

"Were you dating at the time Marcus Tucker died?"

"Yes. We'd been dating for a few months."

"Was Mr. Tucker pleased with your relationship?"

"No. He was upset she was dating me. I don't think he liked her talking to boys at all."

"Any reason why?"

"I never much understood why. Best I could understand, he was just controlling. I mean, he always wanted to know where she was. He bossed her around."

"How did she react?"

"She didn't like it. Who would? While she was with me, she often complained about her father's constant nagging."

"Did she mention any plans to address it?"

"She did."

"And what did she say?"

Jake jumped to his feet to stop this train. "Objection. Hearsay. Plus, none of this testimony is proper rebuttal to anything Ms. Moore testified to."

"Ms. Robb?"

"Everything about this is proper rebuttal. Mr. Fox asked Ms. Moore about the defendant's state of mind at that time. Mr. Dickerson's testimony goes to rebut that point."

"I'll allow it," Judge Dubose ruled. "Mr. Fox, like I said, you'll have your shot to address anything you want on cross-examination."

"Junior, what did Ms. Tucker tell you about how she disliked her father butting into her dating life?"

"She said she couldn't stand it anymore. Rose told me about how he was always up in her business, telling her what to do. She didn't think he would let go of her. That he'd try to boss her around even if she went off to college or on her own."

"Did Ms. Tucker express any desire to take action instead of just complaining?"

Tommy looked right at Rose.

Krista broke it up. "Mr. Dickerson, please answer my question. Did she ever express plans other than complaining?"

"She started talking about how she'd be happy once Marcus was gone."

"Did she ever tell you a reason that she might want her father *gone*?"

A beat or two of silence passed, with Tommy frozen on the stand.

"Mr. Dickerson," Judge Dubose said, "please answer Ms. Robb's question."

"I'm sorry, Rosie, but I gotta tell them," Tommy said.

"Tell us what?" Krista asked.

"One night, Rose and I were down by the lake. She told me that Marcus had been touching her."

Several jurors gasped.

"Inappropriately?" Krista murmured.

"Very inappropriately. Ways a dad should never touch a daughter."

Rose fisted her hands, the knuckles turning white, and jumped up. "Liar!"

"Mr. Fox, control your client!" the judge said. "Ms. Tucker, I don't need to remind you that you are on thin ice in my courtroom. One more outburst, and I'll have you removed."

"But—" Rose pleaded.

"But nothing. Be. Quiet. Ms. Robb, continue."

"At any point, did she say she wanted to kill her father, Marcus Tucker?"

"Yes. The weekend before this all happened, she told me she had a plan. She said he wouldn't be around anymore to bother us. I asked her what that meant, and she said he wouldn't be alive much longer."

"Did you believe her?"

"I don't know what I believed. But the next week Mr. Tucker turned up dead, and now she's on trial. So I don't know that it mattered if I believed her or not. She was going to do it."

"Objection."

"Sustained. The witness will limit his testimony to what he saw or perceived. I will not allow any commentary lacking personal knowledge."

"I'll move along. Junior, did she ask for your help?"

"Not directly."

"What do you mean?"

"Rose asked me if I could get my hands on Rohypnol."

A murmur flashed through the jurors.

"The date-rape drug?"

"Yes. Roofies. I thought it was a strange request. But I still wanted to impress her."

"Did you secure the drug for Ms. Tucker?"

"I'm not proud of it, but I did."

"You gave it to her?"

"Yes."

Krista said, "Thank you for your time today, Junior. I have no further questions."

"Mr. Fox?" Judge Dubose said. A few seconds passed. "Mr. Fox, do you have questions for this witness?"

"Your Honor, may I have just a few more seconds to confer with my client?"

"Make it speedy, Mr. Fox."

Jake turned to Rose, who whispered in his ear. "You must believe me, Jake. Tommy is making all of that up. I said none of what he just said on the stand. I didn't ask him for drugs. My father never touched me."

"Why would he lie under oath? What motive could he have for risking it?"

"I don't know. It's true Marcus didn't want me to date him. He didn't like that he was older than me. He thought I was asking for trouble. But I never said I was angry with Marcus or that I intended to kill him."

Jake scratched his head and then looked from Rose to Tommy to the judge.

"Mr. Fox, is your little reverie over? Can we get on with the trial?"

Jake's head reeled. The jarring testimony had caught him off guard. Tommy was nowhere in Krista's disclosures, and she was likely wrong that the rules did not require her to disclose Tommy. But the judge's ruling would stand on appeal.

Why is this kid doing this to Rose?

He had no idea how they had missed Tommy. But with no idea what he would say, cross-examination was dangerous. His answers, made-up or otherwise, might bury Rose for good. But he could not let his testimony go in unchallenged. His heart hammered in his chest.

"Mr. Fox?" The judge's voice called him back to the present. "Do you have questions?"

"Just a couple, Your Honor." Jake stood at counsel's table. "Mr. Dickerson, you were not present the night that Mr. Tucker was killed, were you?"

"No. I was home playing video games."

"Do you know what happened at the Tucker place that night?"

"I know what she told me before."

"You claim she said those things, but did you see what happened at the home?"

"No. I wasn't there, so I didn't see her kill him. What difference does that make?"

Jake ignored his answer, not wanting to probe a hostile witness he knew nothing about.

"Since you didn't witness anything at the Tucker place that night, your testimony cannot contradict the descriptions provided by other witnesses."

"She said what she said."

"You have no direct evidence of that night."

"No."

"No further questions."

"Mr. Dickerson, you can step down. Ms. Robb, do you have any further witnesses?"

A smug smile bloomed across Krista's face. "The prosecution does not."

"Mr. Fox, rebuttal?"

"Judge, may we approach?"

The judge called them to the bench.

"I need a recess until tomorrow morning," Jake said.

"I'll not delay this trial, Mr. Fox."

"Considering this surprise witness, I need the afternoon to consult with my client about our next move. And given her Fifth Amendment rights, it's critical that we have time to discuss the decision."

"Are you suggesting you might put Ms. Tucker on the stand?"

"Yes," Jake said.

CHAPTER FIFTY

JAKE FOLLOWED Rose to the conference room at the end of the hall. He slammed the door, rattling the glass in the doorframe.

"What in the world was that?" Jake asked Rose. "Who is this Junior?"

"Hold on, now," Hitch said. "Let the girl get a word out."

"I swear, Jake. Everything Tommy just said is a lie. I never told him those things… because they aren't true. Marcus never touched me, ever. I never asked Tommy for roofies. That's crazy. Believe me."

Jake rubbed the heels of his palms into his eyes, twisting them as if trying to grind out his present situation.

Think, think, think.

"You believe me, don't you, Hitch?"

"I'm not the one that counts, little one. The twelve people sitting in that jury box are the only ones that count."

"It can't be that bad," Rose said.

"Motive," Jake said to no one in particular.

"You said it," Hitch chimed in.

"Wait, what? I don't understand. Talk to me, Jake."

"Motive, Rose. Until now, Krista's case was circumstantial

at best. She could present their discoveries in the house. Your panties being in Marcus's bed was unhelpful, but it was a fluke with no direct explanation."

"I have no idea how they ended up there," Rose confessed.

"That might not matter now."

"Hitch, tell me what's going on."

"Before Tommy," Jake continued, "the jury was going to have to guess if you hated Marcus… hated him enough to kill him."

"But now…"

"Now," Hitch said, "Tommy just told them you hated him. And… he told them why."

"Exactly," Jake said. "He made it all sound like premeditated—"

"Murder." Hitch finished his sentence.

"But it's not true," Rose said. "Tommy is lying."

"It doesn't matter if it's true," Jake said. "What the jurors believe is the only thing that matters. They don't have to be right."

"Get him back on the stand. Make him take it back."

"Rose," Hitch said, "Jake did the best he could. What if we put Tommy back on the stand and he doubles down? It will only make it worse. He could get up there and weave a detailed story, dig your hole deeper."

"Then put me on, Jake."

Jake stared at Rose.

"It's risky to put you on the stand. Krista will trick you… tear you up."

"She doesn't scare me."

"She should. She scares me. She's on a mission, even beyond convicting you." Jake exchanged looks with Hitch, who shrugged.

"What? You think she should go on?"

"She is the client, Jake. It's her life at stake."

"She's a child."

"I'm not a child. They're trying to put me in jail as an adult. I'm not a child in this."

"The testimony from that Tommy kid may have decided for you, Jake," Hitch added.

"Tell me it's not that bad," Rose said.

"Tommy was twice as bad as you think," Hitch responded.

"Krista wants to bury you, Rose," Jake said. "She wants to stomp on you to climb the next rung on the political ladder."

"Maybe we raised reasonable doubt," Hitch said. "They have no direct evidence. It's all surmise. Nobody saw someone kill Marcus. It's a fifty-fifty coin flip, but it's better than a suicide mission."

"You said it," Jake retorted.

"On the other hand, you might not have much of a choice," Hitch said.

"A showdown between Krista and Rose? The press in the gallery will eat it up. It plays right into Krista's desires. She'll smell blood and go for the kill in the most violent fashion. Make a scene for the papers."

"Who knows? It might work. Maybe, if the jury believes Rose killed Marcus, they'll deem it justified."

"Hitch, he *never* touched me!" Rose said.

"I'm not saying he did," Hitch said. "But if the jury believed Tommy, they might also think that even if you *did* kill Marcus, that he had it coming. They could let you walk."

"Hitch…" Rose groaned.

"I'm just giving you the skinny, kiddo. You gotta consider all angles. Especially if you're going to testify. A prison cell is no consolation prize."

"I can do it, Jake. Put me on," Rose said.

Jake looked at Rose's emerald eyes. Slight flashes at the edge of his vision foreshadowed an oncoming migraine. He rubbed his temples, trying to ease the tension, then stepped away to stare out the conference room window. The air-conditioning leaked a cool draft from the ceiling. Below him, the walkways in front of the courthouse crisscrossed the lawn. Flowers in deep reds and violets lined the concrete paths as the sprinklers rotated in the freshly mulched beds.

"What are you thinking, Jake?" Hitch asked.

Jake raised his hand, holding Hitch's questions at bay. Tears welled in the corner of his eyes as Lucy stepped out from the bushes below and walked to the middle of the grass, staring up at him.

What's the path, Lu?

The wind left his lungs, and warmth pulsed through Jake as he stared at his daughter.

What a waste, Lu. You're so beautiful.

"Jake?" Hitch called from behind him.

"You sure you're up to this?" Jake asked over his shoulder as he gazed at Lucy.

"I can do it," Rose implored.

Lucy let loose one of her killer smiles.

"It may be crazy, but let's get her ready, Hitch."

CHAPTER FIFTY-ONE

"GET IN THERE, LITTLE LADY," the guard commanded, thrusting Rose into her cell. Rose rubbed away the sharp pain in her arm where the brute's fingers had dug into the muscle while he'd escorted her through the jail.

"Hey, no need to manhandle me," Rose said, putting on a brave face.

"Yeah, leave her alone, you big ox," Cassie said.

The guard lunged at Cassie as if to intimidate her back into the cell. The door clanged shut. Rose grabbed the bars and stared down the guard.

"No need to be so rough. I'm innocent, you know."

"Darlin', everyone in this jail says they're innocent," the guard said with a cruel smile.

"I *am* innocent," Rose said.

"She *is* innocent, Helen," Cassie chimed in.

"Don't you call me by my first name."

"Innocent," a voice called from a cell across the corridor.

"Innocent!" others chanted.

The calls echoed like morning birdsong. Soon every female detainee was chanting, "Innocent! Innocent!" The sound grew and bounced off the pewter-gray walls and steel bars.

"Knock it off!" The guard, Helen, glared at them, but no one stopped. She turned in a circle, scanning the women in their confines. "Go ahead, scream yourselves hoarse! It doesn't hurt me one lick." The fireplug of a woman strode to the steel door. The door buzzed and slid open. She stepped through and disappeared around the corner. Upon her departure, the women clapped, and the noise subsided to a tolerable hum.

"See, I told you so. You're a celebrity with all these girls."

Rose rolled her eyes, collapsed onto her bunk and buried her face in her pillow. "Why's it always so hot in here?"

"Not sure fixing the air-conditioning is a priority. Doesn't seem that they were successful, though. I'm dying to hear. Tell me what happened. Tough day in court?" Cassie asked.

"Miserable."

Cassie sat on Rose's bunk and placed her hand on her shoulder.

"Want to talk about it?"

"Not really."

"Come on, fill me in. I've been bored all day. Give me the juicy details."

"I hate boys."

"Who doesn't, sister? Although… it is a pain that some of them are good kissers."

Rose rolled onto her back. "Why are they such jerks?"

"Come on, spill it."

Rose sat up, tucking her feet under her legs and cradling her pillow in her lap. She wrinkled her nose at the stale, humid air permeated with the odor of sweat and disinfectant.

"My boyfriend—ex-boyfriend—Tommy… or Junior, or whatever he's calling himself these days, testified against me today."

"How bad was it?"

"He may have sunk me."

"Hey, don't think like that. I'm sure it wasn't that terrible. What'd your lawyer say?"

"That's why I'm back so late. He was grilling me in a conference room for hours after court."

"Why?"

"So I can testify tomorrow."

"No way. You can't go on the stand. That's crazy. You sure your lawyer knows what he's doing?"

"I told him to put me on the stand. I *want* to tell the jury what happened."

"And you think they're going to listen to you?"

"They're going to have to believe me. I don't have a choice. If they don't, I'm in here for the rest of my life."

"Come on now. Ten years, tops," Cassie quipped.

"It's no joke."

"Okay, sorry. You're right, this is not a joking type of thing."

Rose ran her fingers through her long hair, scratching her scalp to chase away an itch. She mussed it and let it cascade down her face and shoulders.

"Want to practice?" Cassie asked.

Rose sighed. Exhaustion plagued every inch of her body. "I already practiced 'til I was brain-dead."

Cassie reached out and pushed Rose's hair away from her eyes, tucking it behind her ears. "If you don't mind me asking, how old are you, anyway?"

Rose looked down at the mattress. Cassie used a single finger to lift Rose's chin, the long nail grazing her skin.

"How old?"

"Fifteen."

"Good gracious. You're just a baby. The girls in the yard said the government was trying you as an adult. I don't think any of them knew you were fifteen."

"Surprised?"

"It seems a little young to be accused of murdering someone."

"I didn't—"

"I didn't say you did. I'm just saying. Fifteen? Wow."

"It's not that young."

"I'm twenty-three. Trust me, with as much living as I've done, I wish I could go back to being fifteen. I'd make a bunch of different choices." Cassie trailed off for a moment as if lost in memories and regrets. Then she shook her head, seeming to clear her thoughts.

"Let's talk about something else," Rose said. "I'm tired of thinking about the trial."

"A distraction, eh?"

"Absolutely. What's your life like outside?" Rose asked.

"Not much to tell, really. Got an old man and a job. Love to party. Gotta blow off some steam, you know. I have most days to myself because I work nights and weekends."

"Doing?"

"Mostly I strip over at the Jaguar Club."

A soft laugh escaped Rose.

"Hey now, no judging. I only have a few more good years to flaunt these," Cassie said as she cupped her breasts. "Someday my girls will sag, and I'll be a has-been. Might as well make the most of them while they're still bouncy."

"Sorry, no judging. I'm an alleged murderer, remember?"

"You're no killer."

"What's it like? Stripping."

"The men can get crazy, but the bouncers and tips are good. I like the music. Plus, I enjoy dancing. People are always gonna pay to get drunk and stare at naked women. Might as well be me taking their money… Besides, I don't do it all the time. If I'm not up on the pole getting ogled, I help my old man with his business."

"The guy who put you in here."

"That's him. Zach… He's quite a gem."

"Why would you go back if he's such a jerk?"

A patina coated Cassie's face for a moment, and she looked past Rose. "He'd find me anyway. He always finds me. It's best not to make him mad… I just do what he says, even if I hate it." Cassie smoothed out the wrinkles in Rose's blanket and shook her head. "No worries, though. He'll calm down and take me back. I got my stripper assets. I got special ways of apologizing."

Lost for what to say, Rose fumbled out a response. "What's Zach do… I mean for work?"

"Odd jobs when he works. I tried to get him to take classes down at the community college. Maybe some computer classes. Be a regular guy, you know?" Cassie said wistfully. "But he ain't the school kind. I guess sometimes you just gotta let fellas be fellas. So he futzes around the trailer. Or he heads out to the shooting range. Zach loves to shoot paper targets with that rifle of his. Sometimes I think he looks at them more than me."

Rose tucked her face into the pillow. She wasn't sure where they came from, but fat tears ran down her face.

"Hey, hey. Why are you crying on me?"

"Why does he hate me?"

"Who?"

"Tommy."

"You sure he hates you?"

"Cassie, he got up on that stand and told lie after lie."

"Maybe it didn't hurt your case so much."

Rose blurted out, "He told the world my dad raped me!"

"What?"

"He testified that I told him my dad diddled me."

"Did he?"

"No! Never! It was a lie. That's what I'm telling you. Everything Tommy said was a lie. It was like he hated me… like he was *trying* to put me in prison."

"Babe, it can't have been that bad."

"Oh, it's bad all right. Now the jury thinks I shot my father because he was a pervert." The sobs overwhelmed Rose, coming in waves until she hyperventilated. "Why is it so dang humid?" Rose gasped, her voice thick with sorrow.

Cassie hopped off the bunk, grabbed the rubber cup by the sink, filled it, and brought it back to her.

"Here, take a drink. The water's cool. It will do you some good."

Rose wiped the snot from her nose with the cuff of her fatigues and then reached for the cup. Cassie helped her steady it in her hands before she took a sip. Rose focused on the Celtic cross tattoo on Cassie's wrist, trying to slow her racing mind.

"There now, there you go. Yeah, take another drink. See? It helps."

Rose gulped in air between swigs. Cassie sat next to her on the bed and began rubbing the small of Rose's back.

"Shhh. It's going to be okay. You got this. I'm sure your lawyer…"

"Jake."

"Yeah, Jake. I'm sure he has something figured out. If not yet, he'll spend the entire night finding a way to help."

"I hope so."

Rose tucked her head into Cassie's shoulder, and Cassie ran her fingers through Rose's hair to calm her.

"Lights out!" Helen called. A moment later, the guard flipped a switch, and blackness enveloped them.

As she sat there in the dark with Cassie, Rose's heartbeat slowed.

"Hey, Rose?" Cassie whispered.

"Yeah?"

"Knock knock."

"Who's there?"

"Cows."

"Cows who?"

"No, silly. Cows *moo*. Owls *hoo*."

Rose chuckled and brushed away tears with her sleeve.

Cassie hugged her tight. "You know what? I think you're going to do just fine tomorrow." Then she whispered to no one in particular, "Forgive us our trespasses."

CHAPTER FIFTY-TWO

AFTER MIDNIGHT, Jake smiled and shook his head as his truck ambled up Margie's drive. He clicked his headlamps from bright to low beams as he neared the figure sitting on the steps to his home. She held up her hand to block the glare. Hope's tight black leather jacket, white T-shirt, and jeans cloaked her in a simple sensuality. Jake parked, killed the lights, and exited his truck.

"If you keep stalking me like this, showing up on my stoop, I'm going to call the sheriff."

"I hear she can be a real hard case."

"Rumor has it."

Mr. Snuffles and Tiny shuffled up from somewhere in the dark lawn to greet Jake. Their happy grunts reminded him he'd been away from the house a lot.

"Somebody seems to like you," Hope said.

"They tolerate me." Not to be undone, Ted sprinted up to Jake, his docked tail wagging and wobbling his hind end as Jake petted him. Ted dropped a tennis ball, begging Jake to throw it. The dog's energy seemed endless, even past midnight. Jake picked it up and heaved it far into the grass toward the lake.

"Have you heard what they say about the men that animals like?"

"No, I haven't heard that one."

"Kind hearts," Hope said.

"Is that so?"

"It's what they say… whoever 'they' are. I'm not sure I believe them," she said, and winked.

Jake sat on the steps next to Hope. "What do they say about dog-tired trial lawyers?"

"Jury's still out." Hope smiled at her own pun, reached to the side, and pulled out a six-pack of beer. It was missing a can.

"You got a head start on me, Sheriff."

"Rough day."

"Mine, too."

"I heard."

"Why didn't you knock on Margie's door and wait up there? She'd love to see you."

"I wanted to be alone… Mull my thoughts for a while. Besides, if I did, I'd be eyes deep in a second piece of some god-awfully good peach pie with a side of ice cream. And I'm trying to watch my figure."

She's not the only one.

Jake's heartbeat lurched. He cleared his throat, trying to chase a sudden flood of not-so-pure images from his mind. He held out his hand.

"You getting drunk by yourself, or you planning on sharing?"

"I had one a while ago." Hope dislodged a can from the plastic rings and handed it to Jake. He popped the top and gulped nearly half of it in a long slug. The beer tasted good going down. He smacked his lips and let out a groan.

"Now that hits the spot."

"Thought it might."

Tiny and Snuffles climbed the stairs, their hooves clacking

on the painted wood. They circled up behind Hope and Jake and laid down on the porch, flashing their bellies.

"They're suckers for a tummy rub," Jake said.

"Who isn't?" Hope said, flashing him a grin.

Surprised, Jake spit out his current swallow of beer and coughed.

Hope chuckled and then reached out, scratching her nails across the pigs' stomachs. They sighed contentedly, as if her touch had already lulled them to sleep.

"How's Grace?"

"Still shaken up. Pretty mad at me for locking her up at my parents'."

"Is she safe at their place?"

"Oh, yeah, more than safe. I have a deputy parked in the driveway. And all day my dad has been cleaning an arsenal of guns that would make a militia nut proud."

"Remind me not to upset your father."

"Probably a good idea."

A light blinked on Margie's porch. She walked out in a vibrant housedress, her gait suggesting she was still half-asleep.

"What are you all doin' out there in the middle of the night?" Margie asked.

"Just talking, Margie," Jake said.

"It's just me, Ms. Moore," Hope called out.

"Sheriff? Well, I declare… You two need to get to bed. Jake, you have Rose's trial tomorrow."

"Yes, Margie, I'll turn in soon."

"My word. I can't believe…" Margie's voice disappeared behind the closing door, the glass rattling in the jamb. They watched her shuffle past the living room window toward her bedroom, her bright muumuu almost glowing.

"I should hire her at the department. She'd make a good security guard."

"Or snooping gossip," Jake responded. Hope drained her beer and pulled another from the bundle.

"What's got you at the bottom of the bottle tonight?" Jake asked.

Hope rested her forearms on her knees and bowed her head.

"I think I've lost Beth." Her words bore a thick patina of regret.

"Wait. You saw her?"

"Not exactly."

Jake set down his near-empty can and chucked the ball for Ted. "Now I'm confused."

"I drove up to the casino over the state line to check out a lead."

"By yourself?"

"Yeah, I sort of didn't think that through." Hope handed Jake another beer.

"Wow… Someone just threatened you and Grace, Hope."

"I told you. It wasn't my brightest move, but that's not the story."

"Promise me you won't do that again."

"You got it. Can I tell my story now?"

"Yeah, sorry. Spill it."

"I'm up there, bored at a slot machine, when I spotted a guy with a double-braided beard dragging a dolled-up girl through the lobby. So Todd and I chased after them."

Jake pushed down the sting of jealousy. "Who's Todd?"

"Sorry. Special Agent Strickland. He's with the Oklahoma State Bureau of Investigation."

"I thought you went to the casino alone."

"I did. Strickland just sort of showed up there… Anyway, we pursued them into the parking lot. The girl's dress got tangled in a car mirror, and she tripped. The guy bolted and left her behind. It turns out the girl wasn't Beth, but she was another victim."

"Where's the girl now?"

"Strickland took her to the hospital. He'll watch over her until her parents can pick her up."

"Do you know where she lives?"

"She called from the hospital. Her mom and dad are from Pratt County. So only a few hours away. In fact, they might already have her."

"Good for her."

"She's got a long recovery ahead of her. She'd been missing for eighteen months, and they'd been prostituting her the whole time. Multiple times a day."

Jake pushed away the horror-show thought of Rose, Grace, or Beth in a similar plight.

"She's gone," Hope said. "Beth is gone."

"Hey, you don't know that to be true. You just gotta keep looking for her."

"Worst thing? I owe an update to the judge and his wife. I hate calling them to say I have no news."

"At least you saved one girl today. You should be happy about that result."

"I am. But Beth is still out there… maybe dead."

"You can't think like that. Just keep working on it. You'll find her."

"We can only pray you're right." Hope slapped her knee. "Enough about my lousy day. Tell me about this Tommy kid."

"How'd you know about him?"

"I ran into Hitch at the liquor store on my way out here."

"Figures. Not much to tell, really. Kid comes in and testifies that Rose drugged Marcus and shot him in the head because he was molesting her."

"Holy…"

"Exactly right."

"Is it true?"

"Rose swears Marcus never touched her. She says Tommy's testimony was all a lie."

"What are you going to do?"

"Well, I'm pretty sure the jury believes him. Without other witnesses, I'll call Rose to testify. She's the only one that can dent his credibility."

"Krista will eat her up."

"Therein lies the risk."

"And Rose is okay with testifying?"

"She's adamant. She wants me to put her up. She wants to tell her story."

"Geez, I wouldn't want to be you."

"Thanks for the support."

"That's not how I meant it."

"I know, but… I feel it sliding away from me." Jake's words floated away into a long silence, punctuated by the occasional swig of beer.

"I didn't mean it, you know."

"Mean what?"

"That you were just trying to save Rose to bring back Lucy."

Jake gave a half-hearted nod. Then the words leaked out from somewhere deep in his soul. "She haunts me, Hope."

"I know. She broke your heart." Hope pulled close and gently kissed Jake on the edges of his mouth. Jake held still, and then he pulled back.

"Don't do that," she murmured.

"What?"

"Pull away." She dropped her voice and whispered as she traced the edge of his ear with her lips. "I'm not here to hurt you."

Jake closed his eyes, the ache in his heart palpable. "I get it." He turned to Hope and leaned in to her warmth.

"I thought I told you kids to go to bed!" Margie yelled from her window.

"I'm just heading out, Ms. Moore," Hope answered, her lips lingering near Jake's for a brief moment.

"It's nearly mornin'!"

"We're going."

"Good." The sash on Margie's window clamped shut.

"She sure watches over you," Hope said.

"Like a hawk. You good to drive? You could stay in my guest room."

"Best not," Hope said. "I'm not good with certain temptations." She stood. "You can keep the rest," she said, pointing at the beer. She turned and walked toward her cruiser. "Good night, Counselor."

Jake called after her. "See you tomorrow?"

"I might could fit you in," she said, as she opened the door and unleashed another glorious smile.

"It's settled, then," Jake said.

"Don't push your luck, Jake Fox. Don't boss around a woman with a gun."

Jake watched her pull a K-turn in the drive and roll away. He kept looking until her taillights disappeared down the highway.

Jake waved his hands at the pigs and Ted. "All right, boys, let's go get some shut-eye. Morning will come soon enough."

CHAPTER FIFTY-THREE

THE CEILING FANS creaking in the courtroom accented the silence all around them. Judge Dubose stared down his nose—his glasses perched on the tip—at the involved parties and the standing-room-only crowd. He cleared his throat.

"Mr. Fox, you've had your recess. Before we bring in the jury, I want to know. Are you closing, or putting Ms. Tucker on the stand?"

"Your Honor, Rose will be our next witness."

Murmurs rippled through the sea of onlookers. The crush of humanity in the room let off a mix of perfume and sweat. A loud harrumph arose from Gert and her gaggle of gals. Reporters scribbled down notes. The judge banged his gavel.

"Enough of that nonsense, please. I will remind everyone in the courtroom that I expect a high level of decorum. Ms. Tucker's testimony will be met with complete silence. Do I make myself clear?" The gallery answered with a hush, and the judge turned his attention to Rose.

"Ms. Tucker, please stand." He waited for her to get on her feet. Her hands fluttered briefly as if she did not know what to do with them. "I would be remiss if I did not remind you of your rights. Under the United States Constitution, you are not obliged to put on a defense. The burden always remains on the government to prove every element of the accused crime beyond a reasonable doubt. As a defendant, you can assert your Fifth Amendment right to remain silent. You need not testify. I will instruct the jury that they must not hold your silence against you. Said another way, they cannot assume you are guilty because you did not speak up to defend yourself. I must advise you that it is a rare case where a defendant agrees to testify. It is the exception, not the rule. Once you take the stand, you lose the right to appeal that decision and claim that it is a reversible error that you testified. You might, however, claim ineffective assistance of counsel if you believe your lawyer's advice to testify was reversible error. I will also say, however, that such claims rarely succeed. I share all this because it's a significant choice. One you should not take lightly. Do I make myself clear?"

Rose swallowed as if trying to find her voice. "Yes, Your Honor."

"Very well. What is your decision?"

The color drained from Rose's face. She swayed slightly on her feet and smoothed the navy-blue dress that Margie had brought straight from the cleaners, freshly pressed. She glanced at Jake, then Hitch, and finally the judge.

Margie whispered behind her, "You can do this."

"Judge," Rose started with a nervous vibrato, "I understand all that you have told me, and I would like to testify."

The crowd let off its excitement by shifting in their seats mutely and looking around.

"You choose to do this willingly?"

"I do."

"Very well, Ms. Tucker, approach the bench and be sworn." The judge made quick work of the oath, and as soon as Rose sat down, he turned to the bailiff. "Bring in the jury."

Jake watched as the jury shuffled through the doorway,

their eyes widening as they noticed Rose on the witness stand. Once they had taken their seats, the judge pushed forward.

"Mr. Fox, your witness."

"Thank you, Judge." Jake rose and walked to the lectern with his yellow legal pad.

"Good morning, Rose. How are you this morning?"

"I feel like I'm about to throw up."

Several members of the jury chuckled. Some women looked concerned.

"Sorry, I shouldn't have said that."

"It's okay."

"I'm just so nervous."

"That's understandable. Let's start with some straightforward questions. Where did you grow up?"

"I was born here in Haven and have lived here all my life."

"You go to school here?"

"Yes. I recently finished my sophomore year in high school. I'm looking forward to being a junior."

"Any plans after you graduate?"

"I want to attend college to be a nurse."

"Why?"

A glow of excitement bloomed on Rose's face. "Well, I like science. I'm good at science. And I like helping people. Nursing seems like a good fit."

"I bet you will be a very successful nurse. Did Marcus raise you?"

"My mom ran off and left us when I was young, and I don't remember anything about her. I hear rumors now and again that she's around somewhere. She didn't much care for us, so I'm not sure I have to care much about her. Marcus, he raised me by himself since I was a toddler."

"You lived with him out at the house by the lake?"

"Yes. My grandfather left that house to Marcus, and we lived there the whole time. I've never known anywhere else."

"Your father… What do you remember about him?"

Rose's face flushed and tears welled up along the edges of her eyes.

"He was an excellent father. He took care of me. Provided for me. I never went hungry. We weren't rich by any means, but I cannot remember a time that he didn't put my needs ahead of his own."

"He worked in the oil fields?"

"As a welder… a pipe fitter. My dad worked very hard, often from before sunrise to when he would pick me up after school. I'd be studying in the library like Miss Margie said."

"This may be hard to answer, but did Marcus ever mistreat you?"

Rose swallowed hard, as if composing herself against the question. "I assume you're talking about Tommy saying that Marcus molested me… No. Marcus never touched me like that… ever."

"You are sure? There's no shame in telling the truth if he did."

"My father loved me. I loved him. Not once in my days did Marcus ever touch me, or even look at me, inappropriately."

"Did you ever tell Tommy Dickerson that Marcus abused you?"

"No. I never did because it never happened."

"Why would Tommy say those things to the jury?"

"I have no idea what's going through his mind. We only dated a few months. So I guess I didn't really know him at all. Maybe he's mad at me. He shouldn't have come in here and said those things. They are not true."

"You never asked him for Rohypnol, or what he called roofies?"

"Again, no. It never happened. He's making that all up. I have no idea why."

"Let me take you back to the night Marcus died. Tell the jury in your own words what occurred."

"It was late. Marcus and I were home alone. We'd just

washed up the dinner dishes together. I was sitting down at the table with my books to do homework. Marcus was pacing through the house, and he must have seen something because he went to the front window. That's when it all went crazy."

"What do you mean?"

"Something had gone wrong. Marcus became upset. He started to tell me to get out of the house. To go hide."

"Did he tell you why?"

"Someone was coming up the driveway. I'd never seen Marcus scared before. But he was scared that night."

"What scared him?"

"People coming to the house."

"Did you see them?"

"Not at first. When Marcus freaked out, he just wanted me out of the house."

"Did you leave?"

"Yes. He told me to leave through the back door and hide."

"Where did you go?"

"I ran to the well house out back."

"Did you see anything from in there?"

"I was peeking through a crack in the concrete wall, and I saw them beating on Marcus."

"Who attacked him?"

"I didn't know them. But it was two men and a woman. One man had a long beard. It was braided. He had two braids."

"And the woman?"

"She had long, fire-red hair."

"It was dark. How did you observe all this?"

"They had left on their headlights, so I could see them in the glow."

"What happened next?"

"They hit Marcus a couple more times and then took him inside our house."

"Did you stay in the well house?"

"Marcus liked to be prepared. Under the shed is a tornado shelter. I went down there and waited."

"How long?"

"I was scared. I was also exhausted, and couldn't keep my eyes open. I fell asleep on the bunk. I woke up, and it was almost morning."

"What did you do when you woke up?"

"I peeked through the crack in the wall. The men were gone. So I went into the house."

"What did you find?"

Rose drew in a deep breath, and her bottom lip began to quiver. "Something was wrong. I could tell it as soon as I stepped through the back door. I was looking for Marcus, and I found him. In his room." Sudden, heavy sobs overwhelmed Rose. The bailiff rose and brought her a box of tissues.

"Are you able to continue, Ms. Tucker?" the judge asked.

"I'm so sorry, Your Honor. I don't mean to…"

"You just take a moment to compose yourself."

Rose wiped her eyes, took a deep breath, and continued. "I found my dad in his room. He was dead. They had shot him in the head and left him on his bed."

"What did you do?"

"At first, quite honestly, I fell apart. I rushed to him. I wanted to help. But I could tell he wasn't alive."

"Did you touch him?"

"I guess I shouldn't have. I was in shock. My father lay murdered right in front of me."

"Did you touch items in the room? Did you touch the gun?"

"I fell to the floor when I saw Marcus. I didn't see the gun until my knee crashed down on top of it. I picked it up and then tossed it away. There was blood everywhere. All over my hands." Rose's lip quivered. "It was horrible."

"Do you know how to shoot a gun, Rose?"

"Marcus made sure of it. He'd taken me to the gun range to

practice just the day before. But I don't know why his gun was out. Marcus kept it in a gun safe. He said he'd give me the combination when I turned eighteen."

"You didn't have access to his guns."

"No, not unless he was with me."

"I need to ask you about the underwear found in Marcus's bed."

"They're mine, but I don't know how they got there. Last I knew, they were all in my drawer."

"How do you know that?"

"I'd just done my laundry that morning. I washed and folded all my clothes and put them away. The only underwear not in a drawer was the set I was wearing."

"I know your father cared for you very much. If he were here today, what would you say to him?"

"That I love him… miss him… I need him now more than ever. But he's not coming back. All I can do is hope for a future that makes him proud."

"Rose, I'm going to ask you a very direct question. Did you shoot your father, Marcus Tucker, in the head?"

"No. I did not shoot him. I did not kill him."

"Judge, we pass the witness."

"Ms. Robb, cross-examination?"

CHAPTER FIFTY-FOUR

KRISTA STOOD and secured the brass buttons on the charcoal-gray blazer above her matching pencil skirt. The severe cut of her clothes accentuated all her angles. She'd pulled her hair back into a tight braid and paid particular attention to her makeup. Jet-black eyeliner accentuated the intensity in her brown eyes. She stepped in front of the lectern and paced back and forth like a mountain lion trapping a lost calf, never taking her gaze from Rose.

Jake glanced at Rose, who looked smaller and smaller in the witness chair.

Dear God, what have I done?

"Ms. Tucker, let's play one of Mr. Fox's favorite games. Did anyone see you in the well house?"

"No, ma'am. I was alone."

"Other than you, did anyone see these men hit Marcus?"

"The woman."

"Ah, yes, the redhead. Did anyone else see the redhead?"

"Just Marcus, ma'am."

"So that would be a no."

"I guess, no."

"And other than you and her, nobody saw anyone hit Marcus."

"No."

Rose dropped her head and shook it side to side. "Nobody else saw them supposedly drag Marcus into the house."

"I suppose not."

"You heard the crime scene technician testify that they found no tire tracks, no footprints, did you not?"

"I heard him say that, but it had rained."

"The rain, yes, yes, the rain. So nobody else saw these men and a woman attack Marcus, and nobody can find any trace that they were on your property, conveniently because of the rain."

"I don't—"

"You've been sitting right there, the whole trial. Did you hear anyone corroborate your sighting of these mystery people?"

"Josiah mentioned the SUV."

"Yes, an SUV mysteriously appearing in the night. It sounds like a fable, does it not?"

"Objection," Jake shouted.

"Withdrawn," Krista said and continued to pace, her stiletto heels knocking out an ominous rhythm. She moved nearer to Rose on every pass, closing in on her. Jake's mouth filled with cotton. He looked at the water pitcher but didn't want to reach for it.

"Remind me what you did when you walked into the house, after you woke up in this tornado shelter."

"I went inside and found Marcus. He was lying there dead."

"That must have been a shock. You walk in, and your father is lying lifeless on the bed. Did you call the sheriff?"

"No. I remember thinking about it, but I did not. Marcus had told me to go to Miss Margie's house."

"So, hours after your father was shot, you woke up, found him dead, and then took a stroll to Ms. Moore's home."

"I ran to Margie's. I went along the path by the lake. I didn't know where the killers were. I was scared."

"Did you have your phone when you found your father?"

"Yes, I'd picked it up off the kitchen counter when I got back in the house."

"Wait. You had just seen your father beaten and dragged into the house the night before, but you were able to fall asleep in the cellar, and you stopped to pick up your phone first thing on your return."

"I hid in the well house because those men were still there. I was exhausted… I passed out, more like it."

"And you cared more about grabbing your phone than finding the father you claim was in mortal danger."

"No. I grabbed the phone because—"

"Did you pick up the phone before you looked for your father? It's a yes or no question."

"Yes, but—"

"And when you found him, you claim you were so distraught that you lost track of all the items you touched."

"That's not what I said. I couldn't remember all that happened because I was in shock over finding my father with his head blown off."

"Your fingerprints are on the gun, correct?"

"Yes."

"Your fingerprints are on the door and doorknob, yes?"

"Yes."

"Your fingerprints are on the bottle of bourbon that just so happened to have a date-rape drug in it."

"Yes, that is all true, but I explained all those things."

"You have excuses for all those things, Ms. Tucker. Am I wrong?"

"I just know what happened," Rose said, grabbing a tissue from the box.

"You tested positive for gunpowder residue. You had recently fired a gun."

"Yes, Marcus had taken me for target practice."

"Did anyone see you shooting?"

"No. Marcus took me over to the back side of his friend's ranch. We went often. But it's in the middle of nowhere. Nobody was there."

"So no one saw you."

"That doesn't mean it didn't happen."

"But we only have your word for it, correct?"

"Yes."

"Just like we have to take your word for everything else in your story."

"I—"

"Your word is all the jury has to go on, correct?"

"But I can explain all of it."

"Only if you're telling the truth."

"I am telling the truth."

"How do we know?"

"You just have to trust me."

Krista's mouth widened into a malicious grin accented by her blood-red lipstick. "So you're innocent only because you say you're innocent."

"Because I didn't do it."

"No, Ms. Tucker, because you *say* you didn't do it. That's all you are giving the jury. There is no hard evidence. Mr. Dickerson sat there, swore an oath, and explained to the jury that you asked him to procure Rohypnol for you."

"I did no such thing."

"Because you say so?"

"Because I didn't."

"What possible motive could Tommy Dickerson have to lie? Go ahead, we'll wait. Tell us, why would he lie?"

"I don't know. I can't understand anything he said on the stand. I just know he's lying."

"Again, solely because you say so."

"Because I know so."

"Did you shoot your father because he raped you?"

Rose shot forward in the witness chair. "He never touched me!"

"Your Honor," Jake said, "she's badgering Ms. Tucker."

"She chose to take the stand, Mr. Fox. And you advised her to do so. I suggest you take any issue you have up in redirect of the witness."

Krista shot Jake a smug look, a flash of excitement in her eyes.

She's really enjoying herself.

Jake clenched his fist, the anger seeping into his muscles snapping the pencil in his grip.

"Mr. Dickerson says you confessed to him that your father was touching you inappropriately."

"Tommy Dickerson is a liar."

"It's convenient for you that every other witness is supposedly a liar. How about Mr. Hunter? He saw you hit your father and scream that you'd be better off without him. Is Mr. Hunter a liar too?"

"We were arguing. I wasn't talking about killing Marcus. I was just talking…"

"So that wasn't a threat because you say it wasn't."

"I was upset. I didn't mean it the way you're twisting it."

"I'm not twisting anything. Those are your words—'better off without him'—are they not?"

"Yes, I said them, but—"

"But you don't want them to have any meaning, not now, because you're in this courtroom on trial for following through and killing your father."

"You're distorting my words."

"I'm just repeating them. What about telling Mr. Dickerson that you were going to kill your father?"

"I never said it."

"Sounds to me like something someone would remember if they heard it."

"I didn't—"

"I know you say now that you didn't say those things. But Mr. Dickerson and Mr. Hunter said you did. They said those words came out of your mouth, and it's your word against theirs, correct?"

"But I'm the one telling the truth."

"What about that? They're just telling us what they heard you say in the past. So which Rose Tucker are we supposed to believe? The one in the past or the one here today on trial?"

"I'm not lying."

"How do we know? Which *you* is the jury supposed to believe?"

"Because—"

Krista interrupted her. "Because you say so, Ms. Tucker. Is that what you were going to say? For your story to be correct, everyone else has to be wrong or lying."

"Objection."

"Withdrawn. I pass the witness."

"Mr. Fox, any redirect?"

"Yes, Judge. Rose, did you see those men and that woman?"

"Yes. They attacked Marcus. I'm certain."

"And you found him dead later?"

"Yes."

"How can you ask this jury to trust your version of events over other things they have heard?"

"I don't know. I'm just asking them to believe me. I loved my father deeply. I would never hurt him. I didn't kill him."

"No further questions."

CHAPTER FIFTY-FIVE

"SHE'S IN HERE, MR. FOX," the deputy said, as he led Jake into a room with the holding cell, where the judge had ordered Rose to spend lunch. Deep frown lines adorned her face, and dark circles had taken up residence under her eyes. Jake worried the jury might misinterpret Rose's haggard look as her giving up or becoming resigned to a conviction.

"Did y'all finish?" she asked. The judge had recessed for a two-hour lunch, allowing the lawyers to finish the jury instructions and verdict form. True to form, the judge had denied all of Jake's objections and given Krista everything she wanted.

Jake pulled over a folding chair and sat in front of the steel mesh that separated him from Rose.

"Yes, it's all done. Closing arguments are next."

"Do you think they'll believe me?"

Jake felt the young woman staring into his eyes, as if probing his soul or searching for the truth.

"I don't know. Krista's cross-examination was strong. She made the case about you and asked whether you were telling the truth. She also worked hard to show them they shouldn't believe or trust you."

Rose folded her hands in her lap and dropped her head.

"Was it right for me to testify?" Her question reminded Jake of when Lucy as a kid, asking him if she was in trouble.

"As hard as it was, I believe you did the right thing. The jury should appreciate your guts, and the things you said ring true. But we won't know until they come back with a verdict. If you believe in prayer, this might be a good time."

"My dad never enjoyed attending church. But he taught me to pray when I was little. Sometimes I would pray for rain for all the frogs around our house. They come out more when it's wet, and I liked to catch them."

"That sounds like a nice prayer. I was thinking more about a prayer for staying out of jail."

"I know. I just have so many memories of my father." She looked at Jake. "I miss him so much. I'll have let him down if I end up in prison."

"Rose, you have let no one down. This incident has developed a life of its own. You've done your best. That's all Marcus would have ever wanted."

Jake heard the deputy open the door behind him. "Five minutes, Mr. Fox," he said, as he walked forward and turned the key in the cell's lock. Rose stood, and together they walked out into the courtroom. She took a seat at the defense table. Hitch took a chair next to Rose and held her hand.

Jake noted her mumbling under her breath, and then he heard a quiet, "Amen."

"Praying for frogs?" he asked.

"That and a little something extra."

"All rise," the bailiff called, and the judge scurried to his seat. "Bring in the jury."

As they shuffled in, Jake noticed a few of the women with lingering looks on Rose.

That could go either way.

"Ms. Robb," Judge Dubose said, "please proceed with the prosecution's closing argument."

Krista stood and buttoned her blazer. Stepping behind the

lectern, she waited, making sure the jurors were focused solely on her. Then she began.

"Rose Tucker killed her father, Marcus Tucker. She planned the murder, and then she executed on that plan. On that night, she slipped Rohypnol into her father's bourbon bottle and waited for him to become disoriented. Then she walked into his bedroom with a handgun, pressed it under his chin, and pulled the trigger. It was cold, calculated, and what the law calls 'malice aforethought.

"Why would a child who is supposed to honor her father execute him? We know. That home held a dark secret. Marcus had been molesting Ms. Tucker. Who knows how long such heinous acts took place? A few of you may perceive her action of killing him as justified. Our society takes a low view of pedophiles. There are statutes on the books to protect children from them. Law enforcement can remove such vile individuals from our society. But the law does not allow revenge killings. Vigilante justice is just as illegal as the reprehensible conduct of Mr. Tucker. He deserved a long time in prison. But the law did not allow Ms. Tucker to gun him down.

"Her side of the story? Ms. Tucker has concocted a wild fable of mystery men and a shadowy redhead invading her home, beating Mr. Tucker, and then shooting him. She presents no evidence of these people. Indeed, as far as the record is concerned, they are ghosts. She asks you to believe in these fantastical creatures as you do the Easter Bunny, pretending they are real even though experience and logic tell us they do not exist. Do not buy into her ruse.

"Let's walk through the evidence as we have seen it, as the witnesses testified under oath. The sheriff's office found her fingerprints all over the murder scene. On the gun. On the drugged bottle of booze. Mixed with her father's blood on the door and doorknob to the bedroom, where the sheriff found him dead. They even found the defendant's blood at the murder scene. Ms. Tucker tested positive for gunpowder residue. She had fired a gun. Those findings are objective facts that prove every element of the crime.

"She had the opportunity. That night, before the thunderstorm hit Haven, Ms. Tucker was alone with her father on their property. You've all seen photographs. The home rests in an isolated and private location. No witnesses around. She testified she was there the entire night. Now she claims she was asleep in a tornado shelter out back while ghosts slaughtered her father. Her excuses crumble, leaving only her admission from the stand: she was there all night.

"She had the motive. The sheriff's department found the defendant's underwear in her father's bed. Outrage over her father's abuse filled Ms. Tucker, and hate-filled thoughts consumed her. Mr. Hunter overheard the defendant yelling at her father that she 'would be better without him.' He described her as agitated and angry. She became violent toward her father. Mr. Hunter then saw her punch Mr. Tucker in public. You also heard from Mr. Dickerson. He testified that Rose Tucker told him she would stop her father from interfering with their relationship. She told him Mr. Tucker was defiling her and that he would not be around much longer.

"She had the means. The defendant shot Mr. Tucker with his own gun he kept in his house. Not long before, Rose Tucker asked Tommy Dickerson to provide a drug whose sole purpose is to incapacitate unwitting victims: Rohypnol, a date-rape drug. Mr. Dickerson did as requested and delivered the drug to the defendant. Make no mistake, Ms. Tucker had the means to drug and overpower Marcus Tucker, and then shoot him.

"These facts make logical sense. You heard a prosecution witness testify that most homicide victims know their assailant, and a substantial number of homicides have a family member involved. That happened here. The evidence proves that the defendant had the means, motive, and opportunity. She committed this crime. Rose Tucker killed her father. We ask that you find her guilty of murder." Krista strutted to the prosecution table and sat down.

The judge turned his head. "Mr. Fox. Your closing argument, sir?"

Jake took a deep breath and started his closing before he even stood up from the table.

"Ms. Robb argues the prosecution has provided clear evidence of means, motive, and opportunity. But when you stand back and analyze the case she presented, you see nothing but shaky circumstantial evidence. You find a rush to judgment.

"Analyze what is missing. No witnesses testified they saw Rose shoot her father. Indeed, the prosecution failed to present a single eyewitness to the actual event. Ms. Robb asks you to guess, just as she is, about what happened that night. She denigrates Rose for claiming several men and a woman attacked her father that night. She sneered they were 'ghosts.'" But Ms. Robb's case is every bit as ephemeral.

"Analyze what the prosecution failed to do. The sheriff's department considered no other suspect. Immediately, they homed in on Rose and stopped all other avenues of inquiry. They ignored her eyewitness account of what happened to Marcus. They disregarded the long red hairs found at the crime scene, deeming it unimportant due to the sheriff's presence and red hair. But Rose told them of another redhead: Marcus's assailant. Yet they ignored her. They mention that Mr. Hunter witnessed Rose and Marcus arguing, even that Rose took a swing at her father. But Mr. Hunter himself testified that he believed it was the ordinary friction between a protective father and a teenage daughter. Even the undergarments ballyhooed by Ms. Robb make little sense. The clothes had been laundered. They showed no signs of being worn. The prosecution skipped detailed analysis and latched onto a theory that Marcus had abused Rose. But Ms. Robb has no evidence—none—of Rose ever being in Marcus's bed.

"Finally, analyze who Ms. Robb attacks. It is clear from her testimony that Rose adored Marcus. A tragic act of violence ripped him from her. Did the State show any compassion for a daughter who lost her father? No. Instead, Ms. Robb engaged in a disgusting campaign of victim shaming. She spun tales of Marcus violating Rose without a shred of evidence that any such acts occurred. She denigrated Rose's eyewitness account. Ms. Robb called her a liar and berated her on the witness stand.

"The prosecution's case collapses because the gaps in the evidence are catastrophically large. When you look at the case, rather than find solid evidence, you discover not just reasonable doubt but substantial doubt. That doubt requires that you acquit Rose on the charge that she murdered her father, Marcus Tucker."

Jake turned to return to his chair. The jury now held all the power.

CHAPTER FIFTY-SIX

JAKE WENT to the restroom down the hall, away from the others. He cracked open the window so he could hear the melee below. The trilling of the cicadas spilled through, and the humid breeze carried the sweet scent from the tall lilac bushes down below.

With the case submitted to the jury, they all would have to wait. But that didn't stop Krista from using the tense moment to speed up her ambitions.

She had called a press conference on the courthouse steps. Throngs had shown up to egg on her mischief. Gert and her gaggle stood on the sidewalk holding up signs: "Honor thy Father, Don't Murder Him," "Patricide Is the Work of the Devil," "Give Me that Old Testament Justice." Jake doubted whether Gert's gals believed in any of their signs, but it was a way to draw the television cameras for their five minutes of fame in this out-of-the-way town. The only thing missing was a band. Within moments, Krista was at the microphone, guaranteeing her appearance in every statewide newspaper by morning.

Bile rose in the back of Jake's throat.

She did this on purpose.

"Thank you, thank you... Let's quiet down." The crowd followed her instructions. "I appreciate all of you coming today. Today is another great day for the rule of law and for the justice system in our great state of Texas. In this state, we take the sanctity of life seriously and will not tolerate murders. We are a law-and-order state, and my office has worked tirelessly to ensure the laws are enforced." The crowd cheered for her.

"I want to introduce a dignitary who has come to support our crime-fighting efforts."

For the first time, Jake noticed the tall gentleman standing behind Krista in an obviously tailored suit. Jake's mouth fell open.

"I'll be a son of a..."

"So help me welcome," Krista continued, "the governor of the State of Texas, Earl Saxby."

Jake watched the silver-haired man with broad shoulders, chiseled features, and a tan face take to the microphones, soaking in the group's adoration.

"Thank you, Krista Robb," Governor Saxby said. "How about her, folks!" The crowd cheered again. "It's my pleasure to join you fine people here today. I'm sorry that we have to gather under such somber circumstances. But I am pleased that you have such a strong district attorney to protect your community. Ms. Robb is a talented lawyer. She comes from a fine Christian family. Her father and I were roommates at the University of Texas. And I'll tell you a secret. A court of appeals vacancy may arise soon, and I will have the privilege of appointing a replacement before the next election. I am confident that the slot will benefit from a tough prosecutor!" The crowd erupted and started chanting.

When the chants died down, the governor continued, "The case Ms. Robb is prosecuting is a tragedy. A child murdering her father highlights the fraying of our moral fabric. This is a rot we cannot let grow. This one jury verdict could serve as bulwark against lawlessness and the breakdown of the family. If children lose their respect for their parents, if they move away from the basic Biblical teachings to honor your parents, then the future of this community, of this state, and of the nation is bereft. I am honored to join y'all today. We must ensure that what we teach our children and how they behave comports with our history and traditions. Thank you." The governor stepped away to rapturous applause.

"Thank you, Governor Saxby. Your presence is an honor, as is your understanding of the importance of pursuing this case. As I just explained to the jury, Rose Tucker is not a child who deserves our sympathy for the crime she committed. No, she is an adult who, with cold and calculated precision, murdered her father in his bed. I will tell you, the testimony was tough. We had to hear evil things. Marcus Tucker was a criminal in his own way, abusing his daughter in the manner he did. We all empathize with her plight. But that abuse did not give her the right to circumvent our laws and murder him for her own vengeance. No matter the circumstances, we all must follow the law. We look forward to a verdict of guilty."

Krista triumphantly raised her hand, then joined the governor as they descended the stairs. They disappeared into the first floor of the courthouse. Jake paced in the bathroom, fuming. He considered going to the judge and moving for mistrial because of Krista's conduct. On the second floor of the courthouse, the jury was deliberating. Outside, Krista had whipped up a frenzy with her words blaring from loudspeakers. Certainly everyone in the courthouse had heard them.

She had just accomplished something Jake had never considered. She had the Texas Governor put his stamp of approval on Rose's conviction. It gave cover to the jury. Jake stormed out of the bathroom, the door slamming behind him.

Calm down, Jake. Talk to Hitch before you go to the judge. Keep your cool.

He reached the conference room door where Hitch, Margie,

and Rose were waiting. He took a deep breath and entered. Inside, he saw Rose staring out the window as if stunned into silence.

"You heard it?" Jake asked.

"The dead in the cemetery heard it," Hitch responded. "What are you going to do?"

"Move for a mistrial, maybe. I don't know."

"Good luck with that," Rose said in a weak voice. Then, after a moment, she said, "They are all going to believe it. Believe it all… The whole town hates me."

Jake's heart sank, because it could very well be true.

CHAPTER FIFTY-SEVEN

JAKE AND CREW huddled while the grandfather clock in the corner drummed out seconds. The jitters from the press conference had dissipated… some. The jury had deliberated for hours. They had sent a note to Judge Dubose, requesting dinner and expressing their desire to work late into the night for a verdict. The judge commanded the lawyers to stay close in case the jury had questions. Hitch suggested going to their office in the town square, where the chairs were comfortable.

Jake asked the judge that Rose remain with him so he could counsel his client through the ordeal. Krista objected and argued that Rose should stay in the holding cell. Jake opened his mouth to respond, but Hope interceded. She promised the judge she would station a deputy in the lobby of Jake's office. The judge, in one of his more reasonable rulings, allowed it.

Too amped to sit down, Rose paced around the room. She continued to circle the large oval table at a slow pace.

"You're gonna drive me crazy, little one," Hitch said.

"I can't sit still. This is the worst part. During the trial, I could at least look at them, see their faces. Now I can't see anything, and I have no idea what they are thinking."

"I get it," Jake said.

"Why don't you come over and sit down?" Hitch implored.

"I told you I can't."

Margie popped open a container. "Take a cookie, hon I baked them last night. They're delicious. Get your mind off things."

"I can't argue with you there," Hitch said, using his sausage-like fingers to nab two of the delicious treats.

"You don't have any shame, do you?" Margie said.

"When it comes to you and your cooking? I'm plumb powerless." Hitch flashed a sly grin.

Jake noted that familiar crimson blush creeping up Margie's cheeks.

After some additional pacing, Rose finally slumped down in a chair. The pendulum in the clock clacked out its cadence.

Just then, Jake's phone rang.

"It's the court."

Rose's eyes widened. Jake reached out and took her hand.

Could the jury have a verdict?

"You gonna answer it?" Hitch asked.

Jake pushed the red button on his phone. "Jake Fox." Jake nodded at the few words spoken on the other end and then hung up.

"The judge received a note from the jury. Their deliberations have stalled. They are not unanimous."

Cheers and hollers rang out around the table. Hitch slapped the table, knocking a coffee cup on the floor.

"Wait, wait. Don't get too excited. He called to inform us he's sending back a note that they must continue their deliberations until they reach a unanimous verdict."

"Dynamite charge," Hitch said.

"What?" Rose asked.

Hitch answered. "It's a dynamite charge, darlin'. Judges use them to break logjams in the jury room. It basically tells them it's their duty to deliberate until they come to a verdict."

"But some are on my side," Rose said, a big smile on her face. "They could convince the others I'm not guilty."

"Or some could convince the others that they are too tired to care, and they should convict you so they can go back to their normal lives."

The mood in the room deflated, and the bells on the front door jingled.

"I thought you all might be hungry," Darla said as she busted through the door with several white bags from the diner. A jealous grimace flashed across her face when she saw Hitch gnawing on Margie's cookies. "I gave a cheeseburger to the deputy in the lobby. He seems nice." The smell of greasy fries flooded the small room.

"Sorry, Darla, my stomach's too knotted to eat anything," Rose said.

"Well, pass one over. I'll make a dent in it," Hitch said. Rose stared at him. "What? Man has got to eat. You're gonna be guilty or innocent regardless of if I have a full belly."

"Hitch…" Jake chided.

"I'm just yanking her chain. I'm still on team Rose, but my stomach is on team burger."

Margie opened a bag and pulled out a basket of fries. "Do y'all have any ketchup?"

Darla sat down. "It's in the refrigerator in the kitchen." She pointed the way over her shoulder.

Margie pursed her lips and looked Darla up and down. The other woman ignored the glare. With a huff, Margie stood and brushed off her dress. "Anyone need anything while I'm up?"

"I could use one of those beers off the top shelf," Hitch said through a mouthful of burger.

"Court is still in session," Jake said.

"Fine. If there's a pop in there, I'd drink one."

"Comin' right up," Margie chimed in, fluttering out the door on her errand. Upon her return, she popped the top on the soda can and set it down in front of Hitch with a napkin. "Here you go."

"Thank you much, Margie. I appreciate it."

Darla shot a side-eye at the brief exchange and then said, "Hitch, that waitress at the diner, Tizzie, says hi."

Margie blanched. Jake and Rose exchanged a quick glance, searching for a safe haven.

Margie cleared her throat. "She's not much of a cook, if you ask me."

"She is a sweet woman, but I don't know why the men around here are so high on her," Darla piled on.

Hitch slunk down further into his chair, chomping on his burger, apparently trying to avoid the fray.

You wanted to be a small-town playboy.

"I think it's her enormous breasts."

They all turned to look at Rose.

"What? They're huge. I even stare at them when I'm in there."

Hitch let out a loud guffaw and hooted. The rest of them followed suit until they were crying from the laughter.

The phone rang. Jake answered and grunted a few responses. "Thank you, Your Honor." He hung up. "That was the court again."

"We know that," Hitch said. "What did the judge say?"

"The jury called it quits for the evening after the judge's note. They're going home and resuming in the morning."

Agony flooded Rose's expression. Jake glanced up and noticed the deputy in the doorway.

"Miss Rose, I have to take you back." He scanned the table. "I know you're probably not too hungry. But those burgers beat jail food. I'd stick around a might if you'd like to have yourself some dinner."

"Thank you, deputy," Margie said. "What's your name?"

"Patrick James, ma'am."

"Well, Patrick, pull up a chair. We were just discussing the local scenery at the diner."

"Miss Tizzie and her girls?"

The room burst into laughter again.

CHAPTER FIFTY-EIGHT

LATE THE NEXT MORNING, the judge summoned them. Jake and Margie scooted past the sprinklers wetting down the courthouse lawn. Flowers and grasses fluttered in the soft, early morning breeze. They stepped inside and climbed the stairs to see Rose. The judge had refused to let Rose come to Jake's office. Margie gasped when she caught sight of Rose sitting on a concrete bench at the back of the holding cell. Rose's eyes sparked when she saw them.

"That's not right, puttin' her in a cage."

"I know, Margie. I'm doing my best to get her out," Jake said. "Morning, kiddo. Did you get much sleep last night?"

"Not really. It's never quiet in the jail."

"Hopefully that all ends this morning," Jake said.

Rose shook her head. "I can't let myself think those thoughts yet."

Margie stuck her fingers through the steel mesh as if to touch Rose. Rose did not rise from the bench. It was almost as if she was ashamed. "You can't give up hope, hon."

Rose dropped her head and didn't answer. The door opened behind them.

"Morning, Miss Margie," the deputy said.

"Mornin', Estes. How's Idris?"

"Mama's doin' just fine. She complains about sciatica when it acts up, but she's mostly doing well."

"Still singin' in her choir?"

"Yes, ma'am, she's down at the church Wednesday nights and every weekend, singin' up a storm with the rest of her ladies. They traveled to Dallas by bus last month to sing with a large choir at the First Baptist in downtown."

"Good for her. It's good to be active at our age."

"Yes, ma'am, it is. Morning to you, Jake and Miss Rose."

"Morning, Estes," Rose said.

The deputy approached the holding cell, cowboy hat in hand.

"Miss Rose, I hope that jury gets it right today."

Rose looked at him quizzically.

"I used to volunteer with your daddy down at the lodge, and he was quite the man. Yes, ma'am. Marcus was a hard-working man, and boy did he used to brag on you something fierce."

"I appreciate that, Estes."

"I know that it's probably rough right now. Maybe no one's believing you. I wanted you to know, before that jury comes back, that I believe you. I don't think you did that to your daddy."

"That means the world to me," Rose said.

"The judge wants you all inside." The deputy took his keys off his belt and opened the lock. Rose stood and followed Jake and Margie into the courtroom. Again, people packed benches —reporters and Gert at the ready. As they entered, Krista looked up from the prosecution's table. She stood and caught Jake's elbow as he passed. Rose continued on to sit with Hitch at counsel table.

"I have a good feeling this morning," Krista said, gloating.

"Maybe you just woke up on the right side of the bed. For once," Jake said.

"No, I'm feeling pretty confident that jury is going to bring me a guilty verdict by lunch."

"And what makes you say that?"

"It's Friday, Jake. You know they won't want to deliberate on this case into next week."

"They'll do whatever the facts and law compel them to do."

"The facts say she should be in prison. I figure the jury wants to return the verdict, have a quick lunch, and get their life back."

"I wouldn't get ahead of yourself. Juries are fickle. You don't know what they are going to do."

"I would love to be a fly on the wall, though. To hear the final vote where they seal Ms. Tucker's fate."

"What is your problem with Rose?"

"I have it in for any murderer."

"Any murder with publicity," Jake said. "Holding that press conference was low, Krista. Trying to influence the jury… ugly move."

"Trial law is a full-contact sport, Jake. You don't like it, leave your uniform in the locker room."

"Still wanting to be a judge someday? You think preening for all those cameras will make it easier for the folks of this county to vote you on the bench?"

"It doesn't hurt to have the governor on my side. I'd love to get out of this Podunk town."

Jake surveyed the crowd in the courtroom. "Podunk? I wouldn't let your constituents hear you say that out loud. Besides, you've chosen to live here your whole life. You could have moved on at any time."

"And what? Move down the road to Dallas and become a big-firm lawyer, grinding in an office to make my minimum billable hours? How'd that work out for you?"

Jake's neck tingled and flushed at the brazen allusion to

Lucy and his divorce. He paused a moment to push down the foul words on the tip of his tongue.

"That's one thing I can always count on from you, Krista."

"What?"

"You sure won't let decency impede your mouth."

"Bless your heart. Did I hit a nerve?"

"All rise!" the bailiff called. Both Jake and Krista looked up and hurried to stand behind their chairs at their respective tables. Judge Dubose appeared from the door leading to his chambers and took long, solemn strides to the tall leather chair behind the bench.

"Be seated. I have an update on the jury's deliberations. I just spoke with the foreman. They have reached an impasse." A murmur shot through the crowd. "I will not give a numerical split, as the foreman did not inform me. It appears the dynamite charge did not work. He told me the jury split into two contingents. Neither side will budge from their respective positions. The foreman told me further deliberations would not prove fruitful. I then quizzed the jury. I advised them not to tell me their stance on the verdict, but to tell me if further discussion could change their minds. They all said no. Folks, we have a hung jury. I have no choice but to declare a mistrial."

Electricity shot through the courtroom. Rose gripped Jake's hand and squeezed it.

"That's good for us, right?"

"It's great, but we're not clear yet."

The judge spoke again. "Mr. Fox, I assume you do not object to me declaring a mistrial."

"No, Judge."

"Very well. Ms. Robb, you have thirty days to inform the court if you wish to retry Ms. Tucker."

"Your Honor, I don't need thirty days," Krista blurted. "The prosecution is ready to go to trial as soon as the court has space on its docket. We can start Monday."

"That won't be necessary, but we can retry this case three weeks from Monday. I will see you all then." The judge banged his gavel.

"Your Honor," Krista shouted. "We have one more item to discuss."

"And what is that?"

"The matter of Ms. Tucker's detainment. We believe she should be in the custody of the county jail. Remember, she proved to you she does not follow the court's instructions and is a flight risk."

"Mr. Fox, what say you?"

Jake stepped behind Rose and placed his hands on her shoulders. "That's ridiculous, Judge. Ms. Tucker poses no flight risk and is presumed innocent until proven guilty. She has every right to remain free through trial."

"And take off in her truck? I think not. She attacked a deputy right here in front of me. I've seen nothing to change the facts that led me to detain her. Ms. Robb's motion is meritorious."

Rose stiffened under Jake's grip. He could feel her heart thundering.

"Ms. Tucker, I remand you to the custody of the sheriff, and you will remain detained through the next trial."

CHAPTER FIFTY-NINE

ROSE STOOD under the shower head, the near-scalding water coursing through her hair. Steam swirled around her, providing a wet blanket of heat. She ran the bar of soap over her shoulders. It emitted a powdery scent. For a few moments, she allowed the trial stress to wash away. She soaked in the calm. The guards must have taken some sympathy on her because they allowed her to shower alone without the constant chatter and bustling of other prisoners. Nobody bothered her. The sound of splashing water draped the stillness around her. Recent events flashed through her mind like a movie montage. She disappeared into her thoughts. For how long, she didn't know.

How did you end up here?

After a few moments, Rose woke from her reverie and spied her pruney fingertips. Her time was up. She wrung the extra water from her hair and reached for the towel just beyond the transparent shower curtain strung across the mouth of the concrete stall. As she lay her fingers on the rough cotton rag, the plastic sheet was ripped aside by a large, beefy hand. The towel fell to the floor. Rose jumped back, slipping on the slick shower floor. She caught her fall against the wall and peered through the opening.

"Where do you think you're going?" A wolflike grin slid across the guard's face. "We meet again."

Rose watched as Helen pulled on the cuff of her long-sleeved uniform. A black Celtic cross was tattooed on the inside of her wrist.

What?

A slender shank slid into Helen's hand. She pulled back her arm, preparing to plunge the steel spike into Rose.

"Helen! Leave her alone!" Cassie's voice bounced off the concrete walls. The shout stopped Helen before she thrust at Rose.

"You heard Zach. They want her tonight."

"No. Not her," Cassie pleaded. "She's just a baby."

"Did you suddenly grow a conscience? They are all babies! Zach and Lilith take what they want. You should know that, Cas. Zach takes you all the time," Helen sneered. "If you're not going to help me, leave."

"Drop the shank," Cassie demanded. Helen stepped back and held out her arms like a boxer egging on an opponent. "Make me."

Cassie charged Helen, dropping her shoulder and slamming the brick-like woman in the chest, thrusting her backward and into the concrete wall of the shower room. The large woman emitted a groan. Rose hopped from the shower stall into the cramped aisle lined with sinks on one side.

"Help! They're fighting!" Rose called out.

Helen flung Cassie's petite frame to the floor and turned her glare on Rose.

"Shut up, you little tramp," she growled. Helen advanced, light glinting off the shank. "You will not blow this for me." She took a swipe. The tip of the weapon grazed Rose's bare skin, opening a long gash. Rose grabbed her abdomen, and blood leaked over her fingers.

Cassie shook the cobwebs for her head and pulled herself up using the edge of the sink. With a guttural howl, she leapt onto Helen's back, yanking her hair.

"Get off of me, you whore!" Hellen yelled.

"Rose, run! Get out of here! Now!" Cassie shouted.

Rose bolted for the door. As she flung it open, she glanced over her shoulder. Cassie kicked at Helen, causing the guard's legs to buckle to her knees. Cassie pounded a flurry of fists into the larger woman's neck and head. Rose fled down the hallway.

"Help! Fight! Fight in the showers!" The ache in her side exploded as blood dripped down her legs. "Fight!"

Deputy James rounded the corner, and Rose collapsed in his arms.

"What?"

Rose struggled to catch her breath. "In the showers. A guard attacked Cassie."

The deputy spoke into the hand mic attached to his shoulder. "I need all personnel to the showers. We have a fight in the showers, over."

Within seconds, two more deputies burst in, trailed by the sheriff.

"What's happening?"

"A guard attacked Cassie. In the showers," Rose said. Hope dashed down the hall, following the deputies. Rose struggled to her feet.

"Miss Rose, you stay here," Deputy James said.

"Cassie," Rose wheezed. She stumbled toward the fight. Deputy James tucked his head under her arm, holding her up as she struggled down the hallway. Shouts spilled from the washroom.

"We need medical to the showers immediately." Hope's voice echoed off the hard surfaces. Light spilled through the doorway.

A few more steps.

Rose and the deputy limped around the corner. Cassie and Helen lay sprawled on the floor, and blood was pooling at Cassie's side. Rose fought her way free of Deputy James's grip. She rushed toward Cassie, but Hope caught her mid-stride, restraining her.

"Let me go!" She reached out beyond Hope's arms, holding her back. "Cassie!" She stared into Hope's eyes. "What's wrong with her?"

"Back up. Calm down. Medical is on its way." A deputy behind Hope turned Cassie onto her back, picked up Rose's towel from the floor, and applied pressure to her abdomen.

"This one has a pulse. Breath is strong," the other deputy called out as he knelt over Helen. "Looks like she hit her head on the sink. She's bleeding from a cut above her ear."

Cassie's expression contorted as she fought against the pain.

Deputy James walked up behind Rose, holding up a towel for her to cover herself. Rose's hands shook violently as she grabbed it and secured it around her body.

The jail physician and a nurse rushed in and assessed Cassie's wound.

"Rose, what happened in here?" Hope asked.

"I was showering in here by myself."

"Why were you alone?"

"I don't know… I didn't see the guard come into the room. She tried to stab me in the shower. It was awful. She looked like she wanted to kill me. She had that horrible thing in her hand." Rose pointed toward the floor.

"It's a homemade shank," a deputy said.

"They confiscated that from C Block last week," Deputy James said. "I remember because they were showing it off in the bullpen."

Helen groaned as she stirred from her blackout.

"Restrain her," Hope barked at one guard.

"She's one of us," he protested.

"Deputy, I said to restrain her. Now!"

The deputy dislodged his handcuffs from his duty belts and clamped them around Helen's wrist.

"What is that?" Hope approached Helen, who was cuffed on the floor. Kneeling down, she pushed up the long sleeve of Helen's uniform.

"What's the problem, Sheriff?" Deputy James asked.

"It's a tattoo on the inside of her wrist. A Celtic cross."

"Cassie has one, too," Rose said.

"She's right," the nurse said.

"What is going on here?" Hope asked no one in particular. Then she looked at Rose. "Doc, you need to look at this," she said as she pointed.

Rose glanced at the large red stain blooming on her towel. "She got me, too," Rose said, as her knees buckled and she collapsed to the floor.

CHAPTER SIXTY

"MR. FOX, PLEASE HOLD," the judge's assistant said over the speakerphone in Hope's office. Jake's ire skyrocketed as the banal hold music played in an incessant loop.

Hope clicked her fingers in front of his face. "Hey, killer, settle down. Yelling at the judge will not get you what you want."

"It's his fault! She'd be safe at home with Margie and me."

"I know, but you catch more flies with honey than vinegar."

"Thanks for the inane platitude."

"Hey, you're mad at the judge, not me, remember?"

She was in your care at the jail! But Jake pushed that unfair thought out of his mind.

Hope's phone rang. She pulled it from her back hip pocket and stepped to the side.

"You're sure," Hope said. "That's good news. Thanks, Margie… Jake? He's about to throttle the judge through the phone, but otherwise he's doing great. I know. Yeah. I'll keep telling him. Call again when you can." Hope hung up the phone. "That was Margie."

"I heard."

"I told you, you're chewing on the wrong person."

"What did she say?"

"Rose is resting comfortably. They're waiting on a plastic surgeon to stitch her up. Margie's insisting on it. Something about Rose not having a nasty scar in a bathing suit."

"The other girl?"

"She's still in surgery… listed in critical condition. They'll know more in a couple of hours."

The hold music disappeared, replaced by electronic clicks, and then the judge's voice.

"Mr. Fox, do I have you?"

"Yes, Your Honor."

"Ms. Robb, are you on the line?"

"Judge, I'm here."

"Good… Mr. Fox, why are you interrupting my dinner? What is this all about?" A slight slur tinged the judge's words.

"Judge, an incident occurred down at the jail involving Rose Tucker."

"Why am I not surprised?" the judge said.

Anger bunched in Jake's shoulders. Hope signaled with her hands, imploring him to cool it.

"Ms. Tucker didn't do anything, Your Honor. She was attacked tonight in the jail."

"What kind of attack?"

"A guard tried to stab her in the jail showers."

"A guard?" Krista said. "That sounds as crazy as the ghosts she blames for killing her father. When did she conceive this newest fable?"

"It's the truth," Hope said.

"Sheriff? You're there."

"Yes, Judge. I responded to the incident."

"Could someone tell me what's going on in my county?"

"We're investigating, Judge. I don't know all the facts."

"Like you don't know where my daughter is?"

Hope slumped, deflated by the cheap shot. "Your Honor,

we're working night and day to find your daughter. I'm sorry I haven't found her yet."

"You haven't been working hard enough, Sheriff Stone."

"About tonight, I do know. One of our guards attacked two inmates in the shower. Ms. Tucker was one victim."

"Where is she now?" the judge asked.

"We transported them all to County Medical. The other prisoner is in surgery. Ms. Tucker is waiting to be stitched up."

"You have deputies watching her? I don't want her fleeing the jurisdiction," Krista said.

"She shouldn't be in the jail!" Jake said.

"Mr. Fox, I won't allow—"

"Your Honor, I'm sorry I'm pissed, but someone attacked my client tonight. She shouldn't have been there. She wasn't at risk when she was staying with Margie."

"That sounds like the sheriff's problem," Krista said.

"Sheriff, it does sound like you have a lot of problems," the judge said.

"I have the facility on lockdown, and we're working through our investigative protocols. I *will* find out what happened. But, you're right, this is my problem, and I intend to solve it."

"That's not what this call is about," Jake said.

"Mr. Fox, what exactly do you want me to do? It sounds like your client is going to be fine and is getting the medical care she needs. So I don't know why you called."

"I'm asking you to vacate the detention order and release Rose into my custody and Margie's care."

"That didn't work the last time," Krista said.

"She took a joyride! That's not even in the same league as getting stabbed in the jail showers. Rose should never have been there. She shouldn't be there now."

"She punched my deputy in the nose," the judge said.

"After you ordered her detained. The only violence relates to Ms. Robb's crusade to detain Rose. She wouldn't have punched the deputy if Krista hadn't been grandstanding to put her in jail so she could strut around for the cameras."

"She's a danger to the community," Krista said. "I wasn't strutting."

"Like you weren't grandstanding at your press conference on the courthouse steps?"

"I'm the district attorney. I have a responsibility to keep the community informed."

"You were trying to influence the jury."

"That's low, even for you, Jake."

"It's the absolute truth. The entire city block heard you yammering," Jake said.

"Stop it!" the judge said. "I won't have you bickering like children. I don't know what it is with you two, but I've had enough. Sheriff, what say you?"

"Your Honor, I hate to say it, but until I figure out what happened, I'm not sure I can protect Ms. Tucker here. It would be one thing if another prisoner had assaulted her. But it appears one of my guards initiated the attack. Until I complete the investigation, I must assume that she is not the only one. Perhaps it's best that Ms. Tucker stay at Ms. Moore's home for the time being."

"I—" Krista started.

"Judge, I have a few deputies I know I can trust. I could use them to station a deployment at Ms. Moore's home. We can rotate them out on shifts."

"Home arrest?"

"More or less. It'll stretch resources. But I have some funds in my overtime budget. I hate admitting failings at the jail, but I do think it's for the best."

"Ms. Robb."

"Judge, I don't like it at all."

"I don't care what you like. I want to know if you have a substantive legal objection to the sheriff's solution." A long silence followed. "Ms. Robb?"

"Judge, we can agree to home arrest only temporarily."

"Then we'll go with it on a trial run. Mr. Fox, I'm reluctant, but you have what you called for. I will vacate the detention order. I'll enter a new one on home arrest when I get to chambers in the morning. Anything further?... Then this call is over, and I can get back to my steak and wine. Good night." The line went dead.

Jake looked at Hope, a big grin on his face. "I guess you can catch flies with vinegar."

"If you have a sheriff on the call to bail you out."

"That, too... She's coming home. Let's call Margie."

CHAPTER SIXTY-ONE

$100,000.

The drugs swirled through Beth's mind as Zach's truck roared down the highway. Lilith had given everyone in the room high-fives when the last bid for Beth's virginity reached $100,000. A couple of days passed in the cellar while Lilith and Zach worked out the "shipping instructions" with the buyer. He was sending a plane for her at a remote airstrip. Lilith had told Beth she would like her new "owner." Before the sun had risen, Zach rousted her from her sleep. Lilith fed her another pill. The familiar, welcome euphoria swirled through her, and they loaded her into the truck. Nausea swirled in Beth's stomach, and her heart raced as she stared at the taillights on the tractor trailer in front of them. The horrors awaiting her on the other side played in her mind. She was told to prepare for a long flight, and that fresh clothes and a shower would be waiting for her on the plane.

Think, Beth. Think.

"You're going to make your new master very happy," Zach said. "You're making me rich, too." He twirled the braids of his beard as he drove. Zach reached into his shirt pocket. He pulled a cigarette from the pack, field-stripped it, and tossed the filter out a crack in the window. Striking the match, he lit the tobacco, blowing out smoke rings.

"I have to stop," Beth said.

"You peed before we left, Viv. You can hold it."

I hate that name.

"You don't understand. Men never understand." The drugs were making her brave.

"I understand all I need to know about women," Zach said.

"My period just started, numbnuts. So unless you want me to bleed through my pants and all over your upholstery, I have to stop."

"Don't you ruin my truck."

"Then I suggest you stop somewhere so I can get some tampons."

"Just don't bleed on my seats."

"You're such an ignoramus, Zach. It's not like I control the flow."

"All right, I'll stop. There's a truck stop at mile marker seventy. That's just three miles ahead."

"Whatever."

Zach punched the accelerator and sped toward the exit. In just a few minutes, they pulled in front of the store. Lights and big rigs stretched out around Beth as far as she could see. Zach exited first and then opened her door.

"When you get out, you play it cool. The same as we've always done. Understand?"

"Can I have a twenty?"

"What for?"

"My feminine hygiene products, duh."

Zach reached into his jeans pocket and pulled out a bill.

"Cool, remember. You try to run or create a scene, and swear I'll go back to Haven and shoot that little friend of yours, Rose."

The threat caused Beth's heart to race. She nodded. She walked into the store. The clerk waved and greeted them as she rang up other customers. Beth explored, looking through the aisled jammed with random trinkets. One entire aisle displayed jerked meats. They even had ostrich jerky. She spied what she needed on an end cap. Beth selected a box and paid out at the register.

"I'm going to the bathroom now. I'll be right back."

"I'll come with you."

"Look around, Zach. There's a million people here. Women are going in and out of the bathroom. If you follow me, cops will be all over you. Just stay here. I'll be right back."

Beth left Zach and walked to the women's room. She turned the corner. She studied the walls. There was a window positioned about five feet from the wall in the back. Beth ran to it and traced her fingers along the bottom ledge. She felt the latch and pulled. The window popped open, and a cool breeze flowed over her. It was too high for her to climb out., so Beth upended the trash can under the window, scattering paper towels and trash on the floor. A woman appeared from a stall.

"What in the world?"

"Shh. I'm trying to get away from—"

"You're on drugs, is what you are."

The woman backed away from Beth and went into the hallway. Beth could hear her yelling.

"There's a crazy meth head in there tearing the place up and trying to crawl out the window."

Beth climbed up on the trash can and forced herself through the tight sill, dropping to the concrete outside. One hundred feet in front of her, tractor trailers spread out in a dancing sea of running lights.

Beth took off at a full sprint. She looked over her shoulder just in time to see Zach turn the corner, his heavy boots clopping as he ran.

"Viv, you get back here, you little—"

The drugs Lilith had given her made her head swim, and

she felt her legs faltering underneath her. She was fifty feet from the trucks, and Zach was gaining.

I wonder if he'll beat me on the way to my new owner. Maybe they'll beat me together for sport.

Beth dismissed the thought and dug in. Her lungs burned, and an iron taste flooded her mouth. The bitter diesel fumes from all the idling rigs made it hard to breathe. She was out of shape from being held captive, and could feel her strength waning. Zach was right behind her. Thoughts raced through her mind until she settled on her next move. She let out a slight smile and then started screaming at the top of her lungs.

"Fire! There's a fire. Help. It's all on fire!"

Zach cursed her.

"Fire! Fire! Fire!" Beth kept screaming and running for the big rigs. Time stopped, and then truck doors flew open. Men climbed down from their cabs and scurried about, looking for the blaze, the panic of flames around so many gas tanks forcing them to pay attention. More men appeared. In the middle of the group, she spotted a dark SUV with lights in the grill. Getting closer, she noticed the sheriff's star emblazoned on the side. Still screaming, she forcefully pushed through the initial line of men.

"Fire!"

Several of them followed her, asking where it was.

Ten feet.

The drugs must have muted her depth perception because she hit the hood of the truck at almost a full sprint, knocking the wind out of her. The female deputy inside looked up at her and the men swirling around her.

"What the—"

"I'm Beth Dubose," she tried to shout. Beth collapsed in front of the cruiser as the deputy exited the vehicle. Several men had knelt down next to her.

"Give her some air," the deputy shouted. She squatted in front of Beth.

Beth grabbed her ribs and groaned at the pain as she struggled to get her breath back. Through the sea of legs and bodies, Beth spied Zach backing away. He flipped her off, mimed shooting a rifle, and then tucked tail for his truck.

In a hoarse whisper, Beth let out, "I'm Beth Dubose."

"I know. You look just like your picture, even with that beautiful black hair," the deputy said with a warm smile. "Welcome back. We've been looking for you."

Tears of relief poured down her cheeks. Beth reached out her hand. "May I borrow your phone?"

The deputy held out a smartphone, and Beth dialed. It rang.

Rosie, please pick up.

CHAPTER SIXTY-TWO

LILITH JAMMED DOWN the accelerator of her SUV, tearing into the night. The yellow dotted line on the highway blurred. She pounded her palm on the steering wheel. Zach's voice on the car link blasted through the phone.

"Lilith, it's not that bad."

"Not bad? You nimrod! You lost Beth Dubose. You lost a hundred grand. They're going to take it out of our hide as soon as they hear. It's bad, Zach, and you'd better get that through that rock of a head."

"I'll get it under control."

"How? The girl is in the sheriff's custody now. They're going to have loyal cops around her twenty-four seven."

"I have my ways."

"Do nothing. I don't need you to jack this up any further. It's already a disaster."

"Lilith, watch your mouth."

"I'll say whatever I want. You lost the girl."

"Lilith, I'm warning you."

"Or you'll what?"

"The girl can't live in a bubble forever. We can nab her again. Give it a few weeks to die down."

"And what do we tell the buyer? Here's a twenty-percent discount because of delayed shipping? We're not a department store, Zach. These overseas men live by different rules in their countries. Eye for an eye, genius."

"The guy's a pervert. He might pay more because he had to wait. Like mental foreplay."

"You are demented."

"I told you. Calm down. I'll figure it out."

"We'd better get a handle on it soon. I've been called home."

"Wait… Why?"

"They already know, Zach. The deputy that found her radioed it in as soon as they rescued Beth. It was all over the police scanner. The club called half an hour ago and called me back to answer for your stupid mistakes. They'll want to contain this problem."

"What are you going to tell them, Lilith?"

"The truth, Zach. That this is all your fault."

"They'll kill me."

"That sounds like your problem. I didn't get duped by a little girl." She disconnected the call. Zach tried to call back, and she declined. She had bigger things to worry about. The president had called her to the Devil's Vikings' clubhouse to explain how $100,000 had gone up in smoke and how they'd possibly made an enemy of one of their overseas clients. Hopefully a nightmare didn't await her.

I'll blame Zach. They already think he's a loose cannon. Maybe they'll take it out on him. Please let them take it out on him.

Memories of prior horrors she'd endured in the clubhouse —as the old lady of a Devil's Viking—poured through her mind. Some ragged scars never heal. Lost in her thoughts, the flashing lights and blaring siren behind Lilith startled her.

"Son of a…"

Lilith lifted her foot from the gas pedal, slowed her SUV, and lifted the lid on the center console to confirm that her pistol remained within reach. Coasting to a stop, she strained to see the cop in the cruiser's glare.

Relax. It's just a speeding ticket. Charm the pants off the guy and get out of here. Maybe coax a warning out of him.

Lilith's heart raced as she unbuttoned the top buttons on her blouse, pushed up her bosom, smoothed her fire-red hair… checked her lipstick in the mirror.

Easy.

The deputy exited the cruiser and strode to the driver's-side window.

"License and registration, ma'am."

Lilith put on her best seductive smile to turn and hand the officer her documents. Her smile faded. A female deputy greeted her, looked at her ample cleavage, and returned an irritated stare.

"Do you know how fast you were going, ma'am?"

"I wasn't thinking, deputy. My mother had a heart attack, and I'm racing to meet the ambulance in the emergency room. I guess I lost track of my speed. It won't happen again."

"I'm sorry to hear that, but we all have to be safe," the deputy said as she retrieved Lilith's driver's license. She compared the picture to Lilith's face. "Ma'am, I'll be right back."

Lilith could see the silhouette of the deputy typing on a computer. Time dragged by as Lilith stared at the digital clock on the display. She checked the handgun one more time.

Do I want to kill a cop?

The deputy exited her vehicle and strode back to Lilith's window. She could see the paper ticket in her hand.

Finally. Take the ticket and get the heck out of here.

"Ma'am, are you from around here?" the deputy asked.

"I live just outside of Haven."

"And your mother lives around these parts?"

"She's getting older. Momma's mind's not what it used to be. I watch after her. She lives with me."

"That's very nice of you. Any drugs or weapons in the car?"

"No. What does that have to do with speeding? Just give me the ticket and let me get on my way."

"Step out of the truck and place your hands on the vehicle."

"That's ridiculous. I'll just give you the money for the ticket." Lilith reached for her purse. The deputy stepped back and put her hand on her service weapon.

"Put your hands on the wheel!"

"I did nothing."

The deputy did not change her stance. "Exit the vehicle, now!"

Lilith stared at the closed console.

No way you get the gun out before she shoots you. Come on, Lilith, you can still talk your way out of this.

"I'm sorry! Get a grip." Lilith popped the handle on the door and stepped out, her stiletto-heeled boots clicking on the asphalt.

"Turn and place your hands on the vehicle."

Lilith did as instructed. The deputy pulled Lilith's right hand behind her, clasped a cuff around her wrist, then secured the left. Lilith turned.

"This seems to be excessive for a speeding ticket."

"Turn around." Once Lilith complied, the deputy said, "You were going ninety-five miles an hour in a sixty-five. I'm citing you for excessive speed and reckless driving."

"I—"

Another sheriff's vehicle arrived. A second deputy stepped out.

"You can't arrest me for speeding in Texas. I know my rights."

"Ma'am, answer me this. If you're racing to the emergency room to meet your mother, how come you're headed out of Haven and away from County Medical?"

Lilith clenched her jaw and didn't answer.

"That's what I thought. I'm arresting you for reckless driving."

"What if I want my lawyer?"

"He can meet you at the jail. And you're going to need him."

"What's that supposed to mean?"

"We've been searching for a woman who matches your description—long red hair."

CHAPTER SIXTY-THREE

"JUDGE DUBOSE," Hope called out as the judge and his wife burst through the front door of the sheriff's department.

"Where is she?" Natalie asked. Worry lines on the woman's face seemed to have deepened since the last time Hope had updated them on Beth's case. At the time, they'd thought finding their child alive would be impossible. Her pressed and dry-cleaned tailored outfits had given way to a sweatsuit and shawl. A waft of bourbon smacked Hope in the face.

"She's in the back."

"Take us to her now," the judge said, exuding a similar level of inebriation. He had loosened his tie, but he still wore his prim suit, and there was a fresh shine on his shoes.

"The nurse and EMTs are finishing up. We can go back in a minute."

"They can wait."

"Judge, they're interviewing her. We need to know what happened to Beth while they had her. They're evaluating her and asking difficult questions. She needs to feel comfortable answering. I must know who did this to her. Understand what they did to her."

Natalie slumped over the counter and dropped her head onto her arms. Sobs leaked from her.

"You'll have to forgive my wife. She doesn't have the constitution for stress."

Natalie rounded on the judge, pounding her fists into his chest. "Don't you do that, Harlan. Don't you belittle me!"

The judge grabbed her arms and wrestled them to her side. "Nat! Get ahold of yourself. Not here. Not in public."

Deputy James stood up from his desk and walked toward the couple. Hope signaled for him to hold fast.

"Judge… Ms. Dubose. You don't want Beth to see you like this."

"Why not? Right, Harlan? She's seen it all." Natalie's voice trailed off. "She's seen more than she deserves."

"Nat!" the judge yelled.

Deputy James took a step forward.

"Sheriff?"

They all turned and noticed a surprised young woman in purple scrubs peeking through a doorway. "We're done with Beth. Are these the parents?"

"Yes."

"Sir, ma'am, she's back this way." The nurse held the door open as they all shuffled through. The nurse passed by them and stopped at a closed door down the hall.

"She's shaken, so take it easy when you first see her," the nurse said. She pushed the door open and stepped inside. The ensemble followed, and Beth came into view.

Beth looked up from a chair next to the examination table, her exhausted features blooming into an enormous smile. Natalie wrestled her arm from the judge's grip and bolted for the teen girl.

"Beth!" Natalie rushed forward and flopped to her knees, wrapping Beth in an embrace that seemed as if she was trying to crush them both into one body. "I can't believe…" She pushed fat, joyous tears from her face. "Look at you. Your hair? It's black. Did you do this? Do you like it? If you do, it's beautiful. If you don't, we can change it. We'll get an appointment at the salon. They'll be so happy to see you." Natalie's excitement rambled out of her mouth until Beth touched her fingertips to Natalie's lips. She reached out, pulled a tissue from a box, and dabbed up a few tears from her stepmother's cheeks.

"Good to see you too, Nat." Her voice dropped to a whisper. "So good to see you, too."

Natalie buried her face into Beth's shoulder, sobs wracking her body. "It's going to be better. I'm going to be better. You and me. We'll go to lunch. Talk. Shop. Girl time together. Maybe a little gossip. I'm never going to let you out of my sight."

Beth looked both ecstatic and confused. She glanced up at Hope, who could only shrug. From the corner of her eye, she stole a glance at the judge. He gazed down upon his daughter, stoic, like the expression he wore on the bench. Straightening his tie, he fidgeted with his hands, seemingly unsure how to occupy himself.

"Hi, Dad," Beth said over Natalie's shoulder.

"How are you, Beth?"

"Seen better days."

"Did they…?"

"Let's talk about other things. I'm just happy I'm home."

"You are… you are so home," Natalie blubbered. The tint of bourbon now permeated the air in the tiny room. She turned to Hope. "Can we take her home now?" Natalie implored.

"Yes, ma'am. I'd like a deputy to follow you all. Look around the place. I'm not sure this is over yet."

"What's that crack supposed to mean?" the judge asked.

"Sir. Your daughter escaped tonight from what we think is an organized gang taking girls and selling them on the dark web. We know little about them, so we want to ensure you all are safe."

"You never know much, do you, Sheriff?"

"Everything okay in here?" Deputy James said from the doorway.

"My focus, Judge, is the safety of you and your family."

"You don't have to worry about that, Sheriff. I came out of pocket and hired my own security since the county can't protect us. We can take care of ourselves."

Natalie glowered at the judge. "We'll take you up on that ride," Natalie said. "Beth and me."

"I'll drive them home," Deputy James said. He stared at the judge. "You okay to drive, Judge? I could have a deputy drive your car home, and I'll bring him back."

"What are you saying, Deputy?"

"I'm saying that I like a good bourbon, but maybe it's time to hand over the keys. No shame in being careful." Deputy James held out his hands. The judge's face flushed beet red. He jammed his hand into his suit pocket and pulled out his keys, slapping them into the deputy's hand.

"Let's get on with it," he said. "Nat? Beth? You coming?"

"We're right behind you, Harlan," Nat said as the judge disappeared around the corner.

Natalie stood and smoothed her clothing. "Look at me." She laughed. "I'm a mess."

"I think you look beautiful," Beth said.

Natalie took Beth's hand as they started for the door, and Beth stopped in front of Hope.

"Thank you."

"You're the one who escaped. You're the brave one."

"No… I mean, thank you for always believing. Being alone and hopeless is truly awful. The idea that someone is looking for you… I prayed someone, maybe a guardian angel, still kept me in her thoughts. I'm forever grateful."

"Welcome home."

CHAPTER SIXTY-FOUR

HOPE SHUT the door behind her, pulled out a chair, and set the soda can down in front of Lilith, whose lips parted into a smug smile. Condensation beaded on the cool aluminum can, twinkling in the ultraviolet light from the bulbs buzzing above them.

"Trying to make friends, Sheriff?"

"Thought you might be thirsty." Hope sat in the chair, placed a manila folder on the metal table in the interrogation room, and stared into Lilith's gaze.

"I understand you haven't asked for a lawyer yet."

"True."

"Why?"

"I wanted to chat with you first. I've done nothing wrong. Why did you drag me in here?" Lilith asked.

"Let's say curiosity. We've been on the lookout for a woman with red hair."

Lilith scoffed. "Go look in the mirror, Sheriff. Is that your best police work, arresting every ginger and harassing them?"

"Some are more interesting than others. Those who lie to my deputies pique my interest."

Lilith responded with silence. Hope reached into the folder and laid Lilith's booking photo in front of her.

"I've shown that photograph to a few people," Hope said.

"Print it in the newspaper if you like. Why do I care?"

"One of them, a young woman, believes she saw you the night someone murdered Marcus Tucker."

Lilith shifted in her chair. "I look like a lot people. My daddy used to say have a common midwestern face."

"I'm not sure your outfit is that common. I'd say you're unique."

"This is thin gruel, Sheriff. My hair? My clothing? Did you even go to the police academy?"

Hope nodded and opened the folder again, flipping a plastic evidence bag on the table.

"What's that?"

Hope tapped her finger on the clear plastic baggie. "We recovered those long red hairs from the murder scene." Lilith's stare morphed into a glare. "I'm going to have those tested against a sample you're going to give me, and I'm willing to put big money on the chance that they match."

Lilith worried her tongue across her teeth. "What if I don't give this sample to you?"

Hope pulled her phone from her hip pocket and placed it on the table, typing in the digits for a number so that Lilith could see. "I have a Judge Maddix just a phone call away. I'll have a warrant within minutes to take the sample. When it comes back positive, the district attorney will charge you for first-degree murder." Hope paused, allowing the statement to settle with Lilith. "As I hear it, she's looking for high-profile cases to supercharge her career. A real news hog."

"You think a threat scares me?"

"Probably not. You look like you've been around the block. But I'm thinking the death penalty will. I'm guessing the district attorney will conclude that you kidnapped Marcus before killing him, and that elevates the crime to capital murder. She'll convict you and put a needle in your arm." Hope sat back and watched the range of emotions wash behind Lilith's eyes. "I hear it's a lonely place, that execution room. Just you… a doctor… a prison chaplain if you wish."

"I'm not a religious person."

"I'm told everyone finds God when that thin, hollow steel tube slips into a vein."

Lilith grabbed the soda and popped the top. A hiss escaped as the carbonation departed the can. Hope noticed the slight trembling in Lilith's hand.

"Maybe my lawyer can kill the indictment."

"Maybe so. Then you can go back to your life, right? I bet those you're working with will help you. They seem to be quality people."

"Sounds like you're making up fantasies. Do you believe in unicorns, too?"

"What happens if I hold you for a couple of days, and a whisper goes out to the press that you're cooperating with the sheriff's department? Then I let you go. If you have no cronies, no harm, no foul. If you do…"

With a gulp, Lilith drank and stared at the red hairs in the bag. "You have no idea who you're messing with."

"You? I see nothing more than a hoodlum."

A predatory grin spread across Lilith's face. "Careful what you wish for, Sheriff. Once you lance that boil, I'm not sure you're ready for what comes out. It could get nasty."

"Enlighten me."

"They won't appreciate your snooping. You threaten them, and they'll come for you… and those you love. They play by no rules."

Anger flashed through Hope at the allusion to Grace.

"The Devil's Vikings?"

Lilith pursed her lips, as if contemplating. "Maybe. Maybe not. Perhaps that's just the surface. Are you willing to keep digging?"

"I'm going to do my job."

"Even if it unearths the ugly underbelly of this entire town? If it exposes pillars of the community? Do you expect those people to give up easily? Come clean and ruin their own lives? Give up all that cash?"

"If that's where the trail leads…"

"You're naive. Once I open my mouth, we're both dead."

"Sounds like a threat."

"It's reality."

"We'll protect you."

"Here in the jail? You know that's not true." Lilith grabbed the cuff of her leather jacket and pulled it up, exposing the intricate black lines of a Celtic cross tattooed in on the inside of her wrist. "They're everywhere. But I'm sure you already know I'm telling the truth. Even in your own jail."

Images of Helen and Cassie's tattoos flashed through Hope's mind.

Lilith chuckled. "You're so easy to read. Just find the tattoos, you're thinking, and you'll find them. But what about the real powerbrokers, those without tattoos? People in this town have an appetite for what all that we sell. They sneak up to the casinos for the taste of a young girl. It's an appetite as old as the cavemen. They love the money we distribute. How do you plan on finding them? Those who take a paper bag of cash to look the other way. You can't protect me? You can't protect those around you."

Hope feigned standing up. "Then it sounds like you prefer a lethal injection."

Lilith held up her hand as if commanding Hope to sit back down. "Just between us girls, suppose I could give you the shooter?"

"The bullet that killed Marcus?"

"It sure wasn't Rosie."

"How do you know it wasn't her?"

Lilith glared again at the evidence bag. "If your theory is

that I was there, then you must think I saw who pulled the trigger."

Hope's stomach churned at the way Lilith had said Rose's name. "How do you know about Rose?"

"I'm not illiterate. I could have learned her name from the papers. But that's not the truth. I know more about little Rosie than you ever will." Lilith's eyes flashed as she took another sip from the can.

Hope steepled her fingers on the table. "Maybe I can talk to the district attorney, see what she can do."

Lilith inhaled and closed her eyes. "They'll come for both of us."

"Let them. They don't know me."

"It will be a war. Nobody will be safe," Lilith said as she plucked several hairs from her scalp and laid them on the table. "But that's a story for another time."

CHAPTER SIXTY-FIVE

THE WONDERFUL SCENT of the prime rib in Margie's oven filled the home. And joyful chatter spilled from the flurry of activity in the kitchen. A soft knock caught Jake's attention. "Someone's happy to see me," he said when he opened the door, soaking in Hope's beautiful smile. Her black leather jacket accentuated her athletic form and the slight bulge of the gun at her hip. Hope's T-shirt hinted at all her curves, from her tight-fitting jeans down to her black cowboy boots.

"You like what you see?" Hope asked, mischief in her gaze.

Caught deep in an impure reverie, Jake cleared his throat and changed the subject. "Long day at work?"

"You know it." Hope held up two bottles of wine, one red, one white. "I didn't know what Margie might have for a late dinner, so I wanted to come to prepared. Something smells delicious."

"She's outdone herself."

"Peach cobbler?"

"Peach and blackberry."

"Ice cream?"

"Homemade vanilla."

"I'm in serious trouble. You'll have to roll me out of here."

"Mom's a sucker for cobbler," said a voice behind Hope. Jake glanced over Hope's shoulder at the beautiful young woman who stepped out of the shadows onto the porch. Her blonde hair shone even more vibrantly than Hope's. Her features mimicked the sheriff's, but there was something intimately familiar about her mannerisms.

I must have seen her around town before. Maybe at the diner?

Jake shook the thoughts from his mind.

"Jake, meet Grace. Grace, this is—"

"Jake. Hello, Mr. Fox. It's a pleasure to meet you," Grace said, extending her hand for him to shake.

"Likewise," Jake said, still mildly stunned by the feeling that he knew Grace from somewhere.

"Mom won't stop talking about—"

"Grace!" Hope's face bloomed crimson.

The younger woman flashed an impish grin that made her look like Hope's twin. She reached out and plucked the two bottles of wine from her mother. "I'll ask Margie which one she wants me to open." She pushed past them and headed toward the dining room. "Nice to meet you, Mr. Fox," she called over her shoulder. "You're right Momma. He's kinda cute."

Hope wiped her palms on the back of her jeans, not meeting Jake's gaze. "Sorry about that. I don't know where she gets that smart-aleck mouth."

"Oh, I have a pretty good idea," Jake said.

"You two close that door," Margie chided. "You're lettin' out all the air-conditionin' and lettin' in these dang flies."

"Yes, Margie." Hope pushed the door shut. "She has that tone, you know. Like when she was hushing us in the library in high school. I just snap to attention."

"Try living with it."

"Is that Hope?" Rose shouted as she rounded the corner, running up to the sheriff and almost tackling her. "Did Lilith say anything more since you called?"

"She's gone silent, kiddo. She says she won't say more until she hammers out a deal with Krista. We'll see how that goes. I'm hopeful."

"But it's true—Krista is going to drop the charges? That much is true?"

"It's looking that way. I don't see how she couldn't. Deputy James was observing behind the one-way glass while I questioned Lilith. He heard everything she said and vouched for it with the DA. Krista said she'd get back to us, but there's no way she can retry you. My testimony, corroborated by the deputy, would destroy her in court. It's only a matter of time."

"I can't believe it!" Rose spun and danced a jig. She then planted an exaggerated kiss on Hope's cheek, nearly knocking her over. "I'm free!" She pulled Hope into a tight embrace, coaxing out a soft chuckle. When she finally let go, Hope reached up and pushed Rose's hair from her face.

"We're going to get the guy who killed your father," she said.

Rose disappeared into a moment of sorrow. "I hope whoever did it rots."

"I promise," Hope said. "We won't forget about Marcus."

"Thank you... How's Beth?" Rose asked.

"Her parents have her now. We'll see how it goes. It will be touch and go for the next few days. But she'll be sleeping in her own bed. That should help." Hope shook her head. "That family's an odd one, though," Hope said to no one in particular.

"But Beth—she's going to be okay?"

"It's going to take some time. I'm not sure she fully understands all that happened. Thankfully, it looks like they didn't rape her."

"How in the world..." Jake started.

"As a virgin, she was too valuable on the dark web to spoil. As best I can tell, they had sold her as a white slave to some man overseas."

"That's a thing?" Jake said.

"I'm afraid we're going to learn a whole bunch we don't want to know about how cruel life can be," Hope responded.

"I hope they all rot, too," Rose said.

"You and me both," Hope said.

"What are you going to do about the Vikings?" Jake asked.

"We'll have to chase down those loose ends. Maybe I can get more information from Lilith. I have a sinking feeling this all goes much deeper than we can imagine, but that story has yet to be written."

A loud, booming voice spilled out of the kitchen. "You should have seen it, Margie. There we were in court, Jake and me..."

"Sounds like someone is having a good time," Hope said.

"Hitch is in there retelling war stories to Margie," Jake said.

"He realizes Margie was at the trial the whole time, right?" Hope asked.

"Not when he's lost in a story and a few scotches. I'm not sure she minds, though. She's been in rapt attention since he got here a couple of hours ago."

"Young love," Hope chided.

"Young something," Rose said. "Those two really should get a room."

Hope raised her eyebrows in mock surprise.

"Rose! Come on back, hon. Grace and I are just about to set the table," Margie called.

Rose pecked Hope on the cheek. "You're the greatest, Hope. You're my hero."

"Hey... I helped," Jake said.

"Oh yeah. You too, Jake," Rose called over her shoulder as she rounded the doorway into the kitchen.

"You want me to open one of those bottles of wine?" Jake asked.

"In a second, Counselor. I was hoping you could explain a little law to me," Hope said, as she pulled up close to Jake's mouth. "Can you explain to me the statute of limitations again? I think it might apply to an issue I have."

"It's when a law prevents someone from raising an issue…" The explanation disappeared in the softness of Hope's lips as she quieted him with a deep kiss, pulling away slowly with his bottom lip teased between her teeth.

"Is that so?" Hope said.

"Let me see if I can explain it again."

Heat coursed through Jake as he explored every mystery and riddle of Hope's warmth. He grazed her hair, still damp from a shower, the lavender scent of her shampoo intoxicating. He could have stayed there all night.

"You two are always up to somethin' in the dark," Margie said from behind them. "It's… kind of nice. When you all finish gettin' frisky, we're about to say the blessin' for supper."

"Yes, Ms. Moore. We're coming," Hope said through a soft laugh, as she rested her forehead on Jake's chest.

"Well, come on," Margie said.

"Jake, get your butt in here," Hitch called. "I've told you, son. If you want applause, join the circus."

Jake pulled back and wrapped his hand around Hope's to lead her toward their feast.

A glint of light caught his eye. It danced along the wall beside them. It made no sense at first. Then the simple reflection in the glass of the front door gave it away as the red dot of a laser beam settled in the middle of Hope's back. To a sniper, that was center mass.

"Hope!" Jake yelled. He lunged and slammed into her body as the crack of a rifle echoed across the lake. They crashed to the floor. Glass shards splintered on top of them.

"Everybody down! On the floor!" Hope ordered, reaching for her gun.

Pain exploded through Jake's chest, as if someone had hit him full force with a sledgehammer. He tried to speak, but the wind had been knocked out of him. Hope dragged him closer to her, out of the way of the windows. He could see the blood on her palms when she lifted them.

"Grace! Hurry, bring something to stop the bleeding! Margie, call 911!"

Grace sprinted around the corner in a crouch and pushed her mother out of the way. She tore open Jake's shirt and wadded dishtowels on the gunshot wound, her nursing skills kicking in reflexively.

Jake felt Grace searching for his pulse. A headache thundered through his brain.

Hope moved and cradled Jake's head in her lap. Staring down at him, caressing his cheek.

"You're going to be okay," she said, her voice wet with tears.

"My body feels so heavy. I'm so tired," he whispered.

"Keep him alert," Grace directed her mother in a stern, clinical voice.

"Ambulance is on the way!" Hitch called.

"I'm so tired…"

"Don't you dare leave me, Jake Fox! You look right here at me," Hope said, struggling to give him a reassuring smile.

Jake opened his mouth to speak, but something trapped the words inside. Darkness and flashes of light swirled on the edge of his vision.

"Talk to me!" Hope yelled.

Jake's words came out as gibberish, and his world faded to black.

CHAPTER SIXTY-SIX

JAKE WIGGLED his bare toes in the bright, verdant grass. He walked to the end of the dock and dunked his feet in the cool morning water. The lake stretched out in front of him like a peaceful, welcoming path, a layer of fog undulating as the day warmed. Beyond, the lakeshore disappeared into the infinite shimmer of a cerulean sky. A glow like a fresh, welcoming sunrise lay beyond. Mystery surrounded him. A large bass violently broke the still surface of the lake, chasing a chartreuse dragonfly that escaped with an erratic buzz into the sky. Jake flicked the water with his toes, an incredible peace calling him. The familiar smell of spring flowers blew past him in the breeze. He heard the soft padding of bare feet as they approached on the wooden planks. He spoke before he turned.

"Does it always feel like this here? So peaceful?"

"Even better," the soft voice called from behind him.

"I could use some peace," Jake said, taking in the surrounding scene.

He glanced over his shoulder, feeling the sudden warmth of a powerful love that connected to everything around him. She stepped up next to him, lowering herself, dangling her legs over the dock's edge. Minnows swirled as if trying to play with her toes.

Jake reached out and folded his fingers around the soft, innocent skin of her hand. He choked on his words. "I still love you, Lu." He closed his eyes at memories of his daughter chasing grasshoppers in the grass. He turned and soaked in the loving gaze from those amazing emerald eyes.

"I love you, too, Daddy. So much."

"The pain never fades… I don't know that it will ever fade."

"It will," Lu said, twirling her hair as she watched the wispy black water striders skitter beneath them, running from the tiny fish.

"When?" Jake asked, squeezing her hand.

"I can't tell you," Lu said. "I don't have answers. I only know, now, on this side, that joy requires pain so that you can tell the valleys from the peaks."

"Were the valleys too deep, Lu?"

Lu pushed the tears from her cheeks with the back of her hand, her voice just above a whisper.

"So deep, Daddy."

"I could have helped. Could have saved…"

"Shh… You did nothing wrong."

"Why did you leave me?"

Lu opened her mouth as if to answer and then fell silent.

"I want to be with you, Lu. Like this… Happy, holding your hand. Listening to your stories. I want to hear your laugh again. Dear god, I miss your simple, sweet laugh. Life has been so empty." Jake paused and watched an osprey circle peacefully, scanning the lake and sailing on the thermal updrafts. "I don't know that I can live without you anymore. The ache… The valleys may be too deep."

"I miss you, too, Daddy. I'm glad we get to visit from time to time."

"Is this it? Are we together now… forever? Are we finally a family again?"

In a small, quiet voice, Lu said, "I don't think it's time."

"I could stay, though. If I choose, I could stay with you."

"Yes. If you choose. You can stay here with me."

Jake closed his eyes and felt warm, salty tears dampen his cheeks. Lu turned to him and pushed them away with her thumbs.

"But they need you."

"Then I can't be with you. I have to live without you."

"Who knows the future?"

"Will I understand one day? Someday, will it all make sense?"

"Someday… I promise."

Lucy stood, turned, and started to walk away. She looked back, giving him that killer smile. "I can wait."

Oh, sweet Lucy.

He had a vision of Hope, Rose, Margie, Hitch, and Grace all laughing at a dinner table. But the fierce desire to be with Lu tore at his soul. Then he closed his eyes, and… he chose. The peace gave way to a torrent of pain coursing through his chest. Jake opened his eyes.

Hope's mascara streaked her face as she hovered over him, panic rimming her gaze.

"Jake!… Grace! He's back."

Follow our next Kickstarter!
www.JakeFoxBooks.com

ABOUT THE AUTHOR

Michael Stockham

Michael Stockham has worked as a big-firm lawyer for over twenty years after receiving his law degree from Cornell Law School. He's a sought-after litigator, speaker, and podcast guest expert. You can reach him at Michael@MichaelStockham.com or on LinkedIn.

Jake Fox: Ties That Blind is the first in the Jake Fox series of nine legal thrillers. For a sneak peek at the next book, visit: www.JakeFoxThrillers.com. To find out about the next Kickstarter, visit: www.JakeFoxBooks.com.

Michael Stockham's first novel, *Confessions of an Accidental Lawyer*, attracted several awards and over 3,000 rave reviews on Amazon.

A lifelong lover of books, Michael received two degrees in creative writing: a Bachelor of Arts from the University of New Mexico and a Master of Arts from Texas A&M University.

Blessed by two grown daughters who are Clemson University Tigers, Michael lives in Dallas with his wife, Kiersten, along with three dogs and two potbelly pigs.

www.MichaelStockham.com

ACKNOWLEDGMENTS

Thank you to all my Kickstarter backers! I appreciate your support: Tracy Adams, Dave Armour, Kimberly Armour, Levi Browde, Dana Brown, Aiza Gutierrez, Jeni Lawrence Colarusso, Austin Epstein, Kadan Epstein, Riley Epstein, Susan Epstein, Jesse Hereda, Julie Husa, Ana Koz, Ali Martineau, Nicole McKenna, Lane Palmer, Carolyn Przekurat, Amy Staples, Cormick Stockham, Kiersten Stockham, Peydinn Stockham, Aurora Winter, and Yale Winter.

Becoming a bestselling author has been a long-time goal for me, but the task was daunting, especially with my schedule as a trial lawyer. Thankfully, I found Aurora Winter, founder of SamePagePublishing.com. Collaborating with her makes the process of writing a book fun and interesting.

Aurora is intensely curious, listens deeply, and coaches with compassion and skill. She helped me discover and structure a gold mine of content. She is also there to catch me and coach me when the goal seems too big (or an overly critical inner voice tells me it is impossible). I appreciate working with Aurora and want to acknowledge her contribution and support.

It is a blessing to have someone so thoughtful and kind to work on the project of launching as a Thought Leader, speaker, and author. If you would like to write a book but have no idea how to find the time, I recommend Aurora Winter's award-winning books, which include *Turn Words Into Wealth* and

Marketing Fastrack. For her VIP solutions, visit www.Same-PagePublishing.com.

ALSO BY MICHAEL STOCKHAM

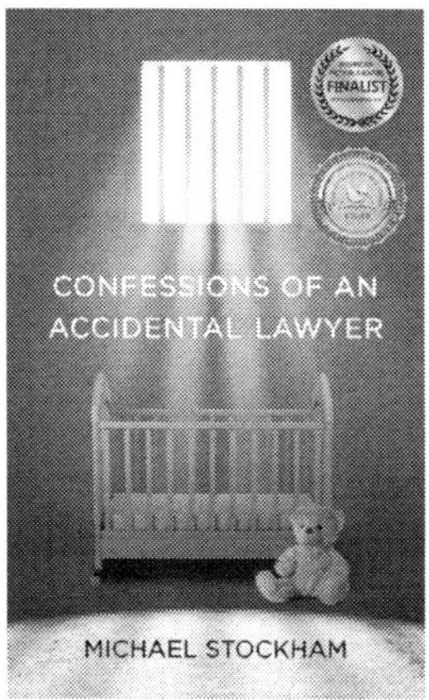

CONFESSIONS OF AN ACCIDENTAL LAWYER

Battling against a Texas prison, a young lawyer fights for a fair trial in a prison-friendly town as witnesses and evidence evaporate.

Scarred physically and emotionally by a botched delivery, his wife struggles to realize their dream of a healthy baby and a happy family.

Trapped in solitary confinement, an inmate fights for medicine to keep his failing heart pumping.

Torn between career and family, with the lives of a prisoner, his wife, and his unborn child on the line, the young lawyer struggles to ensure that his client, his family, and his integrity all survive.

www.MichaelStockham.com

Printed in Great Britain
by Amazon

bbef2291-ffc8-4bde-b154-a09cdd8f8e9eR01